Praise for the novels of #1 *New York Times* bestselling author Debbie Macomber

"Whether [Debbie Macomber] is writing light-hearted romps or more serious relationship books, her novels are always engaging stories that accurately capture the foibles of real-life men and women with warmth and humor."
—*Milwaukee Journal Sentinel*

"No one tugs at readers' heartstrings quite as effectively as [Debbie] Macomber."
—*Chicago Tribune*

"Debbie Macomber is undoubtedly among America's favorite authors [with] a masterful gift of creating tales that are both mesmerizing and inspiring...."
—*Wichita Falls Times Record News*

"Popular romance writer Macomber has a gift for evoking the emotions that are at the heart of the genre's popularity."
—*Publishers Weekly*

"Macomber...is no stranger to the *New York Times* bestseller list. She knows how to please her audience."
—*Oregon Statesman Journal*

"[Debbie Macomber] is skilled at creating characters who work their way into readers' hearts."
—*RT Book Reviews* on *Dakota Home*

"[Macomber] demonstrates her impressive skills with characterization and her flair for humor."
—*RT Book Reviews*

"Prolific Macomber is known for her portrayals of ordinary women in small-town America. [She is] an icon of the genre."
—*Publishers Weekly*

Dear Friends,

Here, just in time for another Valentine's Day, are two of my early stories. *The Way to a Man's Heart* was published in 1989, *Hasty Wedding* in 1993.

It's always interesting to look at the books I wrote that long ago and to see the ways in which my writing and my approach to storytelling have changed. *And* the ways they haven't... Romance, and, in fact, love in all its manifestations—for family, friends, community—is of major importance to me. I think you'll see that in these stories...and in everything I've written since.

The old saying about "the way to a man's heart" refers to food, and since the heroine in the book of that title works in a diner, it's an appropriate choice. But as both stories show, there are *many* ways to reach men's hearts. (And for them to reach ours!) These stories are also in the classic "opposites attract" vein, which remains an enduring romance theme. It's also one of my favorites....

I hope you'll enjoy this excursion into the past. As you may know, I love hearing from readers. I take your suggestions and opinions seriously; in fact, reader feedback has changed the course of my writing more than once. You can reach me through my website, DebbieMacomber.com, on Facebook and Twitter, or through regular mail at P.O. Box 1458, Port Orchard, WA 98366.

Warmest Regards,

Debbie Macomber

DEBBIE MACOMBER

A Man's
HEART

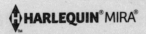 HARLEQUIN® MIRA®

ISBN-13: 978-0-7783-1587-2

A MAN'S HEART

Copyright © 2014 by Harlequin Books S.A.

The publisher acknowledges the copyright holder
of the individual works as follows:

THE WAY TO A MAN'S HEART
Copyright © 1989 by Debbie Macomber

HASTY WEDDING
Copyright © 1993 by Debbie Macomber

Recycling programs
for this product may
not exist in your area.

Dedicated to Cheryl Adler
for her determination and dedication in setting
the impressive goal of climbing Mt Rainier *and*
marrying my brother, who was an equal challenge....

Also by Debbie Macomber

Blossom Street Books
The Shop on Blossom Street
A Good Yarn
Susannah's Garden
Back on Blossom Street
Twenty Wishes
Summer on Blossom Street
Hannah's List
The Knitting Diaries
   "The Twenty-First Wish"
A Turn in the Road

Cedar Cove Books
16 Lighthouse Road
204 Rosewood Lane
311 Pelican Court
44 Cranberry Point
50 Harbor Street
6 Rainier Drive
74 Seaside Avenue
8 Sandpiper Way
92 Pacific Boulevard
1022 Evergreen Place
A Cedar Cove Christmas
   (*5-B Poppy Lane* and
   Christmas in Cedar Cove)
1105 Yakima Street
1225 Christmas Tree Lane

Dakota Series
Dakota Born
Dakota Home
Always Dakota

The Manning Family
The Manning Sisters
The Manning Brides
The Manning Grooms

Christmas Books
A Gift to Last
On a Snowy Night
Home for the Holidays
Glad Tidings
Christmas Wishes
Small Town Christmas
When Christmas Comes
   (now retitled *Trading
   Christmas*)
*There's Something About
   Christmas*
Christmas Letters
Where Angels Go
The Perfect Christmas
Angels at Christmas
   (*Those Christmas Angels*
   and *Where Angels Go*)
Call Me Mrs. Miracle

Heart of Texas Series
VOLUME 1
(*Lonesome Cowboy* and
   Texas Two-Step)
VOLUME 2
(*Caroline's Child* and
   Dr. Texas)
VOLUME 3
(*Nell's Cowboy* and
   Lone Star Baby)
Promise, Texas
Return to Promise

Midnight Sons

VOLUME 1
(Brides for Brothers and
  The Marriage Risk)
VOLUME 2
(Daddy's Little Helper and
  Because of the Baby)
VOLUME 3
(Falling for Him,
  Ending in Marriage and
  Midnight Sons and Daughters)

This Matter of Marriage
Montana
Thursdays at Eight
Between Friends
Changing Habits
Married in Seattle
  (First Comes Marriage and
  Wanted: Perfect Partner)
Right Next Door
  (Father's Day and
  The Courtship of
  Carol Sommars)
Wyoming Brides
  (Denim and Diamonds and
  The Wyoming Kid)
Fairy Tale Weddings
  (Cindy and the Prince and
  Some Kind of Wonderful)
The Man You'll Marry
  (The First Man You Meet and
  The Man You'll Marry)
Orchard Valley Grooms
  (Valerie and Stephanie)

Orchard Valley Brides
  (Norah and Lone Star Lovin')
The Sooner the Better
An Engagement in Seattle
  (Groom Wanted and
  Bride Wanted)
Out of the Rain
  (Marriage Wanted and
  Laughter in the Rain)
Learning to Love
  (Sugar and Spice and
  Love by Degree)
You...Again
  (Baby Blessed and
  Yesterday Once More)
Three Brides, No Groom
The Unexpected Husband
  (Jury of his Peers and
  Any Sunday)
Love in Plain Sight
  (Love 'n' Marriage and
  Almost an Angel)
I Left My Heart
  (A Friend or Two and
  No Competition)
Marriage Between Friends
  (White Lace and Promises
  and Friends...And Then Some)

Debbie Macomber's
  Cedar Cove Cookbook
Debbie Macomber's
  Christmas Cookbook

CONTENTS

THE WAY TO A MAN'S HEART

One

"Are you ready to order?" Meghan O'Day asked the man with the horn-rimmed glasses who was sitting in the booth beside the window. The gentleman was busily reading. Meghan withdrew the small tablet from inside her starched apron pocket and patiently waited for his response.

At her question, the reader's gaze reluctantly left the page of his book and bounced against her briefly. "The chicken potpie sounds good."

"Rose's potpies are excellent," Meghan said with a congenial smile. She noted that even before she'd finished writing down his order, the man had returned his attention to his reading. She grinned, not offended by his lack of notice. Some customers were chatty and openly friendly, while others preferred to keep to themselves. Meghan didn't mind. It was her job to make sure the clientele were served promptly and their needs seen to efficiently. Since Meghan was an avid reader herself, she didn't fault this gentleman for being more interested in his book than in ordering his meal.

Currently only a handful of customers dotted the

diner, and the chicken-potpie order was up within a few short minutes. The reader, with his nose buried between the pages of his book, barely looked up when Meghan delivered his food.

"Is there anything more I can get for you?" she asked, automatically refilling his coffee cup.

"Nothing, thanks."

As she moved to turn away, Meghan noted that it was Geoffrey Chaucer's *Canterbury Tales,* that had captured his attention so completely. Excitement surged through her bloodstream.

Meghan herself was a devoted lover of classical literature. She set the glass coffeepot on the table and gave the reader a second look. Not bad. In fact he was downright handsome.

He glanced up at her expectantly. The only thing Meghan could do was explain. "I… Chaucer is one of my favorites."

"Mine, too." A slow, endearing smile eased across his face. He glanced down at the page and read in a clear, strong voice: "'Bifel that in that seson on a day, in southwerk at the Tabard as I lay—'"

"'—Redy to wenden on my pilgrimage to Canterbury with ful devout corage,'" Meghan finished reverently.

His face revealed his surprise. If she hadn't earned his attention before, she received it full force now. "You know Chaucer?"

Meghan felt a little silly and shook her head. "Not personally." Her fellow Chaucer fan didn't so much as crack a smile at her attempt at a joke. To her way of thinking, he was much too young to take life so seriously; but then she was only a waitress, not a psychologist.

"You're obviously familiar with his works." He

frowned slightly and studied her as though he should be expected to recognize her and didn't.

"I've read it so many times that I've managed to memorize small portions of it. I guess you could say that Chaucer and I have a nodding acquaintance."

He chuckled at that, and planted his elbows on the table, grinning up her. "So you enjoy reading Middle English?"

"I'll confess it was difficult going at first," she said, feeling mildly guilty for interrupting his meal, "but I stuck it out and I'm glad I did. Frankly, when I read it aloud the first time, it sounded a whole lot like Swedish to me."

His face erupted into a full smile, as if he found her insights a bit irreverent, but nonetheless interesting.

A second volume rested on the seat beside him. He picked it up and ran his hand respectfully down its spine. "If you enjoy Chaucer, then you're probably a fan of Edmund Spenser, as well."

She noted that he was holding a well-read volume of *The Faerie Queene*. He continued to look at her expectantly, awaiting her reply. Feeling a bit chagrined, Meghan regretfully shook her head.

"You don't like Spenser?"

"Isn't he the one who wanted to write twelve books, each one celebrating a different knightly virtue?"

The reader nodded. "He only completed six."

"Actually, I don't think anyone minded." As far as Meghan was concerned, Spenser was a prime candidate for intensive counseling, but she couldn't very well tell her customer that. "I didn't mean to insult your tastes," she added quickly, not wanting to offend him.

The man reached for his fork, all the while studying her as if he were trying to place her. "Do I know you?"

Meghan shook her head. "Not unless you eat at Rose's Diner regularly and I don't remember seeing you before tonight."

"This is the first time I've been here, although I've heard for years that Rose bakes the best pies in Wichita. Generally I'm not in this neighborhood." Still he continued to stare without the merest hint of apology.

"Rose will be pleased to hear that." Feeling a little foolish for lingering so long, Meghan picked up the coffeepot and took a step back. "Enjoy your meal."

"Thank you, I will." He continued to observe Meghan as she turned and headed toward the service counter. Even then, she felt his gaze.

Sherry Caldwell, the assistant manager, joined her there.

"Who's the hunk you were just talking to?"

"I don't know. He came in about twenty minutes ago, started reading Chaucer and ordered chicken potpie."

"He's cute, don't you think?" Sherry asked, eyeing him inquisitively. The assistant manager was a grandmother, but still young enough to appreciate a good-looking man when she saw one.

Meghan didn't think twice about nodding. There wasn't any doubt in her mind that this man was attractive. Everything about him appealed to her, especially his choice of reading material. Although he was sitting, Meghan could tell he was well over six feet. His dark hair was thick, cut short, and styled in a manner that gave him a distinguished air. He wasn't openly friendly, but he wasn't aloof, either. He was more of an introvert, she decided; distinguished and professional, too. Those traits wouldn't normally appeal to her, but they did in him—strongly.

From what she'd noticed, he seemed to be physically fit, but she couldn't picture him gliding down ski slopes or lifting weights. In fact, he didn't look like someone who cared much about muscle tone. He was dressed casually now, but something about him suggested he was more at home in three-piece suits and stiffly starched collars than the slacks and sweater he was wearing now.

"He's not the kind of guy one would expect to come in here, is he?" Sherry pressed.

Meghan shrugged. "I guess not, but we get all types."

Sherry chuckled. "Tell me about it, kiddo!"

The following evening, Meghan kept looking for the man who loved the literary classics, chiding herself for even expecting him to return. It wasn't like her to feel so strongly about a stranger, especially one whom she'd only talked to once and briefly at that. All day she thought about the handsome man who knew and loved Chaucer the same way she did. She would like to know him better, and wondered if he felt the same about her.

Just when the dinner rush had started to lull, Sherry strolled past her and muttered under her breath, "He's back."

Meghan's co-worker made it sound as if an FBI agent had just stepped into the diner and was preparing to consort with the KGB. Meghan was carrying three plates of chicken-fried steak, and daring not to hope, she paused to ask, "Who's back?"

Sherry rolled her eyes. "The good-looking guy from last night. Remember?"

"I can't say that I do." Meghan preferred to play dumb, being unwilling to let her friend know how much she'd thought about seeing "the reader" again.

"The chicken potpie from last night," Sherry returned, obviously frustrated. "The one you've been watching for all night, so don't try to fool me!"

"Chicken potpie?" Meghan repeated, continuing the pretense and doing a poor job of it. "Oh, you mean the guy who was reading Chaucer?"

"Right," Sherry teased. "Well, he obviously remembered *you*. He requested your section." Sherry wiggled her finely penciled brows up and down several times.

"He did?" By now Meghan's heart was doing cartwheels.

"That's what I just finished saying."

Meghan wasn't willing to put a lot of stock in this. "I don't suppose it occurred to that romantic heart of yours to assume he was pleased with the food and the service?"

"I'm sure he was," Sherry returned, trying to suppress a smile, and failing. "But I think he's far more interested in seeing you again. After all, he could order the same cooking from any one of us."

Meghan discounted Sherry's reasoning with a soft shrug, feeling disinclined to accept anything more than the fact the handsome man who read Chaucer was back.

"Go get him, tiger," Sherry teased. "He's ripe for the pickin'."

Meghan delivered the chicken-fried steaks and re-filled coffee cups before approaching "the reader's" booth. Once again, his nose was deep in a well-worn leather volume.

"Good evening," she greeted, striving to sound friendly but not overly so—it wouldn't do to let him know how pleased she was to see him again. "You're back."

He closed the book and looked up at her. "I was in the neighborhood and decided to stop in."

"I'm glad you did." Her fingers tightened around the handle of the coffeepot. "I enjoyed our conversation last night."

"I did, too. Very much." His sober gaze continued to study her with undisguised admiration.

Meghan could tell that this man was earnest and serious. He wasn't the type to openly flirt or lead a woman on; in fact he seemed almost uncomfortable. This evening he was wearing a suit and tie and looked more dignified than ever. He was the only man in the entire diner wearing anything so formal.

He set the volume aside and looked up eagerly, reading her name tag. "It's good to see you again, Meghan."

"Thank you…and you too, of course." She set the coffeepot down, pulled her pad from the pink apron and held her pen poised, ready to write down his choice.

Instead of ordering, he held out his hand to her. "I'm Grey Carlyle."

She gave him her hand which he grasped in a firm handshake. Meghan had trouble pulling her gaze from his; his eyes were a mesmerizing shade of blue that reminded her of a midsummer Kansas sky.

"I'm pleased to meet you, Meghan—"

"O'Day," she filled in. "It's Irish," she mumbled, instantly wanting to kick herself for stating something so obvious. If her name wasn't enough of a giveaway, her bright auburn hair and deep blue eyes should have been.

Suddenly there didn't seem to be anything more to say. Grey glanced at the pad in her hand and announced, "I'll order the special—whatever it is."

"Chicken-fried steak," Meghan told him eagerly.

"That sounds fine."

Meghan took her time writing it down, wanting to linger and get to know him better. Instead she asked him, "Would you like soup or salad with your meal?"

"Salad."

She made a note of that. "What kind of dressing?"

He mulled this over as though it were important enough to involve national security. "Blue cheese, if you have it."

"We do." If they didn't she would stir up a batch herself.

"I don't suppose you've read Milton?" He turned over the book on the tabletop and showed her the cover.

Meghan held the order pad against her breast and smiled down on him. "I loved *Paradise Lost* and *Lycidas*, but the whole time I was reading his works I had the impression he was trying to get one up on Dante." The minute the words were out, Meghan wanted to jerk them back. She could feel the color sweep into her cheeks, and it was on the tip of her tongue to tell him she hadn't meant that.

The faint quiver of a smile started at the corners of his full mouth. "'Get one up on Dante'—I never thought of it quite like that before," he murmured. "But actually, you could be right."

A bell chimed softly in the background, reminding Meghan that one of her orders was ready and there were other customers who expected to be served. "I'd better get back to work," she said reluctantly. "I'll have your salad for you in just a minute."

"Before you go," he said abruptly, stopping her. "I'd like to know where you attended college?"

She cast her gaze down and shrugged, feeling slightly awkward. "I haven't."

"You haven't been to university?" Surprise elevated his voice.

Meghan looped a strand of shoulder-length hair over her ear and met his confused gaze.

"Do you mean to tell me you've done all this reading on your own?"

"Is that so unusual?"

He reached for his water glass. "Frankly, yes."

"If you'll excuse me now, I really have to get back to work."

"Of course. I'm sorry for detaining you this long."

"No, don't apologize. I enjoy talking to you. It's just that—"

"I understand, Meghan. Don't worry about it."

She stepped away from the booth, feeling uneasy with him for the first time. Literature was the one love of her life—her passion. She'd started reading early English literature when nursing her mother after she'd taken a bad fall. High school had given her enough of a taste for the classics that she'd sought out and begun to investigate major works on her own, later. While at home, she'd had ample opportunity to explore many of the literary greats, and in a short time had devoured volume after volume, making a whirlwind tour of six hundred years of English literature.

As Meghan headed toward the kitchen, she noticed Grey frowning. Now that he knew she didn't have a degree to back up her opinions, he probably wouldn't ask her what she thought of the classics again. It would have been better if she'd kept her thoughts to herself than to spout them as if she knew what she was talking about. The habit of blurting out exactly what she was feeling was one that continually plagued her. Grey Carlyle was a man of culture and refinement. Her guess was that he was a doctor or an attorney, or someone else equally distinguished. Obviously he knew a good deal more about literature than she ever would.

* * *

Greyson Carlyle watched Meghan move away from the table. In fact he couldn't stop looking at her. He'd embarrassed her when he'd started asking her about college, and he hadn't meant to do that.

When he'd first stepped into the diner the night before, he hadn't given her more than a second glance. It wasn't until she'd quoted Chaucer with such a deep-rooted love that he'd so much as looked at her. Once he *did* notice her, however, he found himself completely enthralled. It wasn't often a man could walk into a restaurant and meet a waitress as lovely and intelligent as Meghan. In fact, meeting Meghan had been downright unexpected. He loved the way her Irish blue eyes lit up and sparkled when she spoke of Chaucer and Milton. She knew these men and savored their works in much the same way he appreciated their craft and keen intelligence.

The things Meghan had said utterly intrigued him, for over the years, Grey had become far too accustomed to having his own opinions spouted back at him. Rare was the student who would have told him that Middle English sounded like Swedish. He couldn't keep from smiling at the thought.

The fact was Grey hadn't been able to stop thinking about the waitress all day. Hearing her outrageous statements was like sifting through sand and discovering pieces of gold.

He'd gone home the night before and found himself chuckling just thinking about Meghan O'Day. In the middle of a lecture the following morning, he'd paused remembering how the young woman had told him no one was sorry Spenser had only completed six of the twelve books he'd planned. He'd broken into a wide grin and had to restrain himself from bursting out laughing right there in front of his students. The freshman class had sat there staring at Grey as if they expected him to leap on top of his desk and dance.

Grey didn't know who'd been more shocked—his students or himself. But he'd quickly composed himself and resumed the lecture.

If Grey was going to be thinking about a woman, he chided himself later, he should concentrate on someone like Dr. Pamela Riverside. His colleague had been less than subtle in letting him know she was interested in getting to know him better. Unfortunately, Grey wasn't the least bit attracted to her.

Instead his thoughts centered on one Irish waitress with eyes warm enough to melt stone—a waitress with a heart for the classics.

He was getting old, Grey determined. It took someone like Meghan O'Day to remind him that life didn't revolve around academia and boring social functions. The world was filled with interesting people, and this waitress was one of them.

That evening, as he walked off the campus of Friends University, Grey impulsively decided to return to Rose's Diner. He would be discussing Milton with his students in the next day or two, and he longed to hear Meghan's thoughts on the seventeenth-century poet. He was certain she would have something novel to say.

"So?" Sherry asked, cornering Meghan the minute she approached the kitchen with Grey's order. "What did he want?"

Meghan stared at her friend and blinked, pretending not to understand. "'The reader'?"

"Who else could I possibly mean?" Sherry groaned.

"He wanted the special."

"I don't want to know what he ordered! Did he tell you why he was back again?"

Meghan chewed on the corner of her bottom lip. "Not actually. He asked what I thought of Milton, though."

"Milton? Who in heaven's name is Milton?"

Meghan smiled at her friend. "John Milton. He wrote *Paradise Lost* and *Paradise Regained* and plenty of other, lesser-known works."

"Oh, good grief," Sherry muttered. "It's those high-falutin Greeks you're always reading, isn't it? When are you going to give up reading that antiquated stuff? Wake up and smell the coffee, Meghan O'Day. If you're going to get anywhere in this life you've got to start reading real writers—like…Stephen King and… Erma Bombeck, God rest her soul." Sherry hesitated, then nodded once for emphasis. "Take Erma—now there's a woman after my own heart. She's got more to say in one newspaper column than those Greek friends of yours say in twenty or thirty pages."

"Milton was English," Meghan corrected, smiling inwardly at her friend's mild outburst.

"What's so intriguing about what these people wrote, anyway?"

"It's not the writer so much," Meghan said carefully, not wanting to insult her co-worker. "It's what they had to say about the things that affected their lives."

"Stephen King doesn't do that," Sherry countered. "And he's done all right for himself."

"He has, at that," Meghan agreed. It wouldn't do any good to argue with Sherry, but she wanted her to understand. "Listen to this," Meghan asked and inhaled deeply. When she spoke, her low voice was soft and well modulated. "'Know then thyself, presume not God to scan; The proper study of mankind is man.'"

Sherry was giving her an odd look. "That's Milton?"

"No. Alexander Pope. But don't the words stir your soul? Don't they reach out and take hold of your heart and make you hunger to read more?"

Sherry shook her head. "I can't say that they do."

"Oh, Sherry." Meghan sighed, defeated.

"I'm sorry, I can't help myself. That sounds like a bunch of mumbo-jumbo to me, but if that's what turns you on, I'll try not to complain."

When Meghan had finished adding salad dressing to the small bowl of lettuce and chopped tomatoes, she delivered it to Grey's table.

"Can I get you anything else before your dinner comes up?" she asked, setting the salad in front of him along with a narrow tray of soda crackers.

"Everything's fine," he replied, and looked up at her. "Listen, I'd like to apologize if I embarrassed you earlier by asking you about your college education."

"You didn't embarrass me." It *had* somewhat, but she couldn't see that telling him that would help matters. Years before, she'd yearned to go to college, dreamed of it, but circumstances had kept her home. She didn't begrudge her lack of a formal education; it was part of her life and she'd accepted the fact long ago.

"I don't mean to pry," Grey said, frowning just a little, "but I'm curious why someone who loves the classics the way you do, wouldn't pursue your schooling?"

Meghan dropped her gaze. "The year I graduated from high school my mother fell down a flight of stairs and broke her hip. She needed surgery and was immobile for several months because of complications. With three younger brothers, I was needed at home. Later, after Mom had recovered, the family was strapped with huge medical bills."

"You're helping to pay those?" Grey pressed.

"They're mostly paid now, but I'm twenty-four."

"What's that got to do with anything?"

Meghan laughed lightly. "I'd be years older than the other freshmen. I wouldn't fit in."

Grey's brows drew together, forming a deep V over his eyes. Apparently he was considering something.

"I was wondering," he said, and hesitated. "I mean, you hardly know me, but there's a lecture on the poetry of Shelley and Keats at Friends University tomorrow evening that I was planning to attend. Would you care to go with me?"

Meghan stared back at him, hardly able to believe what she was hearing. This distinguished man was actually asking her out on a date.

When she didn't immediately respond, he lowered his eyes to his salad. "I realize this is rather spur-of-the-moment."

"I'd love to go," she blurted out, scarcely able to disguise her enthusiasm.

"Shall we meet here in the parking lot...say, around seven-thirty?"

"That would be fine," Meghan responded eagerly. "I'm honored that you'd even think to invite me."

"The pleasure's all mine," Grey insisted with a boyishly charming smile.

"Until tomorrow, then," she said.

"Tomorrow," he repeated.

An hour later, Grey stood beside his car, his hand on the door handle, his thoughts excited and chaotic. He'd found a kindred spirit in Meghan O'Day. The minute she'd softly quoted Chaucer, his heart hadn't been the same. When he heard the reason she hadn't gone on to college, Grey knew he had to ask her to the lecture. Once she'd sampled the feast of rich works to be served the following night at the university, she would be hooked. He wanted this for her. Even if she was a few years older than the majority of the students, he knew she'd fit in. He could tell her this, but it wouldn't be nearly as effective as giving her a taste of what could be in store for her behind those walls of learning.

Grey wasn't an impulsive man by nature, but when he was with Meghan he found himself saying and doing the most incredible things. This invitation was just one example.

With an unexpected burst of energy, Grey tossed his car keys into the air and deftly caught them behind his back with his left hand. He was so stunned by the agile move that he laughed out loud.

A light snow had just begun falling when Meghan walked toward Grey in the well-lit parking lot in front of Rose's Diner the following evening. Snow had arrived early this year; Wichita had already been struck by two storms and it wasn't yet Thanksgiving.

"I hope I didn't keep you waiting long," Meghan said, strolling up to his side.

"Not at all."

He smiled down at her and the chill that had permeated Meghan's bones was suddenly gone, vanished under the warmth in his eyes.

Grey tucked her hand into the curve of his arm. "I think you'll enjoy this evening."

"I'm sure I will. Shelley and Keats are two of my favorites, although I tend to like Keats better."

Grey opened the car door for her. "I find their styles too similar to prefer one over the other."

"Oh, I agree. But I happened to read some of Shelley's letters," Meghan added conversationally, "and I've had trouble thinking objectively about him ever since."

"Oh?" Grey walked around the car and joined her in the front seat. "What makes you say that?"

Meghan shrugged. "His notes to his friends were full of far-out abstractions and so dreadfully philosophical. If you want my opinion, I think Shelley was stuck on himself. In fact, I've come to think of him as a big crybaby."

Grey's eyes widened. "I thought you said you liked Shelley?"

"Oh, dear," Meghan replied, expelling her breath. "I'm sorry. I've shocked you again, haven't I?"

"It's all right," he said, the frown slowly unfolding. "As it happens, Shelley is my all-time favorite and I'm having one heck of a time not defending him. You're right, though. He was big on himself. But who could blame him?"

"No one," Meghan agreed.

"You know what I like best about you, Meghan?"

She shook her head.

"You're honest, and that's a quality I admire. You aren't going to tell me something just because you think I want to hear it."

Meghan cocked her head to one side and expelled a sigh. "That—fortunately or unfortunately, as the case might be—is true. I have a bad habit of blurting out whatever I'm thinking."

"I find it refreshing," he said, reaching for her hand

and squeezing her fingers. "We're going to enjoy tonight. And when the lecture is finished, we'll discuss Shelley again. I have the feeling your opinion's going to change."

Grey drove across town to Friends University. Although Meghan had passed the campus several times, she'd never actually been on the grounds. As she looked around at the ivy-covered structures, her gaze filled with longing. Some day, some way, she would find a way to further her education here.

"It really is lovely here, isn't it?" she said, once they'd parked. Grey walked around and opened her car door, his impeccable manners again impressing Meghan.

"Just standing here makes me want to curtsy to all these buildings," she commented, smiling.

"Meghan," he said kindly, tucking her hand once more into the crook of his arm. "I don't understand. You so obviously love literature, you aren't going to feel out of place once you sign up for a few classes. Yes, you would be older than the majority of first-year students, but not by much and really what would it matter?"

"It's a bit more than that," she said, looking away from him.

"If you can't afford the expense surely there are scholarships you could apply for."

"Yes, I suppose I could. But I haven't."

"Why not?"

She looked away, feeling uncomfortable. "The last thing I want to do is sit in some stuffy classroom and listen to some white-haired professor," she said defensively.

"Why not?"

Grey did a good job of disguising his shock, but Meghan could see that her words had rattled him. It seemed that his voice tensed a little, but Meghan couldn't be certain.

"If you really must know," she said nervously, "colleges and professors frighten me."

"Meghan, that's ridiculous. They're people like and you me."

"Yes, I suppose it *is* absurd, but it's the way I feel. I'm afraid a professor would look down his learned nose at me and think I'm full of myself."

"Listen," he said, placing his hands on her shoulders and turning on the pathway so that he faced her squarely. "There's something you should know."

In the distance, Meghan could hear footsteps approaching. Grey dropped his hands, apparently wanting to wait until the group had passed him.

"Evening, Professor Carlyle."

Grey twisted his head around and nodded. "Good evening, Paul."

"Professor Carlyle," Meghan muttered. "*You're* a professor?"

Two

Meghan felt the surprise splash over her, drenching her to the bone. Grey Carlyle was a university professor, specializing in English literature, no doubt! She couldn't believe how incredibly obtuse she'd been. Just looking at him, reading Chaucer and Milton in his crisp three-piece suit, precisely knotted tie and boot-camp polished shoes should have been a dead giveaway. Only Meghan hadn't figured it out. Oh, no. Instead she'd danced all around him in an effort to impress him with her dazzling insights and sharp wit—all the while making a complete nincompoop of herself.

Her gaze met his and quickly lowered. "I should have guessed," she muttered, forcing a smile.

"Is my hair that white?" he coaxed. "Do I really come off as so terribly stuffy?"

His words were a teasing reminder of the things she'd said about college and professors. "You could have gone all night without repeating that," she whispered, feeling the warm color rush into her face.

"I'm sorry, but I couldn't help myself."

"You're not the least bit sorry," she countered.

Grey chuckled and rubbed the side of his jaw. "You're right. I'm not."

"I should be furious with you, letting me go on that way!" Meghan continued, still not looking at him directly. If those students hadn't arrived when they did, there was no telling how much more she would have said.

"But you're not angry?"

"No," she said, releasing a pent-up sigh. "I probably should be, but I'm not." She'd done this to herself, and although she would have liked to blame Grey, she couldn't.

"I didn't know how to stop you," he admitted, frowning. "I wanted to say something—let you know before you'd embarrassed yourself. I suppose I just assumed you'd have figured it out. It was my own fault; I should have said something earlier."

"That's the problem," Meghan admitted with a rueful smile. "My tongue often outdistances my mind. I get carried away and say the most absurd things and then I wonder why everyone is giving me odd looks."

"Friends?" Grey prompted, holding out his hand.

His look was so endearing and so tender that Meghan couldn't have resisted had she tried. From the first moment she'd noticed Grey Carlyle reading Chaucer, she'd been attracted to him. Strongly attracted. Lots of good-looking men had passed through the doors of Rose's Diner, and plenty had shown more than a casual interest in her. But this was the first time Meghan had ever dated anyone she'd met at the restaurant after such a short acquaintance.

"Friends," Meghan agreed, slipping her hand into his. His touch was light and impersonal, and Meghan experienced a sensation of rightness about their being together.

Perhaps it was best that she hadn't guessed his occupation earlier. If she had, she might not have been so candid.

They started walking toward the ivy-covered brick buildings. The pathway was lined by small green shrubs. "I wish now I'd worn my other shoes," Meghan commented casually. The one good thing about this date was that she'd cleaned out her closest while searching for the perfect outfit. After trying on anything and everything that was the least bit suitable, she'd chosen a red plaid skirt, white blouse and dark blazer, with knee-high leather boots.

Grey paused and glanced down at her feet. "Are those too tight?"

"No, especially since I've stuck my foot in my mouth a couple of times, but my other shoes are more subtle."

"Subtle?" he repeated.

"All right," she muttered. "More dignified. If I'd known I was attending this lecture with a full-fledged professor, I'd have dressed more appropriately for the occasion. But since I assumed you were just a regular, run-of-the-mill, classical literature lover, I thought the boots would do fine."

"You look wonderful just the way you are."

The open admiration in his gaze told her he was telling the truth. "It's nice of you to say so, but from here on out, it's my black patent-leather Mary Janes."

He burst out with a short laugh. The sound was robust and full but a little rusty, as though he didn't often reveal his amusement quite so readily.

Again he securely tucked her hand in the curve of his arm. "This is a prime example of what I was talking about earlier."

"What is?" Meghan wasn't sure she understood.

"Your honesty. There isn't any pretense in you, and I find that exceptionally rare these days."

Meghan was about to make a comment, when they strolled past a group of students.

"Hello, Professor Carlyle," a blond girl said eagerly and raised her hand. When Grey turned toward her, the teen smiled brightly. "I just wanted to be sure you knew I was here."

Grey nodded.

From all the smiles and raised hands directed toward Grey, Meghan guessed he was a popular professor. Heaven knew *she* liked him! Now that was an understatement if there ever was one. But at the same time she'd be a fool to hope that a man like Grey Carlyle would ever be romantically interested in her—and Meghan was rarely foolish. Obtuse, yes; foolish, no! She might amuse him now, but that wasn't likely to last.

Gavin Hall was only a short distance from the lot where Grey had parked his car. The auditorium was huge, and by the time they were seated near the back of the hall, it was more than a third filled.

Two men sat near the podium. The first Meghan recognized from the newspaper as Friends's president, Dr. Browning. The other man was obviously the speaker. To Meghan's way of thinking, he resembled a prune, though she chided herself for the uncharitable thought. The lecturer seemed to wear a perpetual frown, as though everything he saw displeased him. Either that or he'd recently been sucking lemons.

"There seems to be a nice turnout," Meghan commented, impressed by the number of students who appeared to have such a keen interest in Keats and Shelley.

Grey straightened the knot of his tie and cleared his

throat. "Actually," he whispered out of the corner of his mouth, "I bribed my class."

"I beg your pardon?"

Grey didn't look particularly proud of himself. "Dr. Fulton Essary is a colleague of mine and a distinguished poet in his own right. We've had our differences over the years, but basically I value his opinions. I wanted a good showing tonight, so I told my classes that every one of my students who showed up would automatically receive an extra fifty credits toward his overall grade."

"Ah," Meghan said softly. "That was why the blond girl made a point of letting you know she was here."

"Exactly." Grey withdrew a piece of paper from the inside of his suit jacket and unfolded it as quietly as possible. As he scanned the auditorium, he started checking off names.

Within five minutes the lights dimmed and Dr. Browning approached the podium to make his introduction. Shortly afterward, Dr. Fulton Essary stepped up to the front of his audience and delivered his speech—in a dead monotone.

For one hour and five minutes Dr. Essary summarized the life and works of Percy Bysshe Shelley and John Keats. Although Meghan admired the talents of both nineteenth-century poets and was familiar with their styles and literary accomplishments, she was eager to learn something new.

Unfortunately, nothing she could do kept her thoughts from wandering. Dr. Essary was terribly boring.

After the first half hour, Meghan started shifting in her seat, crossing and uncrossing her long legs. At forty-five minutes, she was picking imaginary lint from the lap of her skirt.

The only thing she found riveting was the fact that someone who planned to talk for this amount of time could reveal such little emotion concerning his subjects. He might as well have been lecturing about the Walt Disney characters, Mickey and Minnie Mouse.

If anything in Keats's and Shelley's lives had personally touched him, Meghan would have never known it.

Once he finished there was a round of polite, restrained applause followed by what Meghan felt was a sigh of relief that rolled over the audience. The floor was opened for questions, and after an awkward beginning, one brave student stood and asked something that Meghan couldn't fully hear or understand.

Slowly Grey moved his head toward Meghan's and whispered, "What do you think?"

It was in her mind to lie to him, to tell him what he wanted to hear; but he'd claimed he admired her honesty, and she wouldn't give him anything less now. "The man's a bore."

Grey's eyes widened at the bluntness of her remark.

Meghan saw his reaction and immediately felt guilty. "I shouldn't have said that," she told him, "but I couldn't help it. I'm disappointed."

"I understand you may have found his delivery lacking, but what about content?"

Apparently the question-and-answer session was over with the one question, because just as Meghan was about to whisper her response, everyone started to stand. Happily leaping to their feet more adequately described what transpired, Meghan mused.

She supposed she wasn't the only one to notice, but it seemed to her that the hall emptied as quickly as if someone had screamed "Fire! Run for your lives!" Grey's students couldn't get out of there fast enough. Personally, she shared their enthusiasm.

Once they were outside, Grey helped her on with her coat, slipping it over her blazer, his hands lingering on her shoulders. "You were about to say something," he coaxed.

Meghan stared up at him blankly while putting on her gloves.

Burying his hands in the pockets of his thick overcoat, Grey matched his long strides to her shorter ones. "You didn't like the lecture?"

"I...I wouldn't exactly say that."

"You called the speaker a bore," he reminded her, frowning.

"Yes, well..."

"Is this another one of those times when your tongue got away with you?" he teased, but the amusement didn't quite reach his eyes.

Meghan slipped her hands inside her coat pockets, forming tight fists, uncertain how she should respond. She probably wouldn't be seeing Grey after tonight, so there wasn't any reason to pad her answer. She wasn't sure she could, anyway. After an hour and five minutes of such insipid drivel, she was having trouble holding her tongue.

"Perhaps referring to him as a bore was a bit of an exaggeration," she started, hoping to take the bite out of her blunt remark.

"So you've changed your mind." That seemed to please Grey.

"Not entirely."

His face fell. "You can't fault Dr. Essary. Honestly, Meghan, the man's a recognized genius. He's published his doctorate on Shelley and Keats. Mention the name

Dr. Fulton Essary and the literary world automatically associates him with the two poets. His own published works have been compared to theirs. He's known all across America."

Meghan had never heard of him, but that wasn't saying much. Unfortunately, as far as she was concerned if someone were to mention the name Dr. Fulton Essary, her response would be a drawn-out yawn.

"I won't argue with you," she said, carefully choosing her words, "but there's no passion in the man."

"No passion? Are you saying he should have ranted and raved and pounded his fists against the podium? Is this how you think he should have delivered his lecture?"

"No—"

"Then just exactly what do you mean by passion?" Grey asked, clearly frustrated by her lack of appreciation for his colleague.

"Essary compared Keats to Shakespeare for the richness and confidence of his language, and I couldn't agree with him more, but—"

"Then what's the point?"

"The point is that for all the feeling your associate relayed, Keats could have written 'Mary Had a Little Lamb.' If what he was saying was so profound—and I think it could have been—then it should have come from his heart. I didn't feel anything from this friend of yours except disdain, as though he were lowering himself to share his insights to a group of students who are constitutionally incapable of understanding Keats's and Shelley's genius. Nothing he said gripped me, because it hadn't touched him."

Grey was silent for a minute. "Don't you think you're being unnecessarily harsh?"

"Perhaps, but I don't think so," she murmured. "Ask your students what they think. I'm sure one of them will have courage enough to be honest."

"It was a mistake to have brought you here," Grey said when they reached his car, his mouth a thin line of impatience.

He was angry and doing a remarkable job of restraining himself, Meghan noted. For that matter, she wasn't particularly pleased with him, either. He'd asked her what she thought and she'd told him. It was as if he expected her to say whatever it suited him to hear. Nor was she pleased with what he seemed to be implying. He made it sound as though she couldn't possibly know enough to make an intelligent evaluation of a man as brilliant as Dr. Essary. Good heavens! Even his name was pompous-sounding! All this evening did was reinforce the fact that she would never make it as a college student. If her supposed friend thought her stupid, what would strangers think?

Ever the gentleman, Grey helped Meghan into his car, firmly closing the passenger door and walking around to the driver's side.

The ride back to Rose's was an uncomfortable one. Grey didn't say a word and neither did Meghan. The silence was so loud she could barely hear anything else. It was in her mind to say something to ease the tension, but one look at Grey told her he wasn't in the mood to talk. Now that she thought about it, neither was she. She did feel badly, however. Grey had invited her to the lecture and she'd gone with an open mind, eager to learn; instead, she'd come away feeling depressed and sorry.

He eased his car into the restaurant parking lot and moved to turn off the engine.

"Don't," she said quickly, sadly. "There's no need for you to get out. I apologize for ruining your evening. Despite everything, I'm grateful you invited me to the lecture—I've learned some valuable lessons. But I feel badly that I've disappointed you. I wish you well, Professor Carlyle. Good evening." With that, she opened the car door and climbed out.

As she was walking away, Meghan thought she heard him call after her, but she didn't turn around—and he didn't follow her.

It was just as well.

Three

Grey couldn't remember a time when a woman had upset him more. Streetlights whizzed past him as he hurried back to Friends University, and he realized he was traveling well above the speed limit. With a sigh of impatience, he eased his foot off the gas pedal and reluctantly slowed his pace.

Grey had asked Meghan to Dr. Essary's lecture, believing she would be stimulated and challenged by the talk as well as the man. He'd liked Meghan, been attracted to her warmth and her wit; but now the taste of disillusionment filled him. In the space of only a few hours, he'd discovered that although she appeared intellectually curious, she wasn't willing to listen and learn from those who clearly had more literary knowledge than she. Being a professor himself, he felt it was like a slap in the face.

His invitation had been impulsive; and every time he acted spontaneously, Grey lived to regret it. This evening was an excellent example.

Meghan was a mere twenty-four-year-old with nothing more than a high-school education. She had no right to make such thoughtless statements about a man as eminent as Dr. Essary—a man who'd made a significant contribution to the world of literature. Just thinking about Meghan's comments infuriated Grey. The other man was brilliant, and she'd had the audacity to call him a bore. To worsen matters, she'd gone on to claim that Dr. Essary had revealed little emotion for his subject. Why, anyone looking at him would know differently. All right, Grey admitted, his esteemed colleague could use a few pointers on the proper method of delivering a speech of that length, but the audience wasn't a group of preschoolers with short attention spans. These were college students—adults.

What had upset Grey most, he decided, was Meghan's claim that Dr. Essary had displayed no passion. Of all the silly comments. Good grief, just exactly what did she expect—tears, dramatic gestures, or throwing himself down in front of the audience?

Grey had delivered plenty of lectures in his career, and his style wasn't all that different from that of his associate. No one had ever faulted Grey. No one had claimed he was a bore—no one would dare!

Back at Friends University, Grey sat inside his car for several minutes while the disillusionment worked its way through him. Rarely had he been more disappointed. Indignity burned through him like a fiery blade, hotter than what Meghan's comments warranted.

After a moment he slammed his hand against the steering wheel in a rare burst of emotion.

As he climbed out of the car, the lights from a coffeehouse called Second Life from across the street attracted his attention. A number of Friends students were known to hang out there. Grey started walking in the opposite direction to the faculty reception in honor of Dr. Essary, but stopped after only a few feet. Frowning, he abruptly turned around and headed toward the café.

Meghan secured the tie of her bright yellow housecoat around her waist and set the teakettle on top of the burner. Her apartment near Marina Lake was small and homey, but Meghan felt little of its welcome after this evening's disaster.

To prove exactly what kind of mood she was in, she'd walked in the door and gone directly to her bedroom to reach for her yellow robe. In fact, she hadn't even bothered to undress first.

Do not pass go. Do not collect two hundred dollars.

That was the way she felt—like a loser in a board game.

She'd blown her date with Grey. It was another one of those "open mouth and insert foot" incidents. He'd asked for her honesty, and she'd told him exactly what she thought of his friend. From there, the evening had quickly disintegrated. She should have known he wanted her to lie, and gone on and on about how wonderful the lecture had been.

Meghan didn't know if she was that good a liar. But it was clearly what he'd wanted to hear, and she should have given it to him and saved herself some grief.

So this was to be the end of her short-but-sweet relationship with Grey Carlyle. Unfortunately, it would take a while to work through the regret. Knowing the way she did things, it would take her a few days to pull herself together, to dissect the evening and put the incident into perspective so she could learn from what had happened. At the end of this blue funk she should walk away a little wiser.

The kettle let loose with a high-pitched whistle that broke the silence of the tiny kitchen. Meghan poured the boiling water into the teapot, added the herbal leaves and left them to steep for several minutes. She was just about to pour herself a cup when there was a knock at the door.

She glanced across the living room as though she expected there was some mistake. No one could possibly be coming to visit at this hour—unless, of course, it was one of her teenage brothers; but even that was unlikely this late in the evening.

"Who is it?" she asked.

"It's Grey. Could we talk a minute?"

Grey! Meghan's hands were trembling so badly she could hardly manage to twist the lock and pull open her front door. In that short time span, she didn't have a chance to school her reaction or her thoughts. The only thing she felt was an instant surge of jubilation. The smile that spread across her face came from deep within her heart. Meghan knew without even trying, there was no way to restrain the look of sheer joy that dominated her features.

"Grey," she said, stepping aside so he could enter her apartment.

He did so, standing awkwardly just inside the door. His gaze seemed to rest somewhere behind her and refused to meet her own. His expression was brooding and serious. The smile that had sprung so readily to her face quickly faded.

"I can see this is a bad time," Grey commented, once he looked directly at her and her yellow housecoat.

"No…this is fine," she replied hurriedly. "Would you

like to sit down?" Embarrassed by the load of laundry that was piled on one corner of the sofa, she rushed over and scooped it up with both hands, smiled apologetically and deposited the clean clothes on the seat of the recliner.

"You look as if you were ready for bed," Grey observed, remaining standing. "Perhaps it would be better if I returned at a more convenient time."

"No, please stay." She removed the housecoat and draped it over the back of the chair that contained her laundry. "I bought this robe several years ago when my family was on vacation in Texas," she felt obliged to explain. "Whenever I'm feeling depressed or unhappy about something, I put it on and pout for a while. My mother calls it the Yellow Robe of Texas."

Grey cracked a smile at that. "You're pouting now?"

"I was, but I'm not anymore." Meghan was delighted to see him, if only to let him know how much she regretted the way their evening had gone. She wanted to tell him how she'd felt when he'd lashed out at her, which had only driven home her own point that she wasn't cut out for college-level literature courses.

"I just put on a pot of tea. Would you like some?" she offered.

"Please."

Meghan moved into the kitchen and brought down her two best china cups, along with sugar and milk, and set them on a tray. When she turned around, she discovered Grey standing behind her, looking chagrined, his hands in his pockets.

"Aren't you the least bit curious why I'm here?"

With her heart in her throat, she nodded. The last person she had ever expected to see on the other side of her door was Grey Carlyle—*Professor* Grey Carlyle. "I'm equally curious to know how you knew where I live."

"When I went back to Rose's—I hoped you'd still be there—anyway, another waitress, I think her name was Sherry, gave me your address."

Meghan should have known the assistant manager would be willing to go against company policy for Grey. Normally the information would have had to be tortured out of her co-worker.

Grey freed one hand from inside his coat pocket and jerked his splayed fingers through his hair as though he weren't particularly pleased about something. "I told her you'd left something in my car that I thought you might need. I don't usually lie, but I felt it was important we talk."

Meghan's fingers tightened around the serving tray. "I understand."

Grey took the tray from her hand and set it on the round oak table that dominated what little space there was in her cramped kitchen. With him standing so close, the area seemed all the more limited. Despite herself, Meghan lifted her gaze to his.

Grey raised his hands to the rounded curves of her shoulders and his eyes caressed hers. "I owe you an apology."

"No," she said, and shook her head, more than willing to discount his words. "I should be the one to make amends to you. I don't know what came over me, or why I felt it was necessary to be so insensitive. I'm not often so opinionated—well, I am, but I'm usually more subtle about it. If it means anything, I want you to know I felt terrible afterward."

"What you said was true," he admitted bluntly, frowning. "Dr. Essary *is* an arrogant bore. The reason I took exception to your description of him is because Essary and I are actually quite a bit alike."

"I'm sure he's a fine man of sterling character—" Meghan stopped abruptly. "I beg your pardon?" She was sure she'd misunderstood Grey. He couldn't possibly mean to suggest that he was anything like his colleague. She didn't know Grey well, but everything about him told her Professor Carlyle was nothing like the other man.

"After dropping you off, I drove back to the university campus. I'll admit I was upset…more than I have been in a long time. I sat in my car fuming, feeling confused. I couldn't seem to put my finger on why I should be so insulted." He paused, pulled out a kitchen chair and gestured for Meghan to sit down. She did and he took the seat across from her.

"You were defending your friend, the same way he would have supported you," Meghan reassured him, silently chastising herself for her arrogant ways.

"Not true," Grey contradicted, his frown growing darker and more intense. "Fulton and I have never considered ourselves in those terms. You might even say there's friendly rivalry going on between us."

Since they were both sitting, Meghan poured the tea, handing Grey his cup. She didn't feel nearly as shaken now.

"Something you said, however, struck a note with me," he continued. "You suggested I ask my students what they thought. You seemed confident at least one of them would open up to me."

Meghan did vaguely remember suggesting that.

"A group of my pupils were having coffee after the lecture. I joined them and asked for their honest opinion." He hesitated, looking mildly distressed. "I asked. And by heaven, they gave it to me with both barrels."

Hearing that others shared her sentiments didn't cause Meghan to feel better about what had happened between her and Grey, but it helped.

While he was talking, Grey added both sugar and milk to his tea, stirring it in as though the sweetener were made of some indissoluble compound. "I took a long hard look at Fulton," Grey continued, "and what I saw was a sad reflection of myself."

"Grey, no." Her hand automatically reached for his.

"Meghan, you don't know me well enough to contradict me."

"But I do.... I realize we've only talked a few times, but you're not anything like Dr. Essary. I know it as surely as I'm convinced we're sitting here together."

He captured her fingers and squeezed lightly. "It's kind of you to say so, but unfortunately I know differently. My life has been filled with academia and its importance. In the process, I've allowed myself to become jaded toward life, forgetting the significance of what I thought were trivial matters. In the last few years, I've immersed myself in a disapproving, wet-blanket attitude."

"I'm sure you're mistaken."

His smile was sad, his features grim. "I've laughed more with you in the past few days than I have all year. I look at Fulton, so deadpan and serious, and I recognize myself. Frankly, I don't like what I'm seeing. If you feel there's no passion in him, you're right. But there's none in me, either. It's not something I'm proud to admit. Fun is often associated with frivolity. And as a learned man—an educator—I've looked upon fun as a flaw in the character of a man." He studied his cup as though he expected the tea leaves to spell out what he should say next. "I owe you much more than an apology, Meghan. In only a few short days you've revealed to me something I'd been too blind to recognize until now. I want you to know I'm truly grateful."

Meghan didn't know what to say. "I'm sure you're putting more stock than necessary in all this. The minute I met you I saw an intense, introverted man of undeniable intelligence who loved Chaucer and Milton the same way I did. I'm nothing more than a waitress at a popular diner, and you shared your love for the classics with me. If anything, that made you more appealing to me than a hundred other men." Meghan understood all too well the differences between them. Grey was accustomed to a refined, academic atmosphere while she was fun loving and slightly outrageous. From the moment she'd started talking to him Meghan had recognized Grey's type. He was analytical, weighing each fact, cataloging each bit of information before acting. Impulsive actions were as foreign to him as a large savings account was to her.

"What I saw was a bright, enthusiastic woman who—"

"Who doesn't know when to keep her mouth shut," Meghan finished for him.

They both laughed, and it felt good. Meghan took a sip of her tea, feeling almost light-headed. She realized it had taken a good deal of courage for Grey to seek her out and apologize.

He glanced at his watch, arched his brows as though he were surprised by the time, and stood abruptly. "I'm sorry for interrupting what remains of your evening, but I wanted to talk to you while I still had the nerve. The longer I put it off, the more difficult it would have been."

Meghan appreciated what it must have cost him to come to her, and her estimation of him, which was already high, increased a hundredfold. She didn't want him to leave, but she couldn't think of an excuse to delay him.

"I know how difficult it was for you to stop by. I'm glad you did."

"I am, too." He edged his way to the front door.

Meghan's mind was racing frantically in an effort to prolong his leaving. She thought to suggest a game of Monopoly, but was certain he'd find that childish. Cards weren't likely to interest him, either.

"Thanks for the tea."

"Sure," she said with a shrug. "Any time."

His gaze fell on the yellow robe that had been carelessly draped over the recliner and smiled. "Good night, Meghan."

She went to open the door for him, but his hand at her shoulder stopped her. She turned, and his narrowed gaze met hers in a lazy, caressing action. His eyes were filled with questions, but Meghan couldn't decipher what it was he wanted to know. A contest of wills seemed to be waging within him as his look continued to embrace her. Meghan returned his gaze, not understanding but wanting to help in any way she could.

"Every time I act on impulse I regret it."

She blinked, not knowing what to make of his comment. "Sometimes it's the only thing to do," she murmured. "My mother always claimed I should follow my heart. That's good advice—I suggest you do the same."

The frown left him, to be replaced by a determined grin. "You're right. Sometimes doing what seems natural is by far the best thing. I have the distinct feeling I won't regret this." With that, he lowered his head to hers and she felt the warm brush of his mouth across her own. He slipped his arm around her waist and gently pulled her against him, half lifting her from the floor. He touched the upper part of her lip with his tongue, lightly, and moistened the outline of her mouth.

A choppy rush of air escaped from her lips at this subtle attack on her senses. Meghan moaned softly and leaned into him, letting his weight absorb her own. Then, moving her head farther back, Grey rubbed his lips against hers, applying a gentle pressure until her mouth parted in welcome, eager for a more thorough exploration.

Meghan shouldn't have been so surprised that he would kiss her, but she was. She flattened her hands against his chest, her fingers clenching handfuls of his shirt as she gave herself over to the wealth of sensation that rocked through her.

It was a short kiss as kisses went; his mouth lingered over hers for only a heartbeat more and then quickly withdrew, leaving her hungering for more.

"I'd like to see you again," he said in a voice that sounded unlike his own, strained and reluctant. "Soon."

"Yes."

"Tomorrow night, at six? Dinner, a movie, anything you want."

Meghan made some kind of appropriate response, but the minute he was gone, she leaned against the door, needing its support. Several different emotions buzzed around her head. She felt disappointed that the kiss had been so short, and at the same time electrified and thrilled. With that brief kiss had come an immeasurable flash of excitement. She lifted her fingertips to her lips and examined them, half expecting there to be some lasting evidence of his touch. Her heart was pounding so hard, she felt as if her ribs were about to collapse. It wasn't that she'd never been kissed before; but no one had ever caused her pulse to react like this.

No one.

Four

The dishwasher was humming softly in the background when Meghan stepped into the shower late Saturday afternoon. She'd gone shopping and splurged on a new outfit, and had gotten home later than she would have liked. Normally she would have waited until the dishwasher was finished, but there wasn't time.

From the moment Grey had left her apartment the night before, her mind had been filled with romantic daydreams. She imagined him wining and dining her and then leading her onto a dance floor. Her fantasy showed him wrapping his arms around her and gazing into her eyes with undisguised admiration. Visions of him holding and kissing her filled her mind. Everything about this night was going to be perfect. They'd had such a rocky beginning, and she longed to make everything right.

Halfway through the shower, the water went freezing cold. Crying out in protest, Meghan turned off the knob and reached for a thick towel. A faint gurgling sound could be heard in the background. Thinking she should probably look into what was happening, Meghan wrapped the towel around her body and traipsed into the kitchen. Her wet hair fell over her face and she impatiently swatted it aside as she investigated the scene. An icy cold, wet sensation struck her toes the instant she moved onto the linoleum floor.

Meghan gasped and hurried back onto the carpet on her tiptoes.

Her dishwasher had overflowed.

"Oh, great," she moaned, running into the bathroom for some towels. As luck would have it, there was only one dry one and she was forced to search frantically through her laundry hamper for something to sop up the liquid. In her desperation she was tossing clothing left and right, hurling her panties and bras above her head.

Gathering up what she could, she hauled an armload of soiled clothes into the kitchen and quickly spread them over the floor. The first thing she had to do was to soak up as much water as she could as fast as possible. The whole time she was working, she was glancing at the clock.

What towels she could locate, plus a couple of shirts and two pairs of jeans, looked like mismatched puzzle pieces across her linoleum by the time she finished spreading them around. Still, water was puddled everywhere.

In an effort to help her clothes absorb as much as possible, Meghan danced over them, stomping her feet in a wild kind of jitterbug.

The doorbell chimed and Meghan froze. Please, she prayed, don't let that be Grey! Her gaze swung to the kitchen clock. It was still five minutes early. If there was an angel watching over her, then it wouldn't be Grey at her front door.

"Who is it?" she called out, holding the front of her

housecoat together with one hand, bunching the material together so tightly her nails threatened to bend. Her hair was half dry by this time and stuck out in several different directions.

"It's Grey."

Meghan's faith in heavenly assistance quickly faded. She couldn't answer the door dressed in her robe and underwear with her hair resembling something out of a science-fiction movie. If that wasn't bad enough, her kitchen floor looked as if several bodies had recently been vaporized.

"Meghan?"

"Ah...I'm not quite ready," she responded, forcing a cheerful note into her voice. "Would it be possible for you to come back in a few minutes?"

Silence followed her request.

"That is if it wouldn't be too much of an inconvenience," she tried again, desperately hoping he would agree. When he returned she'd explain, but she couldn't let him see her like this.

"I did say six, didn't I?" he pressed.

"Yes," Meghan muttered.

"It's obvious that something else, or more likely *someone else*, has come by," Grey called back to her. "How long would you like me to disappear for? An hour? Two? Will that be long enough for you?"

Someone else! Grey thought she was trying to get rid of him because there was a man in the apartment with her? Her shoulders sagged in defeat. Without hesitating any longer, she yanked open the front door and stepped aside.

"You might as well come in and have a good laugh," she said, sweeping her hand in front of her. To her horror, her voice became a high-pitched screech, barely discernible. She tried several times to swallow, but all she could manage was to make more of the same wretched sounds.

She dared not look at him, because once she saw the dismay in his eyes, she was bound to burst into tears, and that would only humiliate her further.

"Meghan, what happened?" He moved into her apartment and closed the door.

Her head hung so low that her chin was tucked against her collarbone. "I was in the shower when I heard funny gurgling noises.... My dishwasher died and there's water everywhere and I look like something from outer space." Desperate for oxygen, she sucked in a huge breath.

"Why didn't you say so in the first place?" Grey said.

He made it sound as though she'd purposely planned the whole disaster to evoke sympathy from him. "I wanted everything to be so special tonight—and then you seemed to think I'm keeping a man in here." She didn't dare admit that he was the only male she'd thought about from the minute he'd stepped into Rose's Diner. Her shoulders jerked up and down each time she tried to breathe.

"Meghan," he said, appealing to her with his hands. "I don't know what to say. I'm sorry, I thought—"

"I know exactly what you thought," she interrupted as the situation and his initial reaction started to get the better of her. "As you can see, something *has* come up and I won't be able to go out tonight." Pointedly she walked over to the door and opened it for him.

"The least I can do is help," he insisted.

Somehow the picture of Professor Grey Carlyle under a sink refused to take shape in her mind. This was a man familiar with George Bernard Shaw—not water pipes and broken-down dishwashers.

"I doubt that you know the least bit about plumbing," she remarked stiffly.

"I don't," he agreed, and then added under his breath, "and even less about women, it seems."

With her chin tilted at a defiant angle, Meghan stood with her back straight, her fingers tightening around the doorknob. "I appreciate the offer, but no thanks."

"You're sure you'll be all right?"

"Positive," she said, and flipped a damp strand of hair out of her eyes with as much dignity as she could muster, which wasn't much.

He proceeded to walk out but paused just outside the apartment door to exhale sharply and murmured, "I'm sorry, Meghan."

"So am I," she responded, feeling both miserable and defeated.

Ten minutes later, after Meghan had dressed and run a brush through her hair, she phoned the apartment manager, who was gone for the evening—naturally. Given no other choice, Meghan phoned her father.

Perhaps she'd been a bit hasty with Grey, she mused in the quiet minutes that followed her call home. He'd only been trying to help. Unfortunately his offer had followed on the heels of his implication that she was hiding a man in her apartment. For him to even suggest such a thing was enough to set her teeth on edge.

Both Meghan's parents arrived within the half hour.

"Hi, Mom. Hi, Dad," she greeted, hugging them both, grateful for their love and support.

Her father carried a toolbox with him. At fifty, Patrick O'Day was in his prime—healthy, fit, and handsome to boot. Meghan had always been close to both parents.

"What happened in your kitchen? A mass murder?" her father teased, then laughed at his own joke as he stepped over the sopping array of clothes.

"Thanks for coming over," Meghan told him sincerely. "I don't know what I would have done. The apartment manager wasn't in and more than likely he wouldn't be able to get anyone here until Monday morning, anyway."

Colleen O'Day removed her coat while studying Meghan. "Weren't you going out with that professor friend of yours this evening?"

In her excitement Meghan had phoned her mother and told her all about meeting Grey. "*Was* as in past tense! Obviously, something came up."

"Meghan, darlin', you must be so disappointed."

She nodded. There didn't seem to be anything more to say. This evening wasn't turning out the least bit the way she'd hoped.

When it came to Grey, she felt like someone eager to appear in a circus performing in the high-wire balancing act. Although she wanted badly to do it, she couldn't seem to find her footing. Each time she tried, she nearly slipped and fell.

"You look tired," her mother said next.

Meghan felt exhausted. For most of the day she'd been running on nervous energy, not taking time to eat lunch. Breakfast had been a glass of orange juice while on the run.

"It's not your dishwasher—you've got a broken pipe down here," her father shouted from beneath the kitchen sink.

"Surprise, surprise," Meghan answered with a soft

chuckle. With her mother's help she removed the clothes and towels that littered the floor, placing them inside the empty laundry basket.

Her father had nearly completed the repair when her doorbell chimed. The teakettle whistled at almost the same second, and frustrated, Meghan paused, not knowing which to attend to first.

"You get the door," her mother suggested, "and I'll take care of the tea."

It was Grey. He'd changed out of his pin-striped suit and into slacks and a sweater. He stood in front of her, holding a large book at his side.

"Before you get upset," he said, "I want you to know something."

Meghan's fingers curled around the doorknob. "You should know something, too," she returned.

"What?"

"I *have* got a man in my apartment—a handsome one who openly admits he loves me. This guy's crazy about me. Would you care to meet him?"

Anger flickered in Grey's eyes, and his mouth narrowed.

"Meghan?" her mother called out from behind her. "Who is that at the door?"

Reluctantly Meghan stepped aside. "Mom and Dad, I'd like you both to meet Professor Grey Carlyle. He teaches English literature at Friends University."

Grey stepped into the apartment, but his gaze centered on Meghan. "Your father?" he whispered.

She gave him a saucy grin.

"Professor Carlyle, how pleased we are to meet you," Colleen O'Day greeted, looking absolutely delighted to make his acquaintance.

Her father rose awkwardly to his feet and held out his hand to Grey, who shook it. "It seems my daughter was stuck in some hot water," Pat joked, "and had to call on her old man to rescue her."

"We were just about to have some tea, Professor. Please join us?"

Grey turned to Meghan, who didn't give him any indication she cared one way or the other. Actually, her heart was pounding so hard it was a wonder he couldn't see it beating against her sweatshirt.

"Thank you," he said, smiling up at Meghan's mother. "I'd enjoy a cup of tea."

"Pat?" Colleen asked, while Meghan brought cups down from the cupboard.

"Please." His reply was muffled as he was back under the sink.

"Can I do anything to help?" Grey asked, setting the book on the tabletop.

For the first time, Meghan could see the title, and when she did, she regretted her earlier display of anger. Grey had gone out and bought a book on plumbing repairs. Her insides went all soft at the thought that he should care so much.

"I'm almost finished here," her father told him. "I'll be with you in a couple of minutes. You sit down and I'll be there once I get this blasted fitting secure."

Her mother was busy pouring tea, which Meghan delivered to the small round table.

"I hope you're still hungry," Grey said when she approached him.

Her gaze shot to him and she blinked, not sure she understood.

"I've got two Chinese dinners in my car."

"I—"

"Why, that's thoughtful, isn't it, Meghan?" her mother interrupted. "Pat, don't you think we should be heading home? Danny needs to be picked up from the theater soon."

"I was going to have tea," he objected, and then hesitated, apparently reading his wife's expression. "Right," he said evenly. "I forgot Danny. Now that your pipe's fixed, Meghan, I guess I'll be leaving." Her father picked up the pliers and the other tools he'd been using and placed them inside his toolbox.

"Speaking of dinner," Colleen O'Day said, "why don't you come over to our house tomorrow for Sunday dinner, Professor? We've hardly had a chance to get to know you, and that way you could meet Meghan's three younger brothers."

Meghan's sip of tea moved halfway down her throat and refused to go any farther. It took several attempts to swallow it. Meghan didn't know what her mother could be thinking. Grey didn't want to meet her family. Why should he? He and Meghan barely knew each other, and every time they even tried to date, the evening ended in disaster.

"Thank you, Mrs. O'Day, I'd be honored."

Meghan realized his acceptance was only an excuse to be polite. After her parents left, she would let Grey know he shouldn't feel obligated.

"Okay, princess, everything seems to be working." To prove his point, Pat O'Day turned on the kitchen faucet, and after a few sputters the water gushed out normally.

"Thanks, Dad," she told him, kissing him on the cheek.

"It was a pleasure to have met you both," Grey said, in what Meghan was sure was his most courteous voice.

"You, too."

"We'll see you tomorrow at three, then," her mother prompted.

"I'll be there."

"Now, you two young folks try to enjoy the rest of your evening," Colleen O'Day suggested.

"We'll do that," Grey promised, his gaze reaching out and capturing Meghan's.

Five

Meghan braced her feet on the chair beside her, her knees raised as she held the small white box of spicy diced chicken directly below her chin. Grey might be accustomed to eating with chopsticks, but she wasn't.

"You're doing great."

She smiled lamely. "Right! I've got five different kinds of sauces smeared over the front of my sweatshirt and soy sauce dribbling down my chin." The piece of chicken that was balanced precariously on the end of her chopstick fell and landed in her lap, proving her point.

"Here." Grey handed her a paper napkin.

"Thanks."

Grey set aside the white container and reached for a small bag. "Are you ready for your fortune cookie?"

"Sure." She held out her hand, eager to discover her fate.

Grey gave her one and then promptly opened his first.

Meghan giggled at his shocked expression. "What does it say?"

"Ver-r-y inter-r-esting," he said in a feigned Chinese

accent. "Cookie say professor must beware of waitress who read Shakespeare."

"Very funny," she returned, having a difficult time holding in her laughter. Setting aside the take-out container Meghan ceremonially split open her own fortune cookie.

"Well?" Grey prompted.

"It says I should beware of man who insists women eat with chopsticks."

Grey grinned. "I guess I asked for that."

"You most certainly did," she chided. "I don't suppose you want to hear my views on Shakespeare, do you?"

"Dear heavens, no. When it comes to literature, we can't seem to agree on anything."

"Literature," she echoed, "and just about everything else." That could very well be true, but when he was looking at her like this, his blue eyes warm and filled with humor, every argument she'd ever presented him with turned into melted ice cream. She was forced to pull her gaze away for fear of what he would read in her eyes.

"You'll be pleasantly surprised to know I'm crazy about Willie boy," she announced, popping half the fortune cookie into her mouth.

"Willie boy?"

"William Shakespeare."

"My faith in you has been restored," he said solemnly, dipping his head slightly.

"Oh, come now, Grey. Who couldn't like Shakespeare?"

"The same person who finds fault with Edmund Spenser is questioning my reserve toward another English great?" he asked, his eyes as round as paper plates. "I'd like to keep the peace as long as possible, if I can."

"Okay, okay. Forget I asked that." Still smiling, she

stood and started to deposit the empty cartons into the garbage can.

Grey helped her. "Are you willing to discuss something else?" he asked.

He was so casual that Meghan assumed he was about to pitch another joke her way. "Now that all depends," she replied and tossed a wadded paper sack from behind her back. Her throw was a dead ringer, landing in the garbage can as though it were impossible for her to ever miss. Stunned, her mouth sagged open. "Did you see that?"

"Meghan, I'm serious."

She dropped her hands to her sides and turned to face him. "I know," she teased, laughter bubbling up inside her, "but I'm hoping once you get to know me, you'll lighten up a little."

His responding smile was feeble at best. "Meghan, would you please listen to me?"

The smile drained from her eyes when she realized that something was indeed bothering him. "Yes, of course."

He buried his hands in his pockets and walked over to the sink, staring at it for a couple of seconds before turning to face her. "Earlier, when I met your parents…"

"Yes?"

"I saw your face when your mother invited me to Sunday dinner. You weren't pleased. The fact is, you don't want me there, do you?"

Her first thought was to confirm his suspicion, but she realized it wasn't entirely true. She *did* long for him to meet her family, only she feared the outcome. "You're more than welcome," she said blithely, hoping to casually dismiss any reserve he'd sensed. "It's just that…"

"What?"

"I don't want you to feel obligated. Mom's one of those warm, wonderful people who insists on sweeping everyone she meets under her wing. I'm afraid you might feel pressured into joining my family just because my mother issued the invitation. If the plumber had been here, she probably would have invited him, too," Meghan said, making light of her parent's offer. "It's just Mom's way."

"I see."

From the stiff tone of his voice, it was clear Grey obviously didn't. "You have to understand," Meghan hurried to add. "My brothers would love nothing better than to get you involved in a hot little contest of touch football. And knowing Dad, he'd corner you the minute you walk in the door. He loves chess—anyone visiting is fair game. My dad's a wonderful man but he tends to be something of a poor loser." Meghan realized she was rambling, but she was frantically trying to make him believe that she had his best interests at heart.

She didn't even mention the ribbing her three brothers would likely give him. The annoyed look Grey had told her she was apparently doing a poor job of explaining the situation.

"But what it really boils down to is that I wouldn't fit in with your family," he announced starkly. "That's what you're really trying to say."

"Not entirely." It was; only she hadn't fully realized it. "You're welcome to come if that's what you want," she finished, feeling both frustrated and confused.

"You mean your mother's welcome is sincere, but yours isn't?"

"Oh, Grey, why do you have to complicate this? I told you the reasons I have my doubts, but whether you decide to come or not is entirely up to you."

"I see."

Meghan slapped her hands noisily against the sides of her legs. "I wish you would stop saying that."

"What?"

"*I see*, in that pitiful voice, as though I'd insulted you." Earlier they'd sat and joked and teased each other like longtime friends, and now they were snapping at one another like cantankerous turtles. In the short time since they'd met, they'd muddled their way through several disputes. The last thing Meghan wanted was another one.

"I see," Gray said in exactly the tone she'd been talking about.

Meghan burst out laughing. She couldn't help herself, although it was clear that this reaction was the last thing Grey had expected of her.

"Professor Grey Carlyle, come here."

"Why?" His brows arched suspiciously, he studied her, clearly not trusting her.

"Never mind, I'll come to you." She did so, but the few short steps that separated them seemed more like miles. By the time she stood directly in front of him, Meghan had nearly lost her nerve. Boldly she slipped her arms around his neck, tilted back her head and looked squarely into his eyes.

Grey held himself stiff, with his hands hanging loosely at this sides, his brow puckered. "Kindly explain what you're doing!"

"You mean to tell me you don't know?" she asked softly. His mouth was scant inches from her own. Their soft, short breaths mingled and merged.

Very slowly, Meghan raised her lips to his and graced him with the briefest of kisses.

In response, Grey cleared his throat and moved his

head farther away from hers, yet he didn't disentangle her arms from his neck or make any move to slip her out of his arms.

If he expected to thwart her with a scowl, it wouldn't work. Meghan stood on the tips of her toes and leisurely passed her mouth over his in a soft, almost chaste kiss.

This time neither moved, neither breathed. Kissing Grey the first time should have been warning enough. The second brief sampling only whetted Meghan's appetite for more.

His too, it seemed.

Grey lowered his head until his lips barely touched hers. He held himself completely immobile for a long moment, brushing his mouth back and forth over hers, savoring the velvet texture of her lips. The tip of his tongue outlined first her upper lip and then her bottom one until she felt her knees would buckle if he didn't give her a more complete taste. She moaned softly and he slipped his mouth over hers with a fierce kind of tenderness, molding her mouth to his own.

His fingers were planted on the curves of her shoulders when he gently pushed her away. His breathing was deep and ragged. Meghan's own wasn't any more controlled.

She'd meant to entice him, to take his mind off her mother's invitation to Sunday dinner and the problem that had created between them. Instead, Meghan's plan had backfired.

Everything went stock still. She swallowed uncomfortably and lowered her eyes. She couldn't have met his look, had the defense of Mother Earth depended upon it.

"Meghan?"

"I…I shouldn't have done that."

"Yes," he murmured, "you should have." He lifted his hand to her nape, urging her back into his arms. Without any argument, she went. This wasn't a game any longer. She was trembling, with both excitement and need.

Grey kissed her again, using his tongue to coax her lips farther apart, sending a wild jolt of elation through her.

By the time Grey's lips moved from hers and he buried his face in the curve of her neck, Meghan had no strength left in her bones.

"All right," he whispered into her hair. "I'll conveniently forget the dinner tomorrow. You needn't worry I'll show up—I'll find some excuse to give your mother later."

Meghan tightened her arms around his neck. "I want you there. Only please remember what I said."

He laughed softly. "Meghan, it was obvious from the first that you didn't."

"I changed my mind," she said more forcefully this time. "Just be prepared for…my family."

"I suppose you're going to suggest I throw a game of chess, as well."

"That would be nice, but not necessary. It's time Dad owned up to the fact his strategy stinks."

A long moment passed in which Meghan felt they did nothing more than enjoy the feel of each other.

When her legs felt as if they could support her, she stepped away from him, but her heart was pounding like a charging locomotive. And yet she felt as weak as a newborn kitten.

"Please come," she said in as firm a voice as she could manage and wrote down her parents' address.

"You're sure about this?"

She pressed her forehead against his chest. "Yes."

"Then I'll be there."

Meghan was in the kitchen with her mother, peeling a huge pile of potatoes, when the doorbell chimed in the background. Ripping the apron from the front of her dress, she heaved in a calming breath to regain her composure and hurried into the living room.

Her parents' home was an older style built in the late 1920s, with a huge drawing room. An old brick fireplace with mantel was situated at one end, and bookcases along the other. A sofa, a recliner and two matching chairs with ottomans filled the rectangular area and were positioned around the television, where her father and brothers were watching a football game.

"That's probably Grey," she announced dramatically, standing in front of the TV set. It was the only way to completely gain their attention. "Now, please remember what I said," she cautioned, eyeing them severely.

"Oh, Meghan," thirteen-year-old Danny cried. "You make it sound like we're going to hurt him. He mustn't be much of a man if he can't hold his own in a little game of touch football."

"We've already been through this once, Daniel O'Day. You're not going to ask him to play football with you. Understand?"

"You sweet on this guy, Sis?" Brian asked, eyeing her with sparkling blue eyes and a mischievous grin.

"That's none of your business." As a high-school senior, Brian should know better than to ask. Meghan expected a little more understanding from her oldest brother. It was obvious, however, that she wasn't going to get it.

Her mistake had been revealing to her younger siblings how much she *did* care about Grey.

"Dad... No chess, please."

"Princess, are you going to open the door or not? You're leaving the poor man to freeze to death on the front porch while you give everyone instructions on how to act around him."

"Grey's important to me."

"Oh, gee," fifteen-year-old Chad said, and hit his forehead with the palm of his hand. "We hadn't figured that one out, Sis."

Meghan stood in front of the door, sighed inwardly and smoothed her hands down the front of her dress. At the last moment, she twirled around and faced her father and brothers once more. "Please."

"Meghan, for heaven's sake would you kindly answer the door."

She did as her father requested, her smile forced. "Hello, Grey," she said greeting him with a wide smile and opening the screen door for him. "I'm pleased you could make it."

Grey stepped into the family home, carrying a bouquet of red rosebuds. He was dressed in a suit and tie, looking as dignified and professional as ever.

Meghan looped her arm around his elbow so they faced the O'Day men as a united force. "You remember my dad from last night?"

"Of course." Grey stepped forward and the two men shook hands.

Brian stood with his father and Meghan introduced him.

"I'm pleased to meet you, Brian."

"You too, Professor."

"Please call me Grey."

"Can I call you that, too?" Chad asked. He wasn't wearing his shoes, and his socks had huge holes in the toes.

"That's Chad," Meghan said, and prayed Grey didn't notice her brother's feet.

"I'm fifteen. How old are you?"

"Chad!" Meghan cried, closing her eyes.

"He looks too old for you, Meghan," Chad muttered under his breath. "Now I suppose you're going to get all mad at me because I said so."

She offered Grey a weak smile, which was the best she could do.

"I'm thirty-four," Grey answered without a pause. "And you're right, I *am* too old for Meghan."

"No, you're not," Danny piped up, walking over and holding out his hand, which Grey readily accepted. "I'm Danny."

Meghan could have kissed the freckles off her youngest brother's nose at that moment. Grey wasn't too old for her. In fact, their age difference had never come up before as she hadn't given the matter a second thought.

Danny, however, quickly destroyed all her goodwill by adding, "So, you don't play football? I always hoped that when Meghan got married her husband would like sports."

"Danny!" Meghan cried, feeling her face explode with color. "Professor Carlyle and I are just getting to know each other. We aren't going to be married."

"You're not?"

"Of course not. We only met a few days ago."

"Yeah, but from the way you've been acting all afternoon, I thought you were really hot for this guy."

Meghan cast him a look heated enough to boil water.

"All right, all right," Danny moaned. "I'll shut up."

"Meghan," her father advised discreetly, "if you let go of Grey's arm, he might be able to take off his coat and sit down."

"Oh, sorry," she said, smiling apologetically. She cast Grey a knowing glance and whispered, "I warned you."

"So you did," he mumbled back and removed his overcoat, keeping the bouquet of flowers with him.

"Would you like some tea or coffee or anything else before dinner?" Meghan asked him, just as her mother stepped into the room.

"Professor, how good of you to come," Colleen said graciously.

Grey handed her the roses. "Thank you for asking me, Mrs. O'Day."

"Colleen, please," she corrected. "Oh, my! Roses! Really, Professor, you shouldn't have, but I'm glad you did. It's been years since I've received anything so lovely."

"You brought the roses for my mom?" Danny asked incredulously. "What did you bring for Meghan? I thought you were sweet on *her*. You better watch it, 'cause she's got a temper."

"Danny," Meghan whispered, her eyes pleading with his. "Please don't say another word. Not one more word!"

"But..."

"Do me a favor and keep quiet for the rest of the afternoon."

The injustice of it all was nearly more than her youngest sibling could take and he tucked his arms over his chest and centered his concentration on the football game that blared from the television set.

"How are the Chiefs doing?" Grey asked, sitting down in the chair beside her father.

"Terrible," Pat O'Day muttered and sadly shook his head. "The Seahawks are running all over them. What they need is more power in the backfield."

"Dad's something of an armchair quarterback," Meghan explained.

"Do you like football, Professor?" Chad asked, leaning forward from his position on the ottoman, his hands clasped. His gaze was intent, as though the outcome of Grey's relationship with the O'Day family rested on his reply.

"I've been known to watch a game every now and again," Grey answered.

Meghan sighed her relief.

"That's great, because us men usually play a game or two ourselves after dinner," Chad informed him, as though expecting Grey to volunteer to join them.

It was all Meghan could do to keep from jumping up and down and waving her arms in an effort to remind her brothers of what she'd said. They'd promised not to involve Grey in any of this, but it looked as if Chad had conveniently forgotten.

"I'll take the flowers into the kitchen. Thank you again, Professor," Colleen said, gently sniffing them and smiling proudly. She turned toward her husband and sons. "Dinner will be ready in thirty minutes, so don't get so involved in this silly football game."

"Don't worry, Mom," Brian said. "The Chiefs are losing."

Meghan stood, her feet braced apart. She would have remained planted there, had her mother not dragged her back into the kitchen.

"Mom," she protested, looking back at Grey. "It's not safe in there for him. Grey isn't like other men."

"Oh?" Her mother's eyebrows arched speculatively and her eyes twinkled with amusement.

What Meghan really meant to say was that Grey wasn't anything like the other men she'd dated over the past few years. He was special, and she didn't want anything to happen that would destroy their budding relationship.

"I mean—" she hurried to add "—Grey's an only child. His whole life has revolved around academia. All Brian, Chad and Danny know is football. Grey was so smart he was sent to an advanced preschool class, for heaven's sake." Her mother looked impressed and Meghan continued, listing the details of his academic achievements. "From kindergarten he went straight into a gifted-students program. Grey's a lamb among wolves in there with Dad and the boys."

"He'll do just fine," her mother returned confidently.

"But—"

"Now come on, fretting isn't going to do any good, and neither is hurrying in there to rescue him from the fiendish plots of your younger brothers."

Meghan cast a longing glance over her shoulder, knowing her mother was right but longing to run interference. Grey meant more to her than any man she'd ever met. She and Grey were vastly different—almost complete opposites—and yet they shared several common interests.

Meghan's biggest fear, now that she'd had time to analyze it, was that his meeting her family would emphasize how different they were and discourage Grey from continuing their relationship.

"I'll set the table," Meghan offered when she'd finished dicing the tomato for the salad. The dining room was situated between the living room and the kitchen and offered Meghan the opportunity to check on Grey without being obvious. She opened the drawer to the china hutch and brought out the lace tablecloth. While she was there, she stuck her head around the corner and chanced a peek inside the living room. To her dismay, she discovered Grey and her father deeply involved in a game of chess. She groaned and pressed her forehead against the wall. As much as she loved her father, when it came to chess he was a fanatic and even worse, a terrible sport.

By the time Meghan finished setting the table and mashing the potatoes, dinner was ready. She stood with her hands braced against the back of a dining-room chair while the men gathered around the table.

"Professor, please sit next to Meghan," Colleen O'Day instructed, pointing toward the empty chair beside her daughter.

Grey moved to her side.

"I saw you and Dad," she muttered out of the side of her mouth. "How'd it go?"

"He won."

Meghan sighed, appeased. "Thank you," she whispered back.

"Fair and square, Meghan. I didn't throw the game."

"Dad won?" she asked, louder this time, her voice filled with surprise. She blinked a couple of times, hardly able to believe what she was hearing.

"I'm the world's worst chess player, only you never bothered to ask."

A smile quivered at the corners of her mouth and she shook her head. Once her father had claimed his place at the head of the table, the family bowed their heads as Pat O'Day offered the blessing.

Meals had always been a happy, sharing time for the O'Days, and Danny started in talking about what was lacking on the Kansas City Chiefs football team.

The buttermilk biscuits were passed around, followed by Yankee pot roast, mashed potatoes, thick gravy, small green peas and the fresh salad.

"Professor, Meghan was telling me you graduated from high school when you were fourteen," her mother stated conversationally, turning the subject away from football.

"Is that true?" Chad popped half a biscuit into his mouth and stared at Grey as if the older man had recently stepped off a spaceship.

Grey cleared his throat and looked self-conscious. "Yes."

Colleen O'Day looked on proudly. "Meghan was always the one who earned top marks in our family."

"That's because she's a girl," Danny objected. "Girls always do better in school—teachers like them better. Only sissies get good grades." As if he suddenly realized what he'd said, Danny's gaze shot to Grey and he quickly lowered his eyes. "Not *all* boys who get good grades are nerds, though."

Meghan wanted to kick Danny under the table, but she dared not. She was pleased that her mother didn't continue to drill Grey about his education. She could well imagine what her brothers would say if they knew he'd zipped through college and gone directly into a doctoral program. From there, he'd been accepted on the faculty of Friends University where he'd taught ever since.

"What about girls?" Brian asked, directing the question to Grey. "I mean, if you were so much younger than everyone else, who was there for you to date?"

"No one," Grey admitted frankly. "I didn't know many girls, as it was. There weren't any my age in the neighborhood and none at school, either. Until I was in my twenties, I rarely had anything to do with the opposite sex."

"Personally, I don't think they're worth the trouble," Danny said, completely serious. "Brian used to think that way, but then he met Allison and he's gone to the other side. Chad's not much better. There's a girl who calls him all the time and they talk all the time. I think he's turning traitor, too."

"It happens that way sometimes," Grey commented, sharing a knowing look with Meghan and doing an admirable job of disguising his amusement.

"You like my sister, don't you?" Danny continued, and then added before Grey could answer, "I guess that's all right if she likes you. And she does. You wouldn't believe it. From the moment she arrived this morning, all she's done is give us instructions on what we could say to you and what we couldn't. I've forgotten half the stuff already."

"Obviously," Meghan said wryly.

"I think I can understand why Meghan likes you so much," Chad said with a thoughtful stare. "You teach literature, and Meghan really loves that stuff. She's always reading books dead people wrote."

Meghan stood abruptly and braced her hands against the edge of the table. "Anyone for dessert?"

An hour later, Meghan was helping her mother with the last of the dishes. Brian had cleared the table and the other boys had dealt with the leftovers and loading the dishwasher, leaving the few pots and pans that needed to be washed by hand. Grey and her father were in the living room playing a second game of chess.

"Meghan," her mother said with an expressive sigh, "I wish you'd relax. Grey is doing just fine."

"I know," she said, rubbing the palms of her hands together. "I suppose I'm overreacting, but I wanted him to feel at home with all of us, and I don't know if that's possible with the boys."

"He seems to be taking their teasing in his stride."

"What else can he do?" she exclaimed. "Challenge Danny to a duel?"

Her mother laughed at that. "I told you before there was nothing to worry about." She wiped her hands dry and reached for the hand lotion. "You like Grey, don't you, princess? More than anyone in a long while."

"Oh, Mom, I couldn't have made that any more obvious."

Colleen O'Day chuckled. "You're right about that."

"But we're different." She tucked an errant reddish curl around her ear and cast her gaze to the floor. She was Yankee pot roast and Grey was T-bone steak. "I like him so much, but he's intelligent and…"

"So are you," her mother countered.

"Educated."

"You're self-taught. You may not have an extensive education, but you've always had an inquiring mind and a hunger for the written word. Grey wouldn't be attracted to you if you weren't bright."

"But he's dignified and proud."

Her mother continued spreading the cream over her hands, composing her thoughts. "I don't see any real problem there. Just don't wear your purple tennis shoes around him."

Meghan laughed, and then chewed on the corner of her mouth. "I'm crazy about him, Mom, but I'm afraid I'm closing my eyes to reality. I can't understand why Grey is interested in me. It won't last, and I'm so afraid of falling in love with him. I expect him to open his eyes any minute and realize how irrational our being together is. It would devastate me. I'm excited and afraid at the same time."

Her mother was silent for a long moment. "When you were four years old, you were reading."

"What has that got to do with anything?"

Her mother smiled faintly. "From the time you could walk you were hauling books around with you everywhere you went. You were bound and determined to find out what all those letters meant and all their sounds. I don't suppose you remember the way you used to follow me through the house, pestering the life out of me until I'd give up and sit down with you. Once you were able to connect the letters with the sounds, you were on your own and there was no holding you back."

"It's not letters and sounds that I'm dealing with now. It's a man, and I feel so incredibly unsure of myself."

"Let your heart guide you, princess. You've always been sensible when it comes to relationships. You're not one to fall head over heels in love at the drop of a hat. If you feel so strongly about Grey, even if you've only known him a short time, then all I can advise you is to trust yourself."

"There isn't anything else I can do, is there?"

"He's a good man."

"I know."

Meghan's father drifted into the kitchen and reached for a leftover buttermilk biscuit. He paused and chuckled. "I've got to hand it to that young man of yours," he said to Meghan.

"What, Dad?" Meghan fully expected him to comment on the chess game.

"Chad and Danny talked him into playing football. They're in the front yard now."

Six

"But Grey's wearing a suit!" Meghan burst out as though that fact alone would prevent him from participating in any form of physical activity.

"Brian lent him an old sweatshirt of his."

"Oh, dear," Meghan cried, rushing toward the front of the house.

"He doesn't need you," her father called after her. "Your professor friend is perfectly capable of taking care of himself, don't you think?"

"Against Chad and Danny?" she challenged. "And Brian?"

Her father responded with a tight frown. "On second thought, maybe you'd better check on him."

Meghan grabbed her coat from the hall closet on her way out the door. Her first thought was to dash onto the lawn and insist all four of them stop their foolishness this minute. Instead, she stood on the porch with her hand over her mouth as she watched the unfolding scene.

Grey was bent forward, his hands braced against his knees. After shouting out a long series of meaningless numbers, Brian took several steps in reverse and lobbed the football to Grey. The ball soared through the air, the entire length of the yard, and no one looked more shocked than Chad and Danny when Grey caught it.

"Go for the touchdown!" Brian screamed at the top of his lungs.

"No!" Meghan called out. Unable to watch, she covered her face with both hands. A chill rippled down her spine that had nothing to do with the frosty November weather. Part of her longed to run into the middle of their scrimmage. She wanted to yank Grey off the grass before he got hurt, but she had no right to act as his guardian. As an adult, he must have known what he was getting himself into when he agreed to this craziness. He would be lucky, though, if he came out of this with nothing more than a broken bone.

From the hoots and cheers that followed, it became apparent that Grey had either scored or that Chad and Danny had stopped him cold. She couldn't decide which, and dared not look.

"Meghan?"

She whirled around to find Grey standing on the top step of the porch, looking worried. Her breath left her lungs in a sudden rush of relief. "Are you all right?"

"I'm more concerned about you. You're as pale as a ghost."

"I thought Chad was going to tackle you."

"He had to catch me first. I may not know much about football, but I'm one heck of a sprinter."

Meghan's relief was so great that she impulsively tossed her arms around his neck and squeezed for all she was worth. He felt warm and solid against her and she buried her face in his neck, laughing and fighting off the urge to cry at the same time.

Chuckling, Grey wrapped his arms around her waist and swung her around. "I made a touchdown, and according to Brian, that makes me some kind of hero."

"Some kind of fool, you mean."

"You're not going to kiss her, are you?" Danny asked, making it sound the equivalent of picking up a slug.

Grey's gaze delved into Meghan's. He wanted to kiss her, she could tell, but he wouldn't. Not now. Later, his look promised. She answered him with a soft smile that claimed she was holding him to his word, even if it was unspoken.

"I think we better quit while we're ahead," Brian suggested, joining Meghan and Grey. "It's getting too dark, and personally, I don't think Meghan's heart can take much more of this. I thought she was going to faint when you caught that last pass."

"I was afraid Chad and Danny were going to murder him simply because he happened to catch it."

"We wouldn't have done that," Chad said with more than a hint of indignation. "This is touch football, remember?"

Danny scrunched up his face. "I might have tackled him, but I knew Meghan would kill me dead if I did."

Meghan looped her arm around Danny's neck in a headlock and rubbed her knuckles over the top of his head. "You're darn tootin', I would have."

With his arms squirming, her brother escaped and angrily glared at his older sister. "I hate it when you do that!"

Laughing, they all entered the house.

An hour later Grey followed Meghan back to her apartment and parked outside her building.

"Do you want to come up for coffee?" she asked.

Looking at Grey now, she found it difficult to remember that he'd been playing football with her brothers only a short time earlier. His eyes were serious, his expression sober. He seemed reserved and quiet after an afternoon filled with noise and fun.

"I'd love to come up for coffee," he answered automatically and smiled at her softly, "but regrettably, I can't. There's enough paperwork stacked on my desk to keep me up most of the night." He reached out and caressed the side of her face with his finger. "I enjoyed today more than I can tell you, Meghan. You have a wonderful family."

"I think so." She was close to her parents and all her brothers, although she'd wanted to throttle the boys when she saw that they'd managed to drag Grey into a football game. What had surprised her most was Grey's willingness to partake in her brothers' folly.

He continued to gently stroke the side of her face. Meghan knew he planned to kiss her, and she met him halfway, automatically slipping her arms around his neck. He lowered his lips to caress hers in a long, tender, undemanding kiss. Meghan felt certain that he meant to kiss her once and then leave, but instead, he tightened his arms around her waist, bringing her closer to him. The kiss deepened and she was treated to a series of slow, compelling kisses that made her weak with longing. Something special had sprung into existence between them from the first moment they'd met—something delicate and so tangible that Meghan could feel it all the way to the marrow of her bones.

She moaned at the erotic sensations that circled her heart and her head. Grey responded immediately to her small sigh of pleasure by prolonging the kiss. He parted her lips, then teased and tormented her with his tongue until Meghan was dazed almost senseless.

"Oh, Meghan," he whispered into her hair as though in a state of shock himself. "I can't believe the things you do to me."

"Me?" she asked, her laugh soft and mildly hysterical. Surely he must know that whatever physical electricity existed between them was mutual.

Grey moved away from her and rested his head against the wall, taking in several giant gulps of air. "One kiss. I told myself I was only going to kiss you once. You're quickly becoming addictive, Meghan O'Day."

Meghan's breathing was ragged, as well. "I'm sorry you can't come in for coffee, but I understand," she told him when it was possible to do so and sound as if she had her wits about her. "I enjoyed today, too. Very much."

His hand reached for hers. "There's a cocktail party I have to attend next Saturday night. It'll be dry and boring and filled with people who will remind you of Fulton Essary." He paused and grinned wryly, before adding, "They'll remind you a lot of me, too. Will you go with me?"

Meghan's heart leaped to her throat. Grey had boldly walked into her world and was issuing an invitation for her to explore his. Doubts buzzed around her head like pesky mosquitos at a Fourth of July picnic. "Are you sure you want me there?"

"I've never been more confident of anything in my life. You'll do just fine."

Meghan wished she shared his faith in her. "Before you go, I want to tell you about a decision I recently made," she said, smiling up at him. This small piece of news was something she'd been saving all day to tell him. "I've decided to visit Friends tomorrow."

His gaze widened briefly. "'Visit'?"

"You told me one of the reasons you invited me to hear Dr. Essary was to expose me to the richness of education that was available at the university. I've concluded that you're right. My being older than most first-year students shouldn't matter. There's no time like the present to go back to school. I'm so excited, Grey. I feel like a little kid again, and I have you to thank for giving me the courage to do something I should have done long ago."

The warmth of his smile caused her heart to leap.

"Classes don't start until after Christmas, and I'm only going to sign up for two the first time around and see how I do. That way, I can keep working for a while, as well." She felt a spontaneous smile light up her face as the enthusiasm surged through her. "I'm really trying to be sensible about all this."

"I think that's wise."

"When I first leafed through the catalog, I wanted to register for every literature class offered. But the more I thought about it, the more I realized that I've got to ease my way back into the habit of going to school. After all, it's been several years since I graduated."

"Meghan?"

He stopped her, and when she raised her gaze to his, she noted his brow had puckered into a frown. "Did you decide to take any of the classes I'll be teaching?"

She nodded eagerly. "The one on the American novel. But when I saw that we'd be reading *Moby Dick*, I had second and third thoughts."

"You don't like Melville?"

Meghan nearly laughed aloud at the look of dismay

that briefly sparked in his clear blue eyes. "I read the book in high school and found it insufferable. All those allegories! And from what I see, they made such little sense."

Grey's frown darkened.

"He was a great writer, though," she said, hoping to appease Grey before she slipped into a black hole and couldn't find her way out. When it came to literature Meghan often found her views varied greatly from his. For the past two days, they'd been getting along so well that she'd forgotten how vehemently Grey defended the literary greats.

"Were you aware that *Moby Dick* is said to be the quintessential American novel?"

"I imagine Margaret Mitchell was upset when she heard that," Meghan returned jokingly. "Mark Twain, on the other hand, probably took the news in his stride."

"You can't compare those two to Melville."

What had started out in jest was quickly turning into something more serious. "Grey, honestly, Melville was tedious and boring to the extreme. Maybe he would have appeared less so if he'd made even a passing effort to be less obtuse."

He looked away from her and expelled his breath. "I can't believe you actually said that."

"I can't, either," she confessed. Her quicksilver tongue wasn't helping matters any. She didn't want to argue with Grey. She wanted him to be as excited as she was about attending Friends. "I didn't mean to start a fight with you, Grey. I just wanted to thank you for encouraging me."

He nodded. Although Meghan assumed their disagreement had been a minor one quickly forgotten, Grey was silent on the short walk upstairs to her apartment. Brooding and thoughtful, as well, she noted.

"Thank you for bringing me home," she said.

"Meghan, listen." He paused and raked his fingers through his hair, looking uneasy. "I'd prefer it if you didn't sign up for any of my classes. It would be the best thing all the way around, don't you think?"

Those words felt like a bucket of cold water unexpectedly dumped over her head. She couldn't really blame Grey. Already she'd proved how opinionated and headstrong she was. He was looking for a way to avoid problems, and she couldn't blame him. If she were his student, she would be nothing but a nuisance. Her pride felt more than a little dented, but she could do nothing but bow to his wishes.

"Of course. If that's what you want," she agreed stiffly.

"It is."

She cast her gaze downward, feeling wretched and sorry now that she'd even told him her plans.

"Good night," he said, leaning forward enough to brush his mouth over her cheek.

"Good night," she replied, doing her best to force some enthusiasm into her voice.

He waited until she was inside the apartment and the living area was lighted before he left her. "I'll call you later in the week," he promised.

She nodded, forcing a smile. The minute she closed the door after him, the smile vanished. Dropping her purse on the recliner, she walked directly into the kitchen and braced her hands against the countertop and stared sightlessly at her microwave. The lump in her throat felt huge.

Grey was well within his rights to ask her not to register for any of his classes, but she couldn't help taking it personally. She felt hurt and insulted.

An hour later, Meghan didn't feel much better. She sat in front of the television, wearing her yellow robe from Texas and watching a murder-mystery rerun. The phone rang, and heaving a sigh, she reached for it.

"Yo," she answered, certain it was her brother.

"Yo?" Grey returned, chuckling.

Meghan uncurled her bare feet from beneath her and straightened. "Grey?"

"Hello. I took a break a minute ago to make myself a cup of coffee and I got to thinking about something. When I asked you not to register for any of my classes, there was a very good reason."

Meghan already knew what that was, but she didn't volunteer the information.

"The thing is, Meghan, I want to continue being with you as much as I can. If you're taking my American-novel class, it would be unethical for me to date you."

"Oh, Grey," she whispered, closing her eyes as a current of warm sensations washed over her. "I'm so glad you called. I was really feeling awful about it."

"Why didn't you say something?" he chided gently.

She brushed her bangs from her forehead and held her palm there. "I couldn't. I thought you objected because I can be so dogmatic and bullheaded when it comes to literature."

"I hadn't noticed," he teased.

"Oh, stop." But there was no censure in her voice. She felt as if a heavy weight had been lifted from her heart.

"You agree with me about not registering for my classes, don't you?"

"Of course. I should have realized why myself." She

hadn't; and that only went to prove how insecure she felt about her relationship with him.

"Yes, you should have. I'm glad I phoned. I don't want any more discord between us. I guess for some people, politics is a touchy subject—for us it's literature."

Meghan chuckled. "You're right about that."

To enter the administration office at Friends University was like walking into a living nightmare. Bodies crammed each available space, and lines shot out in every direction imaginable. The noise was horrendous.

Once Meghan had managed to get inside the door, she heaved in a deep breath and started asking questions of the first person she could.

"Pardon me, can I register for classes in this line?" she asked a gum-chewing brunette.

"Not here, honey, this one's for those of us needing financial assistance. Try over there," the girl told her, pointing across the room.

Meghan groaned inwardly and was forced to traipse through a human obstacle course, stepping over and around bodies that took up nearly every inch of floor space, until she reached the far side of the building.

She found a line and stood there, praying she was in the right place.

"Hi," a deep male voice greeted from behind her. "You work at Rose's Diner, don't you?"

Meghan turned to face a tall, rakishly good-looking man who looked vaguely familiar. "Yes. Do I know you?"

"There's no reason you should. I eat at Rose's every now and again. I don't know if you've waited on me or not, but I remember you from there. My name is Eric Vogel."

"Hello, Eric. I'm Meghan O'Day," she replied above the noise and they exchanged handshakes. "This place is a madhouse, isn't it?"

"It's like this every quarter."

"Don't tell me that, please."

"You're a senior?"

"I wish," she said. "I haven't been to school in years, and I'm beginning to feel like an alien—in with all these eighteen- and twenty-year-olds."

"How old are you?"

"Twenty-four."

"Hey, me too."

"I guess that qualifies us for a senior-citizen discount," Meghan teased. "I sincerely hope I'm in the right line for registration."

"You are," Eric said confidently, easing the pack off his back and setting it on the floor.

He apparently knew far more than Meghan did, and she was grateful he'd struck up a conversation with her.

"What classes are you planning to take?"

Awkwardly Meghan opened the catalog and showed him the two literature classes she'd chosen earlier, after much internal debate. Eric instantly started questioning her about her choices and it soon became apparent that they shared a love for the classics.

"You'll like Dr. Murphy's class," Eric assured her. "It's a whirlwind tour through six hundred years of British rhyme."

"A poetry-in-motion sort of class, then."

"Right," Eric said with a low chuckle.

The urge to ask her newfound friend if he'd ever taken anything from Grey was almost overwhelming, but Meghan resisted.

"Once we're done here, do you want to go over to The Hub and have a cup of coffee?" Eric suggested. "I'm meeting my fiancée there, and a couple of other friends. Why don't you join us?"

"I'll be glad to," Meghan said eagerly. The line was moving at a snail's pace and by the time they'd finished, it could well be close to noon. The student center seemed as good a place as any to have lunch.

Eric must have been thinking the same thing. "We might as well plan on having lunch together, from the way things are going here."

"It certainly looks that way," Meghan agreed.

Eric continued to leaf through the catalog. "By the way, if you're interested in joining a reading group, there's one that meets Friday afternoons at two. We get together at The Hub, although I've got to confess we don't do as much reading as we'd like. Mostly we drink coffee and seek solutions to world problems. It's a literary group with bipartisan overtones, if you know what I mean. We seldom agree on anything, but love the challenge of a good argument."

The group sounded like something Meghan had been looking to find for years. "I'd love to come," she told him, having trouble keeping the excitement out of her voice.

Meghan had made her first college friend, and it felt good.

Grey's office lacked welcome when he let himself inside on Friday afternoon. He needed to phone Meghan and had put it off all week. He sat in his high-back leather chair and held a hand over his face as if the gesture would wipe out the image that kept popping into his mind.

He'd known Meghan was registering for classes

Wednesday morning and had half expected her to stop off and see him afterward. When he'd talked to her the day before, he'd casually issued the invitation for her to come to his office, but he had a class at one and she had to be at Rose's before three, so the timing was iffy.

It had been pure chance that had taken Grey to The Hub early Wednesday afternoon. The faculty dining room was situated on the second floor and he was joining Dr. Riverside when he happened to catch sight of an auburn-haired woman who instantly reminded him of Meghan.

It *had* been Meghan, and a surge of adrenaline shot through him to have bumped into her so unexpectedly this way. It took a second longer for Grey to notice the two men and another woman who were sitting at the table with her. The four were talking and laughing, obviously enjoying getting to know one another. One of the men, clearly attracted to her and doing his best to make himself noticed, had his arm draped along the back of her chair. He looked like a decent sort—clean-cut, preppy. Although it was difficult to tell from this distance, Grey thought he might have had the fellow in one of his classes a couple of years before.

The other man's arm was looped over Meghan's chair and was in no way territorial, but the emotions that shot through Grey certainly were. He felt downright jealous, and the fact stunned him. He had no right to feel so strongly about Meghan. Knowing he could experience such a powerful emotion toward her after so short an acquaintance shook him to the core. He'd left as soon as he could make his excuses to Dr. Riverside and returned to his office, badly shaken by the incident.

Two days had passed and Grey had yet to erase the

image of Meghan from his mind. She hadn't stopped off at his office that afternoon, which had been just as well; she belonged with her friends. As soon as her classes started up, after the first of the year, she would come into contact with others like the ones she'd met Wednesday. With her vivacious, warm personality, she would soon have scores of new friends. These people would be her own age, and would share the same interests. They would open up a whole world to her—one in which Grey regretfully acknowledged that he wouldn't belong. There was only one thing left for him to do.

Only it wasn't easy.

Thursday, after giving the matter some heavy-duty thought, Grey had felt downright noble deciding to step aside for a man who would be far better suited to someone like Meghan O'Day. There would soon be several vying for her attention and Grey couldn't blame them. It would be all too easy for him to fall in love with her himself.

Meghan was sunshine and bright colors. Unfortunately, Grey's world was colored in black and white. He was staid; she was effervescent—the embodiment of warmth and femininity. And he was nothing more than an ivory-tower professor, secure in his own world and unwilling to venture far into another.

No. As difficult as it seemed now, it was better for them both if he stepped out of her life before either of them was badly hurt.

His feelings now, however, with the lonely weekend facing him were far less admirable. He might be doing the noble thing, but he didn't feel nearly as good about it.

It was hard to release a ray of sunshine. In fact, it was far more difficult than he ever imagined it would be. Meghan O'Day was someone very sweet and very special who drifted in and out of his life, leaving him forever marked by their all-too-brief encounter.

A cold sensation of regret lapped over him. First, he would phone Meghan and cancel their date for Saturday, and then he'd contact Pamela Riverside. Stiff and exceedingly formal, Pamela was far more compatible with him. If nothing more, they understood each other. And if he wasn't the least bit attracted to her, well, there were other things in life that made up for passion and excitement.

Feeling slightly guilty to be using Pamela to forget one sweet Irish miss with eyes as blue as turquoise jewels, Grey reached for the phone.

Meghan was busy folding clothes when her telephone pealed. Humming softly, she walked around the corner and lifted the receiver off the hook.

"Yo," she greeted cheerfully, easily falling into the greetings her brothers used so often. Meghan was in a marvelous mood. Life was going so well, lately. She'd missed seeing Grey on Wednesday and had felt badly about that, but by the time she'd left The Hub, she was shocked by how late it was. There hadn't even been time to run over and say hello.

"Meghan."

"Grey," she whispered on the end of happy sigh. "It's so good to hear from you. There's so much to tell you I don't know where to start," she said with a rush of excitement. "First of all, I'm sorry about the other day. I met someone while registering and we ended up having coffee with a couple of others, and the time slipped away without my even realizing it."

"I'm phoning about Saturday night," he announced brusquely.

"Oh, Grey, I'm really pleased you asked me to attend this cocktail party with you. Nervous, too, if you want the truth. You never did say how formal it was."

"Meghan," he said tightly. "Something's come up, and I'm afraid I'm going to have to cancel Saturday night."

"Oh." Meghan knew she'd been chattering, and immediately shut up.

"I apologize if this has caused you any inconvenience."

Grey sounded so formal that Meghan wasn't sure how to respond. "It's no problem. Don't worry about it."

"Good."

A short awkward silence followed, and Meghan decided the best thing to do was to ignore Grey's bad mood. "Oh, before I forget, Mom wanted me to ask you to dinner again next Sunday. Dad's eager to play chess again and the boys suggested you wear jeans so they won't have to worry about you ruining your suit pants."

"Meghan…"

"Grey, just wear what you're most comfortable in, and don't worry about my brothers."

"I won't be able to make it," he stated flatly. "Please extend my regrets to your family."

"All right," she replied wishing she knew what was wrong.

"I see that it's about time for you to leave for work," he said next, clearly wanting to end the conversation.

Meghan's gaze bounced to the face of her watch. "I've got a few minutes yet. Grey, is something the matter? You don't sound anything like yourself."

"I'm perfectly fine."

"It's not your health that concerns me, but your attitude."

"Yes, well," he said gruffly, "I've been doing a good

deal of thinking over the last few days. It seems to me that since you're going to be attending Friends that it wouldn't do for us to continue to date each other."

An argument immediately came to her, but she quickly swallowed it. It was clear from the tone of his voice that his mind was made up and that nothing she could say would change it. The disappointment was enough to make her want to cry.

"I understand." She didn't, but that wasn't what Grey wanted to hear. He was giving her the brush-off and trying to do it in the most tactful way possible.

"We'll still see each other every now and again," he continued in the same unemotional tone as though it didn't matter to him one way or the other. "In fact it'll be unavoidable, since both your classes are in the same building as the ones I'm teaching."

Meghan wondered how he knew that. She hadn't even told him which classes she'd registered for. It was apparent he'd done a bit of detective work and had sought out the information himself.

"Yes, I suppose that it will be inevitable, won't it?"

"You're going to do very well at Friends, Meghan. If you have any problems, I want you to feel free to contact me. I'll be happy to do whatever I can to help."

"Thank you."

"Goodbye, Meghan."

The words had a final ring to them that echoed over the wire like shouts against a canyon wall.

"Goodbye, Grey," she whispered. By the time she replaced the telephone receiver, her stomach felt as if a concrete block had settled there.

Seven

Meghan's arms were loaded with books when she stepped into the ivy-covered brick faculty building. The directory in the entrance listed Grey's office as being on the third floor.

With doubts pounding against her breast like a demolition ball, she stepped into the elevator. The ride up seemed to stretch into eternity. It had been two weeks since Meghan had last talked to Grey and her mind stumbled and tripped over what she planned to say. She didn't know if she was doing the right thing in approaching him like this, but she found the persistent silence between them intolerable. Men had come briefly into her life in the past, but none had mattered more to her than Grey. She found accepting his rejection of her both painful and nerve-racking.

"May I help you?" a middle-aged woman who sat behind the computer asked when Meghan entered the series of offices. Apparently several professors shared the same assistant, who acted as both receptionist and assistant.

"Yes, please," Meghan answered, smiling broadly. "I'm here to see Professor Carlyle."

Frowning, the gray-haired women leaned forward and leafed through the appointment book. "Is he expecting you?"

"No. If he's busy I could come back when it's more convenient."

The woman gave Meghan a sharp look. "Professor Carlyle is always busy," she intoned. "Tell me your name and I'll ask if he'll see you."

By this time Meghan was convinced she was making a terrible mistake. She seemed to be shaking from the inside out. Dropping in on Grey like this, with such a flimsy excuse, would only complicate an already complex relationship.

"My dear girl, I don't have all day. Your name."

"Meghan O'Day," she answered crisply, then hurried to add, "Listen, I think perhaps it would be better if I came back another time—"

Before she could say anything more, the receptionist had pushed down the intercom switch and announced to Grey that Meghan was outside his office. Almost immediately afterward, a door opened and Grey stood not more than ten feet from her.

"Meghan."

His gaze revealed a wealth of emotion: surprise, delight, regret, doubt. Not knowing which one to respond to first, she forced a smile and said, "I hope I'm not interrupting anything important." She should be more concerned about making a fool of herself, she decided, but it was too late to do anything else now but proceed full steam ahead. She pasted a smile on her face and met his look, praying he wouldn't read the tumult boiling just beneath the surface.

"You're not interrupting anything. Come in, please."

He stepped aside in order to admit her to his office. Meghan walked into the compact room and sat in a leather chair that was angled toward the huge mahogany desk. Grey's office was almost exactly the way she'd pictured it would be—meticulous in every detail. Certificates and honors lined one wall, and bookcases the other two. Behind his desk was a huge picture window that gave an unobstructed view of the campus below.

She noticed that shelf upon shelf of literary works were cramped together on the bookcases so that there wasn't a single inch of space available. In other circumstances, Meghan would have loved to examine his personal library.

"I should have called for an appointment first," she said, avoiding eye contact with him, "but I decided to stop by on the spur of the moment on my way back from the bookstore." She glanced down at the load of textbooks in her arms.

By this time, Grey was seated in the swivel chair behind his desk.

"I'll admit this is a surprise. It's been what, now—two weeks since we last talked?"

Two weeks, three days and four hours, Meghan tallied mentally. "It's been a little longer than two weeks, I guess," she responded, hoping she didn't look half as nervous as she felt. Her stomach was in complete turmoil. She tightened her arms around the load of books, holding them against her breast as though she expected Grey to hurl something at her, which was completely ridiculous.

Now that she was here, she was convinced she'd made a drastic mistake.

Grey looked at her, waiting.

"It's been really cold lately, hasn't it? I feel we're going to be in for a harsh winter."

"Yes, it has been."

His look told her he had better things to do than discuss the weather. "I was on the campus to pick up my textbooks," she tried again.

He nodded reminding her that she'd already told him that.

"How have you been, Meghan?"

"Good. Really good." Her response was eager and she scooted to the edge of her seat. "And you?"

"Fine, just fine."

Not knowing how else to proceed, she said, "I thought I'd take two classes this first time, since it's been so many years since I was in school.… I guess I already told you that didn't I?"

"Yes, I believe you mentioned that before." A heavy silence followed until Grey asked, "How's your family?"

"They're fine. Mom's busy preparing for Thanksgiving." Her grip tightened all the more around the books until the inside of her arms ached from the unnecessary pressure.

A pulsating stillness followed. They'd exhausted the small talk and there was nothing left for Meghan to do but state the reason for her visit, which at best would sound terribly feeble.

"I've been coming to a reading group the last couple of Fridays here on campus," she began, forcing some enthusiasm into her voice. "I was thinking that you might like to join us sometime."

"I appreciate the fact you thought of me, but no," he said crisply.

She hadn't really expected him to accept her invitation, but she hadn't anticipated that his answer would be quite so abrupt. He hadn't even taken time to give the suggestion any thought. "I know you'd like the others," she felt obliged to add. "They share your views on a lot of subjects; they're thoughtful and intelligent and not nearly as opinionated as me." That was only a half-truth, but she was getting desperate.

"I don't have the time for it," he added starkly.

"I know you don't.... I should have realized that." She stood suddenly, with her heart pounding so fast and furiously, she was certain her ribs would soon crack.

"Meghan?"

"It was wrong to have come here. I'm sorry, Grey." As quickly as she could propel her legs, she hurried out of his office. If this were happening in a movie instead of real life, the elevator would have been open and ready to usher her away from the embarrassing scene. Naturally it wasn't, and she didn't have the time or patience to stand still for it.

"Meghan, wait!"

She couldn't. She should never have come to him like this. If making a fool of herself wasn't enough, she felt like crying—which added to her humiliation. If he saw them it would be that much worse.

Somehow she made it to the stairway, yanking open the door as hard as she could and vaulting down the stairs, taking two at a time until she feared she would stumble if she didn't slow down. Grey called her one last time, but she was forever grateful that he didn't try to follow her.

"The party at table twenty-two is waiting for his check," Sherry said as she brushed past Meghan that night at Rose's Diner.

"I've got it right here," Meghan replied, thanking her friend with a grin. She didn't know where her mind was tonight, but she'd felt sluggish and out of sorts all evening. On second thought, she did know where her mind was, but thinking about Grey was nonproductive and painful. She paused and checked through the slips in her apron pocket and took the coffeepot with her as she delivered the tab to table twenty-two.

"Are you sure I can't talk you into a piece of pie?" she asked the elderly gentleman who was waiting there. "Rose's pecan is the special of the month."

"No, thanks," he said, patting his extended belly. "Rose's cooking has already filled me to the gills." He chuckled at his own joke and reached for his check.

Meghan went around the room refilling coffee cups when Sherry strolled past her a second time. "Don't look now, but trouble with a capital T just strolled in."

"Who?"

"Your professor friend," Sherry whispered, giving her a look that suggested Meghan had been working too many hours lately.

"Oh, great," Meghan groaned. She didn't want to face Grey—not after their disastrous confrontation earlier in the day.

"He requested your section, too."

"Sherry," Meghan pleaded, gripping her co-worker's forearm, "wait on him for me. Please, I can't. I just can't."

"Yes, you can!"

"I thought you were my friend."

"I am," she said, looking Meghan straight in the eye. "That's why I'm going to insist as assistant manager that you wait on your own customer. Someday you'll thank me for this."

"There'll be air-conditioning in hell before I do," she told her friend, her teeth clenched.

Sherry giggled and Meghan reached for a water glass and a menu to deliver to Grey's table. Once more, she noted, he sat in the booth by the window. A book lay open on the tabletop and he was intently reading, which meant he wasn't paying any attention to her. That was just as well.

As unobtrusively as possible, Meghan set down the water glass and menu and walked away. From out of the corner of her eye, she watched as Grey briefly picked up the plastic-coated menu and scanned its offerings. Either he made up his mind quickly or he wasn't particularly hungry, because he set it aside no more than a second or two after reading it over.

His novel didn't seem to be holding his attention, either, because he closed that and pushed it away. His brow was pleated, his look brooding.

Meghan gave him an additional three minutes before she approached his table, her tablet in her hand. "Are you ready to order?"

"Why did you run out of my office today?"

"The special is excellent this evening," she announced, ignoring his question. "Liver and onions—which I'm sure is one of your personal favorites."

"Meghan, please." He removed his horn-rimmed glasses, tucked them inside his jacket pocket and stared up at her.

Her eyelids drifted closed as embarrassment burned through her. "Pecan pie is the special of the month."

"I don't care about the pie," he said forcefully, causing several patrons to glance in his direction. Grey smiled apologetically and added softly, "But I care about you."

Her eyes shot open. In his office, she'd felt inane and foolish, but now she was furious. "You care about me?" she echoed with disbelief.

"It's true."

She rolled her eyes. "Oh, please, spare me. You broke our date two weeks ago and I haven't heard from you since. Believe me, Professor Carlyle, I got your message—loud and clear."

"I—"

"You gave me a polite, educated brush-off in what I'm sure you felt was the kindest way possible. I can't say that I blame you. After all, you're a college professor and I'm nothing more than a waitress with a love for the classics. You're educated and brilliant. I'm simply not good enough for the likes of you."

Anger flared into his eyes, sparking them a bright blue. "You couldn't be more wrong."

Meghan doubted that, and sucked in a steadying breath before continuing in a sarcastic tone. "Hey, don't worry about it. I'm a big girl," she returned flippantly. "I can accept the fact you don't want to see me again."

"Then why were you at my office this afternoon?"

Meghan's mouth made trout-like movements as her mind staggered to come up with a plausible explanation. "Yes…well…that was a tactical error on my part." Then she remembered she'd had an excuse for being there—all right, not a very good one, but a reason. "I honestly thought you might enjoy joining the reading group," she claimed righteously, holding her head high.

Grey's gaze scanned the diner. "I can see that an explanation is going to be far more complicated than I thought. How much longer before you're off work?"

It was on the tip of her tongue to inform him he could

wait all night and it wouldn't do any good because she had no intention of talking to him—ever. But that would have been a lie. As much as she longed to salvage her pride by suggesting he take a flying leap into the Arkansas River, Meghan wanted desperately to talk to him. She'd been utterly miserable for the past two weeks, missing Grey more than she'd thought it was possible to yearn for anyone she'd known so briefly. It was as if all the expectation had gone out of her life; and with it, all the fun and excitement.

"Another half hour. Would you like a piece of pecan pie while you wait?"

"Do you have custard pie?"

She smiled—the first genuine one in weeks. She should have known Grey would prefer custard over pecan. "Yes. I'll bring you a piece of pie and tea," she said, knowing he favored tea over coffee.

"Thank you."

While Meghan was slicing the custard pie, Sherry strolled past her and remarked, "Well, my friend, from the looks of things, the temperature in hell is several degrees cooler." She moved on past, chortling as she went.

The last fifteen minutes of Meghan's shift seemed to drag by. Sherry let her go a few minutes early, and Meghan changed out of her uniform in record time.

Grey was waiting for her in the parking lot. "Do you want to talk at your apartment, or would you prefer coming to my place?"

"Yours," Meghan replied automatically

For some reason, Meghan had assumed Grey lived in an apartment near the university, but she was wrong. She followed him to a house, a very nice two-story brick one with a sharply inclined roof and two gables.

She walked in the front door, doing her best not to ogle. The interior was decorated in a combination of leather and polished wood. As his office had been, the walls of his living room were lined with shelf upon shelf of obviously well-read books.

"Go ahead and make yourself comfortable," he said, taking her coat from her and hanging it in the entryway closet. "Would you like some coffee?"

"Please." She followed him into the kitchen where all the appliances were black and the sink was made of stainless steel. Everything was in perfect order, reminding Meghan that her own kitchen looked like something out of the Star Wars movie. Her stomach rumbled and she placed a hand over her abdomen, silently commanding it to be quiet.

"You're hungry. Didn't you have dinner?"

She shrugged. "Actually, I wasn't in the mood for anything tonight." She'd been too depressed and miserable to think about anything as mundane as eating.

"Can I fix you a sandwich?"

"No, thanks," she returned, although the mere mention of food was enough to make her mouth salivate. Now that she had time to think about it, she was famished.

Grey pulled out a white cushioned stool with a wicker back for her to sit on while he busied himself with the coffee. He seemed to be composing his thoughts as he filled the coffee machine with water.

"I saw you in The Hub," he said as he opened the cupboard and took out two coffee cups. The dark liquid had just started to leak into the glass pot.

"When?" She'd only been there a handful of times.

His back was to her. "The day you registered for classes."

He seemed to place some importance on that fact that Meghan didn't seem to understand. "Yes, I was there."

"Making new friends?" he coaxed.

"Yes. That was the day I met Eric Vogel and the others in the reading group."

"I see."

"*What* do you see?" Meghan pressed. He was using those same words again and in that identical tone of voice that she'd come to dread.

He turned around, his face as tight and constrained as his voice. "You and those other students looked right together."

She frowned. "I don't understand."

He gripped the edge of the counter behind him. "No, I don't suppose you do." His gaze studied the polished black-and-white checkered linoleum floor. "A whole new world is about to open up for you, Meghan," he said, smiling wryly. "You've devoted yourself to your family and your job since the time you finished high school. As soon as you start at the university, you're going to meet lots of new friends."

"Yes, I suppose I will." She still had no idea what he was getting at.

"What I'm trying to tell you, and apparently doing a poor job of it, is that you could have any man you wanted."

Meghan was so shocked that for a minute she didn't speak. "Grey, honestly, you seemed to have overestimated my charms." She couldn't very well announce that the only man who interested her was him! "And even if what you're saying is true, and it isn't, what has it got to do with you and me?"

"Everything." He looked surprised that she would even raise the question.

Meghan couldn't believe what she was hearing. Her stomach gurgled again and she pressed her hand harder against her midriff. "Let me see if I understand your reasoning—"

"There's nothing to understand. I don't want to stand in your way."

"Stand in my way?" she echoed, and jumped off the stool. Her stomach was churning and growling again, making her all the more unreasonable. "Oh...just be quiet," she cried.

Grey looked positively shocked.

"I wasn't talking to you."

"Is there someone else here I don't see?"

"My stomach won't stop making noise."

"Good grief, Meghan, why didn't you accept the sandwich I offered?"

"Because I'm too furious with you!" She was pacing now, lost in a free-fall of thoughts and emotions.

"I'll make you something to eat and you'll feel better," he suggested calmly.

"Stand in my way of what?" she pressed, ignoring his offer of food.

"Of finding someone special like Eric or any one of the others. I noticed how interested in you they all seemed to be. Frankly I couldn't blame them. You're warm and witty, and—"

"Miserable."

"I know you're hungry," he persisted, opening his refrigerator. "I'll have a sandwich ready for you any minute." Already he was gathering the fixings on the kitchen counter.

"I don't want a sandwich," she told him, clenching and unclenching her hands at her side.

"Soup, then?"

"You might have asked me how I felt before making that kind of decision. What gives you the right to decide who I should and shouldn't see? Don't you think it would have been better to discuss this with me first? I've been miserable, Grey, and all because you thought Eric and I looked good together. By the way, Eric's fiancée may think differently about that."

He stopped and turned to face her, a frown creasing his brow. "I have the distinct feeling we're discussing two entirely different subjects here. I thought we were discussing making a sandwich."

"A sandwich? We're talking about my life!"

"Oh." He looked both flustered and uneasy.

"Are you really so insensitive?"

"Actually," he said, boldly meeting her gaze, "*insecure* would be a more appropriate word. I didn't realize you'd been hurt by this until today when you came to my office. Frankly, I was more than a little surprised. I assumed you'd start dating any one of the others and quickly forget me."

"Both insensitive *and* insecure, then," she whispered.

A hush followed her statement. Meghan watched, standing as stiff as a new recruit in front of a drill sergeant, waiting. Her chin was elevated to a haughty angle.

Grey had revealed no faith in her or the attraction she felt for him—none. He'd seen her as a flighty teenager easily swayed by the charms and attention of another.

"Will an apology suffice?" he asked after an elongated moment, meeting her look.

"An apology and a sandwich would be an excellent start. Anything beyond that will need to be negotiated separately."

"Meghan, there's no need for you to be so nervous," Grey said as he pulled his car into a parking space outside Dr. Browning's home.

Grey had insisted she attend this party with him at the elegant home of the president of Friends University. Meghan had hoped that Grey would introduce her to his friends gradually, but he claimed this would be much easier. Easier for him, perhaps, but exceptionally hard on her nerves.

"What, me worried?" she joked, doing her best to disguise her nervousness. Grey may have insisted she attend this party with him, but she doubted he would include her in another. Her heart was in her throat, and she hadn't said more than a dozen words to him from the minute he'd picked her up at the apartment. During the half-hour drive to Dr. Browning's home, it was all Meghan could do to keep from wringing her hands.

"You're as pale as a sheet." He reached for her hand, squeezing it reassuringly. "Everyone's going to love you, so stop worrying."

"Right," she said, forcing some eagerness into her voice. She'd never dreaded a party more. In the beginning, she'd been pleased and excited that Grey had asked her to accompany him; it had meant so much at the time. But now Meghan would have done just about anything to come up with a plausible excuse to get out of this formal gathering. Her mind kept repeating the line about fools rush in where angels fear to tread.

Grey came around to her side of the car and opened the passenger door.

Meghan tightened her fingers around her small evening bag and sucked in her breath. "Grey, I know this is going to sound crazy, but I feel a terrible headache coming on…. Maybe it would be best if you drove me home."

"Nonsense. I'll ask Joan to get you an aspirin."

An over-the-counter drug wasn't going to help her, but arguing with him wouldn't do any good, either.

"You're sure about this?" She felt she had to ask him that and give him the opportunity to back out gracefully before she said or did anything that would embarrass them both.

"Positive," he returned confidently.

Meghan's fingers felt like blocks of ice. The chill extended up her arms and seemed to center someplace between her belly and her heart.

"Before we go inside would you do something for me?" she asked hurriedly.

"You mean other than take you home?" he chided gently, smiling at her.

"Yes."

"Anything, Meghan. What do you need?"

She was sitting sideways in the car, half in and half out, wondering if she'd lost her mind.

"Meghan?"

"I…I don't know what I want," she whispered.

"You're cold?"

She nodded so hard, she feared she would ruin her hair, and she'd spent hours carefully weaving every strand into place to make an elaborate French braid. It seemed exactly the way she should style it for this evening, although she rarely wore her shoulder-length curls any way except loose.

"I think I know what you need," he said, and looked over his shoulder before leaning forward slightly and planting his hands on her shoulders.

Meghan blinked her eyes a couple of times, wondering at this game, when Grey lowered his mouth to hers in a soft, gentle kiss that spoke of solace more than passion. He pressed his lips to hers in the briefest of contacts.

Meghan sighed and braced her hands against his forearms, needing something to root herself in reality. Was this Grey holding her? The same man who would normally frown upon kissing where there was a chance of their being seen?

He kissed her a third time and then a fourth as though a sample weren't nearly enough to satisfy him and he needed much, much more.

When he lifted his head, she could feel the color returning to her face and she was beginning to experience the faint stirrings of warmth seep back into her blood.

"There. How do you feel now?"

"Almost kissed."

He frowned slightly. "I suppose that was unfair, but I couldn't think of any other way to get some rosiness back into you cheeks. You looked as if you were about to faint. Are you ready now?"

"As ready as I'll ever be."

He discharged his breath and linked his fingers with hers. "Just be yourself, Meghan. There's nothing to worry about. Try to enjoy tonight."

"I know I will," she murmured, although she knew that would be impossible.

Together, hand in hand, they strolled up to the large Colonial-style home of the university president.

Nearly immediately, Meghan realized her fears were mostly unfounded. The first people she met were President Browning and his wife, Joan. From the moment she was introduced to her, Meghan liked Joan Browning, who was warm and personable—gracious to the marrow of her bones.

"Greyson's mentioned you several times," Joan stated while the two men engaged in brief conversation. "Both John and I have been looking forward to meeting you for weeks."

Meghan did a good job of disguising her surprise. "Thank you for including me."

"Nonsense. Thank you for coming."

They moved into the house and Grey slipped his arm around Meghan's waist. "There, that wasn't so bad, was it?"

"No," she had to agree. Surprisingly, it had been rather painless. She'd liked Joan Browning, who had gone out of her way to make sure that Meghan felt comfortable and welcome.

"Are you ready to meet a few of the others?" Grey asked.

"Not until I've had some champagne," she said lightly, knowing the alcohol would help her relax. One glass was her limit, but she knew some of her nervousness would disappear with that.

Obligingly Grey fetched them each a glassful of champagne, leaving Meghan for a few short moments. He returned and smiled down at her with both warmth and humor.

"Have I told you how lovely you look tonight?"

"About four times, and I appreciated hearing it every time."

He chuckled. "I feel fortunate to have you with me this evening."

"I'm the one who should be saying that," Meghan whispered, knowing all too well that *she* was the fortunate one. "Grey, who's that woman sitting across the room from us?" she asked, when she couldn't ignore the other woman any longer. "She's been sending daggers my way from the moment we walked in. Do you know her?"

Meghan felt Grey tense. "Yes, well…" He paused and cleared his throat. "I'm sure you're imagining things."

"I'm not. Who is she?" Meghan prodded.

"That's Dr. Pamela Riverside." He was clearly uneasy. He finished the last of his champagne in one swallow and set the tall thin glass aside.

"I think it's time you introduced us, don't you?" Meghan asked, realizing that the champagne had given her the courage necessary to suggest such a thing.

"Frankly, no."

Eight

"Hello, I'm Meghan O'Day," Meghan said, greeting the woman with steel-blue eyes who'd been glaring at her for the past half hour. If Grey wasn't going to make the introductions, then she would see to it herself. The minute Meghan had been free to do so, she'd slipped away from Grey, who'd been engaged in conversation.

"I'm Dr. Pamela Riverside," the other woman said stiffly, holding on to her champagne glass as though she expected it to protect her against alien forces. "I...I'm a colleague of Dr. Carlyle's."

"I assumed that you were."

"Greyson's never mentioned me?" the other woman asked softly, lowering her gaze, looking vulnerable and desperately trying to hide it.

"Grey may have, but I don't recall that he did," Meghan said, after searching through her memory and drawing a blank as far as Dr. Riverside went. From his reaction earlier, Meghan was almost certain that Grey hadn't said a word about his colleague. In fact, it seemed obvious that he was doing everything he could to keep the two of them apart.

"I didn't think he had," Pamela responded in a hurt voice that trembled just a little.

Meghan's pulse started to accelerate at an alarming rate. The thoughts that flashed through her mind seared her conscience. If Dr. Riverside was shooting daggers in Meghan's direction, then there was probably a very good reason. Perhaps Grey had jilted the other woman, and had left her with a battered and bleeding heart. The more Meghan studied the female professor, the more she realized she wore the look of a woman done wrong by her man. She was taller than Meghan by several inches, and thin to the point of being gaunt. Her dark hair was styled in a severe chignon that did little to soften the sharp contours of her cheeks and eyes. Without much effort, she could have been appealing and attractive, but her style of clothing was outdated and she didn't even bother with lipstick or eye shadow.

"Actually, there isn't any reason why Grey should have said anything about me," Pamela continued, looking more miserable by the minute. "He's never been anything but the perfect gentleman with me. If I were to tell you anything different, it would be a lie."

"I don't suppose he mentioned me, then, either," Meghan muttered. Grey had always been "the perfect gentleman" with her, as well. Meghan doubted that he would ever be anything else.

"No, I can't say that he did," Dr. Riverside confirmed brusquely, looking pleased to be telling Meghan as much.

That didn't help Meghan to feel any better. In fact she felt downright discouraged. She wasn't so naive to believe there hadn't been women in Grey's past. He might even be involved with someone now, although she doubted it.

"Actually, there isn't any reason he should tell you

about me, either," Meghan admitted with some reluctance.

The beginnings of a smile came over Pamela. "That's where you're wrong."

"Wrong?" Meghan didn't like the sound of this.

"He didn't have to tell me anything about you. I knew almost from the first."

Meghan wondered briefly exactly *what* it was the other woman knew. "I'm not sure I understand," she said, wishing now that she hadn't refused a second glass of champagne. This convoluted conversation wasn't making much sense.

"By my calculations, I'd guess that you and Grey started going out the last part of October."

Meghan nodded, confirming the other woman's conjecture. She wasn't sure how Pamela Riverside had known that, and wasn't convinced she even wanted to know. Meghan was about to ask another question, when Grey casually strolled up and joined them.

"Pamela," he said as a means of greeting her, dipping his head slightly. He held himself as stiff as a freshly starched shirt collar, his hands buried deep in his pockets. "I can see you've met Meghan O'Day."

"We introduced ourselves," Meghan explained.

Grey's deep blue eyes revealed his disapproval, which surprised Meghan all the more. From everything he'd been saying and doing, it was obvious he didn't want Meghan to have anything to do with his colleague. But his efforts to keep them apart only served to pique Meghan's interest.

"There are some people I'd like you to meet," Grey stated, possessively slipping his arm around Meghan's waist. "If you'll excuse us, Pamela."

"Of course," Pamela murmured, but some of the stiffness returned to her voice. "It was nice meeting you, Meghan."

"You, too," she answered, genuinely meaning it. "We'll talk again soon."

"I'd like that."

Grey tensed and then led Meghan away. Although it could have been her imagination, it seemed that he was unnecessarily eager to remove her from the other woman's presence.

An hors d'oeuvre table had been set up, and several of the guests were milling around there, talking. Meghan recognized a couple of professors from her few visits to the Friends campus, but the others were all strangers.

It soon became apparent that there wasn't anyone in particular Grey meant to introduce her to and that he'd used the ploy as an excuse to get Meghan away from Dr. Riverside. He eased them into line and handed Meghan a small plate and napkin.

Once they'd served themselves, Grey escorted her into the family room. Only one other couple had opted to sit there and they were on the other side of the room, deeply involved in their own conversation. Grey directed Meghan to the sofa, sitting next to her but twisting around so that his back was braced against the armrest and he could look at her.

"I suppose you're full of questions now," he muttered disparagingly.

"No," Meghan fibbed. Her head was buzzing, wanting answers, but she'd intended to ask them in her own good time.

"There never has been anything between me and Pamela, no matter what she told you," he volunteered, his voice elevated and sharp. "Never."

"She didn't suggest that there was."

Grey sagged with relief as the tension slackened between his shoulder blades. "Pamela's ripe for marriage and she's going to make some man an excellent wife—but not me!"

He said this with such vehemence that Meghan nearly swallowed her cracker whole. "I see," she said, not meeting his look.

Grey paused and studied her through eyes that had narrowed suspiciously. "I understand now why you dislike it so much when I say that," he mumbled, clearly all the more troubled. "Exactly what did she tell you?"

"Nothing much." There hadn't been time.

He paused and briefly rubbed the back of his neck. "Pamela and I have been part of the university's literature department for several years. We've worked closely together, and I suppose it's only natural for her to assume certain things. Our backgrounds are similar, and through no fault of our own we've often been coupled together." He rearranged the appetizers on his plate, shifting them around as if doing so was vital to their discussion.

"She's in love with you."

Grey's head shot up so fast, Meghan wondered if he'd strained his neck. "She told you that?"

"She didn't need to. I realized it almost from the moment we walked in here tonight."

"I've never done anything to encourage her, Meghan. I swear to you that's true. We've been thrown together socially for years, and I suspect that several of the university staff have assumed that the two of us were romantically involved. But that isn't true, I promise you it isn't."

"Okay," she said, taking a bite of a cheese-stuffed cherry tomato. "Hmm, this is delicious. Are you going to eat yours?"

Grey's gaze was disbelieving, as though he couldn't quite believe that she could comment on an hors d'oeuvre when the fate of their budding relationship hung in the balance. "You mean you aren't angry?"

"Should I be?"

"No," he claimed fervently, pushing his hand through his hair until his fingers made deep grooves in the dark mane. "There's absolutely no reason for you to be!"

"Like I said before I'm not angry."

"You're sure?"

"Positive." She reached for the cheese-stuffed cherry tomato on his plate. If he didn't want it, she did. "As far as I can see, there isn't any reason to be jealous, either. So I won't be."

His jaw sagged open as though he expected an argument and was almost disappointed when Meghan didn't give him one.

"Grey, you don't have to do this," Meghan urged, her gaze holding his. She still had trouble believing that he'd allowed her two youngest brothers to talk him into this craziness. It was the Wednesday before Thanksgiving and Meghan had a free evening in the middle of the week, which was rare indeed. Sherry had given her the night off to compensate for having her work on the holiday.

"To be honest, I'm not quite sure how they talked me into this, either," Grey replied, chuckling lightly, "but it's something I'd like to do—especially since you're able to come with us."

He parked his car in front of her family home and the

minute he did, Chad and Danny burst out the door as if they couldn't get away fast enough.

"It isn't like the boys never get to go to the movies," Meghan reminded him. "They should never have phoned you and asked you to take them."

"From what Chad said, they needed someone over seventeen to accompany them because this movie has a high degree of violence."

"Brian's over seventeen."

"He's busy."

"And you're not?"

"Meghan—" he reached for her hand "—I want to do this. I haven't been to a movie in years, and this was the perfect excuse to see *Chainsaw Murder, Part Twenty-Three.*"

"But you didn't see the others, and if you had, I'm fairly certain you wouldn't be interested in the sequel. In fact, I'm absolutely positive you're going to hate this movie."

"Let me be the judge of that."

"Don't say that I didn't warn you." If what Grey said was true and he hadn't been to a movie in years, then he was about to receive the shock of his life. Horror films weren't what they once were. There were blood and guts and gore enough to affect even the most hard-hearted.

"Hi, Professor," Danny greeted as he leaped into the backseat of Grey's car with the enthusiasm of a herd of charging elephants. "We're really glad you're taking Chad and me to the movies, aren't we, Chad?"

"Yeah." Chad's enthusiasm wasn't nearly as keen as his brother's. "But I didn't know Meghan was coming along," he added, eyeing his sister skeptically.

"I felt I should, since you two blackmailed Grey into

this evening's outing. Whose bright idea was it to call him, anyway?"

"Danny's," Chad shouted.

"Chad's," Danny retorted in the same loud voice as his brother's.

"I don't mind," Grey insisted, reminding Meghan a second time that he'd been a willing victim of her brothers' schemes.

"But I saw the previews to this movie," Meghan told him. "It's really bloody and violent."

"I can stand a little blood."

"Yeah, so can I," Chad said with the eagerness only a teenager could understand.

"Me, too," Danny chimed in.

"Well, as long as it isn't my own blood, I guess I'm outvoted," Meghan murmured, accepting her fate.

Chad released a huge sigh of relief. "I was afraid when I saw Meghan that she was going to force us to go see something else, like a love story. Yuck!"

"It could be worse," Danny muttered under his breath. "Meghan could have insisted we see a musical."

"Come on, you guys, it's not that bad." Grey was good to her brothers. This wasn't the first time he'd gone out of his way to take them somewhere. Her own mother was half in love with him herself, and it was little wonder. Grey had been to the house twice, and each time he'd brought her roses and faithfully mailed her thank-you cards for having him over for dinner. If Grey had set out to win her family, he couldn't have done a better job. They were all as crazy about him as she was. In some ways it troubled Meghan, the way he catered to them all. But it was only natural that, as an only child, he would be attracted to her fun-loving family. He worked so hard to be a part of them—playing chess with her father, subjecting himself to football with her younger brothers. Deep inside her heart, Meghan was thrilled that he cared enough to strive to be one of them. Yet a small, doubting part of herself worried that it was her family that Grey was attracted to, and that being with her was just a bonus. As much as possible, however, Meghan tried to ignore the negative thought.

Grey found a suitable parking place at the Wichita Mall and escorted them into the cinema.

"We don't have to stay with you two, do we?" Danny asked, once he was loaded down with popcorn and a drink. "We'd look like a bunch of wimps if we had to sit with you guys."

"We *can* sit on our own, can't we?" Chad repeated his brother's concern.

"Sit where we can see you, that's all I ask," Meghan answered for Grey.

"Why?" Chad and Danny demanded together. "We aren't little kids, you know."

"In case something happens and we have to leave early, I want to know where you are so I don't have to rove the aisles to find you," she insisted.

The boys rolled their eyes and then glared at each other as though they suspected Meghan had been talking to their mother too frequently. If they had any further protests, they chose to forget them and hurried off on their own.

Carrying the popcorn and drinks, Grey paused at the back of the theater. "Is there any place special you want to sit?" he asked Meghan.

"Near the back, so when the blood and guts start flowing, I can make a quick escape." Grey chose seats in the second to the last row. In contrast, Chad and Danny were in the third row from the front so that the huge white screen loomed in front of them. If they were any closer, their noses would have touched it. Neither one, it seemed, wanted to miss any of the gory details. Once seated, Meghan's two brothers twisted around and when they saw their sister, gave a short, perfunctory wave.

When Grey seemed sure Meghan was comfortable, he handed her a box of popcorn. She shoved a handful of kernels into her mouth, chewing as fast as possible. She figured she should eat what she could now because once the movie started she wouldn't have the stomach for it.

The lights dimmed and Meghan held her breath while the credits started to roll across the screen. The minute the violence started, Meghan covered her eyes and scooted so far down in her seat that her forehead was level with the backs of the chairs in front of her.

"Meghan," Grey whispered. "Are you all right?"

"No."

He scrunched down, too, so his that face was even with her own. "Do you want to leave?"

"Chad and Danny would never forgive me." She kept her eyes closed. "Is the girl dead yet?"

"The girl?"

"The one in the movie," Meghan whispered heatedly. Who else could she possible mean, for heaven's sake?

"Yeah, and her friend, too."

"Oh, thank goodness." Meghan uncovered her eyes and sat upright. "I'm going to have nightmares all week because of this stupid movie."

Grey straightened, and then looped his arm around her back, cupping her shoulder. "Does this help?"

She smiled into the darkness and nodded.

"And this?" Gently he pressed her head close to his shoulder.

"That's even better." Meghan leaned her head against the cushion of his chest as he shared his warmth and his strength with her. Only when she was so close to Grey could Meghan ignore the grisly details of the graphically played-out murder story.

Content, Meghan looked up at Grey and their gazes met in the dark. Grey gently smiled down at her, and the movie, at least for Meghan, faded into oblivion.

What surprised Meghan most was how much a smile from Grey could affect her. Her heart, which had been beating hard anyway, accelerated, stopped cold and then started up again. She longed for him to kiss her, and her eyes must have told him as much, yet she could feel Grey's resistance. Meghan couldn't blame him—she was asking for the absurd. They were in a crowded theater; anyone could see them.

"Meghan," he whispered.

"I know," she murmured, her eyes downcast. "Later."

"No," he growled softly. "Now." He bent his face toward hers, and his breath fanned her upturned face. Their lips met in the gentlest of kisses—velvet against satin, petal-soft, sweet, gentle, addictive.

Grey breathed in harshly and leaned his forehead against her own. "Sweet Meghan O'Day, the things you do to me."

A tornado could have descended on her at that moment, and Meghan wouldn't even have noticed. The mighty wind that would destroy everything in its path wouldn't have fazed her. Nothing could have compared to the rush of emotion that rocked through her. She was falling in love with Professor Greyson Carlyle—head over heels in love with him. Up to this point she'd been attracted to him, infatuated with him and challenged by the differences between them; but her feelings went beyond all that now.

Some time after the cocktail party at President Browning's house and before tonight, she'd willingly surrendered her heart to this man. The precise time and place remained a mystery.

Grey kissed her one last time, and the kiss was long and thorough. Their lips clung to each other and when they broke apart, it was with heavy reluctance.

Meghan hardly noticed the remainder of the film. At several places in the movie the audience gasped at some gruesome sight, but all Meghan did was sigh and lean against Grey, soaking up his warmth.

When the film was finally over, light filled the theater. Meghan straightened and Grey disentangled his arms from around her.

"We might as well wait for the boys in the lobby," Grey suggested. He helped Meghan on with her coat after she stood.

Behind them, she heard two girls whispering.

"That *is* Professor Carlyle," came the first voice, clearly female.

"It can't be," returned the second, also feminine. "Old Stone Face? Think about it. Professor Carlyle never cracks a joke or hardly ever smiles. He just isn't the type to pay money to see this kind of movie. It couldn't possibly be the same man."

"I know you're right, Carrie, but I swear it looks just like him."

"He's got a woman with him, too. Someone young."

A short silence followed. Meghan was sure that Grey

couldn't help overhearing the conversation any more than she could. Catching his gaze, she tried to reassure him with a timid smile, but if he saw it, he didn't respond.

"I read somewhere that everyone has a twin in this world," the whispering continued. "I bet that man's Professor Carlyle's twin."

"She's too young for him, don't you think?"

On the way out of the aisle, Grey kept his arm tucked around Meghan's waist. He stopped at the last row, paused and looked down at the two teenage girls, who remained sitting. They glared up at him, their mouths gaping open.

"Good evening, Carrie…Carol," he said evenly.

Both teens straightened in their seats as though they'd been caught doing something illegal. "Hello, Professor Carlyle."

"It's good to see you again, sir."

With his hand guiding Meghan at the base of her spine, he directed her into the lobby.

Meghan waited until they were near the exit doors before she spoke. "Greyson Carlyle, that was cruel and unusual punishment."

"Perhaps," he agreed, his smile noticeably forced.

Chad and Danny walked out of the main part of the theater looking as though they could hardly wait to see yet another episode of *Chainsaw Murder*. Meghan cringed at the mere thought of having to sit through another sequel to the dreadful horror film. If Grey had any intention of saying anything more to her about what they'd overheard earlier, the chance was gone.

"Wasn't that super rad?" Chad asked, looking to Grey for his approval. "Danny and I want to thank you for taking us—we probably wouldn't have been able to go if it hadn't been for you."

The comment was designed to cause Meghan to feel guilty for not being more willing to accompany her brothers to such important events, but she refused to be so much as tempted by the emotion. If it had been up to her, they would have gone to see a musical—and both Chad and Danny knew it.

"The movie was rad?" Grey repeated, arching his brows and glancing in Meghan's direction.

"Rad means cool, groovy—you know," Chad explained conversationally.

Grey nodded, his blue eyes serious. What humor shone there seemed forced. "Now that you mention it, I *do* know what that means. Banana splits are rad, aren't they? I wonder if you two boys would be game for one?"

"Are you nuts? We'd love it," Danny answered for them both.

"Grey, you're spoiling them," Meghan protested, but not too strenuously. She enjoyed watching Grey interact with the boys, and it was obvious they were equally fascinated with him.

"Oh, Meghan, don't ruin it for us. Grey's not spoiling us. He offered all on his own, without any coaxing."

"Yeah. We didn't even have to ask—" Danny tagged on his own feelings "—Grey's just being a pal."

"That's right," Grey said, and wrapped his arm around Meghan's shoulders.

He led the way outside, keeping Meghan close, but she felt him withdrawing even as he offered to take the boys out for dessert.

"From what I hear about your uncle Harry," Grey said

to Meghan, "I'm going to need all the friends I can find for tomorrow."

Meghan had nearly forgotten that her infamous uncle would be joining the O'Day family for the Thanksgiving festivities the following day. Uncle Harry was a known teaser, who delighted in saying and doing things that were sure to embarrass the younger generation. Usually he had a trick or two up his sleeve, and he delighted in fooling all the family members.

"I don't think you have much to worry about, Grey," Meghan assured him. "Uncle Harry's mellowed out the last several years."

"Does he play chess?"

"Not with my father," Meghan explained, chuckling. The only one brave enough to tackle Pat O'Day was the man whose arm was draped over her shoulder.

"What about football?"

"Loves it, as long it's on a screen and doesn't involve anything more than a few choice words of advice for the referees and coaches. You're in luck. He hasn't personally touched a football in years."

Grey nodded. "Then he sounds like my kind of man."

Following banana splits at the ice-cream parlor, Grey dropped Chad and Danny off at the house, stopping in briefly to say hello to Meghan's parents. Then he drove Meghan back to her apartment. He was unusually quiet the whole way there, and she longed to bring up the incident in the theater, but wasn't sure how. A couple of times she was tempted to make a joke of it, then decided it would be better if Grey mentioned the episode himself. She didn't know why Grey should be so troubled by it, but he obviously was. Their evening had been perfect until two of his students had recognized him and commented.

"You'll come up for coffee, won't you?" she invited, hoping that he would. Then at least there was the chance they would talk this matter out.

"You're not too tired?" he asked, then promptly yawned. He looked almost embarrassed as he placed his hand over his mouth.

"I'm fine. But from the look of it, you're exhausted."

"It's been a hectic week." He yawned a second time, looking chagrined. "Maybe I'd better just walk you to your door and say good-night there."

He escorted her to her apartment door and brushed his lips over hers in the briefest of kisses, leaving Meghan feeling frustrated and cheated.

"Good night."

"Good night, Grey. I'll see you tomorrow."

His answering smile was lame at best. Meghan bit into her bottom lip to keep from calling out for him to come back. Instead, she moved inside her apartment and plopped herself down on the sofa, letting her disappointment work its way through her.

The following morning when Meghan walked into her family home, she was immediately greeted with the pungent smells of sage and pumpkin-pie spices.

"Meghan, I'm glad you're here," her mother greeted and kissed her on the cheek. "Grey just phoned. He told me he tried to catch you, but apparently you'd just left the apartment."

Meghan dipped her finger into the whipped topping and promptly licked it, savoring the sweet taste. Her mother insisted upon using real cream in her recipes and not the imitation products that had become so popular over the years.

"Is Grey going to be late?" Meghan asked, examining the variety of dishes that lined the kitchen counter.

"No," her mother said sadly. "He called to give us his regrets. He won't be able to spend the day with us, after all. Apparently something's come up."

Nine

"Something's come up?" Meghan echoed her mother's words, hardly able to believe what she'd heard. "What did Grey mean by that?"

"I don't know, princess, but he hardly sounded like his usual self." Her mother was busy whittling away on a huge pile of potatoes. Once they were peeled, she let them fall into a large pot of salted water.

Normally Meghan would have reached for a paring knife and lent a helping hand, but she was too upset. She started pacing the kitchen, her arms wrapped around her waist, her gaze centered on the ceiling while her thoughts collided in a wild tailspin. She should have guessed something like this would happen following the incident with two of Grey's students in the theater.

"I was afraid this would happen," she muttered, discouraged and disappointed—in both Grey and herself. She should have insisted they talk about what happened before he left her apartment.

"Did you and Grey have a falling-out, dear?" her mother asked, reaching for another potato.

"Not really." Meghan leaned her hip against the sink

and appealed to her mother with her hands. "Do you think I'm too young for Grey?"

"Sweetheart, what I think is of little importance," she said matter-of-factly. "That's something that should be settled between you and Grey, not you and me."

"I know you're right." Meghan hesitated then exhaled sharply, thinking it might help to discuss the matter with her mother. "Last night a couple of Grey's students were in the theater. They were whispering and we couldn't help overhearing what they said. Those girls seemed to think Grey was too old for me. Honestly, Mom, it doesn't bother me. Dad's eight years older than you and it's never been an issue."

"Seven and a half years," her father corrected as he sauntered into the kitchen. He reached inside the cupboard above the refrigerator and brought out a huge bag of salted peanuts.

"Don't be ruining your dinner, Patrick O'Day," Colleen warned, shaking her index finger at him.

"I won't, but a man's got to have some nourishment." He wrapped his arms around his wife's waist and nuzzled her neck. "You can't expect me to live on turkey and stuffing alone, you know."

"Oh, get away with you." Colleen chuckled and squirmed out of his embrace. "Dinner will be ready by one."

"We're eating early this year, aren't we?"

"I've got to be to work by three, Dad," Meghan reminded her father. She hesitated and glanced at the kitchen clock. If she hurried, there would be enough time for her to drive over to Grey's house and talk some reason into him. With any luck, she would be able to convince him to join her and the rest of her family at least for dinner, if not all day. To allow those two thoughtless students to ruin the holiday would be wrong, but the fact that Grey had allowed the matter to upset him to this extent troubled her even more.

"Mom," she said hurriedly. "Do you need my help in the kitchen, or can I leave you for a few minutes?"

"No, everything's under control—your aunt Theresa's due any time. Are you going over to Grey's? Good—you convince him to come to dinner. Remember the way to a man's heart often leads through his stomach."

Smiling, Meghan nodded, not surprised that her mother had read her thoughts. "That sounds like a good idea," Colleen agreed, surprising Meghan. "Don't come back without him, you hear?"

"I won't." Meghan kissed her mother's cheek, appreciating her understanding. "I shouldn't be any more than an hour. But it might be longer if he proves to be stubborn."

Colleen O'Day laughed softly. "Then I won't look for you for at least two hours."

All the way over to Grey's house, Meghan prepared her arguments. Her mother was right—more than right! Neither one of them could afford to allow what others thought to dictate their relationship. The instant she arrived, she planned on kissing Grey long and hard. *Then* he could tell her she was too young for him. The strategy had merit, and Meghan grinned, knowing full well that Grey wouldn't have a leg to stand on!

Smiling at this novel plan of attack, she parked her car on the street in front of his house. Excited now, she hurried up the steps, rang the doorbell and waited impatiently.

"Meghan." Her name was issued on a rush of surprised pleasure when Grey opened the door.

"Now listen here, Greyson Carlyle, what's this about you not coming over for Thanksgiving dinner," she accused, her eyes flashing with mischief. "Mom gave me some flimsy excuse not even worth mentioning. I want to know exactly what you think you're doing, and I want to know right now." She punctuated each word by playfully poking a finger in his stomach. With each thrust, Grey took a step in reverse, his eyes wide and disbelieving.

"Meghan…"

He tried to get her to listen, but she wouldn't let him. "I can't believe you'd let what two students said disturb you this way. If you're worried about our age difference, then I dare you to take me in your arms. I challenge you to kiss me and then argue the point."

"Greyson, who is this woman?"

The sober, dry voice came from behind Grey, in the direction of the kitchen.

Stunned, Meghan looked beyond him to face an austere middle-aged woman with silver-white hair that was severely tucked away from her face. She wore a dark blue suit and black shoes—and no smile. Meghan blinked, certain she'd inadvertently run into Pamela Riverside's mother.

"Meghan O'Day, I'd like to introduce my mother, Dr. Frances Carlyle."

"How do you do, Dr. Carlyle?" Meghan said, the teasing laughter in her eyes wilting away under the solemn stare of the older woman. Meghan stepped forward and the two exchanged a brisk handshake. Her legs felt as if they'd turned to water and the size of the knot in her throat would have rivaled a golf ball.

"Are you a student of Greyson's?" his mother asked, her gaze boring holes into Meghan. Her tone wasn't openly unfriendly, but it lacked any real interest or warmth.

"No—we're friends," Meghan quickly explained.

"I see."

There was that phrase again. Meghan longed to share a knowing look with Grey, but she dared not.

"Mother was here waiting for me when I returned last night," Grey explained. He motioned toward the recliner, indicating that Meghan should take a seat. Apparently he noticed she was having trouble remaining in an upright position.

"Would you like some tea?" Frances Carlyle asked.

"Please." Meghan accepted, hoping that once Grey's mother had vacated the room, she could talk to him. She wished with everything in her that she hadn't charged into his home, stabbing him with her finger and chiding him at the top of her voice, demanding that he kiss her.

"I'll be just a minute."

Meghan was convinced his mother had told her that as a means of warning her, but as far as Meghan was concerned, a minute was exactly long enough. She waited until the older woman had left the living room and then covered her face with both hands.

"Good heavens, Grey!" she wailed in a thick whisper. "How could you have let me go on that way?" She wanted to crawl inside a hole, curl up and die. Within a matter of two minutes, she'd given his mother the worst possible impression of herself.

"Meghan, listen…"

She lowered her hands. "I feel like such a fool, barging in here like King Kong. And you let me do it."

"Could I have stopped you?"

She shrugged, then admitted the truth. "Probably not."

"I tried phoning you this morning."

Meghan bit into the corner of her bottom lip. "I know. Mom told me." She could have saved herself a lot of grief had she hadn't let her cell phone battery wear down.

"My not coming to dinner had nothing to do with what happened last night," Grey said, reaching for her hand. He reluctantly released it when he heard movement from inside the kitchen. Meghan gave him a reassuring smile; she didn't need his touch when his gaze was so warm and gentle.

"I can just imagine what your mother thinks," she whispered, feeling all the more miserable.

Grey was about to say something more when Frances Carlyle walked into the room, carrying a tray. Grey stood and took it from his mother and set it on the coffee table.

"Cream or sugar, Meghan?"

"Just plain, thank you," she responded, scooting to the edge of the cushion. There were four cups on the tray, but she didn't give the matter more than a passing thought until Pamela Riverside casually strolled into the room with all the dignity of one who knows she has "arrived." The size of the lump in Meghan's throat doubled in size. She turned her gaze to Grey, and her breath jammed in her lungs.

"When I wasn't home last evening, Mother phoned Dr. Riverside," he said, his gaze holding Meghan's and seeming to plead for understanding.

"Dear Pamela was kind enough to come to the airport on such short notice and drive me to Greyson's house," his mother added in a light, accusing tone.

Meghan noted that Grey's jaw tightened slightly. "I would have been more than happy to come for you myself, Mother, had I known you were arriving."

"It was a surprise, and I hated to ruin it. I suppose it was wrong of me to assume you'd be home, but I couldn't imagine what you'd be doing out the evening before Thanksgiving."

"You were with Ms. O'Day?" Pamela asked, stirring sugar into her tea with a dainty flip of her wrist.

"We were at the movies."

"How quaint." Grey's mother smiled for the first time, but once more Meghan read little amusement or welcome in the other woman's gaze.

"That must have been…fun," Pamela commented, seeming to search for the right word, although she did appear genuinely interested.

If Dr. Riverside was the least bit uncomfortable, it would have been impossible to tell. Actually, there was no reason for her to feel any annoyance, Meghan mused. She was the chosen one, basking under the glow of Frances Carlyle's approval. And who could blame her? Not Meghan.

"What movie did you see?" Pamela pressed.

Meghan should have known that one was coming. She lowered her gaze and mumbled the title, hoping the others wouldn't understand and would let it pass. *"Chainsaw Murder, Part Twenty-Three."*

Frances Carlyle gasped softly, doing her best to disguise her shock. "I'm sure I misunderstood you."

"It's not as bad as it sounds, Mother," Grey said, and his voice carried a thread of amusement.

"I never dreamed my own son would lower himself to view such rubbish," Frances said, fanning her face a couple of times as though the room had suddenly become too warm. "Naturally, I've heard Hollywood is making those disgusting films, but I certainly didn't think that sort of rubbish would appeal to you, Greyson."

"I'm sure it doesn't," Meghan inserted, automatically defending him. "My brothers were the ones who wanted to see that particular film and they conned Grey into taking them."

"Your brothers 'conned' my son?" Grey's mother echoed, her look all the more aghast. She held on to her cup with both hands and it looked for a split second as though she were going to drop it. The cup wobbled precariously, then steadied.

"I didn't mean it quite like that," Meghan hurried to explain. Every time she opened her mouth, she dug herself deeper into a pit of despair. She cast a pleading look in Grey's direction, wanting to let him know how sorry she was for muddling this entire conversation. "The boys mentioned how much they wanted to go, and Grey, out of the goodness of his heart, volunteered to take them."

"I hardly think that is the type of movie for young boys."

"They're fifteen and thirteen." On this matter, Meghan actually found herself agreeing with Grey's mother. But she couldn't force her tastes on Chad and Danny, who seemed to thrive on horror films of late.

"Meghan's family had invited me over for Thanksgiving dinner," Grey said, directing the comment to his mother. "I phoned earlier and made my excuses."

Frances Carlyle nodded approvingly. "Pamela and I will be preparing our own Thanksgiving dinner," she explained, and smiled fondly at the other woman. "However, it was kind of your parents to invite him, but Greyson's with his family now."

From the look Grey's mother cast at Pamela, it was all

too apparent that she'd personally handpicked her son's future wife. She'd done everything but verbally announce the fact.

Meghan's heart was so heavy it was a wonder she was able to remain sitting in an upright position. The differences between her and Grey's social position hadn't actually bothered her until that moment. Whenever they were together, Meghan had been swept up in the magic that sparked so spontaneously between them. But it was all too clear that Grey's mother wasn't interested in hearing about magic; she would be far more concerned with passing on the proper genes and balancing out intelligence quotients.

Meghan leaned forward and set her cup back on the tray. She'd barely tasted the tea, but she couldn't endure another minute of this awkward conversation.

"I have to be getting back," she said as calmly as she could. "We're eating earlier this year, because I have to be at work before three."

"What kind of employment involves working on a holiday?" Frances Carlyle asked.

Once more, Meghan had exposed herself without realizing what she was doing. She would have given anything to quietly inform Grey's mother that she was a brain surgeon and was needed for an emergency procedure within the hour. Instead, she calmly announced, "I'm a waitress at Rose's Diner." She didn't bother to look at Grey's mother, knowing the woman's expression would only reveal her disapproval.

"I see," Frances Carlyle said in a tone so like Grey's that it would have been comical if it hadn't hurt so much.

"I'll walk you to your car," Grey insisted.

"That won't be necessary," she said, keeping her voice as even as possible and having trouble doing so.

"Nonsense, Meghan. I'll see you to your car."

Frances Carlyle stood with Meghan and Grey. "There's no need to expose yourself to the cold, son. You can say goodbye to your...friend here."

Certain everyone could see how badly she was trembling, Meghan reached for her purse, buttoned her coat and headed toward the front door.

Ignoring his mother's advice, Grey followed her outside.

"Meghan, I'm sorry," he said, taking her by the shoulders when they reached her car. His eyes were troubled, his expression grim. "I had no idea my mother was planning to fly in at the last minute like this." He frowned and his face darkened momentarily.

"There's no need to apologize. I understand." By some miracle, Meghan was able to force a smile.

"I didn't know anything about this. Apparently Pamela and my mother have been planning this little surprise for the last several weeks."

Meghan would take bets that they'd arranged this about the time Grey had started dating her. She had to give Pamela Riverside credit. Grey's colleague had used the most effective means possible to show Meghan how ill-suited she was to Grey. All the arguments in the universe couldn't have said it more eloquently than those few stilted moments with his mother. Meghan knew that no matter what Grey felt for her, she would never fit into his world. His family had already rejected her with little more than a passing thought.

Meghan had faced this argument before, but always from her own perspective. She'd stood on the other side of the fence, knowing that her family and friends would accept Grey without a moment's hesitation. The one sample of her meeting Grey's colleagues had been slanted in her favor; for the majority of the evening, she'd stayed glued to his side. It was impossible to calculate how the evening had actually gone.

"I'll phone you tomorrow," Grey promised.

"I'm working." She wasn't due in until three, but twenty-four hours wasn't long enough for her to analyze her feelings. If she could delay dealing with this until her head was clear and her mind wasn't clouded with emotions, Meghan knew she would cope better. "When's your mother leaving?"

"Not until Sunday afternoon."

"It probably would be better if you waited until then to contact me, don't you think?" This was Meghan's subtle method of keeping the peace for Grey's sake. She didn't doubt he would get an earful later. His mother was bound to tell him how improper a relationship with Meghan was the minute she drove out of sight. On second thought, Frances Carlyle was intelligent enough to relay the message without ever having to utter a word. She would probably do it in the same manner Pamela Riverside had delivered her own missive to Meghan.

"What my mother thinks or says isn't going to change the way I feel about you," he said tightly.

Meghan loved him so much at that moment that it took every ounce of self-control she possessed not to break down and weep. She raised her fingers and lovingly ran her hand down the side of his face.

"Thank you for that," she said, her voice little more than a broken whisper. She lowered her eyes, fearing that if she looked at him much longer, she wouldn't be able to hold back the emotion straining for release. Her eyes burned and her chest ached.

She started to turn away from him, but his grip on her shoulders tightened and he brought her back against him. Surprised, Meghan raised her gaze to his, only to discover that Grey meant to kiss her. A weak protest rose in her, but she wasn't allowed to voice any objection. With infinite tenderness, he settled his mouth firmly over hers. His hands on her shoulders were strong enough to lift her onto the tips of her toes.

Meghan opened her mouth to him, kissing him back with all the longing stored in her heart. She gripped the front of his shirt, bunching the material with her fists, holding on to him as though she never intended to let go. She moaned softly as his mouth moved with tender ferocity over her own until they were leaning against each other.

"Meghan," he whispered, planting a series of soft kisses over her eyes and cheeks. He threaded his fingers through her hair, keeping her close. "I'd rather spend the day with you and your family. I'm sorry it has to be like this."

"Don't apologize. I understand, Grey." She clung to him, her eyes closed. But when she looked up, she happened to notice his mother standing in the picture window, looking out at them. The older woman's face was creased into a look of disapproval so sharp that Meghan could feel its pointedness all the way across the yard. With some effort, she eased herself out of Grey's arms.

He opened her car door for her. "I'll call as soon as I can, but it probably won't be until Sunday afternoon."

She nodded, and looked away.

"Have a nice Thanksgiving."

"You, too," she said, and slipped inside the car and inserted the key into the ignition.

"Meghan," her mother said softly, taking the chair beside her in the kitchen after the Thanksgiving meal was over. "We haven't had to a free moment to talk since you got back from Grey's. Did you two argue?"

"No. He's got company from out of town."

"You hardly touched your dinner."

"I guess I wasn't hungry." The excuse was weak, but it was the best she could come up. She made a show of looking at her watch. "I suppose I should think about heading off to work."

"Isn't it a little early yet?"

"I'm sure Sherry's swamped," Meghan explained, hoping her mother would accept that rationalization without voicing an objection. "She'll appreciate an extra pair of hands."

"Hey, Meghan," Danny interrupted, strolling into the kitchen, gnawing on a turkey drumstick. "Can you call Grey and tell him we need him for touch football. We're one man shy."

"I already told you he won't be coming today," she replied sharply. She hadn't meant to snap at her brother, but the words had slipped out uncensored before she could put a stop to them.

Danny's eyes rounded and he shrugged expressively, giving her a wounded look. "Well, I'm sorry for livin'. I thought he'd want to come over, that's all."

"I'm sure he did want to join us," Colleen O'Day assured her son, arching a thoughtful brow in Meghan's direction.

Meghan stood, pushing in her chair. Her fingers bit into the cushion on the back of the seat. "I'm sorry, Danny, I didn't mean to jump all over you."

"Will you tell Grey the next time you see him that we missed him?" her brother pressed. "Hey, you're not breaking up with him, are you? Grey's neat. I like him."

"Don't worry about it, all right? What I do is my own business."

"You *are* going to keep dating him, aren't you?" Danny demanded, not satisfied with her answer.

"Who's breaking up with whom?" Brian asked, strolling into the kitchen. Allison Flynn was with him and the two had been holding hands from the minute she arrived. Meghan had watched them during dinner and marveled at how they'd ever managed to eat.

"Meghan and Grey are on the outs," Danny informed his oldest brother. "He's the best thing that ever happened to her and she's dumping him."

"What?" Brian cried.

"Listen, you two, this isn't any of your business," their mother reminded them. "Whatever happens between Meghan and the professor is their own affair."

"I suppose this means you want us to stay out of it. Right?" Danny asked.

"Exactly," Meghan told him sternly.

"But, Meghan," Danny whined, "where would you ever find anyone as nice as Grey? None of your other boyfriends ever took Chad and me to the movies. I like him. Think about that before you go throwing away the greatest guy in the world."

Unfortunately, it wasn't up to Meghan. Grey's mother would be flying out Sunday. Frances Carlyle had four long days to convince Grey how wrong Meghan would be for him, and how perfectly Pamela Riverside would fit into his life.

If Meghan didn't hear from him Sunday afternoon, she would know exactly how successful his mother had been. It was almost comical when she stopped to think about it. Meghan could have saved Dr. Frances Carlyle a good deal of trouble. She'd already made up her mind about where her relationship with Grey was going.

Nowhere.

Grey lay on his bed, his hands linked behind his head, staring at the ceiling. If he lived to be a hundred and ten he would never forget the look on Meghan's face when she met his mother. She'd marched into his house, insisting he kiss her and heaven knew he'd been tempted. Then she'd looked around Grey and discovered his mother standing just inside the kitchen, looking at Meghan as though she were the devil incarnate come to corrupt her only child.

Regrettably, Frances Carlyle was no Colleen O'Day. Grey's mother meant well, but he'd long ago given up letting her dictate his life. One of the reasons he'd accepted his position with Friends University in Wichita was in order to escape his mother's constant interference.

For the past three days, Grey had been forced to hear her list Pamela Riverside's fine qualities over and over again until he'd wanted to shout for her to cease and desist. When that ploy didn't seem to be working, his mother had gone on to tell how she prayed she would live long enough to enjoy her grandchildren. This was followed by a short sigh, as if to suggest that her stay on earth was only a matter of time and Grey shouldn't expect her to hang on much longer.

Actually, his mother had missed her calling; she should have been in the theater. And as for grandchildren, Grey sincerely doubted that Frances would want anything to do with his children until they were old enough to conjugate verbs.

Over the course of the same few days, Grey had tried to talk to his mother about Meghan, but every time he mentioned her name, the subject had been subtly changed. Yes, Meghan was "a dear girl"; it was unfortunate she was so…"common."

Grey chuckled in the dark. Meghan common! His mother had a good deal to learn about the Irish miss. Meghan O'Day was about as common as green eggs and ham. She was sunshine and laughter, unfathomable, unnerving and incomprehensible. And he was in love with her.

Meghan had been concerned that he would be upset by what Carol and Carrie had whispered in the theater the other night. To be frank, he *had* been troubled at first, but he'd tried not to let it bother him. The age difference between him and Meghan was almost ten years, but it hadn't seemed to affect her. If that was the case, he shouldn't allow it to worry him.

The one thing that had shaken him more than anything was knowing that his students referred to him as "Stone Face." He smiled. He had a reasonable sense of humor. Now that he'd met Meghan, it was becoming a little more fine-tuned. His students would notice the changes in him soon enough.

The following afternoon, Grey drove his mother to the airport. He did his best not to show his enthusiasm. This visit had been more strained than usual. Frances tried, but she really wasn't much of a mother—the instincts just hadn't been there. Her idea of mothering had to do with manipulation and control. She loved him as much as it was possible for her to care about anyone, and he loved her. She was, after all, responsible for giving him life and for nurturing him to the best of her capabilities.

Frances hugged him close. "Keep in touch, Greyson."

"Yes, Mother," he said, and dutifully kissed her on the cheek.

"And please consider what I said. It's time you thought about settling down."

If he settled down any more, his chest would start sprouting corn, but he kept his thoughts to himself.

"Pamela is a dear, dear girl. I do hope you'll try to arrange some time to get to know her better."

He answered that with a weak smile.

"She's crazy about you, Greyson, and just the type of woman who will help you in your career. Your father, God rest his soul, would be pleased. Marriage can't be taken any too lightly, especially by someone in your position. You need a woman who will give you more than attractive children. You must marry someone your equal." She paused and looked directly into his eyes. "You *do* understand what I'm saying, don't you?"

"Yes, Mother." Grey clenched his hands into fists, battling down the anger that flared to life so readily. He only needed to hold on a little while longer. She would be gone in a matter of minutes.

"Good." Frances Carlyle nodded once, looking pleased that her message had been received. She gave her son a smug look and headed into the airport.

Grey hurried home. In fact, he could hardly get there fast enough. The minute he could, he reached for his cell, punching out Meghan's number with an eagerness that had his fingers shaking. He let it ring ten times before he cut off the call. Meghan wasn't answering.

Ten

"Hello, Eric, it's good to see you again," Meghan said, draining whatever energy she had by coming up with a smile. For three nights straight, she hadn't gotten more than four hours' sleep. She was exhausted mentally, physically and emotionally. Filling his coffee cup, she handed him a menu, then automatically recited Monday's special—all-you-can-eat spaghetti and meatballs.

"You look terrible," her college friend commented, studying her through narrowed eyes. "What happened? Did you just lose your best friend?"

In a manner of speaking, that was exactly what had happened. Meghan brushed off his concern with a light laugh. "Don't be silly."

"Meghan, sweetie, I recognize men problems when I see them. If you need a shoulder to cry on, you come to Uncle Eric, okay? Or better yet," he said enthusiastically, "let me arrange for you to talk to Don Harrison."

"Who?"

"Don Harrison. You met him two weeks ago at the reading group. Actually, Don's interest doesn't lie so much in the classics as it does in you. He's been pumping me with questions about you every day for the last two weeks, but I've discouraged him because I knew you were seeing someone steadily."

Meghan didn't even remember meeting Don, but that wasn't unusual. The reading group had ten faithful members who showed up every week and nearly as many others who came and went as the spirit moved them.

"Listen," Eric continued, undaunted by her apathy. "I'll call Don and let him know you could use some cheering up. He'll be thrilled to hear it."

"I'd rather you didn't," Meghan told him. She just wasn't in the mood to see anyone new. Maybe in a few weeks, when her heart was on the mend; but not now. It was too soon. And she felt too raw and vulnerable.

"Why wouldn't you want to see Don? He'll provide the right kind of therapy to help you get over this guy who's making you so miserable."

It was apparent that Eric wasn't going to listen to her objections, but she was equally persistent and shook her head. She took the pad out of her pocket, hoping Eric would take the hint and order.

"Give it some thought and let me know, all right?"

"Okay," she murmured. But she had no intention of dating this guy.

"Everything will look better in the morning," Eric said confidently. "Just wait and see. Now don't argue with your uncle Eric, because he's all-wise and he knows all about these things because he's suffered a few broken hearts in his time. By the way, I'll take the spaghetti and meatballs and a piece of the cherry sour-cream pie."

Rarely had she been more woeful, she realized. It took effort just to get through the day. No one had ever told her that loving someone could be so painful. All her life, she'd grown up believing that when she fell in love there would be birds chirping some sweet song, apple trees blossoming in the distance and enchantment swirling about her like champagne bubbles.

What a farce love had turned out to be.

Meghan didn't even know what she was going to say to Grey. Avoiding him, which she'd succeeded in doing for the last couple of days, wasn't going to work forever. Sooner or later she would have to answer her phone. If she didn't, he would simply arrive unannounced at Rose's, and then she wouldn't be able to escape him.

With that thought in mind, Meghan went on her break. She sat in the employees' lounge and after a few heart-pounding moments of indecision, she picked up her phone and slowly, deliberately, dialed Grey's number.

"Meghan, where have you been?" he cried, then promptly sneezed. That outburst was followed by a loud, nasty-sounding cough. "I've been trying to reach you for two solid days."

"I…I've been busy. How did your visit with your mother go?"

Grey emitted a short laugh. "About as well as they ever do. I know she went out of her way to intimidate you Thanksgiving morning, but I'm hoping you didn't let anything she said bother you."

"No, not in the least," Meghan lied. Dr. Frances Carlyle had looks that would make a Mafia hit man tremble. In those few minutes she'd spent with the other woman, Meghan had sat with her back straight and her hands neatly folded in her lap. Words she rarely used kept slipping out of her mouth—words and phrases like *indeed*, *quite so* and *most certainly*.

"My mother often means well," Grey continued, "but

I refuse to allow her to rule my life. And before you say another word, I didn't have anything to do with Pamela's joining us for dinner that day. I'm not interested in her and never will be. I'm hoping you realize that by now."

"You don't need to worry, Grey. Having Dr. Riverside join you didn't bother me in the least." However, Meghan was willing to wager a month's worth of tip money that his mother would convince him Pamela was the woman of his dreams before the year was out. Meghan was all too aware that this ploy to marry Grey off to Pamela hadn't been all his mother's doing. Grey's esteemed associate had done her share—subtly of course, but effectively.

"Good, I—" He stopped abruptly and let loose a series of turbulent sneezes. "Sorry. I can't seem to stop once I get started."

"You sound terrible, Grey." Now that she wasn't so concerned with her own emotional pain, she realized how miserable he seemed to be.

"It's nothing but a nasty cold. I'll be over it in a couple of days, but I'm sure I'll feel better by Saturday. This is probably just a twenty-four hour virus."

Meghan tightened her grip on the telephone receiver. "Saturday night?"

"We've been invited to a dinner party. I mentioned it the other night while we were eating ice cream, remember?"

No, she didn't. Not at first. Then vaguely her memory was stirred. Knowing how nervous she was about attending these formal affairs with him, Grey had offered to let her scoop up the last of his hot fudge topping if she would agree to let him escort her to a holiday dinner party at the home of Dr. Essary. High on her love for Grey and his generosity to her brothers, Meghan had willingly agreed to the exchange. Now she felt like a dimwit. All things considered, the last thing she wanted to do was attend a social function with him.

"Remember?" he coaxed a second time.

"Yes, I guess I do."

Grey coughed and excused himself, returning a moment later. "I'm sure I'll improve before Saturday."

Meghan squeezed her eyes shut as the pain washed over her in swelling waves. "Seeing that you're a little under the weather, and Saturday is up in the air, would you mind terribly if I canceled our date?"

"Meghan, Meghan, Meghan," he chided in a singsong voice that sounded amazingly like his rendition of *I see.* "You're not going to get out of this dinner party that easily. Honey, the more often you accompany me to these functions, the more relaxed you'll become. I want you with me."

"From the sounds of this virus, you're going to get worse before you get better." Meghan had no idea if that was true or not, but she was grasping at straws.

"If I am still under the weather, we'll cancel."

"But I'd like to make other plans. I don't want to be left on hold like this," she said, digging to the bottom of the barrel for excuses.

"I don't understand. What do you mean by 'other plans'?"

"I've been asked out by...one of the men from the reading group, and frankly, I'd forgotten all about the dinner party." This was elasticizing the truth to the very limit. But according to Eric, she could have a date with Don Harrison if she wanted one. She didn't. But Grey didn't need to know that. At this point, her only intention was to convince him she didn't want to see him any longer before either of them suffered any more from a dead-end relationship.

"One of the men from the reading group," Grey repeated. He sounded as though he were reeling from this news; his voice was barely audible.

"Since you're not feeling well, anyway, I can't see where it would hurt any to cancel our plans."

"Is it Eric Vogel?"

"No. I already told you, he's engaged."

"I see." He paused then asked, "And you'd prefer to go out with this other guy?"

"Yes," she whispered, then regrouped her thoughts and stated calmly, "That is, if it isn't too much of a problem for you, since I had committed myself to you first."

This was so much more difficult than she'd thought it would be.

The silence that followed was loud enough to break the sound barrier. What felt like sonic booms slammed against her eardrums until her head was shaking and her whole body was trembling in their aftermath.

"I hadn't realized your social calendar was so crowded."

Meghan recognized the anger in his voice and it was like inflicting a wound upon herself. "I'll call you later in the week and see how you're feeling."

"Don't worry about Saturday night. Go ahead and date your friend or any other men you might meet between now and Saturday." His words felt like a cold slap in the face.

"Thank you for understanding. Goodbye, Grey."

He may have bid her farewell, but if he had, Meghan didn't hear him. All she'd heard was another series of sneezes and coughs.

For a full minute after the line had been disconnected, Meghan kept her hand on the receiver. Taking in deep breaths seemed to help, but it didn't help control her desire to bury her face in her hands. She didn't do that, of course—not when she had customers waiting.

A violent sneeze ripped the flimsy tissue in half, and Grey automatically reached for another. His head felt as if someone had turned him upside down and all his blood had pooled in his sinuses. His chest hurt even worse; it felt as though a two-ton truck had decided to park there and had no intention of moving. He was utterly miserable! And he had three classes to get through before he could head home.

Meghan wasn't helping matters any. She'd come up with this cock-and-bull story about wanting to go out with another man Saturday night, and he'd fallen for it hook, line and sinker.

At first.

He'd been so infuriated with her that he was sure the elevation in his temperature had been due to his short conversation with Meghan the day before.

Once he'd settled down, sat back and reflected on their discussion, he realized she'd been lying, and doing a poor job of it. If he hadn't been so irritated with her, he would have easily seen through her deception.

In the light of a fresh day, Grey downright refused to believe she was interested in someone else. He couldn't very well claim that at age thirty-four he hadn't been in love before now, but the powerful emotion he felt for Meghan O'Day went far beyond anything in his limited experience. He'd been infatuated, captivated and charmed by any number of women over the years. But it was this one sweet Irish miss who laid claim to his heart. He couldn't love Meghan the way he did and not know when she was making something up.

Grey guessed all this nonsense about her dating someone else related directly to his mother's visit. That aristocratic old lady had buffaloed Meghan into believing she wasn't good enough for him. Grey would bet cold cash on that fact. He couldn't blame Meghan for letting Frances browbeat her into such thinking. Grey's mother had done a good job on Meghan, who'd had no experience in dealing with his manipulating parent. Grey, on the other hand, had had a lifetime of practice; and he wasn't about to let his own mother cheat him out of the best thing that had ever happened to him: Meghan O'Day.

Noticing the time, Grey reached for his tweed jacket, his overcoat and his briefcase. He hesitated long enough to line his jacket pocket with tissues. He was through the worst of this stupid cold—at least that was what he continued to tell himself, but then immediately broke into a series of loud coughs that racked his throat and chest.

"Professor Carlyle, are you all right? Perhaps I should make a doctor's appointment for you."

"Don't worry, I'm fine," he said, waving off his assistant's concern.

"If you're not better in the morning, I really think you should see someone."

The first person who flashed into his mind that he should see was Meghan. A slow smile eased its way across his face. The Milton-quoting waitress would make an excellent nurse—unlike Pamela Riverside, who would probably insist he take cod-liver oil and stay away from her in case he was contagious. Naturally, if Meghan were around, he would have to exaggerate the extent of his sickness. But the mere thought of Meghan sitting at his side, running her cool hands over his fevered brow and whispering sweet nothings in his ear, was far more appealing than a heavy dose of antibiotics or Pamela Riverside.

Before he left the building, Grey turned up the collar of his overcoat. Dear grief, it had been cold lately. A fresh batch of snow had thickly carpeted the campus grounds. Several students had taken to building snowmen, and their merriment filled the crisp afternoon air.

Grey heard the sound of Meghan's musical laughter long before he found her in the crowd. A smile teased the corners of his mouth as he paused in the shoveled walkway, holding his briefcase close to his side while his gaze scanned the large group of fun-making young people.

A flash of auburn-colored hair captured his attention and his gaze settled there. It was Meghan, all right. *His* Meghan. Only she was standing with her arms wrapped around another man and her eyes were smiling up at him.

The amusement left Grey's expression to be replaced by a weary kind of pain that struck sharp and deep. It took a moment for him to find his breath. When he did, he held his head high and continued down the pathway as though nothing had happened. He sincerely doubted that Meghan would ever know that he'd seen her.

"Mom!" Meghan cried, flying into the house, her voice filled with alarm. "I need you."

The kitchen door swung open. "Honey, what is it?"

"Grey. He's ill!" She gripped her mother's forearms and swallowed several times before she could continue. Her own heartbeat sounded like a cannon in her ear. "I was on campus earlier and overheard a student comment that Grey hasn't been to school in three days and all his classes have been canceled."

"Aren't you jumping to conclusions?"

"No. When I talked to him Monday night, he sounded like he had a dreadful cold then. Apparently he's much worse now."

Colleen O'Day tucked in a few strands of gray hair behind her ear and casually strolled back into the kitchen where she'd been folding clothes on the round oak table. "I thought you told me you'd decided not to see your professor friend anymore."

"Yes, but he's sick now and—"

Her mother raised her hand as if she were stopping traffic. "Although it was difficult at the time, I bit my tongue, figuring this is your life. You're twenty-four and old enough to be making your own decisions. Whether I happen to agree with you or not, is something else entirely."

"I'm worried about Grey. Surely you can understand that."

Colleen O'Day fluffed out a thick towel and neatly folded it in thirds. "From what you were telling me the other day, you'd decided you didn't much care for the professor anymore."

"Mom," Meghan said with an impatient sigh, "I didn't come here for a lecture."

"Then why are you here?"

"I want you to make your special soup for Grey. I know once he's had some of your broth, he'll feel better. I always did. Remember when I was a little girl how you used to tell me the soup had magical healing powers?"

"Meghan—" Colleen issued her daughter's name on an exasperated sigh and reached for another towel

"—how do you expect to get the soup to him? According to what you said, you have no intentions of seeing him again. Do you expect leprechauns to deliver it?"

"Don't be silly."

"From what you said, you're not worthy enough to lace that distinguished man's shoes, let alone be seen with him. To hear you tell it, the good name of O'Day is sure to tarnish the professor's reputation and possibly ruin his career. You didn't seem to mind, though, because you'd made up your mind that he was too pompous and dignified for the likes of you anyway."

"You're exaggerating, Mother, and that's not like you. I care enough about Grey to want the best for him. Isn't that what loving someone means?"

Her mother held the laundry basket against her stomach and sadly shook her head. "Perhaps I am stretching the facts a bit, but that's because I disagree with you so strongly. Loving a man often does call for sacrifice, but not the kind you're making. But as I said earlier, it's your life. If you want to break your own heart, far be it for me to stand in your way and gift you with forty-odd years of wisdom."

Meghan knotted her fists at her side. "Will you make the soup or not?"

"And who's going to take it to him?"

"You?" Meghan proposed hopefully.

"Me?" Her mother laughed at the mere suggestion. "I'm not traipsing halfway across town to deliver my special healing soup to your old boyfriend, Meghan Katherine O'Day. If you don't care to go out with him any longer, then why should I care if he's ill? He's your friend, not mine."

"How can you say that?" Grey had brought her mother

flowers, complimented her cooking and gone out of his way to let her know how much he appreciated sharing Sunday meals with them. She couldn't understand her mother's attitude.

Colleen O'Day shrugged as though what happened to Professor Carlyle was of little concern to her. "All I know is that my daughter wants nothing more to do with the man."

"He's ill."

"Why should that bother you?" Colleen pressed. "You don't plan to see him again."

Frustrated, Meghan closed her eyes. "Will you make the soup, or not?"

"Not."

Meghan was so shocked, her mouth fell open.

"But I might be persuaded to share the family recipe with my only daughter. It's time she learned of its miraculous healing powers herself. My one wish is that it will loosen a few of her own brain cells so she can see what a terrible mistake she's making."

The two mason jars were securely tucked inside the shopping bag when Meghan entered the faculty building. Grey's office was on the third floor of the same structure, but that wasn't where she was headed.

When her mother had copied the recipe, Colleen O'Day had done so with the express hope that Meghan would deliver the soup to Grey herself and in the process settle her differences with Grey. Unfortunately Meghan couldn't do that, but she hadn't wanted to disillusion her mother with the truth. She planned to deliver the soup in a roundabout manner and pray that her mother never found out.

Dr. Pamela Riverside would take the soup to him.

After some heavy-duty soul-searching, Meghan had devised a plan of action. She was going to show Pamela Riverside the way to this particular man's heart. It was obvious the poor woman needed help. She might balk now, but someday she would appreciate Meghan's efforts.

As Dr. Riverside's office was on Grey's floor, the same receptionist announced Meghan. Meghan didn't wait, however, but saw herself into Dr. Riverside's room.

Grey's colleague was seated behind a meticulously clean desk in a spotless office that wasn't marked by a single personal item other than her books.

"Ms. O'Day," Pamela greeted, rising to her feet. "This is a pleasant surprise."

But she didn't look pleased, which was just as well. Meghan closed the door and stepped forward, not stopping until she stood directly in front of the other woman's desk.

"Do you love him?"

The other woman sucked in her breath. "I beg your pardon."

"Dr. Carlyle! Do you love him?"

"I hardly think my feelings for Greyson Carlyle are any of your business."

"No, I don't suppose you would." Setting the shopping bag on top of the desk, Meghan crossed her arms and battled down an overwhelming sense of sadness. "You're exactly the right kind of woman for him. His mother knows it. You know it. And I know it."

Pamela Riverside cast her gaze downward. "Unfortunately Greyson hasn't seemed to have figured it out yet."

"And he won't with you looking like that."

Pamela slapped her hand against her breast in shock and outrage. "Exactly what are you saying?"

"Your clothes," Meghan cried, waving her hand at the fastidious dark blue suit as though she were a fairy godmother and held the powers of transformation in the tips of her fingers. "I haven't seen you in anything but that same dark suit and jacket in all the times we've met. That thing looks twenty years old."

"I'll have you know I bought this only last month."

"And have five exactly like it hanging in your closet."

Pamela sucked in a tiny breath that told Meghan she'd hit the peg square on the head. "And those horrible shoes have got to go."

With her hands braced against her hips, Grey's associate glared down at her feet. "These are the most comfortable shoes I've ever worn. I refuse to let you—"

"Of course, they're comfortable. That's because your grandmother broke them in for you. Go shopping, Dr. Riverside, throw caution to the wind and try a new department store. Start with a silk teddy and go from there."

The woman's mouth opened and closed several times, as though she couldn't say everything she wanted to fast enough. "If you insist upon insulting me, Ms. O'Day, then perhaps you should leave."

"Take the pins out of your hair."

"I can't believe I'm hearing you correctly."

"Your hair," Meghan repeated, pointing her finger at the professor, unwilling to brook any argument. "And do it now."

With her face growing more pale by the minute, Pamela reached behind her head and released the tightly coiled chignon. The dark length unrolled down her back and she loosened it so that it fell about her face.

The transformation was remarkable. Pleased, Meghan nodded quietly as she studied Pamela's facial features in a fresh light. "Much better. While you're at the department store make an appointment with a beautician. Have her cut about an inch all the way around, and don't ever wear it up again."

"Well, I never!" she barked.

"Well, it's time you did."

Grey's colleague looked so shocked that she snapped her mouth shut.

"He's sick, you know, and in his weakened condition he'll be more receptive to gestures of concern from you. Go shopping and make sure everything you have on is new. Have your hair done the way I said and then go and visit him. And last but not least, take him this soup and tell him you made it yourself."

"I rarely cook. Greyson knows that."

"Lie."

"Ms. O'Day, I'll have you know I'm as honest as the day is long."

"These are the shortest days of the year, Dr. Riverside. Take advantage of it." Meghan paused and drew in a quivering breath. "Make him happy, or by heaven, you'll wish you had." With that, she marched out of the office.

Tears brimmed in Meghan's eyes, making it almost impossible for her to navigate her way to the elevator.

Grey was on the mend. For the last four days he'd been living on orange juice, canned chicken soup and peanut butter—tasting nothing. The chill that had permeated his bones was gone, but the cough that seemed to convulse his intestines lingered on. He hadn't talked to Meghan in those four days, and it felt like four years. His heart was heavy, his head stuffy and his thoughts more twisted than an old pine tree's limbs. The combination left him in no mood for company, and Pamela Riverside had just phoned claiming she had to talk to him; she possessed urgent information that he must act upon immediately.

Given no choice, he'd changed clothes and put on water for tea, awaiting her arrival with as much enthusiasm as the settlers greeted Indians on the warpath in the 1800s. He would have refused to see Pamela if it weren't for the fact that she sounded highly agitated, which in itself was rare. Whatever was troubling her probably was linked to some problem within the department, and he would prefer to deal with it now instead of on Monday morning.

A car door closing echoed in the distance and Grey braced himself for the inevitable confrontation.

"Hello, Pamela," he said, when he opened the door for her, wondering if she even suspected he wasn't particularly welcoming.

She marched into his living room, her eyes flashing with indignation and her hands knotted into tight fists at her sides. "That woman belongs in jail."

"Calm down," he said, leading her to a chair. Once she was seated, he handed her a cup of freshly brewed tea, adding the cream and sugar he knew she favored.

Waving her hand as though directing a world-class orchestra, Pamela announced, "She pranced right into my office as brazen as can be. I demand that you do something, Greyson."

Grey took the seat across from her, braced his hands on the arms of the chair and dug his fingers into the material, praying for patience. Pamela hadn't so much as asked how he was feeling. It was amazing the things that went through his mind at a time like this.

"Don't you even care?"

Frankly, he didn't. "*Who* pranced into your office as insolent as could be?"

"That…girl you've been dating. Meghan O'Something."

Grey couldn't believe his ears. He uncrossed his legs and straightened, digging his fingers deeper into the pads of the leather chair. "Meghan did? Exactly what did she say?"

Pamela's hand went into action a second time. "You're going to love this! She insulted me and threatened me and insisted I lie to you." She said all this in a rush, as though the memory of it were more than she should be asked to bear. When she'd finished, she let a soft cry part from her mouth, then bit down on her lower lip as outrage filled her once again.

"She insulted you?" That didn't sound anything like Meghan, and Grey honestly refused to believe it.

"Yes," Pamela cried. "She made several derogatory statements about my clothes and demanded that I never wear my hair up again. Right in my own office, Greyson. I mean to tell you, I've never been so insulted in my life."

"I see." Grey frowned. He didn't know what was going on in Meghan's loveable, confused mind, but he fully intended to find out.

"I'm sure you *don't* see," Pamela insisted vehemently. Her gaze sharpened all the more. "Something has to be done about this woman…. She belongs in a…mental ward. I'm still shaking. Just look!" To prove her point, she held out her hand for his inspection, and in fact it was trembling.

"You said Meghan also threatened you."

"Indeed, she did." Tilting her head at a lofty angle, Pamela drew in a short breath as if to suggest she needed something more to calm her before she continued with this tale of horror.

Grey was growing impatient. The more he was with Pamela, the more he realized that she'd attended the same school of dramatics as his mother.

"She claimed that if I didn't make you happy, she'd make sure I wished I had. Now I'm not exactly sure what she meant by that, but the whole torrid conversation started out by her demanding answers to what I consider highly personal and confidential questions." She paused long enough to draw in a second quivering breath. "The thing that concerns me most—because it's obvious now more than ever before—is that this…friend of yours is suffering from some kind of mental flaw, which is probably genetic. Did I tell you that she insisted I lie to you?"

Grey gritted his teeth to keep from defending Meghan, but it was necessary that he hear everything before voicing his thoughts. "Yes," he coaxed, hoping to encourage her to speak freely. "About the lying."

"She delivered some disgusting-looking broth and demanded that I take it to you. What I found most amazing was she wanted me to tell you I'd cooked it up myself. Now you and I both know that while I'm an incredibly talented woman in many areas, my expertise doesn't extend to the kitchen. From everything else this loony woman did, I strongly suspect she could be trying to poison you and then blame me for it. Naturally, the more I thought about the situation, the more plain it became that I had to come straight to you."

"What did you do with the broth?"

"I threw it in the garbage right away. Greyson, it was the only thing to do."

Grey nodded. The soup was a loss, but he was grateful beyond words that Pamela had come to him, although he questioned her purpose. "I'm most appreciative, Pamela."

A smug smile replaced the look of fabricated horror. "Just what do you intend to do about this?"

He tapped his index finger over his lips while mulling over the information. When he'd finished, he straightened and eagerly met Dr. Riverside's gaze.

"I believe I'll marry her."

Eleven

"You want to know what I think?" Meghan asked a group of friends who were sitting in a circle on her living-room carpet. She held up a full glass of cheap wine as if to propose a toast.

"What does Meghan think?" three others chimed in, then held up their glasses, eager to salute her insights.

Tears of mirth rolled down her face and she wiped them aside. This get-together with Eric, his fiancée, Trina Montgomery, and Don Harrison was exactly what she needed to see her through these first difficult days without Grey.

"I think," she said, starting again, trying her best to look somber, "Henry David Thoreau wrote *Walden* when he should have been going for a killing on the stock market." She said this with a straight face, as serious as she'd been the entire evening. Then she ruined everything by loudly hiccuping in a movement so jolting that it nearly dislodged her head. Shocked and embarrassed by the involuntary action, she covered her mouth. Until that moment, she hadn't realized how precariously close she was to being tipsy.

"I bet he made all his students use recycled paper," Trina added, then laughed until the tears streamed down her face.

"Right," Don agreed, nodding. "He missed his calling in life, he should have been a—"

"Boy Scout leader," Meghan supplied.

The others doubled over with laughter as though she'd said the funniest thing in the world.

"I love it," Eric said, slapping the floor several times.

"What I said?" Meghan asked, thinking he might be referring to the continued hiccuping.

Eric and the others were laughing too hard to answer her.

The doorbell chimed and the merriment stopped abruptly. Don glanced toward the door, looking mildly guilty. "Shh," he said, putting his finger over his mouth. "We must be making too much of a racket."

"I don't think we were," Meghan said, doing her best to sober up before going to the door.

Trina covered her mouth with her palm, then lowered it to whisper, "Someone might have called the police."

"What for?" Eric chided. "The worst thing we've done all night is make a few derogatory remarks about Thoreau."

The doorbell chimed a second time.

"I think you'd better answer it," Trina whispered to Meghan. "It's your apartment, and it could be one of the neighbors. Tell them we promise to be quiet."

"Tell whoever it is to lighten up," Don muttered. "It's barely eight o'clock."

Getting to her feet was far more difficult than it should have been. Meghan teetered for a second as the room started to tilt and sway. She walked across the floor and stood in front of her door. Taking in a deep, steadying breath, she smoothed her hair away from her face and squared her shoulders.

"Who is it?" she called out in a friendly voice.

Whoever was on the other side obviously didn't hear because her question was followed by repeated loud knocking.

Startled by the unexpected noise, Meghan's hand flew to her breast. She gasped and jumped back a step.

Immediately Don Harrison leaped to his feet. He was short and a little stocky, but exactly the type of friend Meghan needed right now. She doubted that she would ever feel anything romantic toward him, but he was friendly, patient and kind, and Meghan genuinely liked him.

"I'll answer it for you," Don announced, and readjusted the waistband of his pants as if to suggest he was about to walk into the middle of the street with a six-shooter in his hand and gun down anyone who was crazy enough to upset Meghan.

"No...it's all right." Hurriedly she waved off his concern, twisted open the dead bolt and threw open the door. Her gaze collided with a solid male chest. She squinted, greatly relieved that it wasn't the uniform of a policeman that confronted her. Slowly she raised her head, but when she did, her eyes clashed with a pair of deep China-blue ones that were all too familiar.

"What are you doing here?" she demanded.

"Dr. Carlyle," Don exclaimed from behind her. His shock echoed across the room like a cannon firing into the wind.

"He's going to arrest us for what we said about Thoreau," Trina wailed. "I knew something like this was going to happen. I just knew it." She released a small cry and covered her face with a decorative pillow.

"Dr. Carlyle, sir," Eric cried, struggling to come to his feet. "We didn't mean anything by what we said. Honest."

"May I come inside?" Grey asked, ignoring the others and centering his gaze on Meghan.

Had the fate of the free world rested on her response, Meghan couldn't have answered.

The professor's narrowed eyes then surveyed the room, slowly taking in the scene. He focused on each face, finally drawing his gaze back to Meghan. "May I?" he repeated.

"Oh, sure—I guess." Meghan squared her shoulders, then hiccuped despite her frenzied effort to look and act sober.

"Don't let him intimidate you," Don encouraged, placing his arm around Meghan's shoulders.

"I won't," she whispered.

Grey's look swung accusingly back to Don, and the other man immediately dropped his hold on Meghan, retreating several steps under the force of Grey's eyes.

"You're drunk—you all are," Grey announced.

"I'm not," Meghan insisted righteously, then laughed and pointed her index finger toward the ceiling. "Yet."

"I want to know how he heard what we were saying," Eric mumbled, looking confused. "Does he have Superman hearing, or what?"

"I don't want to know how he found out," Trina mumbled from behind the pillow. "Oh no, there goes my quarter grade. I'll never make it out of his class alive."

Don just sat looking dumbstruck and disoriented.

"You need coffee," Grey announced, and moved past all four and into the kitchen.

Meghan lowered herself onto the arm of the chair. Her knees had started to shake and she wasn't sure she could remain upright much longer.

"He walked into your kitchen as if he had every right in the world to do so," Eric interjected, pointing in that direction. "He can't do that, can he?"

"He said we needed coffee," Don reminded the others.

"But how can he walk into a stranger's home and know where everything is and—" Eric stopped abruptly as if a new thought had flashed into his mind. He exchanged knowing looks with Don.

Don was apparently thinking the same way as Eric. His gaze widened considerably. "You wouldn't by chance happen to have met Dr. Carlyle before tonight?" Don asked Meghan then swallowed convulsively.

"I..." Meghan found herself too flustered to talk. "Yes," she admitted in a small, feeble voice.

"He isn't—" Eric glanced toward the kitchen and paled. His Adam's apple worked up and down his throat a couple of times. "No." He shook his head, answering his own question. "It couldn't be."

"What couldn't be?" Trina demanded.

Eric's eyes rounded considerably. "The reason we came over here tonight," he muttered under his breath.

"We came to cheer up Meghan," Trina replied, looking bewildered.

"Because..." Eric prompted.

"Because she was on the outs with her—" Trina stopped hastily then slowly shook her head. "It couldn't be."

"Did you see the look he gave *me*," Don whispered. "I'm lucky to be alive."

Eric turned to face Meghan. "Do you know Dr. Carlyle…personally?"

Without meeting his gaze, she nodded.

"Professor Carlyle wouldn't happen to be the guy you've been so upset over, would he?"

Once more Meghan nodded.

"That's it," Trina lamented, wrapping her arms around her middle. "I'm flunking out of college. My dad's going to disinherit me."

"Don't be ridiculous," said Don, looking disgruntled.

Trina ignored him. "My mother will never forgive me for doing this to her. My life is over—and all because I wanted to help the friend of the man who in two months is vowing to love and protect me for the rest of my life."

"Grey isn't going to do anything to you three," Meghan insisted, feeling close to tears. The wine, which had gone to her head earlier, had settled in the pit of her stomach now and she felt wretched. The walls refused to stop moving and she dared not look at the floor for fear it would start pitching and heaving. She was grateful to be sitting down.

"You obviously don't know Professor Carlyle the way we do," Trina whispered, shooting a worried glance over her shoulder as if she expected Grey to return any minute.

"You're taking a class with him?" Meghan asked Trina.

She nodded wildly. "Eric, too."

"I did last year," Don admitted. "All of a sudden I have this sneaky suspicion that he's going to find a way to go back and flunk me."

"You're all being ridiculous," Meghan told them. She hesitated. "Do you want me to get rid of him?"

"No," all three chorused.

"No way," Don said, moving his hands like an umpire declaring a runner home safe.

"That'll only make matters worse," Eric explained.

It looked as if he planned to say more, but he stopped abruptly when Grey entered the room, carrying a tray laden with four mugs of steaming coffee.

Silently Grey passed the cups around, leaving Meghan to the last.

"I haven't been drinking," Eric proclaimed as he lifted the cup from the tray.

Grey paused in front of Eric and glared down at him suspiciously.

"It's true. I was planning to drive home," Eric persisted, his voice high and a little defensive. "I'm just in a fun-loving mood," he offered as a means of explanation.

"It's true," Meghan confirmed softly.

"Is anyone here capable of telling me what was going on when I arrived? I'm particularly interested in your comments about being arrested for what you said about Thoreau."

Meghan noted that the other three were all staring at their coffee as if they expected something to pop up and start floating on the surface.

"Meghan?" Grey coaxed. "Perhaps you could explain."

She swallowed uncomfortably and shrugged. "We were just having some fun."

"Apparently at Thoreau's expense."

"I don't think he'd mind," she said weakly. "He had more of a sense of humor that most educators give him credit for."

"Is that a fact?"

"I mean it, Grey."

"Grey?" Don echoed. He looked at the others and his

shoulders moved up and down with a sigh of defeat. "She calls him Grey." This was spoken with such seriousness that Meghan wondered at his meaning.

"Maybe we should just leave," Trina suggested, her voice elevated and hopeful. "It's obvious the professor wants to talk to Meghan alone."

"Yeah," Don seconded. "We should all just leave before—" He let the rest of what he was going to say fade.

"You don't need to worry, I can drive without a problem," Eric promised. Before anyone could say anything more, Eric hurried over to Meghan's closet and jerked his coat off the hanger. While he was there, he retrieved both Trina's and Don's jackets.

He was opening the front door before Meghan even had a chance to protest. Now that her head had started to clear, she wasn't sure that being alone with Grey was such a brilliant idea. At least with the others around, there was a protective barrier for her to hide behind.

"I'll see you to the door," Meghan offered.

"There's no need," Grey countered. "I will."

A part of Meghan wanted to cry out and protest that this was her home and these friends were her guests and she would be the one to see them off. But she wasn't feeling particularly strong at the moment, and arguing with Grey now would demand more energy than she could afford to waste.

Grey seemed to take his time with the task, Meghan mused a couple of minutes later. The four were engaged in a whispered conversation for what seemed an eternity; and although Meghan strained to hear what they were saying, she couldn't make anything out of it but bits and pieces.

All too soon, Grey closed the door and turned around to face her.

Meghan lowered her head so much that the steam from her coffee cup was about to bead against her face.

"Hello, Meghan."

"Hi." Still she didn't look up. "I see that you recovered from your cold."

"Yes, it's mostly gone now."

"That's good news. You sounded miserable the last time we spoke."

"I was, but the cold wasn't responsible for that."

"It wasn't?"

"No."

From the sound of his voice, Meghan knew he was moving closer to her. If there had been any place for her to run and hide, she would gladly have done so. Unfortunately her apartment was tiny, and knowing Grey, he would only follow her.

"The cold was a bear, don't misunderstand me," Grey continued. "But the real reason I was feeling so crummy had to do with you."

"Me?" This came out sounding much like a squeaky door badly in need of oiling. "I'm sure you're mistaken."

"Yes. You, Meghan Katherine O'Day. Plotting so I'd see you making a snowman with your arms wrapped around another man. I'll have you know you nearly had me convinced."

He was so close that all she had to do was look up from her perch on the arm of the chair and meet his gaze, but she was afraid he would read the truth in her eyes if she did. She *had* carefully planned that scene and was shocked that he'd figured it out.

He advanced a step.

Meghan swallowed and, losing her balance, slid backward. A soft gasp escaped her lips as her posterior slithered over the material. She was abruptly halted when her back slammed against the opposite arm of the chair. It was a minor miracle that the coffee didn't end up spilling down her front.

"Are you all right?" Grey asked, clearly alarmed.

It took Meghan a couple of seconds to gather her scattered wits. "I'm fine." Although she made a valiant effort, she couldn't right herself in the chair. Grey pried the coffee cup out of her fingers, and once her hands were freed, she used those for leverage, twisting around so she could sit upright. She did so with all the pomp and ceremony her inebriated condition would allow.

"There," she announced, as if she'd accomplished a feat of Olympic proportions. She brushed her palms together several times, feeling utterly pleased with herself. "Now, what was it you were saying?"

Grey was quiet for so long that she dared to chance a look in his direction. She found him pacing the small area in front of her chair much like a caged animal. He stopped and turned to look at her, then threaded his fingers through his hair in what she thought looked like an outburst of indecision.

"I don't know if this is the best time for this conversation or not," he admitted dryly.

"It's probably not." Meghan was more than willing to delay a confrontation. Her head was spinning, and she was sure it wasn't the wine this time, but the fact that Grey was so close to her. He'd always had this dizzying effect upon her. "You shouldn't even try to talk to me now. You probably haven't noticed, but I happen to be…a little tipsy."

"A little!" he shouted. "You're plastered out of your mind."

"That's not entirely true," she protested, just as vehemently. "And if I am, it's all your fault."

"Mine? Where do you come up with that crazy notion?"

That was the last thing Meghan planned to reveal to him. She tilted her head at a regal angle, then pinched her lips together. With a dignified air, she pantomimed locking her mouth closed and stuffing the imaginary key into the front of her bra. Once she'd finished, she realized how silly this must have looked, and decided that if she was ever going to gather her moonstruck wits about her, the time was now.

Her actions seemed to frustrate Grey all the more, and Meghan began to experience a sense of power. She, a lowly waitress, had managed to flap the unflappable Professor Greyson Carlyle.

"All I want to know," he asked with stark impatience, "is why? And then I'll be out of here."

"Why what?"

"Why did you go to Pamela Riverside's office?"

Meghan's head shot up. "She told you?" That much was obvious. Good grief, the woman was said to have a genius IQ, yet she was displaying all the intelligence of a piece of mold. "That's the last thing in the world she should have done."

"Pamela claims you insulted her and threatened her and demanded that she lie to me. Is that right?"

Meghan crossed her legs then cupped her hands over her knees, praying her look was sophisticated and suave, but knowing it wasn't. "In a manner of speaking, I suppose she's right." If it were in her power now, Meghan would like to have another serious discussion with Grey's associate. It was all too obvious that what the woman lacked in clothes sense she also lacked in common sense. The last thing she should have done was confront Grey and tell him about their tête-à-tête.

"Threatening someone else doesn't sound anything like the warm, generous woman I know."

"Maybe you don't know me so well, after all," Meghan muttered.

"After tonight, I'm beginning to believe that myself."

"Then maybe you should just leave…because as you so kindly pointed out, I'm plastered."

"Maybe I should, but I'm not going to—not until I find out why you'd even approach Pamela…especially when I've gone out of my way to let you know I feel nothing for her."

"She's in love with you."

"She doesn't know the meaning of the word."

"That's not true," Meghan cried, defending the other woman and ignoring the woozy rushes of dizziness that enveloped her. Grey had misjudged Pamela Riverside, and Meghan could understand the other woman's frustration. She remembered all too well how vulnerable his colleague had looked the night Meghan had met her at the cocktail party. Pamela had seen Meghan with Grey and had been devastated. His colleague might have her faults, but she was still a woman and as hungry for love and acceptance as any other female. Strangely, for all her brilliance, Dr. Riverside was shockingly naive when it came to men and the male-female relationship.

"Pamela Riverside possesses all the warmth of a deep freeze," Grey continued, his patience clearly tested. "You can argue with me all you want, but I'm not leaving here until you tell me the reason you found it so necessary to go to her office."

"Because." Her voice was so soft and small. She was certain Grey hadn't been able to hear her, so she repeated herself. "Because." It came out more firmly, but unfortunately it made absolutely no sense.

Grey knelt down in front of her and braced his hands on the overstuffed arms of the chair. "Because? That doesn't tell me much."

"She's perfect for you," Meghan pronounced, not daring to look at him. Although she'd tried several times to push the pain-inducing thought from her mind, Meghan kept imagining what Grey and Pamela's children would look like. All she could envision were dark-haired boys with horn-rimmed glasses, and blue-eyed little girls in two-piece business suits and black tie-up shoes.

"Pamela's perfect for me," Grey repeated and shook his head as if the mere thought brought with it a discordant note. "Honestly, Meghan, if I didn't love you so much, that could be considered an insult."

"An insult!" She'd made the biggest sacrifice of her life for him, and now Grey was calmly telling her that she'd affronted him by gallantly relinquishing him to the woman who was far better suited to his lifestyle. The unfairness of it all came crashing down on her like a ton of concrete. "I can't believe you'd say that to me. I was so unselfish, so noble and—" She stopped and jerked her head up. "What was it you just said? The first part, about…loving me?"

Grey's face was so close to her own that his features had blurred. Then Meghan realized that it was the tears in her eyes that had misshaped his visage. Sniffling, she rubbed a hand down her face. His words sobered her faster than ten cups of strong, black coffee.

"I love you, Meghan O'Day."

"But how can you...? Oh, Grey!" She leaned forward and pressed her forehead against his while struggling not to cry. "You can't love me, you just can't."

"But I do. And I have no intention of ever loving anyone else as long as I live."

From somewhere deep inside, Meghan found the strength to break away from him. She stiffened her shoulders and rubbed her cheeks dry of any moisture. Her heart felt like a thundering herd of horses galloping inside her chest. "I'm really sorry to hear that."

"You love me, too," he stated evenly. "So banish the thoughts of coming up with a bunch of lies to convince me otherwise. I'll refuse to believe you, anyway."

Meghan blinked several times, her lashes dampening the high arches of her cheeks. She reached out and lovingly traced her fingers down the side of his face. "I don't think I could lie, even if I tried," she whispered. "Oh, Grey, how could we have let this happen?"

He brushed the wisps of hair away from her cheekbones and his thumbs lingered there as though he couldn't keep from touching her. "You make it sound as if our falling in love were some great tragedy. From the moment I met you, my life has been better. You're laughter and love and warmth and excitement. I'll always be grateful to have found you."

"But your mother..."

"You won't be spending the rest of your life with her. I'm the one you're going to be marrying."

"What?" Meghan was convinced she'd misunderstood him. "Who said anything about getting married?" The thought was so baffling to her that she jumped up in the cushion of the chair and pointed an accusing finger at him, waving it several times. "You've lost your mind, Greyson Carlyle."

"Okay, we'll live in sin. But to be honest, that may put my career in jeopardy. Dr. Browning lives by a high moral standard, and frankly, he's not going to approve."

"I can't marry you." She wouldn't have thought it possible, but her heart was pounding faster and faster until it felt like a timed device ready to explode within her breast.

"Meghan," Grey murmured, rising to his feet. "Would you kindly climb down off that chair?"

"I...don't think I should. What would be better is if you left, and then maybe I could think clearly and we could forget you ever suggested...what you just did." She couldn't even say the word.

"Don't be silly. Now, come down from there before you fall." He held out his hand to assist her, but she pretended not to see it.

"Meghan," he cried, clearly exasperated.

"If I step down, you're going to kiss me."

"I'll admit the thought has crossed my mind," he said with a devilish smile.

"And if you do, it'll weaken my defenses."

"As it should."

It took both her hands to brush the hair off her forehead. "I can't let that happen. In fact I think you should leave—you've got me at a distinct disadvantage here. I'm dizzy and weak, and everything you're saying is making me dizzier and weaker."

"I love you."

"See what I mean," she persisted. She slumped back down in the chair, bracing her heel against the edge of the cushion and resting her chin on her bent knees. To her way of thinking—which she had to admit was unclear at the moment—she could hurt Grey's career if they were to marry. "I'm a waitress," she whispered. "Have you forgotten?"

"No, love, I haven't. Are you ashamed of it?"

"No!"

He knelt down in front of her and grinned. His smile carried with it all the warmth of a July sun. "My feelings wouldn't change if you mopped floors for a living. You're honest and proud, and I'm crazy in love with you. I'd consider myself the most fortunate man in the world if you'd honor me by being my wife."

All the resistance seeped out of her like air whooshing out of a balloon. She was crazy in love with him herself, and had been for weeks. He studied her for a long moment, and her reluctant gaze met his. It didn't take long for her to recognize that everything he said was true. He did love and want her, and she would be a fool to even consider turning him away. A smile courted the corners of her mouth even as a tear ran down the side of her face.

Grey reached out and brushed her cheekbone with his cool fingertips. The moment was so tender, so sweet, that Meghan squeezed her eyes shut in an effort to savor these marvelous feelings.

Grey was right; she wouldn't be marrying his mother. It would take time and patience, but eventually Frances Carlyle would come to accept her. Meghan couldn't allow their lives to be dictated by someone else. Her mind clouded with fresh objections, but her heart quickly overrode those, guiding her to where she belonged and where she wanted to be—in Grey's arms.

She reached out to him, looping her arms around his

neck. He heaved a sigh of relief and crushed her against him, holding her as though he'd snapped her out of the jaws of death.

"Meghan, my love, you've led me on a merry chase."

She wanted to tell him so many things, but she was kept speechless as he rained countless kisses upon her face—moist darts of pleasure upon her flushed features, some burning against her eyelids and others scorching the pulse points in her neck.

"You *are* going to marry me, aren't you?" he asked after a long moment, still kissing her.

"Yes. Oh, Grey, I love you so much."

Grey moaned and returned his mouth to hers, tantalizing her with a series of soft kisses that quickly turned to intense ones that sent her pulse soaring and left her temples thundering. She tangled her fingers in his hair, and arched her body against his.

He kissed her so many times, Meghan felt spineless in his arms. When he buried his face in the soft slope of her neck, they were both trembling.

"I'm not going to let you change your mind," he said on a husky note.

"I have no intention of doing so," she assured him.

Grey paused and reached inside the pocket of his tweed jacket and brought out a jeweler's box. When he lifted the lid, Meghan gasped at the size of the diamond resting between the folds of black velvet.

He removed the ring, reached for her hand, and gazing into her tear-rimmed eyes, he slipped it onto her finger.

With that simple action, the waitress became forever linked with the professor.

Epilogue

"Meghan," Grey called up the stairs from the living room, "hurry or we're going to be late. We should have left five minutes ago."

Squirting on some cologne, Meghan rushed into the bedroom and searched frantically for her dress heels. Grey's side of the room was meticulously organized, while hers was a disaster area. She could hear him moving up the steps to find out what was taking her so long. Angry with herself for not knowing where her shoes had disappeared, she got down on her knees and tossed whatever was on the floor onto the top of the bed.

"Meghan, we're going to be late," Grey said a second time, standing in the doorway. Their nine-month-old son, Kramer, squirmed in his arms, wanting down so he could crawl to Mommy and play her silly game.

"I can't find my white heels," Meghan cried, lifting up the bedspread and peeking underneath.

"Honey, you shouldn't be crawling around down there in your condition," Grey muttered, lowering Kramer to the carpet. Soon all three were on the floor looking for Meghan's shoes.

"I'll have you know you're responsible for my condition," Meghan teased, her gaze locking with his.

"I know." Grey's look caressed her and his hand moved around her waist to pat the gentle swelling of her abdomen. "I worry about you having the two so close."

"It's the way I wanted it," she reminded him. Still kneeling, she turned and looped her arms around his neck and playfully kissed him, darting her tongue in and out of his mouth in a familiar game of cat and mouse, letting her kisses tell him how much she loved and desired him.

"I think we should have waited. Irish twins—I still can't believe it. Kramer born in January and this baby due in December." His hand rested against the sides of her stomach, caressing her there.

Making gurgling noises, Kramer agilely crept between his parents, his headful of bright red curls leading the way. Once he'd maneuvered himself into position, he stood upright, looking around. He hurled his small body against Meghan, laughing as though to tell her he'd won their game. From the moment he was born, he'd been a sweet, happy baby.

"Oh, Kramer," Meghan exclaimed, swinging him into her arms. "You're going to be walking soon, you little rascal."

Kramer squealed with delight as she raised him above her head.

"That's just what we need," Grey said, frowning just a little.

"What?" she asked, busily keeping her son's eager hands out of her hair.

"Kramer walking at ten months. My mother already believes he's a genius, and if he starts walking that early, it will only prove as much in her eyes."

"She surprised me," Meghan admitted thoughtfully. Her mother-in-law had delivered several surprises over the past year, all of them pleasant ones.

"Surprised *you*?" he returned with a short laugh. "You could have bowled me over with a dirty diaper when I realized she was going to be the doting-grandmother type. When Kramer was born, I thought she was going to buy out the toy store."

"Dirty diapers *do* bowl you over," she reminded him, smiling.

He shrugged. "That was just a manner of speech."

"Your mother loves Kramer."

"And you," he said. "She told me not so long ago how you've become much more than a daughter-in-law to her." He paused and rubbed the side of his face. "To hear her tell it, she was the one responsible for getting us together."

"I suppose she's right. Only she used reverse psychology."

"She absolutely insists you get your degree."

"I will, in time—so she needn't worry. But for now, I'm more concerned with raising my family. I've got a year in already and will take more classes when I can."

Grey's eyes brightened and he quickly crawled across the floor, holding up one pair of white high-heeled shoes that were partially hidden behind the dresser. "Here they are."

Kramer crawled after his father, his little knees moving at top speed.

Meghan quickly rose to her feet, slipped on the white shoes and reached down for her son. "This'll be your first wedding, son, so behave," Meghan told him, nuzzling his neck playfully.

"I think it was nice of Pamela to request that we bring Kramer along this afternoon," Grey said.

"He stole her heart, right along with your mother's," Meghan pointed out. "She wouldn't think of excluding him on this important day."

Grey stood, brushing any traces of lint from his pant legs. "Do you think Pamela and Fulton are going to be happy?"

"Yes, I do," Meghan replied, setting her son down and reaching inside her closet for a light coat. "I was the one who was shocked when Pamela came over to tell us she was marrying Dr. Essary. I hope I was able to hide my surprise."

"What I can't figure out is why we didn't realize it sooner. The two of them make the perfect couple, when you stop to think about it."

"What amazes me is how falling in love has changed the two of them. They're completely different people than when I first met them."

"I'm completely different, too," Grey reminded her. "Thanks to one sweet Irish miss who stole my heart and changed the way I view everything from Milton to French toast."

Clinging to the skirt of his mother's dress, Kramer Carlyle struggled into a standing position. Gurgling happily, he looked at his father and took two distinct steps, then promptly fell onto his padded bottom.

"I knew it all along," Meghan said with a happy laugh. She leaned over and picked up her son. "We've got ourselves a little genius."

* * * * *

HASTY WEDDING

Prologue

Why did it have to be her? Reed Tonasket asked himself as he strolled into the Tullue library. Clare Gilroy was standing at the front desk, a pair of reading glasses riding the bridge of her pert nose. She glanced up when he entered the front door, and as always, Reed experienced a familiar ache at the sight of her.

He guessed she was holding her breath, as though she were afraid. Not of him, but of what he might do. He had a reputation, well earned during his youth, as a rabble-rouser. Being half-Indian added flavor to the stories circulating town about him. Some were true, while others were fiction in the purest form.

His grandfather, in his great wisdom, had wanted Reed to appreciate the part of himself that was not Indian. From ages ten to twelve, Reed had attended school off the reservation. Until that time, Reed had thought of himself as part of the Tullue tribe, not white. He hadn't wanted to become like the white man, nor had he been eager to learn the ways of his mother's people. But his grandfather had spoken, and so Reed had attended the white man's school in town.

Those years had been the worst of his life. He'd fought every boy in the school who challenged him, and nearly everyone had. Usually he was obliged to take on two or three at a time. He defied his teachers, resisted authority and became the first boy ever expelled from the Tullue school district while still in grade school.

Perhaps it was his blunt Indian features that continued to feed the rumors, or the way he wore his thick black hair in heavy braids. It amused him that he caused such interest in Tullue, but frankly, he didn't understand it.

In reality he was pretty tame these days, but no one around town had seemed to notice. Certainly Clare Gilroy hadn't. Whenever he came into the library, she eyed him with concern, as though she suspected he was going to leap atop a bookcase and shout out a piercing war cry. Then again, Reed could be overreacting. He had a tendency to do that where Clare was concerned.

Reed longed to reveal his feelings for her, but words were not the Indian way. He couldn't think of how to tell Clare he was attracted to her and not sound like a fool. Nor was he convinced his love was strong enough to bridge their cultural differences. He was half-Indian and she was a beautiful Anglo.

Reed walked to the back of the library toward the mystery section. He could feel Clare's gaze follow him. It pleased him to know he had her attention if even for those few moments, which wasn't something likely to happen often.

Then why her? Why did he lie awake nights dreaming of holding her in his arms? Why was it Clare Gilroy he wanted more than any woman he'd ever known? He could find no logic for his desire.

Even now he had trouble remembering that he wasn't

pure Indian. His blood was mixed, diluted by a mother who was blond and pure and sweet. She'd died when he was four, and the memories of her remained foggy and warm. He understood well his Indian heritage, but he'd ignored whatever part of him was white, the same way he ignored his desire for this uptight librarian.

If Reed had required an answer for his preoccupation with Clare, it was that she intrigued him. She presented a facade of being proper and untouchable. Yet he sensed a fire in her, an eagerness to break free of her self-imposed reserve. He saw in her a fragile spirit yearning to soar. In his mind he gave her the Indian name of Laughing Rainbow because he felt in her a deeply buried joy that was ready to burst to life and spill out into the full spectrum of colors. Colors so bright they would rival that of a rainbow.

That she was involved with Jack Kingston didn't set well with Reed. He'd waited, dreading the time he learned of their marriage. The white man wasn't right for her, but Reed could do nothing. He wasn't right for her, either. And so, like a green seventeen-year-old boy, he dreamed of making love with the one woman he knew he could never have.

One

"If Jack said he'd be here, then he will," Clare Gilroy insisted, although she wasn't the least bit convinced it was true.

Erin Davis, Clare's closest friend, glanced at her watch and sighed. "You're sure about that?"

"No," Clare admitted reluctantly, lowering her gaze. When it came to Jack, she wasn't sure of anything. Not anymore. Once she'd been so positive, so confident of their relationship, but she felt none of that assurance now. They'd been unofficially engaged for three years, and she was no closer to a commitment from Jack than the evening they'd first discussed the possibility of marriage.

Come to think of it, Jack never had actually proposed. As Clare recalled, they'd sort of drifted into a conversation about their future and the subject of marriage had come up. No doubt she was the one to raise it. Jack had suggested they think along those lines, and ever since then that was all he'd been doing. Thinking.

In the meantime, Clare was watching one friend after another marry, have children and get on with their lives. She loved Jack, honestly loved him…she must, otherwise she wouldn't have been so willing to wait for him to make up his mind.

"We'll give him five more minutes," Clare suggested, knowing Erin was anxious. This dinner party was important to her best friend. Although Erin and Gary were planning a Las Vegas wedding, they were meeting with family and friends for this dinner before flying to Nevada the following afternoon with Clare and Reed Tonasket, who was serving as Gary's best man.

"Five minutes is all we'll wait," Clare promised. No sooner had the words slipped from her lips than the telephone rang. She hurried into the kitchen, knowing even before she answered that it would be Jack.

She was right.

"Clare, I'm sorry, but it doesn't look like I'm going to be able to get away."

Disappointment swamped her. "You've known about this dinner for weeks. What do you mean you can't get away?"

"I'm sorry, babe, but Mr. Roth called and asked if I'd come over this evening to give him an estimate. We both know I can't afford to offend a member of the city council. Roth's got connections, and his account could be the boost I've been waiting for."

Clare said nothing.

"I'm doing this for us, babe," Jack continued. "If I can get this landscaping contract, it might lead to a project for the city."

Again Clare said nothing, gritting her teeth.

"Are you going to be angry again?" Jack asked, using just the right amount of indignation to irritate Clare even more. Jack had a habit of purposely doing something to upset her and then making it sound as if she were being unreasonable. At times it seemed as though he intentionally set out to annoy her.

"Why should I be angry?" she asked, knowing her voice was brittle, and not caring. Not this time. "It's only a dinner party to honor my best friend. Naturally I'll enjoy attending it alone."

"Which brings up another thing," Jack said, his voice tightening. "Rumor has it Gary Spencer's asked Reed Tonasket to be his best man. That isn't true, is it?"

"Yes."

"I don't like the idea of you flying off to Vegas with that Indian. It isn't good for your reputation."

"Really? Then why don't you come along?"

"You know I can't do that."

"Just like you can't make the dinner party?"

"You're in one of your moods, again, aren't you? Honest to Pete, there's no reasoning with you when you get like this. I'm working hard to get this business on its feet and all you can do is complain. Fine, you go ahead and be mad. Now if you'll excuse me, I've got an appointment to keep."

Clare was still holding on to the receiver when the line was disconnected. The drone in her ear continued for several seconds before she set down the receiver. Oh yes, she was in one of her moods again, Clare silently agreed. This sense of annoyance came over her whenever another friend married, or delivered a baby.

She was thirty-two years old and sick and tired of waiting for Jack's struggling business "to get on its feet." She was tired of holding on to empty promises.

"That was Jack," Clare announced when she joined Erin. As always, she kept her frustration and anger buried deep inside, not wanting her friend to know how upset she was. "Something's come up and he won't be able to come with us after all."

Erin didn't say anything for a moment, but when she did, Clare had the impression there was a whole lot more her friend would have liked to have said. "We should leave then, don't you think?"

Clare agreed with a curt nod and forced herself to smile. "Here you are marrying for the second time, and I haven't managed to snare myself even one husband," Clare joked as they walked out the front door.

Clare had put a lot of stock into this evening, hoping that once Jack was around Erin and Gary he'd see how happy the two of them were. Both had been through disastrous first marriages, and after several years of being single and despairing of ever falling in love again, they'd met. Within eight months, they'd both known that this time, this marriage would be different.

Gary was the football coach for the local high school. Clare loved sports and each autumn made an attempt to attend as many of the home games as she could. In a town the size of Tullue, with a population of less than six thousand, football was a wonderful way to spend a Friday evening. Jack had gone with her a couple of times, although he wasn't nearly as interested in local sports the way she was.

Clare had inadvertently been responsible for Erin meeting Gary. Erin had stopped to talk to Clare after a game, and because she'd got held up, she'd met Gary on her way to the parking lot. The two had struck up a conversation and the relationship had snowballed from there. Although Erin had been her best friend since high school, Clare couldn't ever remember Erin being this happy.

The dinner party was being held at The Tides, which

was the best restaurant in town. Until Jack's phone call, Clare had been looking forward to this evening, but now she could feel a headache coming on. One of the sinus ones she dreaded so much, where the pressure built up in her head until it felt as though a steel band was tightening around her forehead.

"It looks like everyone's here," Erin said animatedly as they pulled into the parking lot.

By everyone, Erin meant her mother and stepfather, her father and stepmother, and Gary's elderly aunt. His parents lived on the East Coast and weren't able to fly in. Following a short honeymoon in Vegas, Gary and Erin were heading east so Erin could meet his mother and father.

Naturally Reed Tonasket would be attending this dinner. It made sense that he'd have a date with him. That meant that Clare and Gary's maiden aunt would be the only ones without partners. Clare groaned inwardly. She'd smile, she decided, and get through the evening somehow. It wouldn't be the first time she was odd woman out.

The Tides had set aside their banquet area for the dinner. It was a small room overlooking the Strait of Juan De Fuca, the well-traveled waterway that separates Washington State from Vancouver Island in British Columbia. As Erin predicted, everyone had arrived and was waiting when the two of them walked in.

Gary stood and wrapped his arm around Erin's shoulders, leading her to the chair next to his own. The only other seat available was the one on the other side of Reed Tonasket.

Clare didn't hesitate; that would have been discourteous, and being rude to anyone was completely alien to her. It wasn't that she disliked Reed, or that she was prejudiced, but he intimidated her the same way he did most everyone in town. His size might have had something to do with her feelings. He was nearly six four, and built like a lumberjack. By contrast Clare was slender and nearly a foot shorter. Although it was only the middle of June and summer didn't officially arrive in the Pacific Northwest until August, Reed was tanned to a deep shade of bronze. Clare knew that like most of the Skyutes, he lived on the reservation. She'd heard that he carved totem poles, which were sold all around the country. But that was all she knew about him. Just enough to engage in polite conversation.

What troubled Clare most about Reed was the angry impatience she sensed in him. She was familiar with several Native Americans who frequented the library. They were graceful, charming people, but she found little of either quality in Reed Tonasket.

"Hello," she said, taking the seat beside him. Since they'd be spending the better part of two days in each other's company, it made sense to Clare that she make some effort to be cordial.

His dark eyes met hers, revealing no emotion. He nodded briefly, acknowledging her. "I'm Clare Gilroy," she said. He didn't give any indication he recognized her from the library, although he was a frequent patron.

"Yes, I know."

He wasn't exactly a stimulating conversationalist, Clare noted. "I...I wasn't sure you remembered me."

His eyes, so dark and bright, made her uncomfortable. They seemed to look straight into her soul. It was as if he knew everything there was to know about her already.

"Has everyone had a chance to introduce themselves?" Gary asked.

Reed nodded, and Clare wondered if not speaking was a habit of his; if that was the case, she was about to spend two very uncomfortable days in his company.

"You don't have a date?" Gary's aunt Wilma leaned across the table to ask Clare. "I seem to remember Gary saying something about you bringing your young man."

Clare could feel heat seeping into her face. "Jack… my date couldn't come at the last minute. He has his own business. He's been working very hard at getting it established." She didn't know why she felt the burning need to make excuses for Jack, but she did, speaking quickly so that the words ran into one another. "He got a call from an important man he's hoping will become a client and had to cancel. I'm sure he regrets missing the dinner, but it was just one of those things. It couldn't be helped." She realized as she finished that she was speaking to the entire table of guests.

"How unfortunate," Wilma Spencer murmured into the silence that followed Clare's explanation.

They were distracted by the waitress who delivered menus, and Clare was eternally grateful. She had little appetite and ordered a small dinner salad and a crab cake appetizer.

"That's all?" Reed questioned when she'd finished.

Flustered, Clare nodded. "I'm not very hungry."

His dark eyes, which had been so unreadable only a few minutes earlier, clearly revealed his opinion now. He was telling her, without uttering a word, that she was too thin.

Erin had been saying the same thing for weeks. Clare had defended her recent weight loss, claiming she was striving for an understated elegance, a fashionable thinness that suited her petite five-foot-four frame. Erin hadn't been fooled, and it was unlikely she was deceiving Reed Tonasket, either. Clare was unhappy, and growing more so every day as she battled her suspicions that Jack had no intention of ever marrying her.

"Look, the band's going to play," Erin said excitedly, looking with wide-eyed eagerness toward Gary. Their gazes met and held, and even from where she was sitting, Clare could feel the love they shared.

Love had taken her friends by surprise. They'd both been wary, afraid of repeating the mistakes of their first marriages. Even though it was apparent to everyone around them how perfectly suited they were, Erin and Gary had taken their time before admitting their feelings for one another.

Dinner was served, and the chatter around the table flowed smoothly. Clare found herself talking with Aunt Wilma, who at seventy-five was as spry as someone twenty years younger. The meal was festive, filled with shared chatter and tales of romance and rediscovered love.

Erin and Gary told of how they'd met following a football game, crediting Clare, who blushed when she became the focus of the group's attention. Funny, she had no problem linking up her friends with prospective husbands, but she couldn't find love and companionship herself.

Following the dinner, Reed stood and waited until the table had quieted before proposing a toast to the happy couple. Clare sipped her wine. Although she was happy for Erin and Gary, the lonely ache inside her intensified. Rarely had she felt more alone.

Dessert arrived, a flaming Cherries Jubilee that produced sighs of appreciation. Erin dished up small servings and passed them down the table, but it seemed Erin, who was looking longingly toward the band, was more interested in dancing than sampling dessert.

As soon as everyone had a plate, she reached for Gary's hand and led him onto the dance floor. Erin's parents and their prospective mates joined the wedding couple.

Soon everyone at the table was on the dance floor with the exception of Reed Tonasket, Clare and Aunt Wilma. The feeling of being excluded from the mainstream of happy couples had never felt more profound.

Aunt Wilma, bless her heart, kept her busy with small talk, although Clare answered in monosyllables, sloshing through a quagmire of self-pity. Reed hadn't exchanged more than a few words with her the entire evening, and the burden of carrying the conversation was beyond her just then.

"Would you care to dance?"

His invitation took her by surprise. It was all she could do not to ask if he meant to dance with *her*. His eyes held hers; the same dark eyes she'd found intimidating before were warm and intriguing now. Before she realized what she was doing, Clare nodded.

He held his hand out and guided her onto the crowded floor. The dance was a slow number, and he turned Clare gently into his arms as though he feared hurting her. His arms circled her, drawing her close to the solid length of his body. Soon she was wrapped in the shelter of his embrace, in the warm muskiness of this man.

They fit together as though they'd been made for each other, and her heart beat steadily against his chest. Together they moved smoothly, with none of the awkwardness that generally accompanies a couple the first time they dance together. Clare swallowed, surprised by how easily she adapted to his arms, by how right she felt being held by him. Even her headache, which had been pounding moments earlier, seemed to lessen.

Something was happening. Something Clare couldn't explain or define. They were closer, much closer than when they'd first started dancing, but Clare couldn't remember moving. Her heart was more than beating, oddly it seemed to be pounding out a rhythm that matched the hard staccato of Reed Tonasket's heart. His hold on her was firm, commanding, as if he had every right in the world to be this intimate.

A scary excitement filled her. Her body ached in a strange, embarrassing way. Her breathing went shallow as she battled these inappropriate sensations.

Reed's eyes found hers, and their gazes met and locked. Clare could feel the heat in him. It reached out and wrapped itself around her, enfolding her as effectively as if keeping her prisoner. For a wild moment she seemed incapable of breathing or swallowing.

Myriad feelings tingled to life, feelings she didn't want to feel, not now, not with this man when it should be Jack. Clare closed her eyes, concentrating instead on matching her steps with his. That didn't work, either; instead she felt every nuance of his intense, magnificent body. Battling down a bevy of fluttering, inarticulate feelings, she opened her eyes and stared into the distance.

Without speaking, Reed seemed to be commanding her to look at him. Feeling the way she did, Clare decided it would be best to avoid eye contact. He may be able to hide his emotions, but she couldn't. Reed would know in an instant how confused and shaken she was.

The urge to look up at him was nearly overwhelming. She wasn't going to do it, she determined a second time.

She didn't dare. Yet, the urge to do so grew stronger, more intense as his unspoken request seemed to draw her gaze upward.

No, she silently cried, I can't.

"You're not feeling well, are you?"

Despite her recent conviction, Clare's gaze shot to his. "How...how'd you know?"

"Headache?"

She nodded, amazed he could read her so accurately, unable to drag her gaze away. "I'll be better by morning."

"Yes," he agreed, and his lips grazed her temple as though to ease away the pain with his touch. The kiss was so gentle, so overwhelmingly sweet that tears sprang to her eyes.

With what felt like superhuman strength, she broke away. Color burned in her face, pinkening her cheeks. She felt jolted and dazed and for some odd reason...reprehensible to the very core of her being.

"I...have to go," Clare said abruptly. She needed to escape before she did something that would humiliate her. "I've got a million things to do before the flight tomorrow," she offered as an excuse. "Would you be kind enough to make my excuses to Erin and Gary for me?"

"Of course." He released her immediately and guided her back to the table. Clare swiftly gathered her purse, and with little more than a nod to Aunt Wilma, hurried out of the restaurant.

Clare didn't know what had prompted her to behave this way. She'd practically made a spectacle of herself. That was it. She wasn't herself, Clare mused, searching to find some excuse, some reassurance as she hurried out of the restaurant and into the parking lot.

The day had been a whirlwind of activity as she'd

driven with Erin into Port Angeles, fifty miles east of Tullue, to shop for a new outfit for the honeymoon trip.

After such a hectic afternoon, Clare couldn't be blamed for indulging in a few unorthodox fantasies. Circumstances were further complicated by Jack's canceling at the last minute. But no matter what excuses she offered, when it came right down to it, Clare had to admit she was thoroughly fascinated by Reed Tonasket.

Not sexually fascinated…no, not that; Clare was the first to concede she was something of a puritan. Her experience was limited and what little she'd encountered had always been—she hated to admit—boring. But in Reed she sensed hunger, raw and primitive, as elemental as the man himself. Heaven help her, she was intrigued. That was only natural, wasn't it? Especially when she'd be spending the better part of two days in his company.

Reed's reputation with the ladies only added to her curiosity. Although Clare wasn't privy to a lot of what was said about him, she'd heard rumors. There were those who claimed no woman could refuse him. After experiencing his blatant sensuality, Clare tended to believe it.

Once she was home, Clare leaned against her door and turned the lock. Her heart was racing, and the headache had returned full force. Already the pressure was building up in her sinuses. Stress. These headaches came on whenever she was under an abnormal amount of anxiety.

She walked into her bedroom, ignoring the suitcase, which was spread open atop her mattress, and sat on the edge of the bed. Covering her face with both hands, her long brown hair fell forward. Impatiently she pushed it back, regretting now that Erin had convinced her to wear it down. She exhaled slowly, then breathed in a deep, calming breath. The last thing she needed now was one of her infamous headaches.

She lay back and closed her eyes, hoping to relax and let the tension drain out of her body. But when her head nestled against the pillow, Reed Tonasket leaped, full-bodied, into her imagination. He wore that knowing look, as if he were capable of reading her thoughts, capable of discerning how much he'd affected her.

The doorbell chimed and, groaning inwardly, Clare moved off the bed. Jack Kingston stood on the other side of the door, his handsome face bright with a smile. For a split second, Clare debated if she should let him inside.

He was always so persuasive, so convincing. She had every reason in the world to be angry with him, but if the past was anything to go by, before the end of the evening, she'd end up apologizing *to him*. It went like that. He'd hurt or disappoint her, and before the night was over, she was asking his forgiveness.

"Clare," he said, kissing her softly on the cheek as he casually strolled inside her home with the familiarity of a long-standing relationship. "I've got wonderful news."

"You're going to marry me," she said smoothly, crossing her arms. She didn't suggest he sit down, didn't offer him coffee. In fact she did nothing.

Her lack of welcome didn't appear to phase Jack, who moved into her kitchen and opened her refrigerator, peering inside. "I'm starved," he announced, and reached for a cluster of seedless grapes.

Clare reluctantly followed him. "What's your news?"

Jack's brown eyes brightened. "It looks like Roth is going to give me the contract. He wanted to think about it overnight, which he says he does as standard procedure, but he was impressed with my ideas and the quotes

I gave him. I like the man, he's got a good head on his shoulders. It wouldn't surprise me if he decided to run for mayor sometime in the future."

"Congratulations," Clare returned stiffly.

Jack hesitated and eyed her suspiciously. "Do I sense a bit of antagonism?"

"I'm sure you do. I just spent one of the most uncomfortable evenings of my life." But not for the reasons she was implying. It shook her that she could look at Jack and feel nothing. There'd been a time when she'd lived for those rare moments when he'd drop by unannounced, but those times had wilted and died for lack of nourishment. Perhaps for the first time, she saw Jack as he really was—self-centered and vain. If she let him, and so far she had, he'd string her along for years, feeding her blank promises, keeping her hopes alive. It astonished her that she hadn't realized it earlier.

"Aren't we being a bit selfish?" he asked, arching his thick eyebrows.

"Not this time," Clare answered smoothly. "If anyone was selfish it was you. This dinner's been planned for weeks—"

"I've got to put the business first," Jack interrupted calmly. "You know that. I don't blame you for being disappointed, but really, babe, when you think about it, I did it for us."

"For us?" The excuse was well-worn, and she'd grown sick of hearing it.

"Of course." He popped another grape into his mouth, not threatened by her words. "I don't enjoy working these long hours any more than you enjoy having me miss out on these social events that are so important to you. I hated not being there for your friends' dinner party this evening, but it was just one of those things. Someday all this hard work is going to pay off."

"What if I were to say I didn't want to marry you anymore?"

Jack's hand was halfway to his mouth. He paused, the grape poised before his lips. "Then I'd say you don't mean it. Come on, babe, you're talking nonsense."

"Actually I'm grateful you put off setting the wedding date. I seem to be a slow learner and it's taken me this long to realize we're nowhere near being compatible. Marriage between us would have been disastrous."

Jack stood immobile for a moment, as though he wasn't sure he should believe her. "Are you in one of your moods again?"

"Yes," she returned evenly, "I guess you might say I haven't recovered from 'my mood' earlier this evening."

"Clare…"

"Please don't say anything. I didn't know anyone could be so blind to the obvious."

"I want to marry you, Clare," Jack refuted adamantly, "but when the time's right. If you think you're going to pressure me into setting the date because you're angry, you're wrong. I'm not going to allow you to manipulate me."

"This isn't a pressure tactic, Jack. I'm serious, very serious. It's over."

"You don't mean it."

Arguing with him wouldn't help, she should have known that by now. With her arms crossed, she leaned against the refrigerator door. "You're wrong, Jack, I do mean it." Her voice faltered just a little—with regret, with sadness. She'd wasted three years of her life on Jack, when it should have been obvious after the first month how ill suited they were. Erin had tried to tell her, but Clare hadn't listened. She hadn't wanted to hear the truth.

Jack stalked to the far side of her kitchen, opened the cabinet door under her sink and tossed what remained of the grapes into the garbage. "You're trying to pressure me into marrying you, and I won't have it. If and when we marry, it'll be on my timetable, not yours."

"Whatever," she said, growing bored with their conversation. She wasn't going to change her mind, and wondered briefly how she could have endured the relationship this long.

"Come on, Clare, you're being unreasonable. I'm not going to put up with this. I said I'd marry you and I will, but I don't like being blackmailed into it."

"Jack," she said, growing impatient, "you're not listening to me. I've had a change of heart, I *don't* want to marry you. You're off the hook, so stop worrying about it."

"I hate it when you get in these moods of yours."

"This isn't a mood, Jack, it's D day. We're through, finished. In plain English, it's over."

"I refuse to allow you to back me into a corner."

"Goodbye, Jack."

His eyes rounded with surprise. "You don't mean this, Clare, I know you. You get all riled up about one thing or another and within a day or two you've forgotten all about it." Frustration layered his words.

"Not this time," she said without emotion as she led the way to her front door. She opened it and stood there waiting for him to exit.

Jack's eyes followed her across the living room floor, but he stood where he was, just outside her kitchen, as though he wasn't sure he could believe what was happening.

"Don't be hasty," he warned in a low voice. "We both know you don't mean it and that tomorrow you'll have a change of heart."

"I do mean it, Jack. It took me three years to wake up and smell the roses. I'm not exactly a fast study, am I?" she asked dryly.

"You're going to regret this."

Clare didn't answer.

Jack's gaze narrowed. "You're being unreasonable because of Erin and Gary getting married, aren't you? I swear I hate it when one of your friends asks you to be in their wedding party. It never fails. You become completely irrational. This time you've gone too far. It's over, Clare, you just remember that, because once I walk out that door, I'm never coming back, and that's final."

Once again, Clare decided it was best to say nothing.

"Don't try to phone me, either," Jack added, as he cut across her lawn to where he'd parked his pickup truck. "You've pushed me just a little too hard this time." He pulled open the door and leveled his gaze at her.

"Goodbye, Jack," she said evenly, then stepped back and closed the door.

Two

Clare had done it. She'd actually severed her ties with Jack. She wasn't sure what she expected to feel, certainly not this sense of release, of freedom, as though a heavy burden had been lifted from her shoulders.

For months, perhaps even years, she'd been wearing blinders when it came to Jack's faults and the unhealthy twists their relationship had taken. It'd bothered her, but she'd chosen to overlook their problems all in the name of love. And the promise of marriage.

At some point she'd cared deeply for Jack, but her feelings had died a slow, laborious death. So slow that she hadn't realized what was happening until she'd danced with Reed Tonasket. She would never have felt the things she did in Reed's arms if she truly loved Jack.

The memory was followed with an instant surge of renewed embarrassment. Groaning inwardly, Clare placed her hands over her reddening cheeks and closed her eyes. When he'd asked her to dance, Clare had fully expected to feel awkward in his arms. The last thing she'd anticipated was a full scale sensual awakening.

Reed had known what was happening, too. He must

have. It mortified her to recall the erotic way in which their bodies had responded to each other, as though they were longtime lovers. It'd flustered her so badly, she'd hurriedly left the restaurant, unable to cope with what had passed between them.

To complicate matters even more, they were ~~~ each other again in only an hour. It would have been ~~ much better if she could have put some time and distance between last night and their next meeting. She needed time to gain perspective, to think this matter through. But the luxury of that was being taken away from her.

Within a short while Clare would be with Reed again. For the next two days they'd be sharing one another's company. To her dismay she hadn't given a single thought to how she'd spend her time with Reed following Erin and Gary's wedding. They'd be together almost exclusively from that point onward. Clare sincerely doubted that Erin and Gary would feel responsible for entertaining them the first hours of their honeymoon.

Jack had been concerned about her traveling with Reed. His apprehension was only token, she was sure, nevertheless, he'd made a point. Clare didn't know Reed, really know him that is. Until recently she'd viewed him as unruly and even a tad dangerous. Rumors about him had been floating around town for years, but Clare had never paid much attention to hearsay. To her way of thinking, not half of what was said could possibly be true. It couldn't be, otherwise Gary, who was decent and honorable wouldn't have asked Reed to stand up as his best man.

Clare wondered about the relationship between the two men. If she'd had her wits about her the night before, she would have asked Reed herself. It would have

never been more confident of anything in my life. Erin's the best thing that's ever happened to me."

"I thought so."

"I'd given up hope of ever finding a woman I'd want to marry," Gary continued, "and now that I have I'm so impatient to make her my wife I can hardly stand it."

"From what I've seen of Erin, I'd say she feels the same about being your bride."

"I want a houseful of children, too. I imagine that surprises you. Every time I think about Erin and me having a baby I get all mushy inside."

"That doesn't surprise me."

"What about you?" Gary asked. "Have you ever thought of marrying?"

"No," Reed answered honestly.

His quick response seemed to catch Gary by surprise. "Why not?"

"I'm half-white, half Indian."

"So?"

Reed didn't answer. He hadn't found acceptance in either world. Certainly not in the white man's society. He was looked upon as a hellion although he hadn't done anything in years to substantiate the rumors. With his father's people he was respected, mainly because of his art. He'd been reared by his grandfather, taught the Indian ways until they became as much a part of him as breathing. Nevertheless there was a distance between the tribal leaders from an incident that happened when he was a youth. He'd been passed over for an award he deserved, because he was only half-Indian. In some ways Reed was responsible for the rift, but not in all.

"Then you've never been in love," Gary said dismissively, and glanced at his watch. "I've waited six years for this day, and I should be a little more patient."

"Do you want to go to the chapel and wait there?"

Gary nodded. "Anything would be better than pacing this room."

The same way hotels around the world supplied room service and a variety of other amenities to their guests, Las Vegas provided a wedding chapel. Gary had made the arrangements for his and Erin's nuptials with the hotel staff weeks earlier. Following the ceremony, the four of them would share in an elegant dinner, and from there Gary and Erin would adjourn to the Honeymoon Suite. Reed would take Gary's room for the night and Clare would sleep in Erin's. They were scheduled to fly out early the following morning.

"I appreciate you coming down with us," Gary said as they headed out of the elevator.

"I was honored you asked."

"Oh, Erin," Clare whispered when her friend appeared. "I've never seen you look so beautiful."

"I'm going to cry… I know I'm going to make an absolute fool of myself and sob uncontrollably through the entire ceremony."

Clare smiled at her friend's words. "If anyone weeps it'll be me."

"How are you feeling?" Erin asked, studying her, her gaze revealing her concern.

"Much better," Clare assured her friend. "The headache's almost gone."

"Good." Erin nervously twisted the small bouquet of white rosebuds between her hands, closed her eyes and exhaled slowly.

By tacit agreement they made their way to the elevator and the wedding chapel. Clare's heart swelled with shared happiness. Jack claimed she got in one of her moods every time one of her friends married, and for months Clare had listened to him, believed him. Because he'd been so adamant, Clare hadn't recognized her own feelings.

She wasn't jealous of Erin, she was joyous. Despite tremendous odds, Erin and Gary had found each other, let go of their pasts, learned from their mistakes and were ready to try their hands at love again. Clare saw in them courage, strength and love, and she deeply admired them both.

Gary and Reed were standing outside the chapel, waiting. Clare's gaze was immediately drawn to Reed, and for an instant she didn't recognize him. He looked completely different, but, without staring, she couldn't figure out what it was that had changed. Her heart fluttered wildly as though she were the bride, and she lowered her gaze, fearing she might have been too obvious.

It was crazy, but she wondered what Reed thought when he first saw her. It didn't seem possible that he experienced the same wondrous sensation that had struck her. Her dress was a lovely shade of pale blue with a spray of tiny pearls spilling over the shoulders and across the yoke. Erin had chosen it for her, and it closely followed the shapely lines of Clare's breasts and slim hips. Clare became so involved with what was happening between her and Reed that she was only fleetingly aware of what was going on with Gary and Erin. It seemed there was some paperwork that needed to be completed before they could proceed with the actual ceremony. Erin and Gary were busy with that, leaving Clare and Reed to their own devices.

"Is Erin as nervous as Gary?" Reed surprised her by asking. To the best of her memory it was the first time he'd initiated a conversation.

"A little. Erin's afraid she's going to end up weeping through the ceremony." How odd her voice sounded, as though it were coming from the bottom of a deep pit. Having Reed focus his gaze on added to her nervousness.

She was aware of everything around her, the tall white baskets filled with a wide array of colorful flowers, of gladiolas and irises, roses and baby's breath. Their soft scents lingered in the room, delicate and sweet.

Clare found the need to look at Reed irresistible, and she subtly centered her gaze on him. He was dressed in a black tuxedo, which complimented his dark looks. The petite pleats of the shirt front added a decidedly masculine accent.

"You'll need to sign here," Gary said, but Clare was so enraptured with Reed that she didn't realize he was speaking to her.

"Clare," Erin said gently, "we need you to sign these papers."

"Oh, of course," she faltered, embarrassed.

"If you're ready, we can begin the ceremony." The official reached for his Bible, and the four of them formed a semicircle in front of him.

Over the years, Clare had been a member of several wedding parties. Some had been simple ceremonies such as she was involved with now, and others elaborate affairs in which she marched down the center aisle of a crowded church to the thundering strains of organ music.

None had affected her as this wedding did. It must be

because it was Gary and Erin marrying, Clare decided, when an unexpected lump filled her throat. It had to be that.

As the justice of the peace spoke, the urge to cry increased. Each wedding she attended had touched Clare in some way. The very nature of the ritual was compelling and rendering to the heart.

Moments earlier she'd spoken to Reed of Erin's concern, but if anyone was threatening to break into sobs, it was Clare herself.

As Erin's soft voice rose to repeat her vows, Clare's gaze was drawn back to Reed's. Their eyes met as if guided by some irresistible force, and locked. This awareness, this fascination she felt toward him flowered...no, it was much stronger than flowering, it *exploded* to life. Tears, which had been so close to the surface, filled her eyes until Reed's tall figure blurred and swam before her.

Whatever was happening, whatever was between them, was so powerful it took all her strength not to move to his side. He felt it, too, she was certain of it. As powerfully as she did.

Her lips were moving, Clare realized, although she wasn't speaking. With her eyes locked with Reed's, she found herself repeating the same wedding vows as her friend. *To love, to cherish, always...*

When it became *Gary*'s turn to repeat his vows, his voice was strong and clear with no hint of nervousness. By holding her gloved finger beneath her eye, Clare was able to drain off the tears. Reed's gaze remained locked with hers and he, too, mouthed the words along with Gary. Clare was vividly aware of how intimate their actions were. Reed was silently beseeching her, echoing her own thoughts and needs.

Suddenly the vows had been said. Even though Clare didn't want the moment to end there was nothing she could say or do that would prolong it. Gary embraced Erin and kissed her, and Clare, desperately needing to compose herself, lowered her eyes. Her breathing was shallow, she noted, and her pulse pounded wildly against her breast.

Clare had only started to collect her emotions, when Erin turned and gave her a tearful kiss. "You're crying," she said, laughing and weeping herself.

"I know. Everything was so beautiful...you and Gary are beautiful." She didn't dare look in Reed's direction and was grateful to realize he was occupied with Gary. It was uncanny that a Las Vegas ceremony could evoke such a wellspring of emotion.

She found it impossible to believe that she'd mouthed the vows along with her friend. Then it hit her. She was so anxious, so eager to be a wife herself that an uncontrollable longing had welled up inside her. She yearned to share her life with a man whose commitment to her was as deep as hers was to him. It was this promise of happiness that had kept her locked in a dead-end relationship for three barren years.

Reed turned to her after all the congratulations had been spoken, and reached for her hand, tucking it into the warm curve of his elbow.

"Are you feeling all right?"

Words eluded her, so she tried smiling, and nodded, hoping that would satisfy him. He was frowning at her, and she realized she'd made an utter fool of herself in front of him.

He raised his hand and gently traced his finger down the side of her face. "We'll talk more later."

His words raised a quiver of apprehension that raced up her spine.

He smiled, and to the best of her knowledge it was the first time she'd ever seen him reveal amusement.

"Don't look so worried," he told her, gently patting her hand.

They were walking side by side, her hand in his elbow, Clare obediently allowing herself to be led, although she hadn't a clue where they were headed. Not that it mattered; in those moments Reed Tonasket could have been escorting her to the moon. As a matter of fact, she was halfway there already.

The wedding dinner was a festive affair. Gary ordered champagne, and the sparkling liquid flowed freely as they dined on huge lobster tails and the best Caesar salad Clare had ever tasted.

The evening was perfect, more perfect than anything she could remember. As dinner progressed, she felt the tension slip away. By the time they feasted on a slice of wedding cake, Clare felt relaxed and uninhibited. The terrible anxiety that had been her companion most of the day had vanished, and she laughed and talked freely with her friends.

With eyes only for each other, Gary and Erin excused themselves, leaving Clare and Reed on their own.

"I can't remember a wedding I've enjoyed more," Clare said, looking over to Reed. Perhaps it was the simplicity, or her special relationship with the couple. Whatever the reason, their love had tugged fiercely at the strings of her heart. "I think it was the most beautiful wedding I've ever attended."

She half expected Reed to challenge her words, but he

didn't. Instead he reached for her hand, gently squeezed her fingers and said, "You're right, it was beautiful."

It might have been her imagination, but Clare had the elated sensation that he was speaking about her and not the wedding ceremony. Reed made her feel beautiful. She couldn't remember experiencing anything like this with any man. He was so different than what she expected, so gentle and concerned. With Reed she felt cherished and protected.

"We have several hours yet— Is there anything you'd like to do?"

Clare didn't need to give the question thought. "I'd love to gamble." They were, after all, in Las Vegas.

"Have you ever been to Vegas before?"

"Never," she admitted. "But I can count to twenty-one and if that fails me, there's a roll of quarters in my purse."

Reed chuckled. "You're sure about this?"

"Positive." She beamed him a wide smile. Rarely had she felt less constrained. It was as though they'd known each other for years. She experienced none of the restraint toward him that she had earlier. Looking at him now, smiling at her, she wondered how she could have ever thought of him as aloof or reserved.

"You'll need a clear head if you're going to gamble," he said, and motioning for the waiter, he ordered two cups of coffee.

"I only had one glass of champagne, but you're right, I want to be levelheaded about this ten dollars burning a hole in my purse."

The waiter delivered two cups of steaming coffee and Clare took her first tentative sip. "How long have you and Gary been friends?"

Reed shrugged. "A few years now. What about you and Erin?"

"Since high school. I was the bookworm and Erin was a cheerleader. By all that was right, we shouldn't have even been friends, but we felt drawn to each other. I guess we balance one another out. I knew she should never have married Steve—I wish now I'd said something to her, but I didn't."

"I didn't meet Gary until after his divorce, but he's talked about his first marriage. His wife left him for another man."

"Steve didn't know the meaning of the word *faithful*. Sometimes I think I hated him for what he did to Erin. She moved back to Tullue when they separated and she was so thin and pale I barely recognized her." The outward changes couldn't compare to what Steve had done to Erin's self-esteem. Her self-confidence had been shattered. It had taken her friend years to repair the emotional damage.

"I remember when Gary first met Erin," Reed said thoughtfully. "He drove out to my place. I was working at the time, and he paced from one end of my shop to the other talking about Erin Davis, asking me if I knew her."

"Did you?"

"No."

"They took their time, didn't they?" It had been apparent to Clare from the beginning how well suited they were to each other. "Erin came to me in tears the night Gary asked her to marry him. At first I thought she was crying with joy, but I soon realized she was terrified." An emotion akin to what she'd experienced herself the night before when she'd first danced with Reed, Clare thought. She paused and guardedly glanced in his direction, unsure what had prompted the comparison.

"I wish I knew you better," she found herself saying. She inhaled sharply, appalled that she'd verbalized the thought.

"What is it you'd like to know?"

There was so much, she didn't know where to begin. "How old are you?"

"Thirty-six."

"We were never in the same school together." It was an unconscious statement. Naturally they wouldn't have been since he must have attended the reservation school. "I...we wouldn't have been in high school at the same time anyway... I'm four years younger than you." Avoiding his gaze, she sipped her coffee. "I guess I know more about you than I realized."

"Oh."

"You enjoy reading." She knew that by the frequency with which he visited the library, although she couldn't recall any single category of books he checked out more than others.

"My reading tastes are eclectic," he said as if he'd read her thoughts.

"How do you do that?" she asked, gesturing wildly with her arms.

"Do what?"

"Know what I'm thinking. I swear it's uncanny."

Reed's dark eyes danced mischievously. "It's an old Indian trick."

"I'll just bet." She reached across the table and picked the uneaten strawberry off his plate. After popping it into her mouth, she was amazed that she would do anything so unorthodox. "Do you mind, I mean… I should have asked."

He studied her more closely. "Are you sure you only had one glass of champagne?"

"Positive. Now are we going to the gaming tables or not? I feel lucky."

"Come on," he said with a laugh, "I hate to think of those quarters languishing away in your purse."

Clare smiled and, linking her hand with his, they left the restaurant.

Reed led her first to the blackjack tables. She was short and had trouble perching herself upon the high stool, so without warning, he gripped her waist and lifted her onto the seat.

The action took her by surprise, and she gasped until she realized it was him, then thanked him with a warm smile. After all her reservations, she discovered she enjoyed Reed's company.

"You betting, lady?" the dealer asked, breaking into her thoughts.

"Ah…just a minute." The table was a dollar minimum bet, and Clare exchanged a twenty-dollar bill for chips. She set out two chips and waited until the dealer had given her the necessary cards.

"You're not playing?" she asked, looking to Reed.

"Not now, I will later."

Clare won her first five hands. "I like this game," she told Reed. "I didn't know I was so lucky."

He said nothing, but stood behind her, offering her advice when she asked for it and keeping silent when she didn't. His hands were braced against her shoulders, and she felt comfort and contentment in his being there.

By the end of an hour there was a large stack of chips

in front of her. "I'm going to wager them all," she said decisively, pushing the mounds of chips forward. To her way of figuring, gambling money was easy come, easy go. Her original investment had been only twenty dollars, and if she lost that, then she considered it well worth the hour's entertainment.

"You're sure?" Reed whispered close to her ear.

"Absolutely positive." She may have sounded confident, but when the cards were dealt, her heart was trapped somewhere between her stomach and her throat. The dealer busted, and she let out a loud, triumphant shout.

It required both hands to carry all her chips to the cashier. When the woman counted out the money, Clare had won over two hundred dollars.

"Two hundred dollars," she cried, and without thought, without hesitation, looped her arms around Reed's neck and hurled herself into his arms.

Three

Stunned, Reed instinctively caught Clare in his arms.

"Two hundred dollars," she repeated. "Why, that's ten times what I started out with." She smiled at him with a free-flowing happiness sparkling from her beautiful brown eyes. Reed couldn't help being affected. He smiled, too.

"Congratulations."

"Thank you, oh, thank you."

It wasn't until the man behind them cleared his throat that Reed realized they were holding up the line in front of the cashier's cage. Reluctantly he released Clare, but needing to maintain the contact with her, he reached for her hand.

"Where to now?" he asked.

Clare tugged her hand free from his and slipped her arm around his waist, leaning her head against his shoulder. "How about the roulette table? I'm rich, you know."

Reed wasn't quite sure what to make of the woman in his arms. He had trouble believing this was the same one who sat so primly behind the front desk of the Tullue library, handing out lectures for overdue books. Her eyes were bright and happy, and for the life of him, he couldn't look away.

It was doubtful Clare was drunk. She'd claimed to have had only one glass of champagne and he couldn't recall her having more. If anyone was drunk, it was him, but not on alcohol. He was tipsy on spending this time with Clare, of touching her as though he'd been doing so for years.

"Clare," he asked, pulling her aside and leading her away from the milling gamblers. His eyes searched hers; he was almost afraid this couldn't be happening.

She smiled up at him and blinked, not understanding the question in his eyes.

He didn't know how to voice his concern without sounding ridiculous. It wasn't as though he could ask her if she realized what she was doing. This wasn't the woman he'd loved from afar all these years.

The amusement drained from her eyes. "I'm embarrassing you, aren't I?"

"No," he denied quickly.

"I...shouldn't have hugged you like that? It was presumptuous of me and—"

"No." He pressed his finger over her lips, stopping her because he couldn't bear to hear what she was saying. He'd dreamed of her in exactly this way, gazing up at him with joy and happiness. He had yearned to hold her, kiss her, make love to her, but never thought it possible.

She pressed her hand to her cheek. "I don't know what came over me... I seem to be doing and saying the most nonsensical things."

Reed could think of no way of assuring her and so he did what came naturally. He kissed her.

Reed had longed to do exactly this for years, and now

that the dream was reality, it was as though he'd completely lost control of his senses.

His lips didn't court or coax or tease hers, nor was he gentle. The need in him was too great to bridle, consequently his kiss was filled with a desire so hot, so earthy he feared he'd consume her.

Taken by surprise, Clare moaned, and the instant her lips parted to him. Dear heaven, she was even sweeter than he ever imagined. Kissing her was like sampling warm honey. She opened to him without restraint, holding nothing back. Her tongue met his, tentatively at first, as though she were unaccustomed to such passionate exchanges, then curled and shyly mated with his. Reed was convinced she hadn't a clue as to how blatantly provocative she was.

It cost him everything to break off the kiss. When he did, his breathing was labored and harsh.

Clare's eyes remained closed, and her sigh rolled softly over his face like the lazy waters of a peaceful river.

"Is…is kissing you always this good?" she asked softly, her lashes fluttering open. She gazed up at him with wide, innocent eyes. Reed couldn't find the words to answer.

"The rumors must be true," she said next, under her breath.

"What rumors?"

From the way her gaze widened and shot to him, it was clear she hadn't realized she'd spoken aloud.

"Tell me," he insisted.

"They say…women can't resist you."

Reed didn't know whether to laugh or fume. It was equally difficult to tell if Clare meant it as a compliment or an insult. His indecision must have revealed itself, because she stood on her tiptoes and planted a soft kiss across his lips. "Thank you."

"For what?"

Surprised, she glanced up at him. "For showing me how good kissing can be."

She didn't know? That seemed utterly impossible. His mind was reeling with a long series of questions he longed to ask, but before a single one had taken shape on his lips, Clare was moving away from him, passing through the crowd and heading for the roulette wheel.

Reed found the noise and the cigarette smoke in the casino irritating. He wasn't overly fond of crowds, either, but he gladly endured it all for the opportunity to be with Clare.

By the time he reached her, she was sitting at the table and had plunked down two twenty-five-dollar chips, betting on the red.

When she won, she whirled around to be sure he was there. Reed grinned and, collecting her winnings, Clare dutifully stuffed the chips into her purse.

"What else is there?" she said, looking around. "I feel so lucky."

"Craps," he suggested, although he wasn't certain he could explain the various rules of the game to her within a short amount of time.

It was a complicated but fun game. Clare was much too impatient to be delayed with anything as mundane as instructions on how to play.

There was plenty of room at the dice table, so Reed decided to play himself, thinking that would be the best way to help Clare learn.

It took a few moments for them to exchange their cash for chips, and Reed noticed how Clare's eyes gleamed with excitement. If she continued to look at him like that, he'd have trouble keeping his mind on the action. Unfortunately craps was one game that required he keep his wits about him.

He placed his bet and Clare followed his lead. They managed to stay about even, until it became Clare's turn to roll the dice. She hesitated when she noticed Reed had placed a large wager.

"I thought you said you felt lucky," he reminded her.

"I know, but…"

"Just throw the dice, lady," said an elderly gentleman holding a bottle of imported beer. "He looks like he knows what he's doing."

"He might, but I don't," she muttered, and threw the dice with enough force for them to bounce against the far end of the table.

"Ten, the hard way," the attendant shouted.

Players gathered around the table and the money was flowing fast and furiously. Reed could see that Clare was having trouble keeping tabs on what was happening. She amazed him. She hadn't a clue of what she was doing, yet she ladled out her chips without a qualm, betting freely as though she were sitting on a fat bank account. He would never have guessed that she could be so carefree and unbridled by convention.

As he suspected, Clare was a natural, and within the next several rolls, she had every number covered. Soon the entire table was raking in the chips. The shouts and cheers caught the attention of the other gamblers, and shortly afterward there wasn't a single inch of available space around the table.

"How much longer?" Clare asked, looking anxious.

"As long as you can keep from rolling a seven," Reed

told her. He didn't know how much money they'd won, but he ventured a guess that it was well into the hundreds.

"Don't even say it," the same older man who'd been drinking a beer chastised him. "She's making us money hand over fist."

"You mean everyone is winning?" Clare said, looking down the table. It seemed everyone was staring at her, waiting expectantly.

"Everyone," Reed concurred.

"All right." She tossed the dice and let out a triumphant cry when she made her point. Chips were issued by the attendants, and Clare wiped her hands against her hips before reaching for the dice again.

"I like this game."

"We love you, sweetheart," someone shouted from the other end of the table.

Clare hesitated, then blew her admirer a kiss before rolling the dice once more. Even before Reed could see what she'd tossed, there was a chorus of happy shouts.

"I can smell money," a man said, squeezing his way into the table, tossing down five one-hundred-dollar bills.

A cocktail waitress came by, taking orders, but everyone seemed so caught up in the action that no one seemed to notice. There was apparently some hullabaloo going on with the pit boss. Clare had held the dice for nearly thirty minutes and it went without saying that the casino was losing a lot of money.

"How am I doing?" she asked, looking to him, her eyes bright and clear. "Oh, heavens, I'm thirsty. Could I get something to drink…something diet."

Reed got the cocktail waitress's attention and ordered a soft drink for himself while he was at it.

On Clare's next roll she hit a seven. After a low mur-

mur of regret she was given a round of hearty applause. Grinning, she curtsied and with her drink in her hand turned away from the table.

"Clare," Reed called after her.

She turned at the sound of his voice. "You forgot your chips."

Since he'd been collecting them for her, it wasn't unreasonable for her to think she'd won for everyone else and not herself. The attendant had colored up the chips for them both and Reed handed her nine black chips.

"I only made nine chips?" she asked, bewildered.

"The black chips are worth a hundred dollars."

For a moment, her mouth opened and closed as though she'd lost the ability to speak. "They're a hundred dollars *each?*"

Reed didn't know it was possible for a woman's eyes to grow so wide. He nodded.

"In other words, I just made *nine hundred dollars?*"

Reed smiled and nodded again. He'd won considerably more, and there were others at the table who'd walked away with several thousand dollars.

"Nine hundred dollars," she repeated slowly, pressing her one hand over her heart and fanning her face with the other. "I need to sit down. Oh, my goodness... all that money."

Reed slipped his arm around her waist and, realizing she was trembling, steered her toward the coffee shop.

"Nine hundred dollars," she continued repeating. "That's almost a thousand dollars. I made almost a thousand dollars throwing dice."

The hostess seated them and Reed ordered coffee for them both.

Clare glanced anxiously around her. "Do you think

we should place this in a safety deposit box? I remember reading something about the hotel having one when we registered. Nine hundred dollars…oh, my goodness, that doesn't even include the two hundred I won earlier at the blackjack table. Oh… I won at roulette, too. If we didn't have to leave in the morning, I'd be rich."

Reed enjoyed listening to her enthusiasm. He enjoyed everything about Clare Gilroy. He fully intended to savor every minute, knowing it would need to last him all his life.

"Let's go for a walk," he suggested once they'd finished. He needed the fresh air, and the crowds were beginning to get to him. Clare would enjoy walking the Strip and it would do them both good.

She followed him outside, keeping her handbag close to her body, conscious, he was sure, of the large amount of cash she was carrying with her.

Reed had never known a time when the Strip wasn't clogged with traffic. Horns honked with impatience, and cars raced through yellow lights. Although it was well after the sun had set, the streets were bright with the flickering lights of the casinos. The sidewalks were crowded with gamblers aimlessly wandering from one casino to another like robots.

It seemed natural for Reed to slip his arm around Clare's waist and keep her close to his side. She might believe he was doing so to protect her from pickpockets, but Reed knew better. If he was to have only this one night with her to treasure, then he wanted to make the most of every minute. He wasn't fool enough to believe she wouldn't return to Jack Kingston the minute they were back in Tullue.

* * *

The evening was bright and clear and the stars were out in an abundant display. A hum of excitement filled the streets as they strolled along, their arms wrapped around each other. Neither one of them seemed to be in a rush. Reed had lost track of the time, but he imagined it was still early.

"I love Las Vegas," Clare said, looking up at him with wide-eyed wonder. "I never knew there was any place in the world like this."

Reed loved Vegas too, but for none of the reasons Clare would understand. For the first time he could hold and kiss the woman he loved.

"Where are we going?" she asked, after a moment.

Reed smiled to himself, then unable to resist, bent down and kissed her nose. I'm taking you to my favorite volcano."

Reed hadn't been kidding. He did take her to see a volcano. It was the most amazing thing Clare had ever seen in her life. They'd stood outside The Mirage, a huge hotel and casino, in front of a large waterfall adorned with dozens of palm trees in what resembled a tropical paradise. After a few moments Clare heard a low rumbling sound that was followed by a loud roar. Fire shot into the sky, and she gasped as the flames raced down the rushing waterfall and formed a lake of fire in the pool in front of where they were standing. It was the most extraordinary thing Clare had ever seen.

Speechless to explain all she was feeling, Clare looked up to Reed and was surprised when she felt twin tears roll down her cheeks. She wasn't a woman given easily to emotion. One moment she was agog with wonder, and the next she was unexplainably weeping.

Reed studied her, and a frown slowly formed. She wished she knew what to tell him, how to explain, but she was at a loss to put all she was feeling into words. "It's just all so beautiful," she whispered.

Reed's eyes darkened before he slowly lowered his mouth to hers. She wanted him to kiss her again from the moment he had earlier. She needed him to kiss her so she'd know if what she'd experienced had been real. Nothing had ever been so good.

The instant his mouth, so warm and wet, met hers, she had her answer. It didn't get any more real than this. Any more potent, either.

Clare couldn't very well claim she'd never been kissed, but no one had ever done it the way Reed did. No one had ever evoked the wealth of sensation he did. She felt as though she were the volcano at The Mirage just moments before it erupted, just before the rumblings began. If he continued, she'd soon be on fire, too, the heat spilling over into a fiery pool.

His mouth moved over hers, molding her lips to his with a heat and need that seared her senses.

A frightening kind of excitement took hold of her, yet she wasn't afraid. Far from it. In Reed she found the man her heart had hungered to meet all these years. A man who generated romantic dreams. In her heart she knew Reed was a man of honor and he would never purposely do anything to hurt her. Nor would he take advantage of her.

She opened her mouth to him, pressing her tongue forward, wanting to participate in the delicious things they'd done earlier. Their tongues met and touched, and she responded shyly at first, then after gaining confidence, more boldly. Their mouths twisted and angled against each other, as they sought a deeper contact.

Reed's breathing came hard and fast as the kiss deepened and demanded more of her. She gave freely, unable to deny him anything. Clare's heart was banging like a huge fist against her ribs. Her own breathing was becoming more labored and needy.

"Clare…" Reed groaned and broke away from her as if he needed to put some distance between them.

"I'm…sorry," she whispered, burying her head against his shoulder. She'd never been so brazen with a man, and she couldn't account for her actions now. It was as if she were living in a dream world, and none of this was real.

His breathing was harsh as it had been earlier, his hands buried deep in her hair.

"Say something," she whispered desperately. "I need to know I'm not making an idiot of myself. Tell me you're not sorry… I need to know that."

"Sorry," he repeated gruffly. "Never…there'll be plenty of time for regrets later." With that he kissed her again with a hunger that left her stunned.

They were kissing on a busy sidewalk and no one seemed to notice, no one seemed to care. People walked around them without comment.

Clare's shoulders were heaving when they broke apart. She raised her hand and her fingers traced the warm, moist seam of his lips. "I'll never regret this, I promise."

His gaze narrowed as though he wasn't sure he could believe her. Not until then did Clare realize that he assumed she was still involved with Jack. A cold chill rushed over her arms as she thought of the other man. He seemed a million years removed from where she was now. It seemed impossible that she'd been involved with him. Reed was everything she'd ever wanted Jack to be.

"It's over between Jack and me. I told him before we left that I didn't want to have anything more to do with him again, and I meant it."

Reed's eyes hardened.

"I've squandered three years on him, and it was a waste of precious time. I'm never going back…the only way for me to move now is forward." She looped her arms around Reed's neck, unwilling to waste another moment talking about Jack. She was in his arms and nothing had ever felt more right.

"Clare, then this is all because of your argument with Jack. You're…"

"No. This is because of you. I can't believe you were there all along and I was so blind. Kiss me again. Please, just kiss me."

His hands gripped her wrists as though he intended to break away from her, but he hesitated when their gazes met. "It's true? It's over with Jack?"

She nodded. "Completely."

"Then that explains it."

"Explains what?"

He didn't answer her question with words. Everything she'd ever heard about Reed claimed he was a man of deed, and in this case the rumors were right. He wrapped his arms around her waist and lifted her from the ground until their faces were level with each other. Clare met his gaze evenly, confidently.

Clare had anticipated several reactions from him, but not the one he gave her. He closed his eyes, and she noticed how tense his jaw went, as though he were terribly angry. Before she could ask, he set her firmly on the ground and backed away from her.

"What's wrong?" she asked, her voice barely above a whisper.

He stared at her for several seconds.

"Reed?"

His shoulders slumped as though he were admitting defeat before he gently took her in his arms and rubbed his chin across the top of her head. "You don't want to know."

"But I do," she countered, not understanding him. At first he appeared angry and then relieved. Wanting to reassure him, she locked her arms around his waist and squeezed. The sweet pleasure she received from being in his arms was worth the risk of his rejection.

"Clare..."

"Tell me," she pleaded.

"All right," he said, bracing his hands against her shoulders and easing himself away from her. "Since you're so keen to know, then I'll tell you. You tempt me too much." He said the words as though he were confessing a crime, as though he hated himself for even having admitted it. Having said that, he turned and moved away from her.

"But I want you, too," she said as she rushed after him. She blushed as she said it, knowing it was true, but desperate not to have him block her out. She'd never admitted such a thing to a man in her life. Reed had stirred awake dormant needs, and she wasn't going to allow him to walk away from her. Not now. Not when they'd found each other.

Reed hesitated and glanced down on her. Before, she'd been so confident he was experiencing everything she was, now she wasn't certain of anything. This feeling of separation was intolerable. She couldn't bear it.

"What is it you want from me?" he demanded, his jaw tight and proud.

Clare hadn't had time to give the matter thought. "I... I don't know."

"I do."

"Good," she said, sighing, "you can tell me. All I know is I feel incredible...better than I have in years. I'm not the same person I was a few hours ago and I like the new me. I've always been so practical and so proper, and when we're together I don't feel the need for any of that."

"If I didn't know better I'd swear you were drunk."

"But I'm not."

"I know."

He didn't sound pleased. If anything, he was weary, as if he weren't sure he could trust her, let alone himself. To Clare's way of thinking, paradise beckoned and nothing blocked the path but their own doubts and inhibitions.

Then it dawned on her, and the weight of her discovery was so heavy that she nearly sank to the cement. She'd always been the good girl. Reed didn't want to become involved with someone like her, not when he could have his pick of any woman in town. She was dowdy compared to women he'd known. Dowdy and plain.

"Whatever you're thinking is wrong," he commented with his uncanny ability to read her thoughts. "Tell me what it is, Clare."

She could feel his frown even with her eyes lowered. "I know what's really wrong...only you didn't want to tell me. I'm...I'm nothing like the women you're accustomed to being with. I'm the bookworm, the do-gooder."

His scoffing laugh effectively denied that.

"Then why are you looking at me like that?" she demanded

"We have nothing in common," he said, once his sharp laughter faded away.

"We share everything," she countered. "We're close in age...we were raised in the same town."

"Different school, different cultures."

Clare wasn't about to let him negate her argument. "We both like to read."

"You live in the city, I'm miles out in the country."

"So? It's a small town. You make Tullue sound like a suburb of New York. We know the same people, and share friends."

"Gary is my only Anglo friend."

"What about Erin? What about me?"

He grinned as though he found her argument silly, and that irritated Clare.

"You're talented and sensitive," she continued.

"You don't know that."

"Ah, but I do."

And he *was* talented and sensitive. He'd known she was suffering from a headache, and been gentle and concerned. He'd been aware of her pain when no one else was aware she was suffering. As for the talented part, she didn't want to admit she hadn't seen any of the totem poles he'd carved, but Erin had told her he was exceptionally talented, and she was willing to trust her friend's assessment.

Reed's eyes, so dark and clear, remained expressionless, and Clare knew that he'd already made up his mind about them, and it wasn't likely he'd budge. To Reed, they were worlds apart and would always remain so. He was right, she supposed, but in this time together, in this town, they'd managed to bridge those differences. If it happened in Vegas, they could make it happen in Tullue.

There was something else, something she hadn't considered, something Reed hadn't said but insinuated. Her heart started to beat heavily. Her cheeks filled with color so hot her skin burned.

"Clare?"

She whirled away from him and pressed her hands to her face, unable to bear looking at him. Never had she been more embarrassed.

"What is it?"

"You think…" She couldn't make herself say it.

"What?" he demanded gruffly.

Dear heaven, it was too humiliating to say out loud. Reed guided her away from the pedestrians, and they stood in the shadow of a streetlight next to one of the casino's massive parking lots.

"Clare," he repeated impatiently.

"You think… I'm looking for casual sex…that I'm after a one-night stand." It made her sick to her stomach to voice the words. Even worse it seemed that all the evidence was stacked against her. She'd been nothing less than wanton.

It had started earlier at Gary and Erin's wedding ceremony. Clare hadn't been able to take her eyes off Reed. Later when they'd first gambled, she'd practically thrown herself into his arms. She kissed him back, seeking more and more of him until she experienced an achy restlessness.

After the things she'd done, after the things she'd said, Clare would never be able to look Reed in the eyes again. He must think terrible things of her, and she wouldn't blame him.

"No, Clare," he said softly, "I wasn't thinking anything of the sort."

She chanced to look in his direction, unsure if she could believe him. She suspected he was only saying that to be kind.

"You're attracted to me?"

"I'd say it was a whole lot more than attracted," she said, having trouble finding her voice, and even more trouble believing he was so amazed. "It isn't just being a part of Erin's wedding, either. I felt it when we were dancing... I knew then...you were going to be someone important in my life. I feel it now even stronger than before. I've been waiting for you all my life, Reed."

"Clare, don't."

No one bothered to listen to her, no one bothered to allow her to voice her thoughts, and it angered her that Reed would be like all the rest. "Would you kindly stop interrupting me?" she said sharply.

He straightened as if caught unprepared for her small outburst of temper. "All right. Go ahead and finish what you want to say."

Now that she had his full attention, she wasn't sure she could. "You think that because I'm here for my best friend's wedding that my head's in the clouds and I don't have the sense the Lord gave me, but you're wrong."

"I'd call it a temporary lack of good judgment."

"I happen to believe otherwise...and my judgment's sound, thank you very much," she continued, fuming. "I'm as sane and sober as the next man." No sooner had the words escaped her lips than a man stumbled out from between two bushes, obviously drunk. Clare blinked and shook her head.

"As sober as the next man?" Reed teased.

"You might think it's because I've won all this money… I bet you do. You might even think I've lost touch with reality. I'm carrying over a thousand dollars in my purse and I'd hand it back to the casino in a heartbeat if you'd listen to me."

"I don't advise you to make the offer."

She was amusing Reed, and that infuriated her. "Maybe we can talk when you take me seriously. I'm baring my soul here and you seem to find it amusing. Let me assure you, Reed Tonasket, I'm not pleased."

He grinned then, and Clare swore she'd never seen a broader smile. He leaned forward and kissed her nose and edged away slowly, as if he wanted to kiss a whole lot more of her.

"My proper librarian is back," he said.

"I'm serious, Reed. I'd gladly give all the money I won tonight if…" She hesitated.

"If what?" His eyes were dark and serious, and she was so enthralled with him that she sighed and held her hand against the side of his face.

"Never mind," she said, turning away from him, walking purposely down the sidewalk. He wouldn't understand, and she couldn't bear to say it.

"Clare, tell me." His long-legged stride quickly outdistanced her. Soon he was walking backward in front of her.

She lowered her eyes, close to tears because it was impossible to explain what she meant in mere words.

He stopped abruptly and caught her by the shoulders. His eyes, so dark and serious, studied her. "Tell me."

Her teeth gnawed at her lower lip. "I waited three long years…thinking, hoping Jack was the one. I was so stupid, so blind to his faults, and all along you were there and I didn't know. And now..." She stopped, unable to continue.

"Now what?" he coaxed.

"It sounds so crazy. You'll think I've gone off the deep end, and maybe I have, but I don't want to lose what we've found. I'm afraid everything will be different in the morning, and more so when we return home. I couldn't bear that, and the only way I can think to keep hold of this is to..." She hesitated again.

Reed exhaled and brought her into the warm shelter of his arms. "I don't want to lose this, either. If you know of a way for us to keep this feeling, tell me."

Clare's fingers caressed his jaw line, lingering there. "It's crazy."

"It's been that kind of day."

"People will think we've gone nuts."

"Folks have been talking about me for a long time. Gossip doesn't concern me."

"Really?" She raised hope-filled eyes to him.

"Really," he assured her.

"Then I have the perfect solution."

"Oh?"

Her heart felt as if it would burst wide open. "You could marry me, Reed Tonasket."

Four

Clare hadn't watched for his reaction, but he stood frozen, as if she hadn't spoken. A long moment of hushed, perhaps shocked, silence followed her words.

"That's the reason you were mouthing the words along with Erin," he stated softly. "You want so desperately to be married."

"No," she said, and shook her head. If he were to accept the validity of her words he had to know the full truth. "You're the reason."

"Me?" He sounded incredulous.

"I know it sounds crazy… I can imagine what you're thinking, but I swear it was you. It was dancing with you, sitting on the plane next to you for two solid hours, and feeling peaceful for the first time in weeks. It was seeing you with Gary outside the wedding chapel and realizing I was going to fall in love with you. I've never felt anything like this before, and…I don't know how to explain it. Something happened during Gary and Erin's wedding, I felt it so strongly, and I thought you must have too."

Reed remained silent.

"You mouthed the words along with Gary," she said in gentle reminder.

"Clare…"

"If you're going to argue with me, then I don't want to hear it. Just listen, please, just listen. When we danced… it was as if we'd been together all our lives. You can't tell me you didn't feel it…I know you did."

"I don't think either of us can trust what we're feeling."

"I trust it. I trust you."

He didn't say anything, and Clare suspected he shared her faith in what was going on between them, only he wasn't willing to admit it.

"It's because you've broken up with Jack," he challenged. His eyes hardened as he mentioned the other man's name. "You're feeling insecure and lonely."

Although she knew Reed was sincere, she couldn't keep from laughing. "I've never felt more confident of having made a right decision in my life. I don't want to marry Jack. I want to marry you, Reed Tonasket. If it were in my power I'd do so this very night."

"Clare…"

"Shh, take me back to the hotel."

Neither of them said a word as they walked back. Clare was collecting her thoughts, collecting her arguments. She felt almost giddy with love. Reed must think she was crazy, and she couldn't blame him; she felt completely and totally unlike herself. Normally she was cautious, carefully studying each action, analyzing situations and events before making a move. This time with Reed felt completely right. Her judgment wasn't shadowed by a single doubt, she knew with a clarity that defied definition what she wanted—and she wanted him. Not for this one night, not for these short hours, but for always. Everything she'd ever longed for from Jack was in Reed.

They entered the hotel and by tacit agreement walked side by side through the casino and headed for the elevator. Neither of them spoke, but the instant the doors closed, Clare was in Reed's arms. She didn't know who reached for whom. Their hunger was explosive, their kisses urgent and crazed.

A bell chimed as the elevator stopped and the doors noiselessly glided open. "Where are we going?" Clare asked. Her question came between heavy breaths as she struggled to regain her equilibrium.

At first it was as if Reed hadn't heard her. He sighed and then said, "My room." He studied her as though he expected her to argue.

Swallowing her disappointment, she nodded.

But he didn't leave the elevator. "If we do go to my room, we're going to end up making love." His gaze narrowed as though he anticipated his words would alter her decision.

Again she nodded, unsure that she could verbalize her agreement. "I want to make love with you," she said, after a moment. "Someday…perhaps soon, I'd like to have children with you."

Reed froze, and she realized she'd told him the wrong thing. The worst thing she could have possibly said. He wasn't looking to make a commitment. He was looking to satisfy their physical need for each other.

"Don't worry, Reed," she whispered, feeling wretched. If she was honest it was what she wanted too. "You don't have to marry me."

He studied her, his eyes dark and unreadable.

"I understand," she said, having trouble maintaining

her composure. After waiting three fruitless years for Jack, she should have realized no man would be willing to commit himself on the basis of a two-day relationship.

Decisively Reed stepped forward and pushed the button that closed the elevator doors. Without a pause he pushed another, then he turned back to her and reached for her hand.

"You're sure this is what you want?" The question was gruff, as though he were angry.

She nodded, although she hadn't a clue what she was agreeing to. "Wh-where are we going?"

His gaze shot to her as if he suspected she were joking. "To the wedding chapel. If we're going to have children, they'll have my name even before we set out creating them."

Clare must be out of her mind, Reed reasoned. Clare nothing, he was the one who'd gone stark, raving mad. He couldn't help believing he was taking advantage of her. She wasn't drunk, but she wasn't herself, either. She wasn't impulsive and while he wanted to believe she was sincere, he strongly suspected this was a reaction to her break-up with Jack.

There were a hundred reasons why they shouldn't marry and only one possible excuse why they should. He loved her and he was far too weak to turn down what she was offering. By all that was right he should escort her to her room, give her a peck on the cheek, and put an end to this lunacy.

In the morning, he knew as sure as anything, she'd regret what they'd done. Not so much a doubt crossed his heart. By noon she'd be pleading with him to quietly divorce her. Even knowing what was bound to transpire, it didn't matter.

If he was battling with doubts about marrying her, his feelings were muddied by his earlier intentions. He fully expected to make love to her when she agreed to go to his room. He hadn't hidden his intentions, nor had he disguised them. He'd been as open and forthright as he knew how to be. But when she'd agreed to make love, he'd witnessed the flash of pain move in and out of her eyes. He was treating her the same way Jack had, using her, taking advantage of her vulnerability.

Loving her the way he did, it wasn't in Reed to hurt her. Even acknowledging their marriage was doomed wasn't enough to turn his course. One thing alone had cemented his determination—the look of love in Clare's eyes. Her gentle acceptance of him forged his resolve. She'd been willing to give herself to him without asking anything in return. She'd even gone so far as to tell him she wanted his children.

Earlier that evening Reed had listened to Gary mention his feelings about starting a family. His friend had claimed he went mushy inside every time he thought about Erin carrying his baby. At the time, Reed had listened and found himself mildly amused.

He understood his friend's feelings now. Having Clare mention a child, their child, had a curious effect upon his heart. He wasn't a man given to sentimentality. Nor was he visionary, but the thought of Clare, her belly swollen with his child, had done incredulous things to his heart.

He wanted this baby, who had yet to be conceived, more than he'd thought it was possible for a man to want anything.

His feelings were tempered, he realized because he'd

never known what it meant to be a part of a traditional family. That privilege had been denied him almost from birth. He recalled almost nothing of his life before he'd gone to live with his grandfather, a widower.

The opportunity to give to his own child what he'd been denied was more than he could resist. This child who was nothing more than his heart's desire. He'd love this baby Clare would give him with the same intensity with which he loved his wife.

His wife.

Reed's mind faltered over the words. Perhaps fate was playing a cruel trick on him, leading him to believe there was hope Clare would ever come to love him. He wasn't fool enough to believe she did now. It wasn't possible— she was in love with an idea, a dream. He happened to be conveniently at hand. Knowing that, though, wasn't enough to deter him from the marriage.

Las Vegas was set up for quick, convenient marriages, but it took over an hour to make all the necessary arrangements. Reed, who was normally a tolerant man, found himself growing impatient. Although Clare was the picture of tolerance, Reed couldn't make himself believe she wouldn't change her mind later. By tomorrow at this time they'd be back in Tullue, and he knew to the bottom of his soul that everything would be different.

"It won't take much longer," Clare assured him, smiling peacefully at him as he paced the chapel.

The ceremony itself was only a formality in Reed's mind. As far as he was concerned, they'd stated their vows earlier with Gary and Erin. The service was necessary for legal purposes. Without realizing what he'd done, he'd married Clare in his heart a few hours earlier.

After the wedding was completed, Reed gently kissed

Clare. They'd never spoken of love, and yet they'd each vowed to love each other for as long as they lived. They'd never spoken of the future, yet promised to spend it together. Reed feared their lives were destined to be filled with ironies.

Reed hadn't a clue where this relationship would lead him, but looking down on Clare with her eyes bright with joy, he realized he was willing to fight to the death to give her the happiness she deserved.

"I'll buy you a wedding ring later," Reed promised after the ceremony.

It seemed to take hours before everything could be arranged, but Clare hadn't minded. While Reed had impatiently paced the chapel, she'd been content, knowing they had the rest of their lives.

When it came time to exchange rings Reed had given her a large turquoise ring as a wedding band. One he'd worn himself. He'd slipped it onto her finger and it was so large, it threatened to fall off her hand. Clare had loved it immediately.

"Would you mind terribly if I had this one sized instead?" she'd asked.

"Wouldn't you prefer a diamond?"

Smiling, she looked to him and slowly shook her head. "No, I'd like to keep this ring…that is if you don't object to my having it." The ring was obviously designed for a man, but Clare saw a delicate beauty in it. Since there was little that was traditional about this marriage anyway, she didn't feel obligated to submit to convention with a diamond.

"All I have is yours," Reed assured her.

"And all I have is yours," she echoed, finding serenity

in his words. Tears gathered in the corners of her eyes. She didn't know what was the matter with her, why she would give in to the weakness of tears when her heart felt as though it would burst wide open with a joy so strong it seemed impossible to hold inside.

"Shall we celebrate?" Reed asked as they left the chapel. "Champagne? Anything you want."

"Anything?" she teased, holding his gaze. "All I want is you, Reed Tonasket," she whispered.

His eyes brightened as he leaned down and kissed her. His kiss was gentle, with none of the urgency or hunger of their exchanges earlier, almost as if he were afraid of hurting her.

She'd always found it difficult to read him, but Clare had no trouble now. Reed was incapable of hiding how much he wanted to make love, but at the same time he restrained himself as if he were afraid of frightening her with the strength of his need.

"My room or yours?" she asked, her voice as soft as satin.

"Mine" came his decisive reply.

Reed led the way to the elevator, but he didn't kiss her. It was as though he were unwilling to cloud her judgment. After he opened the door to his hotel room, he turned and effortlessly lifted Clare into his arms.

She smiled up at him, feeling a bit shy and shaky, but never more confident.

His gaze held hers. "I'll always be who I am," he said in a low, almost harsh voice. "There'll be people who'll look down on our marriage, people who'll make snide remarks about you marrying a Native American. If you want out, the time is now."

Her arms circled his neck and she angled her mouth

over his, kissing him with a thoroughness that left her grateful she was supported by his arms. "I'll always be who I am," she answered, choosing to echo his words. "There'll be those who'll disapprove of you marrying outside the tribe. If you're going to change your mind, I suggest you do it now, because after tonight there'll be no turning back."

Reed's chest lifted in a sharp intake of breath, and she took advantage of the moment to kiss him once more. From that point forward their kisses were no longer patient or gentle, but fiery and urgent, as if they had to cram a lifetime of loving into a single night.

Clare couldn't remember Reed setting her on the bed, but he had. His large hands were having difficulty with the tiny satin-covered buttons that stretched down the front of her dress.

"I'll do it," she promised, even as she worked at the fabric of his shirt. They kissed, their mouths straining against each other while she struggled to get out of her dress and finally abandoned the effort.

Reed grew impatient. "Clare, dear heaven, let's get out of these clothes first," he said, reluctantly breaking away from her. He sat upright on the mattress, his shoulders heaving. She offered him a slow, sweet smile as she kicked the shoes from her feet.

"Be careful, Clare, I'm having a hard time slowing this down." His hands worked frantically at the buttons of his shirt. Mesmerized, Clare was incapable of doing anything more than study him, although she was as eager to dispense with her clothes as he was to have her out of them.

"That's the most romantic thing anyone's ever said to me," she whispered. Reed made her feel beautiful and desirable, and for that she loved him with all her heart.

She shouldn't be wasting this time, but she found far more delight in watching her husband.

Her husband.

Her heart swelled with pride and love. She had no regrets for the time wasted with Jack, not when it had led her to this man and this moment.

His shirt came off first, revealing a powerful torso. Until that moment, Clare hadn't realized how muscular Reed was. He wasn't like other men, who made a point of revealing their brawn.

Reaching out, she ran the tips of her fingers across his broad shoulders, reveling in the powerful display of strength. His skin was hot to the touch, and she flattened her palm against the smooth texture and exhaled sharply, wanting him.

"Do you need help?" he asked, turning questioning eyes to her. The room was illuminated by a soft light. Clare would like to have believed it radiated from the moon, but more than likely it was generated by the brilliant lights that decorated the Strip.

Not waiting for her reply, he bent over her and kissed her deeply, while she impatiently worked free the last of the maddening buttons.

Reed helped her to sit up, then peeled the dress from her shoulders, carefully setting it aside. Clare removed her camisole and the rest of her underthings herself, revealing none of the care Reed had with her clothing. Soon she was completely bare before him. She half expected to feel shy with him, but the thought was pushed from her mind when she read the appreciation and awe in his eyes.

His hands were gentle when he reached for her. His kiss was gentle, too, and incredibly sweet. He pulled back the sheets and gently placed her atop the mattress and then looked down on her, his gaze filled with warmth and love.

Clare's heart felt like it would explode with love. She could think of no way of telling him all that she was feeling.

He inhaled, his eyes holding her. "I don't want to frighten you."

"You couldn't," she whispered, stretching her arms up to him.

He came down on the bed beside her, and gently brushed the hair from her face. "You're so incredibly beautiful."

Clare briefly closed her eyes to the heady sensation his words produced. "You are, too," she whispered.

He kissed her then with such intensity that she felt her breasts tighten. "Reed," she pleaded, not knowing, even as she spoke, what she was asking.

He brought his mouth back to hers and kissed her again and again with a hunger that fueled their need. She was hot, feverish with desire until she whimpered, needing him so desperately. "Please," she begged, "don't make me wait any longer."

His lovemaking brought her such keen satisfaction that she thought she would faint with the sheer intensity of it. She ran her hands over his face, whimpering softly. They were both silent as though they no longer needed words in order to communicate. He kissed her several times, soft kisses, a gentle meeting of their lips, and gathered her fully in his arms.

Clare nestled her face in his neck and closed her eyes, unbelievably tired, unbelievably content. Everything within her life was complete. She'd found love, a love so strong it would withstand everything. She had found her home at last.

* * *

Reed lay awake long after Clare slept. He held her in his embrace, not wanting to miss one precious moment of this incredible night.

Idly he ran his chin across the top of Clare's crown, his thoughts traveling at lightning speed into the future and what it would hold for them. Closing his eyes, he decided not to court trouble. They would face that soon enough.

Reed had always lived on the fringes of acceptance in Tullue. The town and he'd maintained something of an armed truce with one another. That was bound to change now because of Clare. If they were going to make their marriage work, something he badly wanted, then he was going to need to make his peace. But that peace would have to be made with himself first, and it was a commodity he'd always found in short supply.

Reed slept, waking sometime later. He couldn't see what time it was without disrupting Clare, and he didn't want to risk that. She slept contentedly in his arms in the sweetest torture he'd ever experienced. His first thought was that he wanted to make love to her again, then chastised himself for being so greedy. They had time, to make love before they left for the airport. He would let his wife sleep.

His wife.

Reed felt a smile touch the edges of his mouth. He liked the sound of the word.

Clare amazed him. She was warm and generous and more woman than he'd ever hoped to find. Unable to resist, Reed kissed her forehead, and pushed aside her tousled hair.

Clare's eyes fluttered open and she yawned, stretching

her arms above her head. "What time is it?" she asked with half-closed eyes.

"I don't know," he whispered, "your head is on my watch arm."

She scooted closer to his side and Reed bent his elbow so that he could read the dial. "A little after three," he told her.

"Good," she whispered, lifting her head so their eyes met in the dark.

"Good?"

The room was dimly lit, but Reed had no trouble reading the heat in her gaze. Slowly she lowered her mouth to his and kissed him until his breath was quick and shallow.

Their need for each other was as great as it had been earlier, which surprised Reed. He'd never felt more drained, or more complete than with Clare. That his body would be so eager for her again was something of a surprise.

When they'd finished, Clare's mouth sought his in a gentle, heady exchange. "Thank you," she whispered.

Reed didn't understand. She was the one who'd unselfishly *given* to him, yet she was the one offering appreciation. His puzzlement must have shown in his eyes because she traced her finger down the side of his face.

"For loving me…for showing me how beautiful lovemaking can be."

He went to move, to find a more relaxed position for Clare.

"No," she pleaded, stopping him. "Stay where you are." She purred, closed her eyes and smiled. Within moments she was asleep and Reed found himself dozing off, as well.

This was an incredible woman he'd married.

* * *

This was an incredible man she'd married, Clare mused as she stirred awake. Reed was sprawled across the bed, his arms draped from one side of the mattress to the other.

Silently she slipped from the covers and glanced around the room. Her clothes were tossed from one side to the other in silent testimony to their lovemaking. Clare sighed and headed for the bathroom. A long, hot soak in the tub would do her a world of good, and when she was finished, she'd find a special way of waking her husband.

She closed the bathroom door and ran the water, hoping the sound of it wouldn't wake Reed. The hotel didn't offer bubble bath, which Clare would have found heavenly at the moment, but a soak in a tub filled with steaming water was indulgent enough.

She sank gratefully into the tub and was resting her head against the back when a solid knock sounded against the door.

"Come in," she called out lazily.

"I've ordered us some coffee. It's late."

"Late?" Their flight was due to leave at eleven. She hadn't bothered to look at the time. Only on rare occasions did she sleep beyond eight. She'd always been a morning person.

"It's almost nine."

"Oh, my goodness," she said, sitting upright so abruptly that water sloshed over the edge of the tub. "How could we have slept so long?"

The sound of his chuckle came from the other side. "You don't honestly expect me to answer that, do you?"

She reached for a towel and wrapped it around her. "I

can't very well wear that dress on the plane.... I'm going to have to get my suitcase from my room."

She came out of the bathroom in a tizzy, gathering her clothes against her stomach as she progressed across the room.

"Relax," Reed said, stopping her. He gripped her by the shoulders and turned her around to face him.

Clare did a double take, startled by the man who stood before her. Reed had dressed, and he wasn't wearing his tuxedo. His hair was combed, not as it had the day before, but into thick braids that flaunted his Native American heritage.

She wasn't expecting to see him like this. Not so soon. And giving a small startled cry, she leaped away from him.

Five

"What's wrong?" Reed demanded.

"N-nothing…you startled me is all. I'll get dressed and be gone in a moment." She was jerking on her clothes, with little concern to how she looked. Her hands were trembling as she hurried about the room, her head spinning. Something was very wrong, and she didn't know how to make it right.

It would have helped if Reed would say something, but he remained obstinately silent. Once she was presentable, she glanced at this man who was now her husband. "I'll need to go to my room."

He nodded, and the dark intensity of his eyes held her immobile.

"I did more than startle you." His words were ripe with incrimination.

Clare froze and closed her eyes, her heart pounding like a sledgehammer against her ribs. "You looked different is all…I wasn't expecting it," she whispered, turning her back to him. She'd always been a little afraid of him. Now, here he was, looking at her the same way he did when he walked into the library. Aloof and bitter. Their marriage, and even more important, her love, hadn't fazed him. Their night together had been a moment out of time. He didn't intend it to last.

"I am different, Clare," he said. "I'm Native American—and that's not going to change."

"I know, but…"

"You'd forgotten that, hadn't you?" His words were softly spoken, so low she had to strain to hear him. He wasn't angry, but there was a certain resolve she heard in him. A certain conviction, as though this was what he'd expected from her from the first.

"It's not what you're thinking," she told him, hearing the panic in her voice. "I don't regret marrying you…. I went into this marriage knowing exactly who you are."

"Did you?" he demanded.

"Yes…of course I did. Can't we talk about this later?" There wasn't time to discuss it, not now when she was barely dressed and they had to rush to catch a flight home. Later they could talk this out rationally when they'd both had time to think matters through. She wanted to kiss Reed before she left, but hesitated. He was tense and she was flustered. It seemed impossibly wrong that so much could have changed between them in so short a time.

"I'll meet you in the lobby," she said, and quietly left the room.

She was grateful their hotel rooms were only two floors apart. Clare didn't meet anyone in the elevator, and when a couple passed her in the hallway, she kept her gaze lowered, certain they must know she'd spent the night in another room.

Her hands wouldn't quit shaking and she had trouble inserting the key card into the lock. Once she was inside the room, she sank onto the end of the crisply made bed and buried her face in her hands.

Everything was so different this morning, so stark. Reed was cold and seemed withdrawn, and Clare feared it was all her fault. Her mind was crowded with all the if only's.

Where had the time gone? While lazing away in the tub, she'd imagined them sitting down to a leisurely breakfast and making necessary plans for their future. A multitude of decisions needed to be made, and Clare was eager for all the changes marriage would bring into their lives.

Now, however, there wasn't time to collect her thoughts, or for that matter anything else. Forcing herself into action, she quickly changed clothes, then hurriedly packed her suitcase, slamming drawers open and closed in her rush to stuff everything back into her suitcase.

Reed was waiting for her in the lobby when she arrived. He took the key from her and set it on the front desk, then removed the lone suitcase from her hand. "The taxi's waiting," he announced without looking at her.

Clare was convinced when they finally arrived at the airport that they'd missed their flight. Most of the passengers had boarded by the time they reached the departing gate. Because they were late, nearly all of the seats had been assigned, and Clare was deeply disappointed to discover they wouldn't be able to sit together.

Everything was going wrong. It wasn't supposed to work out this way. She'd endured the terrible tension between them in the taxi, knowing they'd have a chance to talk later. If nothing more, she could reach for his hand and communicate her commitment to him in nonverbal

ways while on the plane. Not being seated together was
another mini-disaster in a day that had started out so
right and then gone very wrong.

The flight was scheduled to take two hours, and Clare
was convinced they'd be two of the longest hours of her
life. She was seated by the window, four rows ahead of
Reed, making it impossible to see him or communicate
with him.

Her thoughts remained confused, and try as she might,
she was having trouble naming her fears. She married
Reed, but she felt no misgivings over that. She'd known
exactly what she was doing when she'd married him and
would gladly tell him he owned her heart.

Something had changed that morning when she'd first
seen him, and she needed to discern her reaction to him.
This wasn't the man she'd married. Overnight he'd turned
into the brooding man who'd frequented the library. The
one who'd intimidated and confused her. The man she'd
fallen in love with and married was sensitive and gentle.
He had little in common with the one who wore a bad
attitude like a second skin.

Clare looked out the small window of the Boeing 767
to the harsh landscape far below. All that came into view
were jagged peaks.

"Did you win anything?" asked a delicate-looking
older woman with white hair, seated next to her.

"Ahh…" At first Clare was uncertain the woman was
speaking to her. "Yes, I did," she said, feeling a burst
of enthusiasm well up inside her. She'd nearly forgotten she was carrying a thousand dollars in winnings in
her purse. In cold, hard cash no less. Remembering, she
edged her foot closer to her stash, just to reassure herself it was still there.

"I did, too," the spry older woman claimed excitedly. "Five hundred dollars, on bingo."

"Congratulations."

"I generally win at video poker, but not this time. I wasn't going to play bingo. I can do that any time I want at the Senior Citizen Center, so why fly to Vegas to play there? But my eyes gave out on me on poker and I decided to play bingo for a while. I'm certainly glad I did."

"My...husband and I played craps." It was the first time she'd referred to Reed as her husband, and it felt good to say it out loud. "It was my first time in Vegas."

"I fly down at least twice a year myself," the woman continued. "It gives me something to look forward to."

"I imagine we'll be coming back ourselves." Clare would like it if they could plan their anniversary around a trip to Vegas. It seemed fitting that they would.

A smile touched her heart when she realized for the first time that she shared the same wedding day as Erin and Gary. The four of them could make an annual trip out of it.

"I thought you must be traveling alone," Clare's newfound friend added conversationally.

"No, my husband and I overslept. We're lucky to have even made the flight, but unfortunately they didn't have two seats together." *Husband* definitely had a nice ring to it, Clare decided. Before the end of the trip she was going to sound like an old married woman.

The friendly stranger seemed eager to talk, and Clare was grateful to have someone turn her thoughts away from her troubles. It helped pass the time far more quickly. When they landed, Clare was anxious to talk to Reed and clear away the misunderstanding.

Heaven knows they had enough to discuss. They were

married, and yet hadn't made the most fundamental decisions regarding their new status. Where they'd live had yet to be decided, although Clare hoped he'd agree to move into town with her. The Skyute reservation was several miles outside of Tullue and would require a lengthy commute for her. She'd feel out of place living there, too, and hoped Reed would understand and accept that.

The plane landed in Seattle shortly after noon. The sky was overcast, the day gray and dreary. Las Vegas had been clear and warm, even at ten in the morning.

Because Clare was seated several rows in front of Reed, she was able to disembark ahead of him. Not wanting to cause a delay to the other passengers, she walked out the jetway and waited just inside the terminal.

"It was nice talking to you," the elderly woman said as she came out of the jetway. She was using a cane and moved much slower than the others.

Reed came out directly behind her, and Clare looked to him eagerly, drinking in the sight of him as though it had been days instead of hours they'd been separated. His eyes met hers, his expression closed, his chiseled features proud and dark.

"How was your flight?" she asked, stepping forward and linking her arm with his.

"Fine," came the clipped response.

From the corner of her eye, Clare caught sight of the older woman who'd sat next to her on the plane. She was staring at Clare and Reed, and her friendly countenance had altered dramatically. The smile had left her eyes and she glared with open disapproval at the two of them.

Clare couldn't believe a look could reveal so much. In the woman's hostile eyes she read prejudice and intolerance. She appeared openly shocked that Clare had chosen to marry a Native American. Never had Clare had anyone look at her quite like that, and it left her feeling tainted, as if she'd done something wrong, as if she were something less than she should be.

Reed was looking down on Clare, and he turned, his gaze following hers. She felt him tense before he stiffly said, "I warned you. You can't say I didn't."

"But…"

"Ignore her. Let's get our luggage."

He was outwardly cool about it, outwardly unconcerned, but Clare knew better; she could almost feel the heat of his anger. Clare didn't blame him, she was furious herself. She longed to march up to the woman and demand an apology. How dare that woman judge her and Reed's love! Clare wanted to remind Reed that the woman's prejudices were long outdated but she could see it would do no good.

Reed remained uncommunicative while they waited at the luggage carousel. Clare was conscious every moment of the woman who'd been so friendly only moments earlier, who now blatantly ignored her and Reed.

It didn't help matters any to realize that within a short time she'd be facing her own relatives and friends with the news of her marriage to a man who was half Skyute Indian.

Her parents were wonderful people and she loved them both dearly, but when it came right down to it, Clare didn't know how they were going to react to Reed. Her father had never made a point of asking her not to date Native Americans, but then there'd never been any reason for him to approach her with the subject.

Deep in her heart, Clare feared her father might disapprove of her marriage to Reed. He might not come right out and say so, but he'd make his feelings known.

That wouldn't be the case with her mother and her two brothers. They'd have no qualms about telling her what they thought. Her mother, in particular, would assume that Clare had grown so desperate to marry that she'd acted unwisely. She might even suggest Clare had married Reed as a means of getting back at Jack.

Jack.

She hadn't thought about him all day, hadn't wanted to think of him. Having her parents, especially her mother, regard him so highly could complicate the situation with Reed and her family.

Clare's last conversation with her mother burned in her mind. Ellie Gilroy had urged Clare to be more patient with Jack, to give him time to get his company on its feet before pressuring him on the issue of marriage. The landscaping business was only an excuse, Clare realized. There'd always be one reason or another Jack would find not to marry. It had taken her a long time to recognize that, much longer than it should have. But it was more than Jack's putting her off that was wrong with the relationship. It was much more.

It didn't matter what her family thought, Clare decided, tightening her resolve. This was her life, and she'd marry whomever she pleased and Reed Tonasket pleased her. Having concluded that, she was relieved. This marriage wasn't going to be easy. They knew it would require effort on both their parts to make it work. Clare was willing, and she'd assumed Reed was, too. Now she wasn't so sure.

Their luggage arrived, and Reed silently lifted the two bags and walked away, leaving it for her to choose to follow him or not. His attitude irritated her, still she had no choice but to tag along behind him.

"I...I was sorry we weren't able to sit together," she said, rushing her steps in order to keep pace with his much longer stride. "There's a lot we need to talk about."

Reed gave no indication that he'd heard her. He was so cool, so distant, and that infuriated her even more. If he refused to slow down, then she wasn't going to trot along beside him like an obedient mare.

She deliberately slowed her pace, but it was apparent he didn't notice. If he did, he found it of no concern.

By the time she reached Reed's truck, he had loaded their luggage into the back and unlocked the doors. Once again he didn't acknowledge her.

"Will you stop?" she demanded, standing beside the passenger door.

"Stop what?" he asked in cool tones. Their gazes met over the hood.

"Acting like I'm not here. If you ignore me long enough I'm not going to disappear."

His steely eyes narrowed before he pulled his gaze from hers and jerked open the door. "I won't, either, Clare. This is what you wanted, remember that."

"What I wanted? To be ignored and frozen out? There're so many things for us to discuss, I don't even know where to begin. The least you could do is look at me."

He turned and glared in her direction. His stance, everything about him was tense and remote. She might as well have been pleading with the moon for all the impact her words had on him.

"Never mind," she said, climbing inside the cab and

snapping her seat belt into place. She'd talk to Reed when he was ready to listen, which he obviously wasn't now.

He climbed in beside her. No more than a few inches separated them, but in reality they were worlds apart.

Reed had known it was a mistake to marry Clare. Even as he'd uttered his vows, he'd realized she'd soon regret the deed. He hadn't counted on it happening quite this soon. He'd assumed he'd encounter a few doubts in the morning, but knowing Clare, he expected her to show a certain resolve to work matters out. Clare wasn't the type of woman who'd take something as serious as marriage lightly. Even a Las Vegas marriage.

Her broken engagement had made her especially vulnerable, Reed mused. She'd come to Las Vegas to act as the maid of honor to her best friend when she'd desperately yearned to be a wife herself. Her generally good judgment had been clouded with visions of contented marital bliss. All her talk had been just that.

Talk. She meant well, but he knew better than most the path of good intentions.

It hadn't mattered who she married as long as she could say she was married. It salvaged both her pride and her honor to marry him, and he'd definitely been willing. Since he was the only one with a clear head, he should have been the one to put an end to this nonsense. Instead he'd gleefully taken from her all that she was offering.

Reed had called himself a fool any number of times, but he'd never thought of himself as vindictive. He did so now. Because he loved Clare and had for years, because she represented everything unattainable to him, he'd taken advantage of her.

His reputation with women might have had something

to do with her eagerness to marry him. She mentioned it herself. Perhaps by marrying him she was proving to the world that she was woman enough to handle him. Reed smiled grimly to himself. His reputation. What a laugh that was—and all the result of a lie Suzie Milford had spread several years back. For some odd reason it had followed him, enhanced by time.

Women were more stubborn than men and often had trouble admitting they were wrong. Reed had to find some way to convince Clare it was necessary before she could persuade him otherwise. His love for her had already eclipsed his judgment once, and he couldn't allow it to happen a second time.

An hour passed, and neither of them said a word. Tullue was almost three hours' distance from the airport, which gave him an additional two hours to sort through the problem.

"I need to eat something," Clare said just before they boarded the Edmonds ferry. Her hand was clenched around a brown plastic pill bottle she'd taken from her purse. "I need food in my stomach before I take the medication."

Her headache had returned, and Reed felt a rush of remorse. She was in pain and he'd been so caught up in self-recriminations that he hadn't noticed.

They drove aboard the Washington State ferry and parked. "Do you want me to bring you something back?" he asked, thinking it would be easier for him to climb the stairs up the two decks than for Clare to make the long trek when she wasn't feeling well.

"If you wouldn't mind. Please."

"What would you like?"

"Anything…a muffin, if they have one, and maybe a

cup of coffee." He couldn't be sure, because it had been impossible to view Clare from where he was seated on the plane, but he guessed she'd forgone the snack the airline had served.

It was early afternoon and she hadn't eaten all day. She must be living on adrenaline and pain.

"I'll be as quick as I can," he promised.

She offered him a weak smile and whispered, "Thank you."

Once he was in the cafeteria-style galley, Reed bought them both turkey sandwiches, large blueberry muffins, drinks and fresh fruit.

Clare's eyes revealed her appreciation when he returned.

"Thank you," she said again and reached for the coffee. Peeling away the plastic top, she sipped from the paper cup, then, unwrapping the turkey sandwich, she ate several bites of that. When she'd finished, she removed the cap from the pill bottle and swallowed down a capsule.

Reed reached for the prescription bottle and read the label.

In a heartbeat, he understood. Everything made sense now, it all added up.

Clare hadn't been herself the night before and with good reason. She'd combined a glass of champagne with her prescription drug when the instructions on the bottle specifically advised against doing so. It hadn't made her drowsy or drunk as the warning claimed, but it had drastically affected her personality.

No wonder she'd gazed up at him with stars in her eyes and blown kisses to complete strangers at the far end of the craps table. He doubted she'd even realized what was happening to her,

"I'm sorry about this morning," she said after several minutes. "I didn't mean to offend you…I'm hoping we can put the incident behind us and talk."

"We can talk." Although he didn't know what there was to say. Everything was crystal clear in his mind. If he hadn't been so crazy in love with Clare he would have realized right away that something was drastically wrong.

He was a world-class jackass. The only option left to him was to try to undo the damage this marriage had caused, before it ruined Clare's life.

"First and foremost I want you to know I have no regrets," she said softly, sweetly and, to his remorse, sincerely.

Her words sent Reed's world into a tailspin before he realized she couldn't very well admit she wanted out. Clare wasn't the type of woman who would treat marriage casually. She wouldn't give up without a fight. Unfortunately she hadn't figured out what had prompted the deed. The issue was complex; her reasons for marrying him had been both emotional and physical.

"Aren't you going to say anything?" she asked, when he didn't immediately respond. "I can't stand it when you don't talk to me."

"What would you like me to say?" he asked. He'd never been a man who felt the need for a lot of words. This situation baffled him more than any other.

"You might tell me you don't regret being married to me. There are any number of things you might say that would reassure me that we haven't made the biggest mistake of our lives."

Reed felt at a complete loss.

"You're impossible— How do you expect us to make any worthwhile decisions when you refuse to communicate?"

"What type of decisions?"

She apparently didn't hear his question or she openly refused to answer it. "You certainly didn't have a problem talking to me last night. Compared to now, you were a regular chatty Cathy."

"Chatty who?"

"Never mind." She jerked her head away from him and glared out the side window. "The least you could have done was warn me."

"That I prefer to wear my hair in braids?"

"No," she fumed. "That you intended to change personalities on me. I thought…I hoped…" Her voice broke, and she hesitated.

"I'm not the only one who went through a personality change," he told her quietly, thinking it was best to get it out in the open now and be done with it. "I don't suppose you happened to read the label on your medication before you drank the champagne, did you?"

"No…" She reached for her purse and dug around until she located the bottle. After reading the warning, she raised her soft brown eyes to his. "The champagne…I didn't even think about it. But I wasn't drunk, I mean…"

"No, but you weren't yourself, either. You generally don't eat food off someone else's plate, do you?"

Clare went pale. "So that's what was different."

He was gratified to note she wasn't going to play word games with him. "No wonder you were so uninhibited, blowing kisses to strange men. What about the public displays of affection between the two of us," he continued. "I don't imagine you usually kiss men in the streets. If anyone changed, Clare, it was you."

Her head rolled forward, and she caught it with her hand.

"Marrying me was like everything else about our time in Vegas. Unreal. You no more want to be saddled with me as a husband than—"

"That's not true," she argued. "I want to be your wife, no matter what you say. But you're too...hardheaded, too macho to admit it, so you're trying to put everything on me."

Reed knew he dare not believe she was sincere about their commitment to each other. "Methinks the lady doth protest too much."

She went silent as they pulled into Kingston and drove toward Tullue.

"What do you want to do?" she asked after a time, sounding very much as though she were close to a physical and emotional collapse. Reed realized now wasn't the time to press the issue, although he preferred to have it over and done with. Later would be soon enough.

"I'll follow your lead," he told her when it was apparent she expected an answer. They were nearly to Tullue by then, and Reed was both regretful and, in the same heartbeat, eager for them to separate. He couldn't be near her and not want to hold her. Couldn't be this close and hide his love.

"My lead?"

"As far as I'm concerned, we can do this any way you want. I wasn't the one crossing prescription medication with alcohol." He didn't know why he continued to throw that in her face. Clare was confused enough. "You have every right to bow out of this entire episode," he concluded.

"Bow out?"

"It's a bit late for an annulment, don't you think?" The question had a sarcastic twist.

"You think we should get a divorce?" Her voice broke and wobbled before she regained control. "I'm probably the only woman in the world who can't manage to hold on to a husband for more than twenty-four hours."

Reed had no comment to make. A divorce wasn't what he wanted, but it wasn't his decision to make. After taking advantage of her the way he had, he couldn't allow his desire to dictate their actions.

"What if…if I'm pregnant?"

The subject had been foremost on his mind the night before, the prospect filling his heart and his soul with a profusion of happy anticipation. No more. A child now would be the worst kind of complication, torn between two worlds without the guardianship of parents who would offer love and guidance to an understanding and acceptance of his or her heritage.

"Is it possible?"

"Of course it's possible," she flared, taking offense at his question.

"When will you know?"

She shrugged. "I… There are the home pregnancy tests, but I've never used one before so I don't know how long I'll need to wait for an accurate reading."

They were in the outskirts of Tullue. Within a few all-too-short moments he'd have her home, and they had yet to settle even the most rudimentary of the many decisions facing them. Everything hinged on what Clare decided to do about the marriage.

"I...I don't know what to do," she said, pressing her hands over her ears as though to block out all the questions that plagued her. "I can't think... I was so sure, and now I don't know what I feel."

"Sleep on it."

"How can you be like this?" she cried. "Don't you care what happens? We're talking about the rest of our lives and you make it sound so...so unimportant."

"It is the rest of our lives, Clare. It's much too important to answer here and now when your head aches."

"In other words, live my life in limbo, take all the time I need, but in the meantime what happens with us? Or would you rather I conveniently forgot our little... misadventure?"

"I'm not going to forget it."

"You certainly seem to be giving me that impression." Her eyes were bright, but Reed couldn't tell if she was holding back tears, because she gasped softly and went pale.

"What's wrong?"

She straightened and rubbed the heel of her hand under her eyes. "Nothing. Just...just pay attention to the road." No sooner had she finished speaking than Reed noticed a white pick-up truck pulling behind him.

Jack Kingston.

Reed tensed, welcoming the opportunity to confront the man, to make him pay for the misery he'd caused Clare.

"Don't look so worried," he said, grinning over at her.

"Please, Reed, don't do anything foolish."

"Like what?"

"Start a fight."

He was offended that she'd be so quick to assume he'd be the one looking for trouble. Then again, she might be worried he'd hurt her pretty Anglo boyfriend.

Reed heard Clare draw in several deep breaths as though she needed to calm herself. He noticed her hands were trembling and how she nervously wove a stray curl of hair around the outside of her ear.

The other man followed him for a couple of miles even when Reed slowed to a crawl.

"Reed, please." Clare sounded almost desperate.

"Please, what?"

"Just take me home."

"That's exactly what I intend to do."

"Ignore him, please," she begged, showing more life than she had in several minutes. "It's over between Jack and me. I don't want to have anything to do with him."

"Fine, I'll make sure he understands that."

"No." She sounded frantic.

"What are you so worried about? More importantly who?"

"Jack doesn't like you… He didn't like the idea of me flying to Las Vegas with you and I'm afraid he's looking for trouble."

"No problem, sweetheart, trouble's my middle name." He eased his truck to a stop in front of Clare's house and turned off the engine.

"Reed," Clare said, pressing her hand against her forearm, her eyes beseeching. "Just ignore him."

"Get out of the truck, Clare" came Jack's angry voice from behind her.

"Let's leave," she suggested. "There's no reason we have to put up with this."

"Leave?" Reed spit out the word. "Sweetheart, I've never backed away from a fight in my life, and I'm not about to start now."

Six

"Clare," Jack called a second time. "Get out of that truck."

Clare's mind was whizzing, as she tried to decide the best course of action. Reed seemed almost eager to fight her former fiancé, to prove his dislike for the other man, to defend her honor. She couldn't allow him to do that. Jack wasn't worth the effort.

"I'll never ask much of you," she said, trying hard to keep her voice even and controlled, "but I'm asking you now."

"What is it you want me to do?" Reed's steely gaze bored into hers.

"Don't fight Jack."

"That's up to him," Reed said matter-of-factly. He opened the door and stepped out onto the street.

Jack was out of the truck in a flash. He stormed across the lawn, jerked open the passenger door and offered Clare his hand, as though she required his assistance.

Clare ignored him and gathered her purse and sweater as Reed walked around to the bed of the truck. Jack's gaze moved from Clare to Reed and then back again.

"We need to talk," Jack said to her.

"No, we don't," she countered with a tired sigh. "Now if you'll excuse me I'm going inside. I'm exhausted and definitely not in the mood for company."

"I've done some thinking," Jack called after her, eyeing Reed malevolently, as if he found even the sight of him distasteful, as if he'd welcome the opportunity to prove how much of a man he was by challenging Reed.

Clare watched with a sick kind of dread as Reed carried her suitcase up the walkway leading to the front door.

Having no luck with her, Jack seemed to want to impress her by hassling Reed. He raced down the sidewalk, leaped in front of Reed and shouted, "Stay away from Clare!"

Clare gritted her teeth, not knowing what would happen. To his credit, Reed said nothing, sidestepped Jack and continued walking until he reached her front porch, where he deposited her suitcase.

Jack followed on Reed's heels, waiting for an opportunity to make trouble.

"Thank you," Clare said softly to Reed, when they met as he was returning to his truck. "For everything."

Reed's gaze met hers, and for an instant she detected a hint of a smile. "You can handle this jackass?" he asked.

She nodded. "No problem."

Reed studied her for an elongated moment. Clare wished they could kiss. They'd never had any problems communicating when it came to the physical aspects of their relationship. She'd been so certain marrying him was good and right and now she felt terribly confused. If he left now, she was afraid it would be the end, and she wanted so badly for them to find a way to build their lives together.

"Goodbye," she whispered, knowing it would be impossible for him to stay. "I'll be in touch with you soon."

"You won't have anything to do with Reed Tonasket," Jack flared angrily from behind her. "And that's final."

"Might I remind you, Jack," she said smoothly as she reached her front door and freed the lock, "you have no right to tell me whom I can and cannot see. If I chose to see Reed again, it's none of your business."

"Oh yes it is."

Reed was almost to his truck. If Clare could distract Jack long enough she might be able to prevent further confrontation between the two men.

"I'll make certain he knows it, too," Jack said, walking away from her.

"I might even choose to marry Reed," she said a bit louder. If she'd wanted Jack's attention, she had it then. For that matter she had Reed's, too. His eyes seemed to be warning her, but she chose to ignore the silent entreaty.

"Why is it," Jack demanded impatiently, "that everything boils down to marriage with you? That's what this is all about, isn't it? You think you're going to make me jealous. Well, I'm telling you right now, it isn't going to work."

"Frankly, Jack, I don't really care." Lifting her suitcase, she carried it inside the house and closed the door. She glanced out the window and was relieved to see Reed drive away.

Jack looked as if he didn't know what to do—follow Reed and have it out with him or take his chances with her. He took three steps toward his pickup, abruptly changed his mind and stormed back toward the house.

Clare turned on her radio and ignored him. She had run bathwater and put a load of wash in the machine before the pounding on her door ended. She wasn't going to speak to Jack Kingston. Everything had already been said. As far as she was concerned, the relationship was over. They were finished.

The following morning Clare woke more confused than when she'd gone to sleep. She needed to talk to Reed, before she could put order to her thoughts, but she didn't even know where he lived. Nor did she have his cell number.

She found it frustrating and irritating to be so ignorant about her own husband. He at least knew how to reach her and could come to her anytime he pleased.

Apparently he felt none of the urgency to set matters straight that she did.

If Clare was frustrated Monday, she was downright angry by Wednesday afternoon when Reed showed up at the library. Clare was busy at the front desk when he arrived. If she hadn't happened to glance up just then, she wouldn't have noticed he was there.

Despite her angry disappointment, her heart gladdened at the sight of him, but she took one look at his closed expression and her heart sank. Right away she knew nothing had changed.

It took several moments before she was free to leave the front desk. Reed had walked to the farthest corner of the library, the mystery section. No one else was within hearing distance. With swift, determined steps she followed him.

Reed was waiting for her, and she watched as his gaze moved over her, making her conscious of her appearance. She raised her hand to her head, distressed to note that several strands had escaped her chignon. She'd dressed carefully each morning that week, wondering how long it would take for him to make a showing. If she looked her best, then they might be able to recapture the magic they'd found in Vegas and then lost on their return.

"It took you long enough," she said with tart reproach, then immediately longed to jerk back the words. She'd been starving for the sight of him for days, needing desperately to talk to him.

With everything in her heart she prayed he'd come to offer her reassurances, to prove to her it hadn't all been a wild, impossible dream.

"Did Kingston give you any problems?"

"No. What about you?"

A half smile touched his lips. "I'd enjoy it if he tried."

"Oh, Reed, he isn't worth the effort."

He didn't agree or disagree. He kept his distance, she noticed, when she badly wanted to feel his arms around her. What she badly needed was the security of his embrace...of his love.

"Have you reached a decision?"

The abruptness of his question took her by surprise. "How could I?" she flared. "We have a lot to discuss, don't you think? I've felt so thwarted in all this. I don't even know how to get to your house. Nor do I have your cell number."

"I don't own a phone."

Clare had never known anyone without one, and blinked back her surprise.

"We can't talk now," he said, looking past her. Apparently someone had come into the library, and he didn't want them to be seen together. "I'll come to your house tonight."

"What time?"

He hesitated. "Late," he answered after a moment, "after dark."

"But why..." she began then realized he'd already turned away from her, "so late?" she finished lamely.

Reed had bided his time, waiting three days, hoping Clare would have accepted the reality of their mistake and be willing to take the necessary measures to put their lives back into order.

He was looking to protect her reputation from gossip. He feared his reputation and people's prejudices would tear her apart when it became public knowledge that she'd married him. News of Gary and Erin's wedding had been in the local paper, and Clare's name had already been linked to Reed's in the news piece.

He'd heard through the grapevine that Kingston wanted words with him. Apparently Clare's friend wanted to be sure Reed was going to leave "his woman" alone.

Reed had nothing to say to the other man. Clare had asked him to ignore Jack Kingston, and since there was little he'd be able to do for her, he'd decided to honor her one request. It seemed like a small thing to do for the woman he loved.

When he showed up at the library he'd been fairly certain he could count on them having a few minutes alone together. It wasn't until they were in the far corner of the building between Agatha Christie and Mary Higgins Clark that he realized his mistake.

She'd stood beneath a window, and the light had filtered down on her petite form. The sun, coming from behind her, had given her a celestial look as though she were a heavenly being. An angel, he imagined, but he couldn't decide if she would lead him to heaven's door or deposit him at the gates of hell.

Those few moments with her had knotted his insides with a need so strong he knew he had to leave almost immediately. It demanded every ounce of restraint he possessed not to touch her. Before he could train his mind, the vision of her on their wedding night flashed before him. The sweet smile she wore as she raised her arms to him left him weak in ways that were foreign to him.

The brief encounter at the library forced him to acknowledge how vulnerable he was when it came to Clare. Something had to be decided, and quickly. Since she had trouble knowing her mind, he'd make the decision for them both. A quick divorce wasn't what he wanted, but it was necessary.

He couldn't be alone with Clare and not want to love her. This evening presented an even greater challenge than he'd originally anticipated. He didn't know how he was going to keep from touching her. Nor did he know how he was going to avoid making love to her. He had to find a way to convince her to put an end to this farce of a marriage without letting her know how much he cared.

Reed liked to think of himself as strong willed. It was his nature to close himself off from others. It had also been necessary. He'd isolated himself from the good people of Tullue by choice, preferring to think of himself as an island, needing no one, dependent only on himself.

Now it alarmed his sense of independence to realize how much he needed Clare. Not physically, although his desire for her clawed at him. This one woman, more than any other, was able to reach him in areas of himself he'd assumed were secure. There'd never been anyone in his life he felt as close to as Clare, other than his grandfather.

His relationship to his father's father had been unique. They'd been a part of each other, sharing blood and heritage. It had been his grandfather who'd guided his life, who'd trained him in the ways of the Skyutes. His grandfather had taught him what it meant to be Indian.

The harsh lessons about life he'd learned from the Anglos. Finding himself uncomfortable in both the Indian and the white man's world, Reed had forged one of his own. He'd isolated himself, finding solace in his art, fulfillment in his craft. He made certain he was completely self-sufficient.

For the first time, his hard-won serenity was being threatened. By Clare. She made him vulnerable in ways he couldn't protect. Marrying her had been the biggest mistake of his life. Having shared the physical delights of marriage with her had changed who he was, altered his spirit.

In the back of his mind, Reed had convinced himself that once they made love, this need, this vulnerability she brought out in him would leave.

He was wrong.

Loving her had created an appetite for her that left him physically frustrated and in a permanent bad mood. His life had become a misery and all because of a slip of a librarian who refused to admit she'd made a mistake.

Clare waited impatiently, checking the front window every few minutes. She'd given up answering her phone, letting the machine pick up the messages, hoping to avoid being trapped in a conversation with Jack.

He'd called several times in the past few days, each time threatening to make it the last time he contacted her. In his last message he claimed he would wait until she came to her senses and phoned him.

Hell would freeze over first. She wanted nothing to do with him again.

Jack could continue to be a problem for her though. It'd be just her luck if he decided to show up the same time Reed did. She checked her watch again, wondering how long her husband was going to keep her waiting. It was already after nine, and she was growing anxious. Perhaps she'd misunderstood him. Perhaps he had meant he was coming the following night. His words were suddenly unclear in her mind.

She was looking out the front window for signs of his car when a knock sounded at her back door. Jack or Reed? Clare didn't care any longer. She hurried across the house to her kitchen and opened the door without looking.

"I was beginning to think you'd never come," she chastised Reed, wondering why she found it necessary to lash out at him each time they met. Especially when she longed to hurl herself into his arms and have him reassure her. Her heart fell as she looked at him. A single glance told her he wouldn't welcome her embrace.

She swallowed back the hurt and let him inside her home.

"Would you like some coffee…and really, it isn't necessary for you to come to the back door."

"It is if Kingston's parked outside."

"Jack's watching the house?"

Reed's eyes hardened as he nodded. "He's down the street. Don't marry him, Clare, the man's not good enough for you."

"How can I possibly marry Jack when I'm already married to you?" The idea was ludicrous. It seemed she couldn't make Reed understand it was over between her and Jack any more than she could make Jack accept her decision.

"We're going to straighten out this marriage business once and for all," he said pointedly, not wasting any time. He'd barely arrived, and already he seemed eager to leave. "It was a mistake. A big one. There's only one option left and that's to divorce."

"What do you mean? I…I haven't agreed to a divorce. I…I don't know what I'm going to do yet. I certainly don't appreciate you making my mind up for me."

Reed grinned as if her small outburst had amused him. He pulled out a chair and sat down, crossing his arms over his muscular chest as though he needed to do something to close himself off from her.

He seemed so bitter and hard, and Clare longed to force him to confront his anger toward her and toward life. He needed to put the past behind him. It would have to happen if they were ever to make a success of their marriage.

"I need to know what you're thinking," she said, sitting across from him. The coffee was forgotten. He didn't seem all that eager for a cup, and she didn't want to be distracted.

"I know an attorney in Seattle. I'll contact him and have him arrange for a quiet divorce."

Clare felt the blood run out of her face. It went against the very core of her being to give up on the idea of this marriage without either of them making a minimal effort. "Is…that what you want?"

He was silent for several earth-shattering moments. "It's for the best."

"How can you say that?" she flared. "Apparently you

aren't interested in my opinion," she told him defensively, sarcastically. "You obviously want out of the relationship. It'll take…what, two or three months before everything is final?" She stood, and with arms cradling her middle, walked over to the stove. "Funny, isn't it, that the divorce will take longer than the marriage lasted."

"It's better this way, Clare."

"Better for whom?" she asked in a pain-filled whisper.

An eternity passed before Reed answered. "Both of us."

Clare had no argument. Reed clearly wanted out, and she had no option but to abide by his wishes. It cut deep to let go of the dream, just when she'd believed she'd finally found a man she could love.

"You'll let me know if you're pregnant?"

"How?" she asked automatically, remembering how frustrated she'd been with no means of contacting him. "I don't know where you live."

He gave her simple directions to his home, which she attempted to write on a yellow tablet she'd taken from her drawer. Because her hands were shaking so badly and because her heart was so unbearably heavy, she made a mess of it. Finally Reed took the pad from her hands and wrote everything out himself.

"I have some books due back at the library next week," he said, as if he wanted to warn her he'd be seeing her soon.

Clare nodded. There didn't seem to be anything more for her to say.

Reed opened the drawer and replaced the pen and tablet for her. "If Kingston gives you any problems, let me know."

She trained her gaze away from him, because it hurt

too much to look at him, knowing he was about to walk out of her life and take all her dreams with him.

"I'm sorry it has to be this way."

"Right," she agreed. From somewhere deep inside she found the strength to smile. "I'll…be in touch."

He stood in front of the back door, ready to leave. Clare felt as though the entire state of Washington was bottled up inside her throat. Breathing had become almost impossible. Never had she felt more heartsick or more confused.

She couldn't look at him, certain he'd read the painful longing in her eyes. Pride demanded that she pretend it was as easy for her to let him go as it was for him to walk away from her. But standing there and saying nothing was the most difficult thing she'd ever done in her life.

Her hands folded around the back of her kitchen chair, her nails bending with the strength of her grip.

He opened the door, and suddenly her pride was forgotten. "Reed." She heard the aching inflection of his name in her own voice. It had demanded every ounce of courage she possessed to stop him.

He froze, his back to her. Clare trembled in confusion, raised her hand, then grateful he couldn't see the small entreaty, dropped it lifelessly to her side.

"Thank you for the most beautiful night of my life," she whispered through the pain she couldn't disguise.

Something broke in Reed. It was almost visible. His shoulders drooped, and he inhaled a deep breath and dropped his hand from the doorknob.

Within seconds she was locked in his arms; his mouth, hungry and hard, covered hers. The force of his kiss backed her against the wall and he held her there, urgently kissing her until a soft moan of pleasure eased from low in her throat.

"No more!" He groaned the words, lifting his head from hers. His eyes were squeezed shut as if he dared not look down on her.

"No," she cried in protest, seeking his mouth with her own. She caught his upper lip between her teeth and teased his mouth. A surge of power shot through her when Reed moaned and lowered his mouth to hers for a series of long, frenzied kisses.

Once more he jerked his head up. "This has got to stop. Right now."

"No." Her hands were in his hair, loosening his braids. Once they were free she locked her arms around his neck and angled her mouth over his to gently nibble at his lips.

He trembled, and she felt a surge of power at his need. "Make love to me," she whispered between slow, drawn-out kisses.

His hands stilled. Before she realized what was happening, a shudder went though him and he gently closed his fingers around her wrists and dragged them from his neck. "Our marriage isn't going to work," he said, his dark eyes glaring down on her own. "Pretending it will isn't going to change reality."

Without giving her time to react, he broke away from her and was gone, slipping silently out the door.

The doorbell chimed and, knowing it was Jack, Clare ignored the summons. Shaken, she lowered herself into a chair, her legs no longer capable of supporting her. She buried her face in her hands and drew in several head-clearing breaths.

All wasn't lost, she decided, with the sound of the doorbell buzzing in her ear. She experienced the first ray of hope since the morning after her wedding. She wasn't sure she could trust her instincts, but deep in her heart, she couldn't believe Reed wanted this divorce any more than she did.

"We don't do this often enough," Ellie Gilroy said as she lowered her menu early Saturday afternoon. "I hardly see you anymore," her mother complained.

Clare smoothed the paper napkin across her lap. "I was glad you called, Mom. There was something I wanted to discuss with you."

"I imagine it has something to do with Jack."

Although still young, in her early sixties, Clare's mother looked older. The past few years had been difficult for her parents, Clare realized. Her father had retired, and the two were adjusting to each other's full-time company. Ellie had been a housewife all these years and Clare summed up the problem as one of territory. Her father had invaded the space her mother had always felt was her own.

"I've broken off the engagement with Jack," Clare announced.

"Oh, dear," Ellie said on the end of a sigh. "I was afraid it was something like that. Jack called and talked to your father the other night. When I asked Leonard what Jack had to say, your father told me it was none of my business. You're not seeing a Native American by any chance, are you?"

"A Native American," Clare repeated, her heart in a panic. She would have willingly told her mother she'd married Reed Tonasket, but she couldn't see mentioning her marriage to her family seeing that Reed was planning to divorce her.

"Your father asked me if you knew Reed Tonasket."

"Oh, you mean Reed," she said, knowing she was a terrible liar. She'd never done well with pretense. "He was the best man at Gary and Erin's wedding."

"Ah, yes, I seem to remember something about that now. How was the wedding? Oh, before I forget, I have a gift for Erin and Gary at the house. Don't let me forget to give it to her when she returns. I don't suppose you happen to know when they'll be back?"

"In a couple of weeks."

If Clare had ever needed her best friend it was now. Erin had a way of putting everything into perspective.

"Tell me what's going on between you and Jack?" her mother continued.

"Nothing," Clare returned starkly, not wanting to ruin her day by discussing something so unpleasant.

"But I liked him, Clare. Both your father and I feel he'll make you a good husband."

"I'm sorry to disappoint you, but I don't want to have anything to do with Jack. He's out of my life, only he hasn't seemed to figure it out yet. Apparently he phoned Dad looking to make trouble."

Ellie settled back in her chair. "You know I think your father must have felt the same thing. I asked him about the call and he got short-tempered with me, then later he said he wasn't that sure Jack was the man for you after all."

"I spent a couple of days with Reed Tonasket," Clare said, hoping to sound nonchalant and conversational. "I like him very much."

Clare carefully watched her mother's reaction, but she read none of what she expected. Not concern, and certainly not anxiety.

"Isn't he the one who does such an excellent job of carving totem poles?"

"Yes," Clare answered quickly. "I haven't seen any of his work, but Erin says he's very talented."

"It seems I read something about him not long ago in one of those regional publications."

"Really?" Funny Clare hadn't seen the piece, especially since the library subscribed to several area publications.

"How would you and Dad feel if I were to start dating Reed?" Clare asked, diving headfirst into what she feared were shark-infested waters. Times had changed and so had attitudes. Her parents' generation had a difficult time adjusting to new attitudes.

Her mother's chin came up abruptly and her gaze clashed with Clare's. "You're not asking for my permission, are you?"

"No," Clare admitted honestly.

"Then it doesn't matter what your father and I think, does it?"

"No, but I'd like to know your feelings."

Her mother's sigh was deep enough to raise her shoulders. "You're over thirty years old, Clare. Your father and I finished raising you a long time ago. If you want to become involved with Reed Tonasket, that's your business. I just can't help thinking—" She stopped abruptly. "I'm not even going to say it."

Clare knew without her mother having to say it; nevertheless, she was glad to have aired the subject with her mother. She knew exactly where they both stood.

Needless to say, her family hadn't a clue that she'd done a whole lot more than date Reed. He was their son-in-law…at least for the present.

The lunch with her mother freed Clare. Afterward she felt jubilant that the groundwork for her marriage to Reed had been laid with her family. Clare didn't doubt for an instant that her mother would return home and repeat their conversation with Leonard. Within a week or less, everyone in the family would know she'd broken up with Jack Kingston. They'd also know she was interested in Reed Tonasket.

The urge to see Reed took hold of Clare when she left the restaurant. She stopped first at the house and grabbed the directions Reed had given her to his home, then took a leisurely drive into Port Angeles, where few people knew her.

By the time she turned onto reservation land, some of her bravado had left her. She'd been on the Skyute reservation countless times over the years. The tribal center there was one of the best in the Pacific Northwest and attracted a lot of tourist traffic.

The road twisted and curved beside the Strait of Juan de Fuca and the breeze blew in gently from the cool green waters. Colorful wind socks flapped wildly, and several Native American children played contentedly in the rows of homes that bordered the paved road.

Fishing nets were set out to dry in the warm afternoon sun. Clare noticed a few curious stares as she followed the directions Reed had written out for her.

His cabin, for it could be called little else, sat back in the woods, surrounded by lush green fir trees in what was part of a Pacific Northwest rain forest. Reed explained that he didn't have a phone, and from the looks of the place, she doubted that he had electricity, either.

The dirt road that led to his home was dry now, but Clare could only imagine what the rut-filled path would be like in the dead of winter, washed out by repeated rainstorms.

She parked her car next to Reed's truck, and after a moment or two, climbed out. Glancing around, she was relieved to find he didn't have a dog, at least none that revealed any interest in her.

No one seemed to be around. She stood next to her car for several minutes, thinking Reed would hear her and come, but that didn't seem to be happening.

Her knock against the rough wooden door went unanswered. After coming all this way, she didn't intend on being easily thwarted. They were married, after all, and as his wife, surely she had the right to go inside his—their—home.

The door was released with a twist of the knob. She let it open completely before she stepped inside. It took her eyes a moment to adjust to the dark, and what she found caught her by surprise. Reed's home was as modern as her own, perhaps more so, with large windows that looked out over the strait. Far in the distance she caught sight of Vancouver Island.

His sofa and chair were angled in front of a large basalt fireplace. A thick braided rug rested on the polished hardwood floor. Several oil paintings decorated the walls, and her gaze was drawn to them. She wondered if Reed was the artist.

The kitchen was to her left, the room huge and open. The bedrooms, she guessed, were down a narrow hallway that led from the living room.

It was apparent Reed was close, since there was a cast-iron kettle heating on the stove. Investigating, Clare discovered he was cooking some kind of stew. It smelled wonderful. Her husband was probably a better cook than she was.

Setting her purse aside, she decided to make herself at home. She reached for a magazine and sat in the deep overstuffed chair to wait for Reed.

It didn't take him long. She heard him even before he came through the door, his steps heavy on the wooden porch.

"Clare." He was inside the cabin in three strides.

He wasn't wearing a shirt, and his skin gleamed with a sheen of perspiration. He wore his hair straight with a leather band tied around his forehead. He looked all male, and Clare's heart stopped dead at the virile sight of him.

"Hi," she greeted with a warm smile. "I…I thought you might want to know if I was pregnant or not."

Seven

"Are you pregnant?" Reed asked. The vision of Clare carrying his child, her abdomen swollen with the fruit of his love, was deeply rooted in his heart. A vision he dared not entertain.

"I…I don't know yet. I bought one of those home pregnancy tests."

"In Tullue?" Reed's concern was immediate. With Clare living in such a small town, news of her purchase could create excess talk.

"No…I drove to Port Angeles, to a drugstore there. I didn't see anyone I knew."

"Good."

Her eyes flickered, and for an instant Reed thought he might have witnessed a flash of pain. If that was so, he didn't understand it.

"I read over the instructions," she said somewhat stiffly, further confusing him. "We'll know within a few minutes." She reached for her purse and took out a small brown bag. Inside was a test kit. "It only seemed fitting that we do this together."

"You're angry?" he asked softly.

The way her eyes widened revealed her surprise. "Not angry...nervous, I guess. I could have waited and let nature tell us in due course, but I wanted to know and I assumed you would, too."

"I do." Reed had difficulty identifying the wide range of emotions that warred inside him. His first thought was one of eager anticipation. But Clare bearing his child left his heart and his life wide open. He wouldn't be capable of hiding his joy or his love for her and their child.

If Clare was pregnant, Reed decided he'd move her here with him, shield her from the prejudice and small thinking that had haunted him most of his life. He'd do everything possible to protect her from outside influences.

If the test proved to be negative, he'd follow through with the divorce proceedings. He'd already left one phone message with the Seattle attorney, but he'd make another call on Monday morning.

"Are you ready?"

As ready as he was likely to get.

She hesitated, studying him. "I had lunch with my mother this afternoon," she said casually.

An odd inflection in her voice caught his attention. Either there was some meaning behind her words, or she was hiding her mother's reaction from him.

"Yes?" he prompted, when she didn't continue right away.

"I almost told her we were married, but I didn't, I couldn't...because you're so sure about this divorce thing. I'm happy to be your wife...and it's getting difficult to pretend you don't mean anything to me when you do."

"How much did you tell your mother?"

Clare's gaze fell to the floor. "I told her that I...I wanted to date you."

Reed stiffened. He could well imagine Mrs. Gilroy's reaction to that. It angered him that Clare had approached her family, knowing their approval meant a good deal to her. Needless to say, they wouldn't sanction him as a son-in-law.

"I know you'd rather I kept everything a deep, dark secret, but I've never been one to play games. We're married, and have been for a week now. I'm not going to conveniently forget it because you happen to have had a change of heart."

"What happened with your mother?" he asked again. Her purpose in coming to his home was clear to him now. The pregnancy test was an excuse. This visit had been prompted by the conversation with her mother.

"She said I was old enough to decide whom I dated and we left it at that."

"She wasn't pleased." Reed made the statement because there was no doubt in his mind of what had been left unsaid between mother and daughter.

Clare didn't answer him, and while she was preparing for the pregnancy test he went outside and stood on the porch. She joined him a few moments later.

"We'll need to wait a few minutes."

Reed had the impression they were going to be the longest minutes of his life.

And hers.

"It's beautiful out here," Clare said, wrapping her arm around the post and staring into the lush green growth of rain forest.

Reed glanced to the heavens. The clouds were rolling in, darkening the afternoon sky. A squall would follow shortly. He'd best put his tools away, close up shop and keep Clare with him until after the storm.

Without explanation, he started to walk away from her and she called after him. "Where are you going?"

"To my shop. I need to do a few things."

"Can I come with you? Even a few minutes can seem like a long time when you're alone."

He nodded, knowing in his heart he would treasure every moment of her company the rest of his life. These were precious gifts not to be taken for granted. He hadn't meant to be rude, nor had he intended to exclude her. He simply wasn't accustomed to company, nor was it his way to announce his intentions.

Clare stood a little proud, a little unsure, a few feet from him.

"I'd like to show you my shop," he said, and was rewarded with a smile that seemed to come from the deepest reaches of her heart.

She slipped her hand into his, and the unexpectedness of the action caught him by surprise. He didn't have time to steel himself against her touch, and his hand automatically tightened around hers. He couldn't be with Clare and not want her physically. She'd be in his home several hours, from the look of those clouds, and he wondered how he was going to manage to keep from making love to her…especially if she was already nurturing his child.

"I didn't even know this building was back here," Clare said as they entered the large shop. The log had been cut only a few days earlier, and the scent of cedar permeated the air. Reed had been working on it most of the afternoon. It resembled little more than a long, slightly square red block at this point, but within a few weeks it would be shaped into an eight-foot thunderbird, bear and salmon. The city of Los Angeles had commissioned it for a park that was to be dedicated in early September.

Reed was pleased with his progress so far, although it revealed little of what the finished product would be like.

"I'm afraid I don't know very much about totem poles," Clare said, walking around the cedar log. Her fingertips glazed the ears, face and beak, which were partially shaped from the square wood.

"In our culture totem poles were a substitute for the written word," Reed explained. "Several hundred years ago they revealed the history of a man, his clan and any war victories or favorable events."

"And today?" Clare wanted to know.

"Today they decorate the entrances of parks."

"That's where this one will go?"

Reed nodded.

"What's it going to be?"

Reed carefully explained the design, pointing out the beak of the thunderbird, the shape of bear and the salmon.

"Do those mean anything?"

Reed gauged her question carefully, wondering if her interest was a polite curiosity or genuine. Her eyes met his and he realized her sincerity.

"The thunderbird is a guardian spirit, the benevolent protector of all Native Americans. The bear portrays immense strength and is capable of performing great feats of skill and daring."

"And the salmon?" she promoted.

"The salmon is the symbol of fertility, immortality and wealth." He mentioned several other of the more frequent symbols used by totem pole carvers. The raven, the owl, the loon, casually telling her of the totem poles he'd been commissioned to build through the years.

"I didn't realize how well-known your work has become. My mother mentioned reading about you in an article in *Washingtonian* magazine. I must have missed the piece."

As she spoke, Reed gathered his chisels and hammers and the other instruments that were strewn about the shop.

"I was surprised the local paper didn't pick up on the article and write one of their own." She frowned as she said it, as though irritated that Tullue would slight him.

"They asked for an interview. I declined."

"But why?"

Reed shrugged. "I'm known as a half-breed hellion in Tullue. I couldn't see any reason to correct their impression."

"But—"

"Shall we go back to the house?" he asked, interrupting her. This wasn't a subject he wanted to discuss. No amount of success would change Tullue's view of him. In the eyes of the town he was a troublemaker, and if that was what they chose to believe, he wasn't going to disillusion them with the truth.

Clare was strangely quiet as they walked back to the house. He wasn't sure what to make of her mood, and because he was uncertain, he quietly assembled the wood to build a fire.

"What's this?" Clare asked after a few moments. "I saw it earlier and wondered. It's so beautiful."

She held up a small totem pole he'd carved three years earlier, one made of black walnut wood. He'd carved a rainbow, an eagle and a salmon. The totem was rich with meaning because it represented Clare in his eyes. Laughing Rainbow.

"I carved that several years ago."

"A rainbow?"

"Yes," he said, squatting down in front of the basalt fireplace to build a fire. "You can keep it if you wish." Although the offer was made in an offhanded manner, it would mean a great deal to him if Clare would accept the gift. He'd made it with her in mind, spending several months on the intricate details of the carving. It seemed a small return for all that she'd given him. She continued to wear the ring he'd given her, and, despite his determination to go through with the divorce, he was pleased she had his ring.

"Reed, I couldn't keep this."

"Please. I want you to have it."

"Then I accept. It really is very beautiful. Thank you."

The flames were flickering hungrily at the dry kindling when Reed stood. "I'll only be a few minutes," he said, excusing himself. He needed to wash and put on a shirt.

By the time he returned, the living room had darkened considerably with the approaching storm. Clare was standing in front of the window, her back to him. He could tell even before she turned around that she was troubled.

"Clare?"

"The test…it's negative. I'm not pregnant."

Her voice was a low monotone, and when she didn't immediately turn around, Reed went to her. She must have sensed he was behind her because she turned and wrapped her arms around his middle and buried her face in his chest. Instinctively he held her and he slowly closed his eyes, savoring the spontaneous way in which she'd reached out to him.

"Are you disappointed?" he asked softly, pushing the hair from the side of her face. The pregnancy test results left him with mixed feelings. He didn't have time to contend with those, not when Clare was snuggling in his arms. She was warm and delicate, and the feel of her caused his heart to beat slow and hard, building a heavy need within him.

"I...don't know," she answered with frank honesty. "Now isn't the time for me to be pregnant, especially when our marriage is so uncertain. It would have created a problem, but in other..."

"Yes," he prompted when she didn't immediately finish.

"It might have solved problems, too."

"How's that?"

"You might not be so eager to be rid of me." The hurt in her voice wrapped itself around him like new rope. She didn't understand and he couldn't explain. Every time he held her or kissed her made leaving her more difficult. He couldn't allow himself the luxury of becoming accustomed to her presence in his life.

"Let's sit down," he suggested, hoping that once she was out of his arms, his judgment wouldn't be clouded by the pleasure he received holding her.

Clare sat on the sofa and Reed joined her. They twisted to look into the fire, and before Reed quite understood how it happened, Clare was leaning back against him and his arms were around her. He couldn't remember either of them moving; it was as though they had gravitated naturally to each other. His hands stroked the length of her arms.

"Tell me about your parents?" she asked after several contented moments.

"My father was born and raised on the reservation," Reed explained. "He enlisted in the army and, from what I understand, did quite well. He died in a plane crash. I never knew him."

"And your mother?"

His memories of her were fleeting. Try as he might, he wasn't able to form a clear picture of her in his mind. From photographs he knew she was blond and delicate. And beautiful.

"She fell in love with my father when he was stationed back East. Her family disapproved of my father and wanted nothing to do with either of them when she married him."

"How sad."

"Apparently when my father died, she tried to contact them, but they refused to see her. I don't know what the death certificate says, but my grandfather told me she died of a broken heart. I came to live with him here on the reservation when I was four."

"Do you remember much about her?"

"Very little."

"She must have loved you very much."

Reed was silent. He'd learned a valuable lesson from his mother's life, the lesson of not crossing from one world to another, of the costly price of love.

In his heart, Reed was certain his father had carefully weighed the decision to marry an Anglo, but he'd miscalculated. His death had left Reed and his mother outcasts. No abject lesson could be more potent than what had happened to his parents. Yes, times had changed. Prejudice wasn't as prevalent now as when his parents married. Nevertheless it existed and he refused to subject Clare to such discrimination because of their marriage. Nor was he willing to risk bringing another child into a hostile environment.

The rain started then, in heavy sheets that slapped against the window. A clap of thunder was so loud, it sounded as though a tree had split wide open directly beside them.

Clare's startled gaze shot outside.

"It'll pass soon," Reed assured her. "You'll stay for dinner?"

She nodded. "The stew smells wonderful. I didn't realize you were an accomplished cook, but then there's a lot I don't know about you, isn't there?"

The question was open-ended, and Reed chose to ignore it. The more Clare knew about his life, the more vulnerable he became to her. He wished he knew what it was about her that affected him so deeply. When they were together, he felt intensely alive, profoundly calm, as though she brought him full circle, back to the love that had surrounded him while his parents had been alive.

"I'll check the stew," he said, needing to break away from her. Each moment she was in his arms increased the ache in his heart. He'd always possessed an active imagination, and sitting there with Clare in his arms, so content and peaceful, was slowly but surely driving him insane. The memory of their wedding night played back in his mind, tormenting him.

He wasn't a saint in the best of circumstances. Anyone reading his mind now would recognize he'd never be a candidate for canonization.

"I'll set the table," Clare offered, following him into the other room.

Reed stood in front of the stove, willing his body to relax, willing the graphic images of them together to leave his mind. Clare was either too busy to notice his predicament, or too innocent to realize what she was doing to him.

They sat at the table, across from each other, and it was all Reed could do to eat. The savory aroma from the stew should have appealed to him since he hadn't eaten much during the day. But his mind wasn't on dinner. He discovered Clare occupied his thoughts as keenly as she did when he was holding her.

"Tell me about your family," Reed requested, not because he was curious, but because he felt he should know more about her than he did. The attorney might need information Reed couldn't give him.

"I'm the youngest of three children. My brothers both live and work in Seattle. Danny's the oldest, and is an accountant. Ken's a salesman for a pharmaceutical company. He does a lot of traveling."

"They're both married?"

Clare nodded. "I have six nieces and nephews. Dad was in the logging business, but he's retired now."

"You were born and raised in Tullue?"

She nodded, tearing off a piece of bread.

"What about college?"

"I went to the University of Washington. It couldn't have worked out better. Mrs. Gordon was looking to retire as head librarian and waited until after I'd graduated."

"Why haven't you married?" He realized as he spoke that everything he'd asked her had been leading up to this one question. It was what he really wanted to know, needed to know about Clare.

She carefully set her fork beside her bowl. Reed had trouble reading her expression, but it seemed she stiffened defensively. "Do you want the long, involved story or the shorter version?"

Reed shrugged, leaving the choice to her. She looked very much the proper librarian now, her chin tilted at an angle that suggested a hint of arrogance. Her eyes were clear and her mouth, her kissable, lovable mouth was pinched closed.

"I'll give you the shorter version. No one asked." She placed one hand in her lap and reached for her fork.

"Are Anglo men always such fools?" he asked, amazed they had been blind to her beauty.

"White men are no more foolish than Native American men. Might I remind you, Reed, you seem mighty eager to be rid of me yourself. Don't be so willing to judge others harshly when you…when you're…" She left the rest unfinished.

Reed couldn't bear it any longer. Heaven help him, he'd tried not to kiss her, but the pain he read in her made it impossible.

He loomed over her, and she gazed up at him, her eyes wide and troubled.

"What is it?" she asked.

He hunkered down so their gazes were level. He studied her, wondering anew how anyone could be so oblivious to such warmth and passion.

Then Reed understood.

Others didn't see it because Clare hadn't recognized it herself. "You really don't know, do you?"

Confused, she slowly shook her head.

He tucked his arms around her waist and pulled her forward for a slow, deep kiss. Clare sighed, and her arms circled his neck as she melted against him. Reed went down on his knees, and Clare, who was perched on the edge of her chair, leaned into his embrace. He kissed her again, his mouth moving slowly, thoroughly over hers. Kissing Clare was the closest thing to heaven Reed had ever experienced, the closest he'd ever come to discovering peace within himself. Desire raged through him like wildfire, and he breathed in deeply, reaching blindly for something to hold on to that would give him the control he sought.

It was either stop now or accept that he was going to make love to her right there on his kitchen floor. Reed recognized that fact as surely as he heard the soft cooing noises she made.

When he hesitated, Clare kissed him, her mouth tentative at first, but slowly she gained confidence as she seduced him with her lips and soft murmurs of pleasure.

"Clare…" He groaned her name, needing to break this off while a single shred of sanity remained.

His breathing…her breathing went deep and shallow as she dealt with the pleasure his kisses brought her.

"Reed…please." She found his mouth with her own, and he felt in her the same painful longing he was experiencing. Only Clare, his beautiful, innocent wife, didn't feel she could say what she wanted. The realization had a more powerful effect on him than her kisses.

Reed pulled her forward until she was kneeling on the floor in front of him. His hands stroked the gentle curve of her spine as his lips devoured hers.

"We have to stop," Reed groaned, tearing his mouth from hers. He was fast reaching the point where it would be impossible to control his needs.

"Why?" She found his ear and nibbled softly at the lobe. Desire shot through him like a hot blade.

"Because if we don't, we're going to end up making love," he told her frankly.

"We're...married."

"Clare, no." He reached for her wrists and pulled her arms free from his neck, breaking her physical hold on him. The emotional hold was far stronger and required more strength of will than he thought himself capable of mustering. His legs were trembling when he managed to stand and back away from her.

"I'll see to the fire," he announced, surprised by how weak he sounded. He walked over to the fireplace and added a dry log. The flames licked at the bark and greedily accepted this latest sacrifice.

Miserable, Clare sat back on her legs and waited until the trembling had stopped before she attempted to stand. Carrying their bowls over to the sink, she busied herself by rinsing their dirtied dishes.

"Leave that," Reed instructed.

"It'll only take me a moment," she countered. Occupying her hands with the dishes offered her the necessary time to compose her shattered nerves.

Once again she'd made a fool of herself over Reed. She'd practically begged him to make love to her. Not with words, she couldn't do that, not again. Pride wouldn't allow it, and so she'd used her lips and her heart to tell him what she wanted.

Once more Reed had rejected her.

How ironic that he could be telling her how foolish the men of Tullue were to have passed her over, while he was pushing her aside himself.

Tears brimmed just below the surface, and it was fast becoming futile to hold them at bay. Pride was a powerful motivator, however, and when she'd finished with the dishes, she walked into the living room and reached for her purse.

"I have to get back to town," she said, with little more than a glance in Reed's direction. He stood next to the fireplace, his back to her. "Thank you for dinner and for…the moral support with the test. Let me know what the attorney says." In any other circumstances Clare would have been pleased by how unaffected she sounded, unruffled by their fiery exchange, as if she often passed a rainy afternoon making love.

"You can't go," he said darkly. "The storm hasn't passed."

"It will in a few minutes."

"Then wait that long."

She didn't want to argue with him, but she wanted out before she made an ever bigger fool of herself. Despite superhuman efforts her bottom lip started trembling. If she uttered one more word, a sob was sure to escape with it. Clare couldn't risk that.

"Every time we touch we're playing with fire," Reed said angrily. "It doesn't help any having you look at me like that."

"Look at you?"

"One harsh word and you'll dissolve into tears."

"I'm in full control of my emotions," she shot back, furious that he could so accurately pinpoint her feelings. Her anger was what saved her from doing exactly as he claimed.

His smile was slightly off center, as if it were all he could do not to laugh outright. "Don't pretend you don't know what I'm talking about," Reed said calmly. "If we'd continued we both know what would have happened. We can't, Clare, not again."

His words hit her like a slap in the face. In one breath he was telling her the men in town were fools for not marrying her, and in the next he was quietly arranging to divorce her. She was married, but the opportunity to be a wife was being denied her. One night in bed together didn't constitute a marriage, but apparently that was all Reed had wanted. One incredible night.

She reached for the small hand-carved totem pole he'd given her and hurried outside. Pride urged her to leave it behind, but at the last second she took it, unwilling to forsake the gift.

The rain had stopped, although the sky remained dark and unfriendly, the air heavy and still. Fat drops fell from the trees and the roof as she bounded off the porch and headed toward her car.

"Clare." She heard the desperation in Reed's voice as he followed her.

"The storm's over," she called over her shoulder. "There's no reason for me to stay."

"Listen to me," he said, gripping her by the shoulders and turning her around to face him. His eyes were narrowed into hard slits, his control paper-thin.

"You needn't worry, Reed, I got your message loud and clear, although I have to admit I'm a little surprised by your double standard."

"What are you talking about?" he barked.

"You don't want me as a wife any more than Jack did," she reminded him. The wind was whistling in the woods, a low humming sound, a groaning that seemed to come from the very depth of her spirit. "Don't worry," she continued, refusing to look at him, "you'll get your divorce."

His jaw went granite hard as he clenched his teeth. He looked away from her. His eyes, dark and haunted, burned with frustration. "You don't understand."

"But I do," she countered. "I understand perfectly."

He released her then, or at least his hands did. He didn't try to stop her when she opened her car door and climbed inside. He might not be clutching her physically, but his hold was as powerful as if he had been.

He'd wanted her as badly as she'd wanted him, but something more powerful than physical need was holding him back. Intuitively Clare recognized that whatever it was had restrained him most of his life. He couldn't allow any person to become important to him. He'd let her into his life as much as he'd dared, and now he was pushing her aside the way he had everyone else. She'd come as close as he would allow. He didn't want her, and she had to accept that and get on with her life.

By the time Clare pulled onto Oak Street, thirty minutes later, she'd managed to compose herself. The sky was clear and bright, sun splashing over the earth in vibrant renewal.

The first thing Clare noticed as she approached her home was Jack's truck parked outside. The frustration hit her in waves. She wasn't in the mood to deal with him now, but that option had been taken from her.

She parked her car. Jack was sitting on her front porch, looking beleaguered and defeated.

"Hello, Clare," he said, looking to her with a round, pleading expression.

"Jack." She prayed for strength and patience.

"Clare," he said, standing. "You win, baby, you win."

"I didn't know we were in a contest."

Jack didn't comment. "I can't go on like this. You want

me to tell you how much I've missed you—all right, you deserve that much. I've missed you. You were right about so many things."

It wouldn't be savvy to disagree with him. Clare had never felt less right in her life, about anything or anyone. She'd wasted three years of her life on Jack, then married a man who couldn't wait to be rid of her.

"I'm pleased you think I was right."

"I love you, Clare. I've been miserable ever since we split up. It's made me realize I can't live without you." He got down on one knee in front of her, reached inside his pocket and took out a velvet ring case. "Will you marry me, Clare? Will you put me out of my misery and be my wife?"

Eight

Jack was serious, Clare realized. How often she'd dreamed of him coming to her, his eyes filled with gentle love, as he asked her to share his life. For three years she'd longed for this moment, and now she'd give anything if Jack could quietly disappear from her life.

"Well, say something," Jack said, holding open the jeweler's case for her to examine the solitary diamond. "I know you're surprised."

"Jack…I don't know what to say," she whispered. Not once did she doubt her answer. It amazed her that only a few weeks earlier she would have been overwhelmed, delirious with joy that she would have burst into happy tears. Now she experienced a regretful, embarrassed sadness, knowing his proposal had come far too late, and being so grateful that it had.

"That diamond's big enough to take your breath away, isn't it?" Jack reached for her hand, intending to place the engagement ring on her finger.

Clare lamely allowed him to hold her hand.

"What's this?" he asked, gazing down at the large turquoise ring Reed had given her on their wedding day.

Clare hadn't removed it, not even to have it sized. Instead she'd wrapped tape around the thick band until it was snug enough to stay on her finger.

"It looks like a man's ring," Jack commented.

Clare closed her hand and removed it from his grasp. "Come inside, we need to talk."

"I'll say. There's a lot to do in the next few weeks. You might want to involve your mother and have her help you with the necessary arrangements. I imagine you'd like the wedding fairly soon, which is fine by me. You'd better snatch me up before I change my mind." He laughed lightly, finding humor in his own weak joke.

Clare led the way into her home, set her purse and the totem pole Reed had given her on the kitchen countertop. "Do you want something to drink?" she asked, standing in front of the open refrigerator. Her thoughts whirled like the giant blades of a helicopter, stirring up doubt and misgivings. The last thing she wanted to do was hurt Jack. "I've got iced tea made."

"What I want," Jack said, sneaking up behind her, "is a little appreciation." He grabbed her about the waist and hauled her against him, kissing her neck.

Finding his touch repugnant, Clare pushed away. "Not now," she pleaded.

For the first time Jack seemed to realize something was awry. "What do you mean 'not now'? You're beginning to sound like we're already married. You know, Clare, that's always been a problem with us. You've never liked me to touch you much, but, sweetheart, that's about to change, right?"

Clare recognized the truth of his words, and in the same heartbeat realized the same didn't hold true for Reed. She was anything but standoffish with him. The deep physical longing she experienced whenever they were together had been the cause of much consternation on her part.

"Jack, sit down," she instructed. From somewhere she had to dredge up the courage and the wisdom to explain she wouldn't marry him—and at the same time leave his pride intact.

She pulled out a chair and sat across the table from him. "We've been dating for a long time now."

"Three years," he returned brightly. "Which is good because we've gotten to really know each other. That's important in a relationship, don't you think?"

"Of course." Her fingers were laced atop the table as though she were sitting at attention in her first-grade class, shoulders square, eyes straight ahead. She tried to force herself to relax but found it impossible, especially when Jack's gaze drifted down to the bulky ring Reed had given her.

"Where'd you get that awful ring?" he asked for the second time. "I can't understand why you'd ever wear anything like that. It looks Native American."

Clare lowered her hands to her lap. "We need to discuss a whole lot more than my taste in jewelry, don't you think?"

His tight features relaxed as he nodded. "It's just that I'm eager to put this diamond on your finger." He removed the ring case from his pocket and set it on the table, propping it open. "I checked for clarity and color," he announced proudly. "I got a good deal, too."

"Let's talk about marriage."

"Right," Jack agreed, reverting his attention back to her. "We should set the date right away. Do you want to call your family now? No," he said, disagreeing with himself, "we should do that together. You want to drive over, surprise them?"

"No...let's talk."

"We are talking." His gaze narrowed. "It concerns me that we have so much trouble communicating. I thought you'd go wild when you saw this diamond. I don't understand what's wrong with you."

"I agree it's a beautiful ring," Clare murmured, experiencing a low-grade sadness at the sight of it. She wasn't disappointed to lose out on the diamond. The turquoise band Reed had given her appraised far higher in her mind, even though she realized she'd soon be returning it.

Her melancholy, she recognized, was a result of regret and self-incrimination that she hadn't faced the truth sooner. They'd never been right for each other, she and Jack, and never would be. Jack appreciated little about her and she about him. Their lives together would have been a constant battle of wills, of attempts to mold each person into the other's vision.

"You're darn right, it's a beautiful ring," Jack went on to say. "This half carat set me back a pretty penny."

"I'm pleased we dated for three years," Clare continued softly. "It was time well spent."

"I couldn't agree with you more." Jack relaxed against the back of the chair, confident and serene. "You kept pushing me and pushing me, but the time wasn't right and I knew it."

"I'm grateful for another reason, Jack," she said, her voice dropping, heavy with dread.

"Oh, why's that?" He picked up the ring case to examine the diamond more closely. When he looked up, he was grinning proudly, as if he'd mined the stone.

"I'm grateful for those years, because I've come to realize, I'm not the right woman for you."

Her words were met with stark silence.

"Say that again."

"This last week has—"

"You've got what you want," Jack flared, nearly shouting. "What more is there? I said I'd marry you."

"A marriage between us wouldn't work. You were right to wait, you were right to hold off making a commitment. I think you must have intuitively realized what it's taken me so long to accept. We simply wouldn't have made it as a married couple."

Jack shot to his feet and forcefully jerked his hand through his hair. "There's no satisfying you, is there? You want one thing, then you don't. It's the craziest thing I've ever seen in my life. You hound me for years to marry you, and then when I agree, you have this flash of lightning that says we're no longer compatible. Reed Tonasket has something to do with this, doesn't he?"

"I'm sorry, Jack," she said, meaning it, refusing to answer his demand.

Jack leaned forward, pressing his hands against the side of the table. "What happened, Clare? What changed?"

"I did," she admitted freely.

"This whole thing started when you were spitting mad because I wouldn't attend that stupid dinner party with you. Is that still what's wrong? You want your pound of flesh for that? It's because I missed that dinner that you've been throwing Reed Tonasket in my face, isn't it?"

Clare tensed. "This has nothing to do with the dinner party."

"Then what happened?" he demanded, stalking to the

other side of the kitchen. His feet were heavy, his footsteps reverberating as they hit the floor.

"I…in Vegas I realized—" She stopped abruptly. Any further reference to Reed would be a mistake. She'd already wounded Jack's pride enough without revealing the full truth, although it burned within her. Keeping their marriage a secret was becoming more difficult by the minute.

"It all started when you ran off to Vegas with that troublemaker, didn't it?"

"Reed was Gary's best man," she reminded him. "And I was Erin's maid of honor. You could have come with us if you'd wanted to, remember?"

"Tonasket was with you when you returned," Jack said slowly, his eyes accusing her. "What happened, Clare?" he asked, strolling across her kitchen, his steps much slower now, as though he were dragging the weight of his suspicions with him. He paused in front of her countertop, where he reached for the totem pole. Clare watched as the side of his mouth lifted in a derisive smile.

"I think you should leave," Clare said stiffly, growing tired of this conversation.

"For curiosity's sake, where were you this afternoon?" he asked, looking at the totem pole and pretending to examine its workmanship. "Let me guess. You were with him, weren't you? Is he that good in bed, Clare? I've heard—"

"Get out, Jack."

"Not until I know the truth."

"The truth," she repeated, "is what I've been trying to tell you for the last several minutes. I don't want to marry you…let's leave it at that."

"Oh, no, you don't, sweetheart. You've got some explaining to do."

Clare walked over to her telephone and lifted it from the receiver. "Either you leave now, or I'm phoning the sheriff."

"Threats, Clare?" His face was tight with anger, his eyes flashing with fury. "So you're screwing Reed Tonasket. I should have guessed long before now."

"Get out!" she yelled. "Before I have you arrested for trespassing."

It looked as if he would challenge her, but he changed his mind when she starting punching the numbers on her phone. He stalked across the room, jerked the diamond ring off the table and stormed out of her house.

The windows shook violently when he slammed the front door, but no more forcefully than Clare, who grieved for what she'd been too blind to recognize for three long years.

Reed carefully planned his trip into town. He waited until early Tuesday afternoon, hoping to catch Clare in the library during a slack time. He had information. The conversation with the Seattle attorney had resulted in several things he needed to pass along to her.

Clare had been right about one thing. The divorce would take longer than the marriage had lasted, which was a sad commentary on its own.

But what an adventure it had been. Reed felt honor-bound to follow through with the divorce, but he suffered no regrets over their brief marriage. His few days with Clare were more than he ever thought would be possible.

Reed hungered for the sight of Clare. She'd come to his home and spent an afternoon with him. Her leaving had left him alone in an empty house. He'd stood outside several moments after she'd driven away and experienced an ache that wrapped itself clear around his soul. The need for her had grown with each passing moment since.

Later that same day, he'd viewed, across the horizon, a multifaceted rainbow. He hadn't thought of Clare once since then without remembering the vibrant colors of the sundog.

It didn't help matters that they'd parted with so much left unsaid. Clare had been feeling foolish, with the sting of his rejection fresh in her mind. Although he'd wanted to ease her misery, he couldn't. In order to follow through with the divorce, Reed had to allow Clare to believe he was indifferent to her. Thus far he'd failed miserably, his actions contradicting his words each time they were together. The divorce was necessary because it protected her—and that was his biggest concern.

He drove past the library and noted several cars parked in the lot. Disappointed, he decided to wait an hour and try again. There were errands he needed to run, which would occupy him until then.

He spotted Jack Kingston when Reed came out of the hardware store, his arms loaded with his purchase. The other man parked his truck behind Reed's, blocking off his exit.

"Stay away from Clare," Jack shouted, leaning out of his cab. "I'm warning you, if you come near her again, you're going to be sorry."

Reed ignored him, opening the tailgate and sliding the stepladder onto the truck bed.

"Apparently you didn't hear me," Jack shouted.

Reed continued to ignore him and fished his keys from

his jeans pocket. He half suspected Jack had been drinking, otherwise he wouldn't have the courage to face him.

"Clare isn't your squaw."

Reed paused in an effort to cool his rising anger. Jack could call him any name he liked, but he'd best leave Clare out of it.

Clare had asked him not to fight Jack. It was the only thing she'd ever requested of him, and although he could feel every fiber of his being tighten, Reed would honor her plea. Unless...

Jack climbed out of his truck and grabbed Reed by the shoulder, slamming him against the side of the truck, his face inches from Reed's.

Reed sighed. Jack was making this difficult.

In the back of her mind, Clare had told herself she'd probably hear from Reed by Tuesday. He'd told her he'd be in touch once he'd spoken to the attorney, which he seemed anxious enough to do. It made sense that he'd show up sometime soon to relay the pertinent information.

He didn't stop in at the library, and by the time she closed at six-thirty, Clare felt defeated and more than a little discouraged.

Erin and Gary were due to arrive back anytime, and Clare was anxious to talk to her best friend. Erin always seemed to know what to do in awkward situations.

Clare was headed home when she passed Burley's True Value Hardware store. For a moment she was sure she saw Reed's battered pickup parked in the lot. It might have been her imagination, or simply because she was so anxious to see him again. Whatever the reason, she turned around and pulled into the lot herself.

It would take only a moment to see if he was inside and no harm would come of it. If he wasn't, she'd casually be on her way. If he was, she'd let him know she didn't appreciate the way he continued to keep her waiting.

"Evening, Mr. Burley," she greeted, smiling at the potbellied proprietor as she strolled past the checkout stand. She wandered down the aisles, pretending to be interested in a set of pots and pans.

"I tell you, Alice, I've never seen anything like it," a female voice drifted from the other side of the aisle. "Two grown men fighting like that right out there in the parking lot. Poor Mr. Burley ended up having to call the sheriff."

"What could they possibly have been brawling about in broad daylight like that?" Alice asked. She too sounded equally disgusted by the events of that afternoon.

Clare wandered down the row and glanced both ways, hoping to catch a glimpse of Reed.

"Reed Tonasket was involved."

Frozen, Clare listened.

"Were either one of them hurt?" the second woman asked.

"I couldn't tell how badly, but it seemed the other fellow took the worst of the beating. He got his licks in though. Reed was bleeding pretty bad."

Reed. Clare reached for the shelf when she realized the two women were talking about Reed and Jack. Without thinking, she reached for the carton of pots and pans and carried it to the counter where Ed Burley was working the cash register.

"I understand there was something of a commotion here earlier," she said breezily, drawing her debit card from her purse.

"We had a huge fight on our hands," Ed Burley confirmed. "I was afraid they were going to end up killing one another. I couldn't let that happen—I had to call in the sheriff. I hate to be the one to tell you this, Clare, but Jack was involved."

"*What* happened after that?" she prompted, needing to find out what she could.

"Not much. The sheriff's deputy hauled them both away."

Clare's gaze returned to the parking lot where Reed's truck was parked, and a sick kind of dread took root.

"That'll be $155.36," Ed Burley went on to say.

Clare stared at him blankly until she realized he was quoting her the price for her purchase. Quickly she handed him her debit card. She was halfway out the door when Ed Burley called after her.

"You forgot something," he said, handing her the oblong box of pans. By the time Clare reached her car, her legs were shaking so badly she needed to lean against the side of her vehicle. If she was to faint, folks would attribute it to the heat. The day was downright sultry. The hottest day of the year and much too hot for early summer.

But it wasn't the weather that had affected her so negatively. It was Reed. He'd been in a fight. No wonder he had a reputation as a troublemaker. If he was going to engage in violent behavior, he had only himself to blame.

Then she remembered how eager Jack had been to fight Reed the afternoon they'd returned from Las Vegas. Any excuse would do. It had bothered her then, and it did even more so now.

The two were destined to clash, she realized, but she'd hoped Reed would be able to avoid it. She feared he'd been as eager as Jack and that was what troubled her most.

That chip on Reed's shoulder was sometimes larger

than the red cedar he used to carve his totem poles. It was as if he wanted to live up to every negative thing that had been reported about him. As if he found it his God-given right to feed the rumors.

Fine. He'd pay the price the same way Jack would. She certainly wasn't going to reward his uncivilized behavior by bailing him out of jail, even if she was his legal wife.

Clare realized she was too upset to be driving when she ran a stop sign. She pulled over to the side of the road and waited for her nerves to settle. But the longer she sat there, the more pronounced her feeling became.

Clare was rarely angry. It wasn't an emotion her family dealt with often. Anger was something to be corrected, or ignored.

Sifting through her emotions did nothing to ease her outrage. She was furious with Reed, more angry than she could ever remember being at anyone.

She tried to relax, to breathe in several deep, calming thoughts and exhale her frustration. But she soon discovered nothing would ease the terrible tension that held her as much a prisoner as Reed was in the local jail.

It was a minor miracle that she didn't get a ticket for a traffic violation as she drove home. She hadn't a clue of how many infractions she'd committed.

Parking in front of her home, she walked to the front door and hesitated. Heaven help her, she couldn't do it. She couldn't leave Reed in jail. With an angry, frustrated sigh, she turned around and marched back to her car.

She'd post Reed's bail, Clare decided, trembling. But he'd know beyond a shadow of a doubt how disappointed she was in him. He wouldn't like her going to the jail, but, by heaven, she was his wife—for now at least—and that entitled her to something.

Tullue's sheriff's office housed a holding cell where they kept those arrested until they could be transferred to larger Callam County jail in Port Angeles. Clare wasn't sure what the charges were against Reed. No doubt they were numerous.

She parked and hiked up the stairs of the sheriff's department as if she were attacking Mount Everest. A longtime family friend was sitting at the receptionist's desk, and Clare realized that news of her actions would undoubtedly reach everyone in town. But that did little to change her mind.

"Hello, Clare." Jim Daniels revealed some surprise at seeing her. "What can I do for you?"

"I understand a deputy brought in Reed Tonasket and Jack Kingston earlier."

Jim's gaze slowly rose to hers, his dark eyes questioning. "Reed Tonasket is here."

"What are the charges?" She removed her wallet from her purse.

"Disturbing the peace, but he may get aggravated assault thrown in. From what I understand, Jack Kingston's at the hospital now."

"Any priors?" How efficient she sounded, as though she were an experienced attorney on a routine call. As if she knew what she was talking about when in reality she knew next to nothing.

"One."

"Has the bail been set?"

Jim named off a figure, and Clare opened her wallet and handed over her credit card.

"You're posting bail?" Jim asked as though he were sure he misunderstood her intentions even now.

"Yes," she returned primly.

"This is going to take a few minutes," Jim continued, sounding ambivalent. "There's some paperwork that needs to be completed first."

"I'll wait here."

Still Jim hesitated. "You're certain about this, Clare?"

"Positive." Her words were stiffer this time. She didn't appreciate his concern, nor was she going to accept his censure. She was over thirty years old, and if she chose to bail someone out of jail that was her business.

Clare's back was rigid as she sat in the waiting area, her hands folded in her lap. Jim returned a few minutes later and announced it would take a couple of moments longer, then sat down at his desk. He glanced up at her once or twice as if seeing her for the first time.

Until she'd married Reed, she'd never done anything the town could consider the least bit improper in her life. Everything about her was predictable. Her entire life had followed a schedule with few deviations, a predetermined outline of events.

The one area she'd failed in had been marriage. She'd assumed, that by a certain age she'd have settled down with a good, upstanding man and produced the required 2 or 3 children, the same way her brothers had.

The door opened and an officer escorted Reed into the reception area. Clare's gaze was instantly drawn to his. Before she could help herself, she gasped in dismay. His left eye was swollen and there was a deepening bruise along the side of his face. His nose looked as if it had taken the brunt of the attack. Although she didn't know much about this sort of thing, she feared it might be broken. Dried blood was caked just below his bottom lip.

Reed didn't say a word as the handcuffs were removed. He rubbed his wrists as if to restore the circulation to his hands. The officer said something to Reed, who nodded and moved toward Clare.

She remained silent until they were outside the sheriff's office. Tears blurred her vision.

"What are you doing here?" Reed demanded.

"Me?" she cried. "I'm not the one who got myself tossed into the clinker for disturbing the peace."

"Who told you?" He held himself rigid, his stare as cold as she'd ever seen it.

"Does it matter?" She hadn't expected gratitude, not exactly, but it hadn't occurred to her that he'd be so coldly furious with her.

"Did you post Kingston's bail, too?"

Clare whirled around so fast she nearly toppled down the flight of stairs. "I'm not married to him. You're the one who concerns me."

Reed didn't answer her. He marched down the steps and onto the sidewalk.

Clare raced after him. "Why'd you do it? You...promised me you wouldn't. You said—"

"I promised you nothing."

Clare's entire life felt as if it had been nothing more than empty promises. Empty dreams. Reed walked away from her, but she refused to follow him.

"You shouldn't be here any more than you should be married to me," he told her, holding himself stiffly away from her. How unyielding he looked, unforgiving.

"You're...right on both counts," she cried, swallowing a sob. Tears streaked her face and forcefully she brushed them aside, even more furious that he would see her cry.

"I didn't ask you to come down and bail me out. It would have been better if you—"

"I couldn't leave you there."

It was as though he didn't hear a single word she said. He worked his jaw for a moment, then rubbed his hand along the side of his face to investigate the damage. Clare could see that nothing would get through the thick layer of pride he wore like a suit of armor, so she gave up. He wasn't in any mood to listen to her, nor was he seeking her help. There was nothing left for her to do but go. He'd walk back to his truck and seek her out when he was ready…if he ever was.

Not once did she look back as she drove away. Not once did she allow herself to mentally review her marriage. In another couple of months their relationship would be over; until then she'd try to forget Reed Tonasket meant anything to her.

It sounded good. Reasonable even. But it didn't work. She couldn't stop thinking about Reed, couldn't make herself forget his blackened eye and how swollen his nose was. He should never have fought Jack, she told herself. No matter what he said, he'd promised her he wouldn't.

Technically he was right, he hadn't said it with words. He'd promised with his eyes the afternoon they'd returned from Vegas as he'd carried her suitcase to the front door. Even then it hadn't been easy for him to ignore Jack's verbal attacks, but he had, and he'd done it for her.

Clare might have been able to settle her nerves if it wasn't so blasted hot. Hoping to generate some cross ventilation, she opened both the front and the back door and then lounged on the sofa, waiting for the worst of the heat to pass.

It seemed impossible, but she must have fallen asleep. When Clare stirred some time later she was surprised to find the room dark. It was as though someone had lowered a black satin blanket over her.

Sitting up, she stared into the empty space, her heart heavy.

She hadn't eaten, hadn't changed out of her work clothes. The room was dark, but much cooler than it had been earlier. Silently she moved into the kitchen, her heart and thoughts burdened. She stood alone in the dark.

The night was rich with sound. June bugs chirped in the distance, the stars were out in brilliant display. Not knowing what drew her, Clare moved to the screen door and gazed into the raw stillness of the night.

Her eyes quickly adjusted to the lack of light. It was then that she saw him. Reed. He couldn't have been standing more than ten feet away.

They stared at each other through the wire mesh. All the anger she'd experienced earlier, all the fear and the outrage vanished.

He stood there silent and still for several moments. Distance and the night prevented her from reading his features. In her mind it seemed that he was waiting for something, some sign, some word.

With her heart in her hand, Clare answered him.

She stepped forward and held open the screen door.

Nine

Reed didn't understand what had brought him to Clare's, nor did he question the powerful, unrelenting need he experienced for her. He walked toward her, his eyes holding hers. As the distance narrowed, he could see every breath she drew. His gaze was mesmerized by the small, even movements of her chest as it rose and fell.

His body was hard, tight, coiled with tension. For now this woman was his wife, and he was through denying himself what he yearned for most. He was through denying what Clare had asked to give him.

She stood in the moonlight waiting, silent, holding open the screen door for him. Words weren't necessary. They would have distracted him from his purpose.

He paused in front of her; their gazes locked. They stood no more than a few inches apart, reading each other. Clare sighed and, whether she meant to or not, she swayed toward him. He caught her by the waist and gently drew her forward. She came with a soft sigh, and slipped her arms around his neck.

Their kiss brought him pain, but the small discomfort was far outweighed by the pleasure he received holding

Clare. His face was sore, his eyes and mouth battered, but it would take far more than a few well-placed punches to keep him from his wife.

Lovingly, Clare raised her hands to his face, her fingertips lightly investigating the swelling around his eye. Her troubled gaze found his. "Why?" she whispered.

Reed shook his head. It wasn't important now.

"I…need to know."

Reed hesitated, then said, "He insulted you."

Clare's eyes drifted closed and when she looked to him again, he noted tears and a weary sadness. Her hands gently cupped his face as she raised her mouth to his, her lips tenderly moving over his, as though she were afraid of causing him even more pain.

"Clare." His fingers covered hers as he diverted her from her gentle ministrations. "I'm sorry," he breathed. It was why he'd come to her, he realized. To seek her pardon for his anger when she'd risked so much on his behalf.

"I am, too," she whispered on a half sob. The question must have shown in him, because she elaborated. "For having doubted you…for being so angry."

He kissed her again, and it was a cleansing, a pardon for them both. They were inside the darkened kitchen now, although Reed couldn't recall moving from the back stairs. He knew with a certainty that they were going to make love, and in some deep, unexplainable way that troubled him.

He wanted Clare; his desire for her had been an ever-present torment since Vegas. Yet he resisted her, refused himself, his reasons legitimate and sound, lined up like a row of righteous judges in his mind.

He'd convinced himself it was important for both their sakes to avoid anything physical, especially since a divorce was inevitable. He realized now he was only partially right. His reasons for backing out of the marriage were far more complex than he could acknowledge, deeply rooted in emotions he was only beginning to understand.

When he made love to Clare, he was completely vulnerable to her, his soul was laid bare. Loving her cost him dearly. He lost the ability to hide behind the barrier of indifference. He couldn't love her and remain passive. Marrying Clare had been the most exhilarating experience of his life, and at the same time the most revealing. Because of Clare he could no longer hide.

The desire to run from her vanished, overpowered by his rapidly increasing need. He kissed her again and again, tentative, light kisses in the dark. Her trembling body moved against him, and soon unabated desire seared through them both.

Making soft cooing sounds, Clare broke away from him, her shoulders heaving with the effort. Then, taking his hand, she led him down the darkened hallway to her bedroom.

Moonlight dimly lit the neat, well-kept room, and Reed smiled, remembering the careless way in which Clare had discarded her clothes the night they'd exchanged their vows. He hadn't known her well enough then to appreciate how eager she'd been for him.

He knew her now. Understood her. Heaven help them both, he loved her, and where that love would lead them, he could only speculate.

Clare smiled up at him, and Reed swore her look cut clear through him. Her unselfishness, her generosity had deeply affected him. He kissed her again, taking more time, savoring each small kiss, each sigh. Together they lay upon the mattress, their breathing growing more labored. Reed trembled with impatience.

They sighed in harmony as his mouth locked over hers. Reed found it impossible to refuse her anything, least of all what he wanted most himself. Again his lips claimed hers in a lengthy, deep kiss. By mutual, unspoken agreement, they parted long enough to remove their clothes. Reed's hands shook with the urgency of the task, finishing before her. He turned to help her and soon discovered that his fumbling hands impeded the process.

Clare smiled at him in the moonlight, her eyes eager and happy. The love he felt for her in that moment was nearly his undoing. A yearning, deep and potent, gripped him. He discovered he could wait no longer—his need was too great. He wanted to explain, apologize, but he found himself incapable of doing more than steering her back toward the bed.

Afterwards neither of them spoke. Reed had never been one for words, and he found them impossible now. He needed Clare. He loved her, but he couldn't have said it, couldn't have managed it just then.

Nestled in his arms, she seemed encompassed in lassitude and close to sleep. The same way Reed was himself. He closed his eyes, content and satisfied and she nestled into his embrace and they both slept.

Shortly after dawn, Reed woke. The sun shone through a narrow slice between the drapes. Clare remained in his embrace, and the wealth of emotion he experienced being there with her produced an odd, intense pain in his heart.

He'd never known a woman like Clare. She looked small and fragile, but she had the heart of a lion and a bold, unflinching courage. There'd never been anyone in his life like her.

He wrapped his arm around her shoulders and kissed her crown, savoring her warmth and her softness. She smelled warm and feminine and his body ached with his need for her.

In an effort to divert his mind, he allowed his thoughts to wander in an attempt to judge their future together. He loved Clare more than he had dreamed it was possible to love.

The thought of anyone looking down on her because of him, of calling her the names Jack had, produced a fierce protective anger.

He'd promised himself he wouldn't touch her, vowed he'd do the right thing by her, then broken his own word. When he'd seen her at the jail, he'd wanted to grab her and shake some sense into her. Didn't she realize what she was risking by posting his bail? She opened herself up to speculation and possible ridicule and everything else Reed was looking to protect her from. She'd done it for him. She'd do it again, too. Their lives together would demand a long list of forfeits, and he wasn't sure what she had to gain.

He frowned as he carefully weighed the cost in his mind. A sense of alarm filled him, alarm that she would carry the burden of speculation because of him. He knew she'd do so willingly, without question, with the same courage and generosity that he'd witnessed in her earlier.

He couldn't do it, Reed realized in the next heartbeat.

He couldn't drag her into his world, that isolated island. She didn't belong there, and deserved much better. Nor could he join her in her world. He was who he was, and the ways of the white man had always bewildered him.

He had no option. He loved Clare, and because he did, he had to set her free.

Clare woke slowly, by degrees, more content than she could ever remember being in her life. Reed had come to her, had loved her, had spent the night with her. All night.

She had never known a man like him. They'd make love, sleep for an hour or so, then wake and make love again. It was by far the most incredible experience of her life. Clare found she could refuse him nothing. Each time they'd made love as man and wife had been different. Unique.

They hadn't talked. The communication between them had been made with sighs and moans. Quietly snuggled in each other's arms they'd lain utterly content and listened to the sounds of the night. A whispering breeze, an owl's hooting call. Clare's head had rested over Reed's heart, and she could hear the even, heavy thud of his pulse in her ear. She'd found such simple pleasure in being held by her husband.

Rolling onto her side, she scooted closer to him, intending to wrap her arm around his middle. After the tumultuous night they'd spent, she felt comfortable enough to freely touch him.

Only he wasn't there.

Clare opened her eyes, and even then she was surprised to find him gone. Surely he wouldn't have left her, not without saying something. Not without a warm goodbye. Surely he wouldn't do something so crass after what they'd shared.

She struggled out of bed, reached for her robe, and with quick steps ventured into the kitchen. Part of her was completely confident she'd find him sitting at her table sipping a cup of coffee.

Padding barefoot from one room to the next, she soon realized she was wrong. Reed was nowhere to be found. Her home was as empty as her heart.

One possible explanation piled on top of another. There could be any number of very good reasons why Reed had found it necessary to leave her.

Certain she'd missed something. She searched her home again, looking for a note, something, anything that would remove this terrible sensation of doubt and inadequacy.

Not sure what she should do, she brewed a cup of coffee and sat, holding the mug with both hands, while she collected her thoughts.

They were married. It wasn't as though he'd abandoned her, but if that was the case, then why did she feel so desolate, so...forsaken?

A glance at the clock reminded Clare that she didn't have time to lounge around her kitchen and sort through the uncertainties. Surely Reed intended to contact her at some point during the day.

She dressed, choosing a pale pink summer dress with a wide belt and pastel flowered jacket. It wasn't something she wore to work often, but dark outfits that had become her uniform looked stark and unfriendly. She kept her hair down, too, because she knew Reed liked it that way. He'd never told her so, but he seemed to take delight in removing the pins and running his fingers through its length.

All morning Clare looked for Reed. Her stomach

seemed to be upset, but she wasn't sure if it was nerves or if she was coming down with something.

It wasn't Reed who stopped in to see her. Instead, it was her mother.

Clare recognized the look her mother wore immediately. The pinched lips, the beleaguered, weary sadness in the eyes that said Clare had done something to displease her.

"Hello, Mom," Clare greeted, forcing some enthusiasm into her voice.

"I need to talk to you."

"Go ahead," she said. She hadn't been very busy, and there wasn't anyone at the front desk who required her attention. She could listen to her mother's chastisement and return books to their proper slots at the same time.

"Your father had a call from Jim Daniels this morning."

It certainly hadn't taken the stalwart deputy long to make his report, Clare noted. She'd hoped it would take two or three weeks before word of her posting Reed's bail leaked to her parents.

"Do you have anything to say?"

"Yes," Clare answered calmly. "I'm a woman now, Mother. I'm not thirteen, or eighteen or even twenty-one. I'm not a young lady to be admonished for wrongdoing."

The pinched lips tightened even more. "I see."

"I mentioned to you earlier that I was dating Reed Tonasket. He's a friend…a very good friend."

"Do you have any other friends who get themselves thrown in jail?"

"No," she agreed readily enough. "He's the first."

"Then I hope to high heaven he's the last jailbird you date."

"Personally I don't think it was an experience he's looking to repeat, either."

"I should hope not," her mother said primly. Her black handbag dangled from her arm, and when she sighed, she looked older than her years and troubled. "I can't help being concerned about you, Clare. I'm afraid you're showing signs of becoming…desperate."

"Honestly, Mother." She tried not to, but she couldn't help laughing. In an effort to understand her parent's point of view, she added, "If the circumstances were reversed I'd probably be just as worried about you. All I'm asking is that you trust my judgment." Which was asking a good deal in light of her lengthy relationship with Jack Kingston.

"Your father doesn't know what to think."

"I imagine he's concerned, and I can't say that I blame either one of you. Perhaps it would help matters if I brought Reed over so you and Dad could meet him. Once you got to know him, I'm sure you'd feel the same way I do about him."

"You're serious about this young man, aren't you?"

Clare hugged a novel against her stomach and resisted the urge to laugh. "Very serious."

Her mother's eyes moved away from Clare. "I'll check with your father and get back to you with a time."

"Thanks, Mom." If they'd been anyplace else, Clare would have been tempted to blurt out the truth. She more than liked Reed, she was crazy in love with him. If they continued in the vein they had the night before, Clare would be bleary-eyed from lack of sleep and pregnant by the end of the month.

Pregnant. The desire for children was no longer muddled in her mind. More than anything she longed to give

Reed a child. Her feelings hadn't crystallized when she took the pregnancy test. She hadn't known what she felt when the results proved negative. She'd been a bit apprehensive, then later a little sad, her emotions too confused for her to judge her true feelings.

Clare was utterly confident about what she wanted now. At one time she'd been concerned about where they'd live. Details no longer interested her. Her needs were simple—she wanted to spend the rest of her life with Reed. If he opted to continue living on the reservation, then she'd be utterly content to be there, too. If he chose to move into town, all the better. As long as they were together, nothing else mattered.

Reed came into the library just before closing time, when she least expected to see him. The first thing she noticed was that the swelling had gone down around his eye. Other than a small bruise along his jaw line, it was difficult to tell he'd been in a physical confrontation.

He set several books on top of the counter and waited until he had her attention, which he'd had from the instant he walked in the front door. Unfortunately Clare was occupied with a young mother and her two preschoolers, her last customers for the day.

Reed waited until they'd gone and Clare had locked the glass door behind them. She felt a little nervous with him. A little unsure.

She wanted to know why he'd left her that morning and why it'd taken him the entire day to come back, but she didn't feel she should make demands of him. He had his reasons, and when it came time he'd let her know what had dictated his actions.

"Hi," she said, occupying herself with the last-minute details.

"You look different."

"Thank you." She wasn't entirely sure he meant it as a compliment, but she chose to accept it as such. She lifted a heavy stack of books from the counter, prepared to move them to the large plastic bin, when Reed silently stepped in and took them from her. It was then that she noticed his knuckles. They were scraped, bruised, the skin broken. In her concern about his face, she hadn't realized his hands had taken the brunt of the fight.

"Oh, Reed," she whispered, his pain becoming her own.

He raised questioning eyes to her. His gaze followed hers before he grinned. "Don't worry, it doesn't hurt."

"But I do worry. Jack…"

"He isn't bothering you, is he?"

"No… I haven't seen him since Saturday."

"What happened Saturday?"

"Nothing." She shook her head and resumed her task.

"Clare," he repeated softly, "what happened Saturday?"

"He…stopped by the house with a diamond ring and proposed."

Reed was silent for several moments. "What did you tell him?"

"I wanted to tell him I was already married, but I couldn't very well do that, could I?" she blurted out, growing impatient with his questions. They had a lot more important issues to discuss than Jack Kingston.

"What did you say?" Reed repeated.

Clare flashed him an irritated look, one similar to what her mother had given her earlier in the day. "I told him I wasn't the right woman for him and sent him on his merry way. He doesn't love me, you know. He might have convinced himself he does, but I know better."

A smile quivered at the edges of Reed's lips.

"What's so funny?" she demanded, reaching for her purse, ready to leave.

His smile became full-fledged. "You. I imagine you're able to quell whole groups of rebellious youngsters with that look of yours."

Clare didn't bother to pretend she didn't know what he was talking about. Arguing with him would have wasted valuable time.

"Unfortunately Jack saw the totem pole you gave me and guessed that I'd spent the day with you. He was angry when he left. In thinking over what happened, I'm sure he's relieved to be off the hook. Jack never was keen on marrying me until I wanted nothing more to do with him."

Reed didn't agree or disagree with her. "We need to talk about what happened last night."

"All right," she agreed hesitantly. As far as she was concerned there wasn't anything to discuss. She walked around the front desk and sat down at one of the round tables the library had purchased that spring. There wasn't any threat of someone interrupting them since the library was technically closed and she'd secured the lock.

He didn't make eye contact with her, and that troubled Clare. It bothered her enough for her to speak before he could.

"We can discuss last night—unless you plan to tell me it was all a big mistake," she blurted out. "Because if that's why you're here, I don't want to hear it." If he attempted to trivialize their lovemaking, pass it off as unimportant, an error in judgment, then she would refuse to listen.

Reed didn't sit down. He walked past her, as if he needed time and space to form his thoughts. "You should never have posted bail for me. There's already talk."

"Talk's never bothered me. I knew when I went there what I was risking. It was my choice and I made it."

"Your parents—"

"Don't worry about them," she flared, growing impatient with him. "Stop worrying about what everyone else thinks."

"Your reputation's at stake."

"My reputation," she repeated with a small, humorless laugh. "I'm just grateful the good people in Tullue feel they have something to say about me. It's the first time in my life I've generated so much interest." This last bit was an attempt at humor, but she recognized right away that it was a mistake.

Reed's eyes darkened and his shoulders went stiff.

"I was just joking," she said, making light of her words.

"Your parents…"

"Already know," she finished for him. "Mom was in earlier this afternoon."

Reed's probing gaze searched hers. "You didn't tell her we were married, did you?"

"No, but I wish I had."

"Clare, no."

"Don't look so concerned," she said, frowning. "I told her how important you are to me…much more important than a friend."

"This isn't good," he muttered.

"I'm not ashamed of being your wife. You might prefer to keep it some deep, dark secret, but I happen to—"

"You don't know what you're talking about," he bit off gruffly. He stalked away from her, and Clare realized he was removing himself from her emotionally, as well as physically.

"I told Mom I wanted to bring you over so she and Dad could meet you," she said after a moment, doing her best to keep her voice steady.

"I wish you hadn't done that."

"Why?" she asked innocently. "We're married, Reed, and they have a right to know. I'm their only daughter."

"They don't need to know."

"What is it you want me to do?" she flared back. "Do you want me to wait until we've moved in together before I tell them? Or do you want me to get pregnant first and then casually announce we've been married all along? Is that what you want me to do? Because I find that completely unfair to everyone involved."

"Pregnant." He said the word as though he'd never heard it before.

"Okay, I get it," she continued, "they aren't going to be leaping up and down for joy to know I got married behind their backs. That's going to cause some readjustment in their thinking, but they love me and in time they'll come to love you too."

Reed whirled around to face her, his look wild, almost primitive. His eyes were narrowed and pained. She could see him steel himself against her. Against her words, against her love.

When he spoke, his words were low and harsh. "I'm afraid you've assumed too much, Clare."

"What do you mean?"

An eternity passed before he spoke. "You're not moving in with me."

"Fine, you can come into town," she said brightly, giving a small, dismissive gesture with her hands as though to suggest it made no difference to her. "That'll save me the long drive from the reservation every day, so all the better."

Even as she spoke, Clare realized she was being obtuse. Reed was trying to tell her he fully intended on following through with the divorce.

"The attorney mailed me some preliminary papers for you to read over," he said, removing an envelope from his pocket. He set it on the table in front of her.

Mutely Clare stared at the envelope. It was a plain white one, not unlike thousands of others. This particular one had the name of the law firm printed on the upper left-hand corner. It amazed Clare that something so small, so simple, could be the source of so much pain.

Her heart felt as if it had stopped completely, then she realized it continued to beat, but it was her lungs that weren't functioning. Not until it became painful did she realize she wasn't breathing.

In the past, pride had saved her, granting her the impetus to pretend she was unaffected, unscathed, unconcerned. She could rely on it to carry her for several minutes, long enough, she prayed, before she broke.

"How embarrassing," she said with a frivolous laugh, trying to make light of it. "I've just made a complete idiot of myself, haven't I?"

"Clare..."

"Don't worry, I get the picture. Despite last night you don't want to stay married to me, but an occasional bout of good old-fashioned sex wouldn't be amiss."

He looked as if he wanted to say something, but held himself in check. "If you need me for anything…"

"Be assured I won't," she told him in clipped tones. The temperature would drop below freezing in Hawaii before she'd turn to Reed Tonasket for anything.

"If you're pregnant I'd appreciate knowing it."

"Why? Are you worried that might delay the divorce proceedings?"

"Don't, Clare," he whispered, and it almost seemed he was pleading with her.

She didn't realize how badly she was trembling until she attempted to stand up. "Please go…just go."

He hesitated, his face set and hard with determination and pride. Unfortunately, Reed Tonasket wasn't the only one with an oversupply of pride. It had carried Clare this far. Her heart was shattered, her dignity in shreds, but by heaven there was a shred of pride left in her and she clung to that the way a trapeze artist hangs on to the bar.

"You're right, I'm sure. This quickie divorce is for the best."

Reed's eyes were savage, but Clare was too busy concentrating on maintaining her control to pay him much heed. "I'll let you out of the library," she said, walking to the front door, her keys jingling at her side.

Reed walked out, and she stood there watching him through the glass door until he was out of sight. Somehow she made it home; only when she was parked outside the single-family dwelling did she realize where she was. She remembered nothing about the drive.

Her neighbors were out watering their flower bed, and Mrs. Carlson gave her a friendly wave. Clare returned the gesture, walked into her house, went straight into the bathroom and lost her lunch.

Someone rang her doorbell, but Clare was too distraught to care who it could be.

A short, impatient knock was followed by a small voice. "Clare, are you here? Your car's parked out front."

Clare hurried into the living room. "Erin," she cried, and burst into tears. "I'm so glad you're home."

Ten

Erin didn't seem to know what to do. "What happened?" she asked gently, then bristled. "Don't tell me, I already know. Jack's at it again, right?"

Clare laughed, not fully understanding why she found her best friend's words so amusing. Her life was far removed from Jack Kingston's now. He was a figure from her past, and although it had been only a matter of a couple of weeks, it seemed much longer.

Clare slumped onto her sofa and gathered her feet beneath her. She was feeling ill again and weepy, and detested both. Weakness had always bothered her, but never more than in herself.

"How was the honeymoon?" she asked.

Erin brightened, sinking into the overstuffed chair across from her. "Fabulous. Oh, Clare, marriage is wonderful."

The flash of pain was so sharp that Clare closed her eyes until it passed.

"Clare?" Erin asked softly. "Are you ill?"

Clare nodded. "I…I must have come down with a bug," she murmured.

"Then this doesn't have anything to do with Jack?"

"Not a thing. It's over between us."

"You told me that when we left for Vegas, but I didn't know if you were sure."

"Trust me, I'm sure. Now tell me when you got back and why you'd waste time with me when you've got a husband at home waiting for you."

Erin crossed her long jean-clad legs and smiled. "Gary told me to get lost for a few minutes. He's got some kind of surprise brewing. My guess is that he ordered new living room furniture and is having it delivered, but I'm not supposed to know that."

"I didn't think you were due back until Saturday." Clare had hoped that by then she'd have recovered enough both physically and mentally to welcome Erin and Gary home.

Clare couldn't ever remember seeing her friend more radiant. Love had transformed Erin's life. It had transformed her own, too, but not in the same way. Loving Reed was a mistake, she tried to convince herself. Another in a long list of relationship errors. But her heart refused to listen. If loving him was just another blunder, then why was she grieving like this? When she'd broken up with Jack, there'd been a sense of release, of freedom. She felt no elation now. Only a pain that cut so deep it was nearly crippling.

"How'd you and Reed get along after the wedding?" Erin asked conversationally.

Clare tensed. "Wh-what makes you ask?"

Erin paused, her leg swinging. "You two didn't get into an argument or anything did you?"

Her lifetime friend had no idea how far the "or anything" had stretched. "No...we had a wonderful time together. I won a thousand dollars."

"Gambling!" Erin cried. "I don't believe it. Gary and I were in Vegas and I didn't so much as bet five dollars." She hesitated, and a shy, slightly chagrined smile lit up her features. "Of course we didn't leave the hotel room all that much."

The living room started to spin, and Clare scooted down on the sofa and pressed her head against the arm. "How was Boston?"

"Great. Gary's family is wonderful, which isn't any real surprise, knowing the man my husband is." She stopped abruptly and exhaled sharply. "My husband...I still can't get used to saying that. I never thought it was possible to find a man I'd love so much. I never thought it'd be possible to say the word 'husband' again and feel the incredible things I do."

Pain clenched at Clare's breast; how well she understood what Erin was saying. "Husband" was an especially amazing word to her, too.

"Then you and Reed had a chance to get to know one another a little better?" Erin continued.

For the first time that afternoon, Clare wanted to laugh out loud. "You might say that."

"Good."

"Why good?" Clare wanted to know.

"I like Reed. I never knew him very well—I don't think many folks around town do since he keeps to himself most of the time. Gary knows him about as well as anyone, and claims Reed's both talented and generous. I had no idea he was so actively involved with Native American youths. He's helped several of them over the years, kept them out of trouble, given them pride in their heritage. From what Gary said, Reed's taken in and been like a foster father to a handful of boys over the last several years."

Clare wasn't surprised, although she hadn't known that about him.

"I don't think anyone in town realizes how well-known his artwork has become all across the country, either," Erin continued. "Gary and I saw one of the totem poles he carved while we were in Boston."

"You don't need to list his virtues for me, Erin."

"I don't?" she asked, elevating her voice. "You like him?"

"Very much," Clare admitted.

"Then you wouldn't be opposed to the four of us having dinner together sometime soon? I don't want you to think I'm playing matchmaker here, but I was kind of hoping the two of you would be interested in each other."

Clare couldn't keep the sadness out of her smile. "I... don't think that would be a good idea."

"Why?" Erin returned defensively. "Because Reed's half Native American?"

"No," she returned, defeat coating her words, "because I sincerely doubt Reed wants anything more to do with me."

"That's ridiculous," Erin returned, shaking her head. "Gary said he thought Reed was attracted to you, and I absolutely agree. I saw the look in his eye right before the wedding ceremony. When a man looks at a woman like that, there's interest. In my opinion, Clare Gilroy, you should fan those flames."

"Trust me, Erin, they've been fanned."

"And?" Erin leaned forward expectantly.

"You don't want to know." Her friend was looking at the world through rose-colored glasses. Clare didn't want to drag her back to earth with the sad litany of her own problems.

"Of course I want to know. I thought something was wrong," Erin said suspiciously, then stood and walked over to where Clare was lying down. Pressing the back of her hand against Clare's forehead, she asked, "This is a whole lot more than a flu bug, isn't it?"

"Not exactly, although it's much too soon to know if I'm pregnant."

"Pregnant," Erin repeated in a weak whisper.

"Don't look so startled...you don't need to worry—I'm married. Well, sort of married. No," she said, changing her mind once more. "If I'm married enough to get pregnant then I'm more than sort of married." Clare didn't know if her friend could make sense of her words or not.

Erin flopped into her chair. "Who? When... I did hear you right, didn't I?"

"You heard me just fine." Although she was feeling dreadful, Clare sat upright. "I'm just not sure you're going to find all this believable." She held out her left hand. "The ring belongs to Reed. He gave it to me in lieu of a wedding band. We...we were married a few hours after you and Gary, although it's going to be one of the shortest marriages in Nevada history. Reed's already arranged for a divorce."

Reed straightened and wiped the sweat from his brow with the back of his forearm. His muscles ached; the low-grade throb in the small of his back seemed to be growing more intense. Nevertheless he continued working. He welcomed the discomfort, because the physical pain balanced out what he was feeling emotionally.

It'd been three days since he'd last seen Clare. The

temptation to drive into town and check on her had been nearly overwhelming. He was disciplined in every area of his life, by choice and by necessity. For both their sakes, he'd decided not to see Clare again until it was unavoidable. Until he could steel himself enough to hide his pain and ignore hers.

Clare was a survivor. She was hurting now, but that would pass, the same way his own pain would ease. Over time, prompted by pride.

They'd both needed to deal with several emotional issues, but knowing Clare, Reed was confident she'd find whatever good there'd been between them and cling to that. It was a trait he admired about her.

In the beginning he'd been amused by her Pollyanna attitude, but later he'd come to respect it as being a very special part of this woman he loved. She continually expected the best from others, and because she expected it, she often received it.

Their marriage was the exception, and that troubled Reed. She'd trusted him, believed him and given unselfishly of herself to him. His only comfort was that in the next few months, Clare would uncover something beneficial from their experience.

Reed had to believe that, had to trust in the strength of Clare's character or go insane knowing he'd hurt the one person he truly loved.

A sound of an approaching car caught his ear and he straightened, setting aside the chisel and hammer.

Coming out of his workshop, he noticed the blue sedan pulling into the parking space next to his house.

Gary Spencer.

He spied Reed about the same time, and an automatic smile lit up Gary's face. "Reed, it's good to see you."

"You, too." Marriage agreed with Gary, Reed realized immediately. "Welcome back."

"Thanks."

"Come inside and have something cold to drink." Reed led the way into the cabin, then pulled out a chair at the table for Gary to sit. "When did you get back?"

"A few days ago."

Reed opened the refrigerator and took out two cold cans of soda, tossing the first to Gary. "How's Erin?" he asked, straddling a chair himself.

"Busy, much too busy to suit me. I surprised her with some new furniture, which I'll tell you right now was a big mistake."

"How's that?"

Gary grinned. "Now she thinks the living room walls look dingy and insists we paint the room. The last few days of our honeymoon are going to be spent in the living room instead of the bedroom—the way I planned."

Reed pretended amusement. His own bride...he paused, forcefully pushing the memory of Clare sleeping in his arms from his mind. He had to carefully guard his thoughts when it came to his last evening with Clare. Indulgence came with a heavy price tag. He dared not remember the way she'd opened herself to him with generosity and love, or he'd find it impossible to stay away from her. Giving her time to heal and himself time to forget was essential for them both.

"I have to admit Erin was a good sport about it. She offered to do it herself, said she'd invite Clare Gilroy over to help. Apparently she helped Clare paint her kitchen sometime back and was going to ask her to return the favor. Unfortunately Clare's been sick, so it looks like I'm going to get stuck with the task." Gary raised the aluminum can to his lips and took a deep swallow.

Clare sick. Reed's mind raced. "Anything serious?" he asked, not wanting to reveal his immediate concern.

"I wouldn't know. From what Erin said it's some kind of flu bug. It's wiped her out."

"Has she seen a doctor?"

Gary shrugged. "I don't think so."

Reed relaxed, then tensed. He'd heard of women who suffered flulike symptoms throughout their pregnancies. His mind raced with fear and doubt. Maybe it was possible Clare was pregnant, but how possible, he didn't know. He'd hoped Clare would have the presence of mind to contact him, but in his heart he knew she wouldn't. If he wanted answers he'd have to ask.

Reed returned his attention to Gary, who was staring at him as though seeing him for the first time. His friend's shoulders sagged as he shook his head. "It's true, isn't it?"

"What's true?"

Gary hesitated, as if he were stunned and having trouble talking. "Erin came back from visiting Clare with this incredible story of the two of you marrying. Frankly, I didn't believe it."

Reed frowned. So Clare had told Erin. He wished she hadn't, but there was no help for it now.

"I don't know Clare that well," Gary continued, "but I know she's been under a lot of emotional stress over breaking up with Kingston. I thought she might have made the whole thing up."

"It's true," Reed said, standing. He walked over to the sink and looked out the window, blind to the lush green forest just beyond the house.

"The two of you were married in Las Vegas a few hours after Erin and me?"

"I said it was true." Reed's words were clipped and hard. Gary had waded into a subject Reed didn't intend to discuss.

"Why?" Gary asked incredulously.

The question angered Reed so much he stormed around to face his friend, hands clenched into fists at his side. He didn't understand how other men could be so unconscious of Clare's beauty. She was a woman of strength and courage. Generous and loving. Was the whole world blind to the obvious?

Realizing he'd traipsed onto forbidden ground, Gary swiftly changed the subject. "I heard what happened between you and Kingston. I take it he got the worst of the beating. I don't know if you heard, but he has a busted jaw. His mouth had to be wired shut."

A fitting penalty after the things he'd called Clare. Reed had taken delight in making him retract each and every one. "He'll survive."

"That was one way of making sure he doesn't go near her again. What I don't understand," Gary continued, pausing long enough to take another drink of his soda, "is if you don't want her yourself, why you'd go out of your way to cause trouble with Kingston? From what I understand he intended to marry her until you got your hands on him."

"He isn't good enough for Clare," Reed muttered. He wanted to change the subject to something more pleasant, but he discovered a certain comfort in hearing about Clare and knowing Kingston wouldn't be around to bother her again.

"If you care for her, and you clearly do," Gary said with a hint of impatience, "then why are you so quick to divorce her?"

"That's my own business," Reed said harshly.

"If there's an ironic side to this situation," Gary continued, "it's that Erin and I had talked about getting the two of you together. Neither one of us is much of a matchmaker, but there was such a strong chemistry between you two. We both felt it."

"She didn't know what she was doing when she married me," Reed said, his words low and regretful.

"She was drunk?"

Reed shook his head. "She crossed some medication with alcohol."

Gary's eyebrows folded together as he collected this latest bit of information. "That could explain what prompted Clare," Gary murmured thoughtfully, "although I have a hard time picturing her doing something so out of character."

"She was caught up in the heat of the moment," Reed explained, excusing her actions.

"Maybe that's why Clare agreed to go through with the wedding. But you were stone sober, weren't you?"

Reluctantly, Reed nodded.

A satisfied gleam entered Gary's eyes. "Then tell me, what prompted you to agree to the marriage?"

Reed knew he wasn't going to be able to stay away from Clare any longer. Knowing she was ill, suspecting she was pregnant had hounded him ever since Gary's visit earlier in the afternoon. He should be more patient, bide his time, give Clare the necessary space before he went to her.

He couldn't now. He'd nearly worn a path on the kitchen linoleum worrying about her from the moment Gary mentioned she was sick. His friend was a clever character, Reed realized. He should have known Gary had an ulterior motive, dragging Clare into the conversation. He'd casually brought up Clare's name, then waited for Reed's reaction before questioning him about the marriage.

The fact Gary was able to read him so easily told Reed his feelings for Clare remained close to the surface. If he wasn't able to hide them from Gary, then it would be next to impossible to conceal them from her.

An internal debate had warred inside him the rest of the afternoon. It wasn't until he sat down for dinner, with no appetite, that he accepted the inevitable.

He would go to her.

The need, the urgency that drove him was an additional source of concern. He wondered how long his love for her would dictate his actions, drive him to do the very things he promised himself he wouldn't. The need to protect her, to look after her remained strong, and he couldn't imagine it changing.

Not now. Not ever.

Clare guessed this was more than a simple flu bug the second day she couldn't keep anything in her stomach. She would have called her doctor to make an appointment, but didn't for the simple reason that she was too sick to go into his office.

She felt dreadful, but blamed it on a combination of ailments. Her sinus headache, not surprisingly, was back, and she was suffering from all the symptoms of an especially potent form of flu. On top of everything else the man she loved was determined to divorce her.

It was enough to put a truck driver flat on his back.

When the doorbell chimed, Clare raised her head from her pillow and groaned. She wasn't in the mood for company; she especially didn't want to be mothered, coddled or bothered.

The temptation to ignore the summons was strong, but she realized her not answering would likely cause more problems.

Heaven help her if it was Erin again, dishing up chicken soup Clare couldn't keep down, along with aspirin and plenty of juice. Erin seemed especially worried about her, but Clare wished her friend would devote her attention to Gary and leave her in peace.

The doorbell chimed again and Clare groaned. There was no help for it; she had to get up. It surprised her how weak she was, how the room refused to hold still and how much effort it took to accomplish the simplest of tasks.

She reached for her robe while her feet groped for her slippers, then paused in the doorway, afraid for a moment she was about to faint. There was a good possibility she might get over this bug if people would kindly leave her alone.

"Who is it?" she asked, her hand on the dead-bolt lock.

"Reed" came the gruff reply.

Clare closed her eyes and pressed her forehead against the door. It felt cool against her skin and oddly soothing. "Would it be possible for you to come back another time?" she asked without unlatching the door.

"No."

Somehow she guessed that. With a good deal of reluctance she turned the knob and opened the door. If he hadn't already made up his mind about the divorce, seeing her now would erase all doubt.

Clare didn't need a mirror to know she looked dreadful. Her hair hung in limp strands about her face. She was pale and sickly, hadn't brushed her teeth, and she smelled like curdled milk.

"If you need me to sign some papers from your attorney, just leave them with me and I'll see to it later," she said. Her defenses were down and she didn't have the strength to fight him.

Clare wasn't sure what she expected from Reed. A lecture, a tirade, anger or love—she was beyond guessing anymore. But having him mutter curses under his breath, then lift her into his arms and carry her back into the bedroom certainly came as a surprise.

"How long have you been sick?" he demanded, gently placing her in the center of her bed.

"I don't know that it's any of your concern," she returned with as much dignity as she could marshal, which unfortunately wasn't much.

He picked up the bottle of pills on her nightstand and read the label. "Another sinus infection?"

"No...I don't know why you're here, but if it's because I'm sick, let me assure you—"

"What did the doctor have to say?" he asked, not allowing her to finish.

"Who told you I was sick anyway?" She had a few demands of her own, and one of those included privacy. "Don't answer that, I already know. It could only have been Erin."

"It wasn't. Now for the last time what did the doctor say?"

Clare remained stubbornly silent. She closed her eyes to block him out, hoping he'd take the hint and leave. When he did walk away, she opened her eyes and blinked back tears of disappointment.

Not until she heard his voice coming from her kitchen did she realize he hadn't left her after all. She squeezed her eyes closed and tried as best she could to listen in on the telephone conversation, but Reed's voice was too low for her to hear much. She couldn't figure out who he'd called or why.

He returned looking like someone from Special Forces on a secret mission. Methodically he opened and shut her closet doors, left and then returned a couple of minutes later with her suitcase.

"What are you doing?" she demanded, trying to sit up. If the room would stop spinning like a toy top she might have been able to pull it off.

Reed didn't answer her. Instead he opened several drawers, took out a number of personal items, not stopping until her suitcase was filled.

"Reed?" she pleaded.

"I'm packing."

That much was obvious. "Where am I going?" she insisted, then softly shook her head. "More important, why am I going?"

"You're too sick to be alone" came his brusque response. "I'll be taking you to your parents' house."

"You can't."

Reed turned cool black eyes toward her. "Why not?"

"They're on a camping trip."

"All right, I'll take you to Erin and Gary's."

Clare groaned inwardly. "Don't be ridiculous. I certainly don't want to pass on this germ to them, and furthermore, I'm not keen on sleeping in the bedroom next to a couple of newlyweds."

For the first time since he had arrived, Reed hesitated. She prayed to heaven he was listening, because she didn't have the strength to reason with him.

Unfortunately, he didn't pause long. Reaching up to the top shelf of her closet, he brought down a blanket. He laid it over her, then picked her and the blanket up in one swift, easy motion.

"Reed, please don't do this."

He ignored her as he had so often.

"I'm much better really… I want to stay in my own home, my own bed. *Please.*"

He didn't hesitate, and the frustration beat down on her like war drums. She wanted to pound his chest and scream at him. He'd made it perfectly clear he wanted out of her life. Perfectly clear he regretted their marriage.

Clare didn't know what to believe any longer. She didn't know how he could hold and love her one night and casually mention divorce the next. He bewildered her, frustrated her.

At the moment, Clare's options were exceptionally limited. Despite her protests, Reed carried her outside, opened his car door and carefully deposited her in the passenger side. Before she could complain further, he went back to the house and returned with the suitcase and her purse.

"Will you kindly tell me where you're taking me?" she asked, her voice pitifully weak. He refused to answer her, his jaw as hard as granite. She might as well be reasoning with a statue for all the response he gave her.

"Reed…please tell me where you're taking me."

"Doc Brown's."

"His office has been closed for hours," she told him.

"I know. We're stopping off at his house."

"His house?" Clare couldn't believe what she was hearing. "You can't take me there. Reed, please, you just can't do that." Once again he acted as if he hadn't heard her. If she wasn't so weak, she would have cried.

"He's waiting for us."

"You talked to Dr. Brown? When?"

"Earlier. I let the library know you wouldn't be in for the rest of the week while I was at it." Each response he gave her was like a gift, Clare realized. She didn't understand why he was doing this, or why he appeared so angry. She hadn't asked him to come, didn't want his sympathy, nor was she interested in his pampering.

"You think I'm pregnant, don't you?" she asked after a few minutes. It all added up in her mind now. "It's… only been four days. I doubt I'd have this kind of reaction so quickly, so you can stop worrying."

Reed ignored her and continued driving until they reached the physician's residence.

He left her in the car while he went to the front door and rang the doorbell. Dr. Harvey Brown answered himself. Clare watched as the two men shook hands. Apparently they were acquainted with each other.

Reed returned to the car a moment later and carried Clare into the house, taking her through the entrance and down a picture-lined hallway to what she assumed was the doctor's den. Reed gently placed her in a black leather chair beside the desk.

"Hello, Clare," Dr. Brown greeted, his eyeglasses perched on the end of his nose as he gazed down on her.

"I understand you haven't been feeling well." Before she could answer him one way or the other, he stuck a thermometer under her tongue.

Reed stood in one corner of the room, with his arms crossed. The physician removed his stethoscope from his small black bag. Next he opened Clare's robe and gown enough to press the cold metal over her heart. He waited a few moments, and then, seemingly satisfied, he removed the instrument from his ears.

"I understand you're the one who shut up Jack Kingston," he said, glancing briefly to Reed.

Reed nodded. "We had a difference of opinion."

Dr. Brown grinned. "It's about time someone put that boy in his place."

Reed didn't respond, but Clare thought she detected a slight smile. She continued to watch the play between the two men. Meanwhile Dr. Brown continued his examination, then asked Clare a list of questions having to do with her symptoms.

"Does she need to be hospitalized?" Reed asked, after several moments.

"Don't be ridiculous," Clare flared. She had the flu, but she wasn't that sick.

"That depends on what kind of home care she'll be getting."

"Would you both stop it," she said, straightening in the high-backed leather chair. "If you want to give me your diagnosis, Doc, do so, but I'm not a child and I'd appreciate your talking to *me*."

Clare noted how Reed's gaze connected with that of the physician. They both seemed to find her small outburst cause for amusement.

"First of all," Dr. Brown said, turning to Clare, "I want to know why you didn't come into my office earlier?"

"I couldn't," she told him a bit defensively. "I was too sick."

"Did you talk to my nurse?"

"No," she admitted reluctantly.

"Next time, young lady, you call in and talk to Doris, understand?"

To her mother she was a young lady, to Dr. Brown she was a young lady. Why did everyone insist upon treating her like a child when she was a woman? Even Reed seemed to think she needed a keeper.

"I'm mainly concerned about her keeping down fluids. She's…you're nearly dehydrated now. If that happens I won't have any choice but to admit you."

"I'll make an effort to drink more," Clare assured him. She hadn't realized she was so sick. She *knew* she was ill, of course, just not how ill.

"I don't imagine this bug will hold on longer than a couple more days. It'll take another week or more for you to regain your strength." Although he was talking to her, Dr. Brown was looking at Reed, which infuriated her even more when he'd completely excluded her from the conversation.

"I'll be a picture of health in another week or so," she announced tartly.

"I don't like the idea of her being alone."

"She won't be," Reed said without looking at Clare. "I'm taking her home with me."

Eleven

Clare was silent during the forty-minute drive to Reed's cabin, knowing it wouldn't do any good to argue with him. His mind was set and she'd bumped against that stubborn pride of his enough to know it'd be useless to try to reason with him.

Throughout the endless trip, Clare felt Reed's gaze upon her, but she paid no heed. Understanding this man was beyond her. She didn't know what to think anymore, and feeling as rotten and weak as she did, she wasn't in any shape to accurately interpret his actions.

Perhaps he felt responsible for her. Despite his best efforts to rush into their divorce, they remained legally married. Her guess was that he considered it his duty to nurse her back to health. Whatever his reason, Clare was past caring. He'd made his intentions clear enough. He wanted out of her life, out of their marriage, and had done his level best to be sure she understood.

Now this. Clare was more confused than ever.

When Reed pulled into his yard, he parked his car close to the house. Before she could do more than open the car door, he was there, lifting her in his arms as if she weighed no more than a child.

"I can walk," she protested.

He ignored her objection, as she knew he would, and carried her into his home. He paused in the entryway, seemingly undecided as to exactly where he should take her. After a moment, he headed into the living room and gently deposited her onto the thick cushions of the sofa.

Clare lay back and closed her eyes. Although she'd slept a good portion of the day, the jaunt into town to see Dr. Brown and the drive to Reed's home had exhausted her.

Before retrieving her suitcase, Reed brought her a thick blanket and a pillow. When he'd finished covering her, he stepped back. Her eyes remained closed, but Clare profoundly felt his presence standing over her, watching her. With anyone else she would have felt edgy and uncomfortable, but oddly, with Reed, it felt as if she were nestled in his arms.

Clare had learned more than one painful lesson trying to decipher Reed's actions. She dared not trust her feelings. He didn't want her. Didn't need her. Didn't love her.

With her heart crushed under the weight of her pain, Clare kept her eyes closed, not believing for a moment that she would sleep. Almost immediately she could feel herself drifting toward the beckoning arms of slumber. She resisted as long as she could, which was a pitifully short time, then surrendered.

She stirred later, not knowing how long she'd slept. The sun was low in the sky and the wind whispered through the trees in an enchanted chorus.

Her gaze found Reed in the kitchen, standing before

the stove, stirring a large pot. He must have sensed she was awake, because he turned and glanced at her.

For a moment their eyes met. Clare looked away first, fearing her unguarded glance would reveal her love. She was with him under protest and only because he felt some ridiculous responsibility to take care of her.

"How long have I been asleep?" she asked, struggling with the weight of the blanket to sit upright.

"An hour or so."

It had felt like a few minutes. She should have realized it was longer, since the sun was setting. Bronze rays of light slanted toward the earth, bouncing back.

"I'm making you soup."

The thought of food terrorized her stomach. "Don't. I'm not the least bit hungry."

It was as though she'd told him how excited she was at the prospect of dinner. He set a large bowl of the steaming soup at the table, along with a cup of tea and a glass of water and then came for her.

"I...I don't think I'll be able to keep it down," she confessed weakly.

"You can try." Tucking his arm around her shoulders, he helped her upright. At least he wasn't carting her to the table as if she were an ungainly sack of potatoes, granting her one small shred of dignity.

The soup was thick with vegetables, homemade and delicious. Clare was surprised by how good it tasted. After three days of being so violently ill, her appetite was practically nil, but she did manage five or six spoonfuls. When she finished, she placed her hands in her lap.

"Would you like a bath?" Reed asked. He stood beside her and brushed a thick strand of hair away from her face. His fingers were as light and gentle as his voice.

For the first time since he entered her home, he wasn't bullying and browbeating her. A part of Clare wanted to resist him at every turn, prove he wasn't the only one with an abundance of pride. He might insist upon nursing her, but by heaven she wouldn't be a willing patient.

"A bath?" she repeated slowly. Her strength to fight him vanished completely. "I'm a mess, aren't I? My hair…"

His eyes delved into hers. "No, Clare, you aren't."

It would take a better liar than Reed to convince her otherwise. As though reading her thoughts, he stood, cupped her face in his hands and gazed down on her.

"I was just thinking," he said, and his voice sounded strangely unlike his own, "that I've never seen a woman I've wanted more."

Clare turned her face from his, battling tears. Leave it to Reed to say something sweet and romantic when she looked her absolute worst. Emotions churned inside her and, sniffling, she rubbed the back of her hand under her nose.

"I'll see to your bath," he said, leaving her.

Taking time to collect herself, Clare gathered the blanket around her and moved down the hallway to find Reed sitting on the edge of the tub, adjusting the water temperature.

"I can get my things," she offered, "if you tell me where you put my suitcase."

"It's in the first bedroom on the right," Reed instructed, then stood to help her.

"I can do it," she assured him with a weak smile. "Don't look so worried."

He hesitated a moment, then nodded.

Clare traipsed down the hall, following Reed's instructions. Pausing in the doorway of the bedroom, she realized this wasn't the guest room, as she suspected it would be, but Reed's own. His presence was stamped in every detail, from the dark four-poster bed to the braided rug that covered the floor.

"I'll be sleeping in the guest bed," he explained, scooting past her. He lifted her suitcase onto the mattress and opened it for her, removing a fresh gown.

Clare didn't understand. It made no sense to her that he would give up his own bed. As if reading her thoughts, he explained. "It's more comfortable in here and closer to the bathroom."

"I know but..." Before she could finish, he left the room as if he were as bereft to explain why he'd opted to give her his own bed as she was to understand why.

Sighing, Clare wandered back to the bathroom. Reed was there, sorting through a cupboard. He removed an armful of fresh towels.

"Thank you," she said, and waited for him to leave. It soon became apparent he had no intention of doing so.

"Trust me, I can bathe myself," she informed him primly.

His returning smile was roguish. "You're sure about that?"

"Of course, I'm sure."

"You aren't going to show me anything I haven't seen before," he took delight in reminding her.

Clare felt the color seep into her cheeks. This seemed to amuse him, and, chuckling, he took her by the shoulders, kissed her softly on her cheek and left. The door remained open, but only a crack so he'd be sure to hear her if she were to call for him.

Clare undressed slowly, leaving her clothes in a heap on the floor. The steaming hot water felt heavenly. Sighing, she sank down as far as she could, closed her eyes and leaned back in the tub. Clare didn't know how long she soaked.

"Need me to wash your back?" Reed asked from the other side of the door.

"I most certainly do not."

He chuckled, and she heard him walk away, leaving her to her pleasure. Sinking low in the tub, Clare rested her head against the porcelain base. Slowly a smile came to her.

Reed stood at the end of the bed, watching Clare, who was fresh from her bath. He knew he should leave her to rest, but found himself unable to walk away. She was small and incredibly fragile. And so beautiful she took his breath away.

He invented reasons to touch her, to stay with her, to make himself useful so he'd have an excuse for being there. She'd washed her hair and sat amidst a pile of pillows with a thick towel piled on top of her head.

"I can't remember when I've enjoyed a bath more," she said as she unwound the towel and set it aside.

She must have enjoyed it. Reed swore she'd been in the bathroom a solid hour. Every time he'd gone to check on her, she'd shooed him away, insisting she was fine.

Her hair was all tangled, and after attempting to free the strands with her fingers, she reached for her brush, tugging it through the length. He paused, wanting to offer to comb it for her, but hesitated, knowing she'd have trouble surrendering even the smallest task to him.

"I can do this," she assured him, but it became clear to him after the first few strokes of the brush that the effort exhausted her.

"Let me," he volunteered readily, glad for the excuse

to linger. He knelt on the edge of the bed. The mattress dipped with his weight.

After a moment's hesitation, Clare handed him the brush and then twisted so that her back was to him. Her hair was thick and tangled, and he painstakingly worked the brush through the matted strands, being careful not to hurt her unnecessarily.

His hand was steady and sure, but his thoughts were in chaos, tormenting him. It didn't take him long to realize that volunteering for this small intimacy had been a mistake. His gut knotted as desire flooded his veins. Clare was sick; it was lucky she hadn't ended up in the hospital. He cursed himself for his weakness and continued brushing, hoping she wouldn't guess his thoughts.

Clare's head moved in the direction of the brush as though her neck were boneless. When he heard her soft sigh, Reed knew she was enjoying this small intimate exchange as much as he was himself.

Every cell in Reed's body had stirred to life. He'd scooted further up on the bed than he intended, and Clare's back was pressed full against his chest. When he'd packed her suitcase, he'd purposely chosen a flannel nightgown, wanting to keep temptation at bay. He realized too late that even the sexless gown couldn't conceal her exquisite shape. His hand tightened around the brush as he struggled with himself. Reed had never thought of himself as a weak man. Not until he'd married Clare, that was.

The ache to touch her, to taste her, grew so intense Reed's hand stilled. "I think that should do it," he said. He pulled away from her, although he'd never wanted to make love to her more as he did right then. The ache in him was physical, but he couldn't take advantage of her now when she was ill, despite the fact they were man and wife and she was sleeping in his bed.

"Thank…you." Clare's voice was small as she scooted down in the warm blankets. "I…feel better than I have in days."

Grumbling to himself, Reed left the room. She might feel better, but he certainly didn't.

Clare woke the following morning feeling greatly improved. After being so wretchedly sick, all her body needed now was time to recover. She realized she was hungry, and wondered if Reed was up and about. If not, she'd fix herself something to eat and him, too.

Her suitcase revealed a pair of jeans and a sweater, which she slipped on, grateful to be out of the flannel gowns that had made up her wardrobe the past several days.

The act of dressing weakened her, and, discouraged, she sat on the edge of the bed and regrouped before heading for the kitchen.

Reed was there, in front of the stove, cooking eggs. He smiled warmly when he saw her.

"Morning," she said a bit shyly.

"Did you sleep well?"

Clare nodded, almost embarrassed by how soundly she had slept. She didn't know where Reed had spent the night and felt mildly guilty that she had put him out of his own bed. And disappointed that he'd opted to sleep elsewhere instead of with her.

"You look like you might be feeling a little better," he said as he cracked an egg into a pan of simmering water.

"I feel almost human."

"Good. I've made you some tea and there's eggs and toast. Fruit, too, if you'd like some."

His thoughtfulness brought a curious ache to her heart. That he would so painstakingly care for her physically and think nothing of devastating her emotionally baffled Clare. He seemed to genuinely care for her, although it was difficult for her to judge the depth of his feelings. Every time she dared to hope, to believe he might want to keep their marriage intact, she'd been bitterly disappointed.

Clare was through second-guessing Reed. She'd take it one day at a time and wait him out, she decided.

"Sit down and I'll bring you breakfast," he told her.

Clare sat at the table and he carried over a plate with poached eggs on dry toast. The meal was heavenly. Sitting across from her with his own plate, Reed seemed to enjoy watching her eat.

"Will you be all right by yourself for an hour or so?" he asked when she'd finished.

"Of course."

"I need to run a couple of errands," he explained, carrying her dishes to the sink. "Do you need anything from town?"

She answered him with a small shake of her head.

It occurred to Clare that she should ask him to take her with him. It was apparent the worst of her malady had passed. She had no right to infringe on his hospitality longer than necessary, but he said nothing, and Clare didn't offer.

If he wanted her there with him, then she was content to stay. No matter what it cost her later. There would be a price, Clare realized, but one she would willingly pay.

Reed left shortly afterward, after setting her up on the sofa in the living room. She sat for a time, content to read and enjoy the morning.

The sun came out, bathing the scenery in a golden glow.

After having been cooped up inside for several days, Clare felt the need to breathe in the fresh scent of the morning. Although it was warm, she reached for Reed's light jacket and moved onto the front porch. She stood there for several moments, her arm wrapped around the post for support, surveying Reed's world. It was peaceful, still.

The morning was glorious, and before she even realized her intent, Clare moved off the porch and down the pathway that led to Reed's workshop. Continuing along the trail, she discovered a small lake. Sitting on a stump, she breathed in the beauty of the world surrounding her.

Clouds, like giant kernels of popped corn, dotted the sky, while an eagle lazily soared above her, the sun on its wing. Clare wasn't aware of how long she sat there; not long, she guessed. Time lost meaning as she closed her eyes and listened to the sounds of the forest. Squirrels chattered and scooted up the trees. Bluebirds chirped irritably and fluttered along the trail with gold finches and swallows.

"Clare." Reed's voice had a desperate edge to it.

"I'm here," she shouted back, surprised by how weak her voice sounded.

He came down the path, half trotting, and stopped when he saw her. His relief was evident and Clare realized she should have left him a note. She would have if she'd known where she was headed.

"It's so peaceful here," she said, not wanting him to be angry with her.

He moved behind her and cupped her shoulders. "I love it, too."

"I feel better for being here… I feel almost well."

She was improving each hour. Her body drank in the sunshine and fresh clean air the way a sponge does water.

"Did you finish your business in town?" she asked, looking up at him.

Reed nodded. "I let Erin and Gary know you were with me and why."

Clare wondered if their newly married friends had offered to care for her themselves and guessed they hadn't. If anything, they seemed to encourage the romance between her and Reed.

"Let's get you back before you exhaust yourself."

Clare didn't want to leave this enchanted spot on the edge of the thick evergreen forest, but she realized Reed was right. He wrapped his arm around her as though he suspected she wasn't strong enough to make it all the way on her own. It amazed her how accurately he was able to judge her limited strength.

By the time they reached the house, she was shaking and fatigued, although it was only a short distance.

"I think I'll rest," she murmured, heading toward the bedroom.

Reed gave her a few moments, then came into the room. Her head was nestled in the thick down pillow. He laid his hand on her hair. "Sleep."

Clare smiled, doubting that she'd be able to stay awake much longer. Her eyes drifted closed. "Tonight... I'll sleep in the guest bed."

"You'll stay exactly where you are," Reed whispered. "It's where you belong." He stayed with her until she was asleep, at least Clare assumed he did. Her fingers were laced with his and his hand brushed the hair from her brow until she became accustomed to the feel of his callused palm against her smooth skin.

When Clare woke, the house was quiet. She went into the kitchen and glanced at the clock, surprised she'd slept so long. Reed was nowhere in sight, but she guessed he was probably in his shop, working. Pouring them each a cup of coffee, she carried it to the outbuilding.

"Hello," she said, standing in the open doorway. She'd guessed correctly. Reed was working, his torso gleaming with sweat, his biceps bulging as he chiseled away at the thick cedar log. She found his progress remarkable. When he'd first shown her the project, she'd barely been able to make out the shape of the three figures. The thunderbird in particular caught her eye now. The beak and facial features of the creature were vivid with detail.

"You're awake."

"I feel like all I've done is sleep." Clare resented every wasted moment, wanting to spend as much time as she could with Reed.

"Your body needs the rest." He set aside his tools and took the mug out of her hand.

"Are you hungry?" he asked, sipping from the edge of the earthenware cup.

She shook her head. "Not in the least."

Reed leaned against a pair of sawhorses and drank his coffee, grateful, it seemed, for the break. Not wanting to detain him from his job, Clare took his empty mug when he'd finished, and prepared to head back to the house.

Reed stopped her, his gaze finding hers. Then he bent over and found her mouth with his. The kiss was as gentle as it was sweet, a brushing of lips, an appreciation.

When they pulled apart, Clare blinked several times, feeling disoriented and lost. She must have swayed toward him, because Reed caught her by the shoulders and smiled down on her with affectionate amusement.

It nettled her that she should be so unsettled by their kissing when Reed appeared so unaffected. Confused, she backed away from him. "I'll…I'll go back now," she said, and twisted around.

Clare was still shaking when she returned to the house. Standing at the sink, she tried to put their kiss into perspective. It had been a spontaneous reaction, a way of thanking her for bringing him coffee. She dared not read anything more into it than he intended; the problem was knowing what that was. In clear, precise terms, he'd assured her he meant to follow through with the divorce. She had to accept that because she dared not allow herself to believe he wanted them to stay married.

Clare was on the sofa, reading, when Reed came inside the house a couple of hours later. She glanced up and smiled, now used to seeing him shirtless and wearing braids. It was as though he had stepped off the pages of a Western novel. She recalled the morning following their wedding, how taken aback she'd been by the reminders of his heritage. No longer. To her mind he was proud and noble. She'd give anything to go back to that first morning in Vegas.

"Gary's on his way," Reed announced.

Clare frowned. "H-how do you know?"

"I can hear his car. My guess is that Erin's with him."

It was on the tip of Clare's tongue to suggest she ride back into town with her friends. She was much improved. The worst of the flu had passed, and other than being incredibly weak, she was well. But she didn't offer, and Reed didn't suggest it.

Within a couple of minutes of Reed's announcement, Clare heard the approaching vehicle herself, although she wouldn't have been able to identify it as Gary's car.

Reed had washed his hands and donned a shirt, although he'd left it unbuttoned. By the time the sound of the car doors closing reached her, Reed had opened the front door and stepped onto the porch.

Erin came into the cabin like a woman scorned. "I told you you were sick," she fumed, hands on her hips. "But would you listen to me? Oh, no, not the mighty Clare Gilroy. Reed told me what Dr. Brown said… I should have your hide for this, Clare. You could have died."

Erin had always possessed a flair for the dramatic, Clare reminded herself. "Don't be ridiculous."

"You nearly ended up in the hospital."

"I know… I was foolish not to have made an appointment earlier. I certainly hope you didn't drive all this way just to chastise me."

"I wouldn't bet on it." Gary appeared in the doorway, grinning. "She's been fuming ever since Reed stopped by this morning."

"I'm much better," Clare assured her friend. "So stop worrying."

As though Erin wasn't sure she should believe Clare, she looked to Reed.

"She's slept a good portion of the day. Her fever is down and she ate a good breakfast."

Erin sighed expressively, walked farther into the living room and sat on the end of the sofa. "Your face has a little color," she said, examining her closely.

Clare didn't know if that was due to her improved health or the result of Reed's kiss. "I'll be good as new in a few days," Clare assured her friend.

Gary and Reed were talking in the background. Reed walked over to the refrigerator, took out two cans of cold soda and handed one to Gary.

"So?" Erin whispered, glancing over her shoulder. "How's it going with Reed?"

"What do you mean?"

"You know," Erin whispered forcefully. "Have you two…made any decisions about the divorce?"

Clare's gaze moved from Erin to the two men chatting in the kitchen. "No…it's up to Reed."

"He isn't going to follow through with it," Erin said confidently. "Not now."

"What makes you think that?" Clare dared not put any credence into Erin's assessment, but she couldn't help being curious.

"From the way he looks at you. He loves you, Clare, can't you see it?"

Frankly she couldn't. "Then why does he…"

"Think about it," Erin said impatiently. "Why else would he have hauled you to Doc Brown's house, then carted you home with him? It's obvious he cares."

"He feels morally responsible for me."

"Hogwash."

Erin and Gary stayed for a little more than an hour and then left. Clare walked out to the porch with Reed to see off the newlyweds. When Reed slipped his arm across her shoulders, she drank in his warmth and his strength and smiled up at him.

Reed's gaze narrowed as he studied her, and then without either of them saying a word, Reed took her in his arms. They kissed long and hard, drinking their fill, standing there on the front porch.

"I've wanted to do that all day," Reed admitted, burying his face and his hands in her hair.

"I've wanted you to kiss me, too."

His arm circled her waist, and as he lifted her from the porch, he brought her mouth back to his. Clare didn't need further encouragement. She looped her arms around his neck and sighed with pleasure.

"I need you, Reed," she whispered, running her tongue around the shell of his ear.

Reed shuddered. "Clare, no."

"I'm your wife."

He shook his head adamantly. "You've been sick."

"Make me well." Her hands framed his face as he brought his mouth back to hers. "I need you so much."

"Clare," he groaned her name.

She kissed him again and he moaned once more. "You don't play fair."

"Does that mean you're going to make love to me?"

"Yes," he whispered, his voice low and husky. He carried her into the bedroom, and Clare swore he didn't take any more than a few steps.

Their lovemaking was completely different than it had been at any other time in their relationship. When they'd finished, Reed held her close. Clare buried her face in his shoulder as she sobbed uncontrollably.

Twelve

Reed comforted Clare as best he knew how. He was at a loss to understand her tears, and not knowing what to say, he gently held her against him until the sobs had abated.

"Can you tell me now?" he asked, his voice a shallow whisper.

She shook her head. "Just hold me."

He rubbed his hand across her back, caressing her smooth, velvet skin, and waited. After several moments it dawned on him from the even rise and fall of her shoulders that Clare was asleep.

Asleep!

One moment she was whimpering and confused and the next she was snoozing. A smile came to him as he tucked her more securely in his arms and closed his eyes. Twenty years from now he doubted that he'd understand Clare. He'd thought he knew her, assumed...

Twenty years from now... The words echoed in the silent chamber of his mind. At some time over the past few weeks, he didn't know when, he'd accepted that their lives were irrevocably linked.

Only a fool would try to turn back now. Only a fool would believe it was possible to walk away from Clare.

Clare was his wife. At some point she'd ceased being Clare Gilroy, and he accepted that she was his future. The woman who filled the emptiness of his soul. The one who would heal his bitterness and erase his skepticism.

He didn't know how it would happen, but he trusted that his love for her and hers for him would make a way where his humanness found none.

The time had come for him to wipe out the past and start anew. To forgive those who had wronged him. The time had come for him to get on with his life. He couldn't love Clare and remain embittered and hostile.

Lying there with his wife in his arms, Reed felt as if the shackles were removed from his heart. He was free. Emotion tightened his chest as he recalled the time as a youth when he'd been passed over by the tribal leaders, his talent ignored by the elders. He recalled the incident as if it were only a few days past, and once again anger gripped him.

It was their rejection that had set the course of his life, that had cast his fate as an artist. From the tender age of fourteen onward he'd decided to resurrect the art of carving totem poles. He'd made a good living because of this one slight. His name was becoming well-known across the country, and all because Able Lonetree had received the award Reed had deserved.

Good had come from this unfairness, and for years Reed had been blind to that. He'd held himself apart from his tribe, the same way he'd held himself apart from his mother's people.

The local paper had wanted to write an article about him after the piece had appeared on him in the regional magazine. Reed had declined, preferring to maintain his anonymity with the good people of Tullue.

His reputation as a rebel was the result of an incident that happened when he was nineteen. A fight. He'd stumbled upon two of the high school's athletes bullying a thin, pale-faced youth. Reed had stepped in on the boy's behalf. A fight had broken out, two against one. Eventually they were pulled apart, but when questioned, the youth Reed had been defending changed his story and Reed was arrested for assault.

No doubt the rumors about him would be fed by his recent confrontation with Jack Kingston. So be it. In time, he'd make his peace with Tullue, Reed decided. He wasn't sure how, but he imagined Clare would aid him in this area, too.

A sigh lifted his chest. He felt as though a great burden had been taken from him. He recalled his grandfather and the wisdom handed down to him as a boy. He didn't appreciate what his grandfather had told him about hunting until he'd fallen in love with Clare.

The man who'd raised him had taught Reed to trap and hunt. It was the way of the Skyutes, but each spring and summer they fished instead. Reed could hear his grandfather as if he were standing at the foot of the bed. There was no way in the world a man could mate and fight at the same time. Other than the obvious meaning, Reed had assumed his grandfather was also referring to trapping. Animals couldn't raise their young if they were being hunted. The logic of this was irrefutable, but Reed understood a greater wisdom.

He couldn't love Clare and maintain his war with the world. He couldn't love Clare and live in isolation. He could no longer maintain his island.

As quietly as he could, Reed slipped from the bed, not wanting to disturb Clare. He dressed and wandered barefoot into the kitchen. His first inclination was to wake her and tell her of his decision. There were a large number of items they would need to discuss. First and foremost was her family.

The burden that had so recently left him came to weigh upon his shoulders once again. Clare had told him she'd spoken to her parents about him. At one point, she'd confessed to dating him. But Reed knew dating was one thing, marriage was something else again.

With a sick kind of dread he recalled the reaction his mother's family had had to his parents' marriage. Even in her greatest hour of need, her family had turned their backs on the two of them.

Reed sensed they might have experienced a change of heart following her death, but he wanted nothing to do with them. As a teenager he'd received a letter from the grandmother he'd never known, which he'd read and promptly destroyed. For the life of him he couldn't remember the contents of the letter. He hadn't answered, and she'd never written again.

The thought of Clare being forced to give up her family because of him troubled Reed. If bridges were to be built, he'd have to be the one to construct them. For Clare's sake he'd do it; for the sake of their children, he'd find a way to make their love acceptable to the Gilroys.

Their children. The two words had a profound effect upon Reed. He scooted a chair away from the table, sat down and pressed his elbows against the wood surface. He'd barely become accustomed to the idea of marriage, and already he was looking into the future.

Children.

He wanted a son, yearned for this child Clare would give him. Frowning, he realized his attitude was chauvinistic in the extreme. When the time came for them to have a family, there was every likelihood that their love would produce a daughter.

The instant surge of delight that filled him with the prospect of a girl child came as something of a surprise. His mind envisioned a little girl, a smaller version of Clare, and Reed experienced the same intense longing as he had imagining a son.

The future had never seemed more right.

A sound from the bedroom told him Clare was awake. The water on top of the stove was hot and he brewed her a cup of tea, taking it into the bedroom with him.

Clare was sitting up, the blanket tucked around her front.

"Hello, Sleeping Beauty," he said, sitting on the edge of the mattress. He set the tea on the nightstand and leaned forward to kiss her.

He tasted her resistance, which took him by surprise. Clare had always been so open, welcoming his touch.

"Do you want to tell me what's wrong?" he asked.

With her eyes lowered, she shook her head.

Needing to touch her, he brushed the hair from her face. "I shouldn't have allowed us to make love," he said, blaming himself for any unnecessary discomfort he might have caused her. She was barely over her bout with the flu and he was dragging her into his bed, making physical demands on her. He couldn't be around Clare and not desire her.

Thirty years from now it would be the same. Reed wasn't sure how he knew this, but he did. He'd be chasing her down the hall of a retirement center.

"You're right," she said, emotion tattering the edges of her words. "That shouldn't have happened."

Regret? Was that what he heard in her voice? Reed didn't know. He scooted off the bed and aimlessly strolled to the far side of the room.

"I…I want to go home," she announced.

It was on the tip of his tongue to tell her that she *was* home, but intuitively he realized now wasn't the time. The determined, stubborn slant of her jaw assured him of a good deal more. They wouldn't be able to discuss anything of importance in her present mood.

"I'll pack my things. I'd appreciate it if you'd drive me back to Tullue."

Reed said nothing.

"If you'd leave I'd get dressed." It sounded as if she were close to tears, and not knowing what to say to comfort her, Reed left.

Reed felt at a terrible loss. He'd never told a woman he loved her, and he feared the moment he opened his mouth he'd blunder the whole thing.

Clare appeared a few minutes later, her suitcase in her hand. Once again her eyes refused to meet his.

Reed stepped forward and took the lightly packed bag out of her grasp. He had to say something before she left him. Nervously he cleared his throat. "My grandfather told me something years ago. I didn't realize the significance of it until recently. It had to do with the reasons our tribe fished during the summer months."

Clare cast him an odd, puzzled look.

Reed tensed and continued. "Grandfather claimed a man couldn't fight and mate at the same time."

An empty silence followed his words, and Reed realized he'd botched it just the way he'd feared. Clare continued to glare at him.

"We aren't fighting," Clare said.

"Not fight," he assured her quickly, "but talk."

Her eyes drifted shut, and after a moment she sighed and shook her head. "I don't know what more there is for us to say."

She was wrong, but Reed didn't know how to tell her that without invoking her wrath. He searched for a possible excuse to keep her with him. "Don't you think we should pick up another one of those test kits before you traipse back into town?"

"Test kits?" she asked, scowling. Pain flashed across her features. "Oh, I see you're afraid I'm pregnant."

"Afraid isn't the word, Clare."

"Terrified then."

"No," he countered. "I'd like it if we had children together. I was thinking about this while you were sleeping and I realized how very pleased I'd be if you were pregnant."

"Pleased," Clare cried. "Pleased! No doubt that would feed your pride if I—"

"Clare," he said, losing his patience, "I love you. I'm not looking to bolster my ego. Yes, I want children, but we'll only have them if it's what you want, too. It just seemed to me that as my wife…" He stopped midsentence at Clare's shocked expression. "Clare," he said her name gently, not knowing what to think.

She burst into tears and covered her face with both hands.

If he lived to be an old man, Reed decided then and there, he'd never understand women. He'd thought, he'd hoped this was what she wanted, too, to share his life, his home, his future.

He guided her to a chair and left her long enough to retrieve several tissues from the bathroom. Squatting down in front of her, he pressed the tissues into her limp hand. It was then that he noticed she'd removed the turquoise ring he'd given her the night they were married.

She'd been wearing it earlier that day. He found it interesting that she would continue to wear the bulky piece of jewelry when it was so obviously ill suited to a woman's hand. He had his mother's wedding band and he'd thought to give her that.

If she intended to stay in the marriage.

Perhaps Clare had experienced a change of heart and decided she wanted out. It would be just like fate to kick him in the face when he least expected it.

"You want me to be your wife?" she asked between sobs. Clenching the tissue in her fist, Clare leveled her gaze on him.

"You are my wife, or had you forgotten?" It was difficult to keep the frustration out of his voice.

"I've never forgotten…you were the one who contacted the attorney…who insisted from the very first that we take the necessary measures to correct the…mistake."

Their gazes held. Reed stood the full length of the kitchen away from her. "Was marrying me a mistake?"

"At first I wasn't sure," she admitted softly. "Everything seemed so right in Vegas. I felt as though I'd been waiting all my life for you."

"And later?"

"Later…the morning after, I didn't stop to think. It seemed to me, after we were married, the deed was done. I didn't once consider the right or wrong of it. It never entered my mind that a married couple would entertain regrets quite so soon."

"You didn't know what you were doing," Reed reminded her forcefully, regretting having brought up the subject of their wedding. Each time he did, he felt as though he'd taken advantage of her.

"But I did know what I was doing," she countered. "You make it sound like I was drugged or something. Let me assure you right now, I wasn't. No matter what you say about me crossing my medication with alcohol, I was fully aware of my actions. If I was behaving out of character there were...other reasons."

"Kingston," Reed muttered under his breath. Clare had ended a three-year dead-end relationship with the other man. Reed should have realized much sooner that had dictated her actions.

She must have been near giddy with relief to have Kingston out of her life and desperate that no one else would ever want her. A sickening feeling clawed at his stomach. Just when he'd squared everything in his mind, he found another excuse for Clare to want out of their marriage.

"Yes," she agreed hesitantly, "I think breaking up with Jack had something to do with it, too." Reed hadn't realized she'd heard him say the other man's name. "I've often wondered what you must have thought when I suggested we marry," she continued slowly. "Surely you knew I'd broken up with Jack. I was absolutely certain no man would ever want me again. If you're looking to fault me for anything, fault me for that."

He nodded and buried his hands deep in his pockets.

"I've never understood why you agreed to marry me," she said softly, smearing a trail of tears across her cheek.

"You can question my motivation with good reason. But it doesn't help me understand why you agreed to marry me."

Reed went motionless. It was the same question Gary had posed the other day, the one Reed had skillfully avoided answering. He could steer around his friend's inquisitiveness, but not Clare's.

Reed was a proud man. He'd never given his heart to a woman, but it seemed to him that if he was willing to spend the rest of his natural life with her then he should be equally amenable to confessing the truth.

"Why'd you agree to marry me?" Clare asked him a second time.

"I loved you then just as much as I do now," Reed admitted stiffly.

His words were met with a stunned silence. "But we barely knew one another," Clare argued. "You couldn't possibly have loved me."

Reed lowered his gaze. "There's a library on the reservation, Clare. Every visit I ever made to the Tullue library was to see you, to be close to you, even if it was only for a few minutes."

Her eyes revealed her shock. "But you never said more than a few words to me."

"I couldn't. You were dating Kingston."

"But…" She stood, then sat down again as though she needed something stable to hold her. "Why? You didn't even know me… You don't honestly expect me to believe you were in love with me, do you?"

"It was your eyes," he told her softly, "so serious, so sincere. I saw fire there, hidden passion."

"You've since proved that to be true," she muttered, and her cheeks flushed crimson.

"I saw joy in you. Your spirit is fragile, it is even now. It was why I named you Laughing Rainbow."

"Laughing Rainbow," Clare repeated slowly, then looked to him once more. "The totem pole you gave me... the top figure is a rainbow."

Reed smiled, pleased that she'd made the connection. "I carved that some time ago because I love you. It helped me feel close to you."

"Oh, Reed." She pressed the tips of her fingers against her lips as though his words had brought her close to tears.

They moved toward each other. Reed closed his arms around her and he sighed with relief. He'd never experienced emotion so deep. He trembled at the depth of it, bottled up inside him for so many years.

He felt release as though he'd survived a great battle. Weak, but incredibly strong.

"I don't want a divorce, Reed," she told him. She planted her hands on the sides of his face and spread eager kisses over his features. "I want us to stay married. And...there'll be children. I want them so much." Her voice trembled with happiness.

His arms circled her waist, lifting her so he could kiss her the way he wanted, with her making soft whimpering sounds of need. She lifted her face from his and smiled slowly, her eyes laughing. Reed swore he could have drowned in the gentle love he found in her.

"I could already be pregnant," she whispered.

He longed to lose himself in her, yet when he came to Clare he wasn't lost; instead he'd been found. Her love gave him serenity and peace. Her love was the most precious gift he'd ever received.

Reed promised himself he couldn't make love to her

twice in one day, not when she was recovering after being so ill, but he felt powerless to resist. "You've been sick… weak." He tried to offer her all the reasons why they shouldn't, but one more kiss, one silken caress of her hand convinced him he was wrong. He lifted her in his arms and hauled her back to the unmade bed. She raised smiling eyes to him. "Conserve your strength," he told her, "because you're going to need every bit of it."

Clare laughed, and Reed swore he'd never heard a sweeter sound. "If anyone needs to conserve their strength it's you, my darling husband."

Clare woke early the following morning while Reed slept contentedly at her side. The drapes were open and the morning was gray and foggy. By midmorning the sky would be pink with the promise of another glorious summer day.

Clare had made her decision, and Reed had made his. They were man and wife. Her heart gladdened at the prospect of them joining their lives.

Reed stirred, and she rolled into his arms.

"Morning, husband," she whispered.

Reed's eyes met hers before he smiled. "Morning, wife."

"For the first time since we said our vows I feel married."

"Is that good or bad?" he asked.

"Good," she assured him, "very good."

"How are you feeling otherwise?"

Clare kissed his nose. "Wonderful, absolutely wonderful."

"What about the flu…we didn't…" He left the rest unsaid.

"I think we've stumbled upon a magical cure. I've

never felt better and furthermore, I'm starved." They'd eaten dinner late that evening, close to midnight. Reed was ravenous and had fried himself a thick T-bone steak. Clare was content with soup, not wanting to test her stomach with fried foods.

Afterward they'd cuddled on the sofa and he'd entertained her with tales of adventures from his childhood. Stories of learning to fish with his hands, of hiking deep into the woods and finding his way home, guided by the stars, and what he'd learned from the forest. Before returning to bed, he placed a plain gold band—the band his mother had worn—on the fourth finger of her left hand.

"Do you want breakfast in bed?" Reed asked, tossing aside the blanket and sitting on the end of the mattress.

"Why? Do you intend on spoiling me?"

"No," came his honest reply, "but I'd like to pamper you."

"What if I decide I want to pamper you?" she asked.

A mischievous look came into his dark eyes. "I'm sure I'll think of something."

Clare reached for her robe to cover her nakedness and followed him into the kitchen. She sat in the kitchen and braced her bare toes against the edge of the chair. Her knees were tucked under her chin. "I want to ask you about something you said."

"Fire away." Reed dumped coffee grounds from the canister into the white filter.

"You said something about me having a fragile spirit. What did you mean?"

Reed hesitated. "It isn't a negative, Clare. You have the heart of a lioness."

"But my spirit's fragile? That doesn't make sense."

Reed took his time, seeming to choose his words carefully. "It's because the people you love mean so much to you. I'm afraid you're going to be in for a difficult time once your family learns we're married."

"They'll adjust."

"But in the meantime, you'll suffer because you love them. It hurts me to know that."

"If they make a fuss, then they're the ones losing out." Although she sounded strong and sure, she realized Reed was right. Her family's opinion was important to her. She'd always been the good daughter, living up to their image, doing things precisely the way they'd planned. But her love for her husband was strong and steady. Nothing, not her parents, public opinion, or anything else would give her cause to doubt. Clare was convinced of it.

While the coffee brewed, Reed told her the story of his own parents and how his mother's family had turned away from her following her marriage.

"My parents would never do that." Clare desperately wanted to believe it, but she couldn't be sure. "Times have changed," she continued, undaunted. "People aren't quite as narrow-minded these days."

"If it comes down to you having to make a choice, I'll understand if you side with your family."

Hot anger surged through Clare's veins. "You'll understand? What exactly does that mean?"

"If you're put in a position where you have to choose between me and your family, I'll abide by whatever you want."

"What kind of wife do you think I am?" she demanded.

Reed didn't so much as hesitate. "Lusty."

"I'm serious, Reed Tonasket. You're my husband... my place is with you."

"Here?" He glanced around as if seeing the cabin for the first time, with all its faults. As he'd told her earlier, this was the only home he'd known since he was little more than a toddler.

"I'll live wherever you want," Clare assured him. "Here, Tullue, or downtown New York."

Although Reed nodded, Clare wasn't completely convinced he believed her. "I'm serious," she reiterated.

Reed kissed her, then silently stood to pour their coffee.

His words stayed with her that morning as Clare washed their breakfast dishes. When she squirted the liquid detergent into the water, her gaze fell to the gold band Reed had given her that had once belonged to his mother.

Clare wished she could have known Beth Tonasket. When she'd quizzed him about his mother, Reed hadn't been able to tell her much. His own memory of the woman who had given him birth was limited.

He'd gotten some pictures of her from a box stored in his closet, and Clare had stared at the likeness of a gentle blonde for several moments. Although her coloring was much lighter than Reed's, Clare could see a strong resemblance between mother and son. Of one thing Clare was sure—Beth Tonasket hadn't possessed a fragile spirit.

Clare wasn't sure why Reed's words had upset her so much. She feared it was because they were so close to the truth. Sooner or later she would have to face her parents. Soon the whole town would know she'd married Reed.

She recalled the look on Jim Daniels's face when she'd gone to the city jail to post Reed's bail. It had angered her at the time that this old family friend would be so quick to judge her. He certainly hadn't wasted any time in letting her parents know what she'd done. Her mother had shown up at the library the next afternoon flustered and concerned.

While Reed was busy working in his shop, Clare took down the box of pictures from the shelf, wanting to look them over, learn what she could of Reed's life.

Sitting atop the bed, she sorted through the stacks of old photos and found several that piqued her curiosity. One, a tall proud man in an army uniform, caught her attention. Clare knew immediately this must have been Reed's father.

Studying the photo, Clare felt a heaviness settle over her. How he must have hated leaving his wife and young son, knowing they would have to deal with life's cruelties alone.

"Clare."

"I'm here," she called.

Reed came into the bedroom, pausing when he found her. "I haven't looked through those in years."

"Are you in this one?" she asked, holding out a black-and-white photo of several Native American youths.

Reed laughed when he saw it. "I'm the skinny one with knobby knees."

"They're all skinny with knobby knees."

"There," he said, sitting next to her. He pointed to the tall one in the middle, holding a bow and arrow. "That was taken when I was about eight or so. The tribal leader had held a council and grandfather and I attended. I'd forgotten all about that."

"Will…you be taking our son to tribal councils?"

Reed hesitated. "Probably. Will that bother you?"

"I don't think so. He'll be Native American like his father."

"I'll be teaching all our children the ways of our tribe." He said this as though he expected her to challenge his right to do so.

"Of course," she agreed, though she wasn't sure what that would entail. Skills like trapping, hunting, fishing were often passed down from any father to son.

"I need to go into town sometime today," she told him. Her sick leave was about to expire and it was important that she make out the work schedule for the following week. Although she was much better, Clare wasn't ready to go back full-time. Even if she was, she would have delayed it a day or two so she could be with Reed.

"I'll drive you later. It might be a good idea if we checked in with Doc Brown while we're in Tullue."

"Reed, I'm a thousand percent better than I was when he first saw me."

"I don't want there to be any complications."

Clare grumbled under her breath, deciding it would be a waste of time to argue with him. She had the distinct feeling he was going to turn into a mother hen the moment he learned she was pregnant.

After this past month it would be a minor miracle if she wasn't. When Reed had described her as lusty he hadn't been far off the truth. It embarrassed her how much she wanted him. The future might hold several problems, but Clare was convinced none of them would happen in their marriage bed.

"Someone's coming," Reed announced, straightening. He climbed off the bed.

"Erin?"

"Not this time." He frowned. "It sounds like two cars." His uncanny ability to make out noises fascinated her.

Reed walked onto the porch, and Clare followed him.

She was standing at his side when the two vehicles pulled into view.

One look down the narrow driveway and Clare froze. She felt as though the bottom of her world had fallen out from under her.

The first car was marked Sheriff. Clare recognized Jim Daniels. The second car followed close behind. Inside were her parents.

Thirteen

"Get inside, Clare," Reed said with steel in his voice.

"I don't think that's a good idea," she murmured, moving closer to his side. Her heart felt as though it were on a trampoline, it was pounding so hard and fast.

Clare fully intended to tell her parents she was married, but she'd hoped to do it in her own time, in her own way, when the conditions were right.

"Clare, for the love of heaven, do as I ask."

"I can't," she said miserably. "Those are my parents."

Reed was already tense, but he grew more so at her words. His eyes found hers, and in their dark depths Clare read his doubts and his concern.

"I love you, Reed Tonasket," she said, wanting to assure him and at the same time reassure herself. Reed had claimed she possessed a fragile spirit. At the time Clare had been mildly insulted. His words contained a certain amount of truth, but she wasn't weak willed. No matter what happened she'd stand by her husband.

The sheriff stepped out of the car. The sound of his door closing felt like a giant clap of thunder in Clare's ear.

"Good day, Officer," Reed said appearing relaxed and completely at ease. "What can I do for you?"

"Clare, sweetheart," her mother cried, climbing out of the car. Ellie Gilroy covered her mouth with her hand as if she were overcome with dismay. "Are you all right?"

"Of course I am," Clare answered, puzzled. Blindly her hand reached for Reed's. They stood together on the porch, their fingers laced.

"Would you mind stepping away from Clare Gilroy?" Jim Daniels requested of Reed in a voice that sounded both bureaucratic and official.

"Why would you want him to do that?" Clare demanded defensively.

"He wants to be sure I haven't got a knife on you," Reed explained. He dropped her hand and placed some distance between them. A chill chased down her arms when Reed moved away from her.

"That's the most ridiculous thing I've ever heard in my life." Clare was outraged. Old family friend or not, how dare Jim Daniels make such a suggestion!

"This man is a known troublemaker," Jim insisted.

"That's not true." Clare was so angry she was close to tears.

"Are you here of your own free will?" Jim inquired in the same professional tone he'd used earlier.

He sounded as if he were reading for the part of a television detective.

"You don't honestly believe Reed Tonasket kidnapped me, do you?"

"That's exactly what we think." Her father spoke for the first time. His large hands were knotted into fists at his sides as if he were waiting for the opportunity to fight Reed for imagined wrongs.

Never having crossed the law herself, Clare wasn't familiar with legal procedure, but it seemed the deputy was sticking his neck on the chopping block. She wasn't entirely sure the sheriff's jurisdiction extended onto the reservation. Furthermore it seemed highly peculiar that he would drag her parents into what he believed to be a kidnapper's den.

"I came with Reed of my own free will," Clare explained as calmly as she could. She'd never had an explosive temper, but she feared that much more of these ridiculous accusations would change that.

"I don't believe her," her father said to his friend.

"There's not much else I can do, Leonard."

"Clare." Her mother's eyes implored her. "Are you ill?"

"Do I look sick?" she flared.

"I brought her to the cabin with me when she came down with a bad case of the flu," Reed explained in reasonable tones. "I intended to contact you, but from what I understand you were on a camping trip."

"I was worse off than I realized," Clare explained. Her mother had been in touch with her before they left for camping. Clare had been the one to insist they go. Her parents didn't get away nearly often enough and she would have hated to be the one responsible for ruining their plans.

"Clare was nearly dehydrated and close to being hospitalized," Reed added.

"But did she come of her own free will?" Jim demanded.

"I already said I did," Clare shouted, losing patience with the lot of them.

"She wasn't happy about it," Reed admitted, "but there

were few options available. She needed someone to take care of her, and…"

"She didn't need a jailbird doing it."

"Daddy!"

"The man was recently arrested for aggravated assault," her father stormed. "If he'd attack another man, what is there to say he wouldn't kidnap my daughter?"

Clare couldn't remember ever seeing her father so agitated. He'd always been a calm and reasonable man. She could hardly remember him raising his voice. He seldom revealed emotion of any form.

"Arrest him," Leonard insisted.

"On what charge?" Clare demanded. "I've already told you I'm here because I want to be. I can't believe you're doing this. Reed took me in, nursed me when I was ill and this is the way you treat him?"

"He didn't need to bring you here. There were plenty of other places he could have taken you."

"Dad, you're being unreasonable."

"He admitted himself that you didn't want to come."

Clare clenched her teeth to keep from saying something she'd later regret. "Why doesn't everyone come inside and we'll sit down and talk about this in a civilized manner?"

"That sounds like a good idea, doesn't it, Leonard?"

Clare could have kissed her mother. She started toward the front door, then realized she was the only one who'd moved. Reed, who stood with his arms crossed, hadn't budged. Neither had Jim Daniels or her father. Her mother took one tentative step forward, but froze when no one else moved.

The sound of another car barreling up the driveway diverted everyone's attention.

"Who else could be coming?" her father demanded.

"I think it would help matters a whole lot, dear, if you'd come off those steps and stand by your father and me," her mother suggested in low tones, as if she assumed speaking softly would coax Clare to leave Reed.

"It's Gary and Erin," Reed told her long before the car came into view.

Clare felt as though the whole world had descended on them at the same moment. Gary pulled in behind her parents' car and leaped out of the front seat as though the engine were on fire.

"What the hell's going on here?" he demanded, hands on his hips. Erin stepped out of the car, but held on to the door as she surveyed the scene around them. It was apparent to Clare that their friends had inadvertently stumbled upon the confrontation. Erin looked as shocked as Clare felt.

"It seems Deputy Daniels believes I kidnapped Clare," Reed explained.

"That's ridiculous."

"That's what I've been trying to tell them," Clare cried. "Why doesn't everyone come inside so we can discuss this situation rationally?"

Gary and Erin stepped onto the porch, but hesitated when no one else followed.

"What's the matter with you people?" Gary asked, glancing from one to the other. "Reed didn't kidnap Clare any more than he did me or Erin. He brought her here because she was ill. You should be grateful."

"That's my daughter he took—"

"Dear," Ellie Gilroy said softly, "I don't think it's fair to say Reed took Clare."

Her father glared at his wife but said nothing.

Knowing she would need to face her parents with the truth, Clare was hoping to soothe the waters as best she could before hitting them with the news of her marriage.

"I'll help you with the coffee," Erin said, taking Clare by the elbow and leading the way inside the cabin. Reluctantly Clare went inside, but not before casting Reed a pleading gaze. She wasn't sure what she expected him to do.

"Do they know?" Erin asked the instant they were inside the house. Clare didn't need for her friend to clarify the question. Her parents hadn't a clue she was married to Reed.

"No."

Erin sighed expressively. "I was afraid of that."

"Reed won't tell them, either." Of that, Clare was certain. Even if it cost him dearly, he wouldn't do or say anything that would place Clare in an awkward position with her parents.

"How'd they know you were here?"

"I haven't a clue, unless Doc Brown said something."

"That isn't likely," Erin muttered.

Clare went about assembling the pot of coffee. The temptation to walk back onto the porch and find out what was happening was strong, but it was more important to collect her thoughts.

Erin brought down several mugs and set them in the center of the table. Her father used sugar, so Clare brought over the sugar bowl, a couple of teaspoons and a handful of paper napkins.

"The coffee will be ready in a couple of minutes," she said, stepping outside. She rubbed her palms together as she cast a pleading glance to her parents.

Everything seemed to be at a standstill. No one was

speaking. They stood like chess pieces, reviewing strategy before making another move.

"Mom?" Clare pleaded.

Her mother glanced toward her father, but he ignored her.

"Jim, I appreciate you coming, but as you can see I'm in no danger."

Jim Daniels nodded, but he didn't reveal any signs of leaving.

"It might be best if you left," she said pointedly. "There are several things I need to discuss with my parents. Family matters."

"I want him here," her father insisted.

"Why?"

"That man's dangerous."

Clare was too angry to respond. "He's no more *dangerous* than you are! "

"I wasn't the one arrested for aggravated assault."

"That does it," Clare shouted, slapping her hands against her sides in a show of abject frustration. "Does anyone know why Reed and Jack fought? Does anyone care?"

"Clare." Reed's low voice was filled with warning.

"Reed doesn't want me to tell you, but I will." She folded her arms across her chest the same way Reed had and shifted her weight to her left foot. "I broke up with Jack for a number of excellent reasons."

"We know all that, dear," her mother said.

"What you don't know is that Jack started pestering me afterward. First he started bothering me with phone calls. It got so bad I had to unplug my phone. Then he sat outside my house, watched every move I made."

"You should have got a restraining order against him," Jim told her.

Clare agreed, but she hadn't thought of it at the time. "I…I don't know what led up to the fight, Reed never told me, exactly what he said but Jack apparently insulted me. In my heart I know there was a very good reason. Jack learned that I was…dating Reed, and his ego couldn't take that. Jack never cared for me, but the thought of me having anything to do with another man was more than his petty ego could take."

"According to the statement we got from Kingston at the time of the—"

"Knowing Jack, it was a pack of lies," Clare interrupted. "It was bad enough having Jack hound me the way he was. I knew that once he discovered I was seeing Reed, matters would get much worse. Jack was determined to make my life a living hell. Yes, Reed got into a fistfight with Jack, but he did so to defend me. I haven't heard from Jack once since the fight and I have Reed to thank for that. Jack won't pester me again because he knows if he does he'll have Reed to contend with."

"And me," Gary chimed in.

"I wasn't aware there was a problem with Jack," her father admitted reluctantly.

"We had our suspicions though," Ellie mumbled. "He called shortly after you broke off your engagement, and it was clear to your father, that Jack was trying to make trouble."

"I don't think Jack was ever the man we thought he was," Clare said with a tinge of sadness.

"There's no need to do something foolish because of Kingston," her father said pointedly. "Getting involved in another relationship because you're on the rebound isn't wise."

"Especially with a Native American," Reed supplied, stating what had been left unsaid.

Her father's gaze connected with Reed's. Clare could only speculate what passed between the two men.

"Will you come inside now?" she asked softly.

"Come home with us, Clare," her father insisted, holding his arm out to her. "You've had a bad time. First this business with Jack, and then having to deal with the flu. Let's put all this behind us."

"I am home, Dad."

"Nonsense, your place is with us and—"

"Dad, you're not hearing me."

"Now listen here—"

"Dad," Clare shouted, her voice cracking. "Would you stop and for once in your life listen to what I'm trying to tell you?"

"Clare." Reed's eyes implored her. He seemed to be saying now wasn't the time, but she ignored his silent plea, refusing to put off the truth any longer.

"Mom and Dad," Clare said, moving to Reed's side. She slipped her arm around his waist. "Reed and I are married."

Fourteen

"You're married? You and Reed? Oh, dear." Ellie Gilroy pressed her hand over her heart. "I do believe I need to sit down."

Clare's father gripped his wife by the elbow and directed her inside Reed's home, his former hesitancy gone.

Jim Daniels would have followed right behind him if Leonard Gilroy hadn't turned and said, "We'll take it from here, Jim. We appreciate your time and trouble."

"No problem. Give me a call anytime."

By the time her mother was seated in the living room, Clare had poured her a glass of water and brought it to her. Ellie studied Clare as she sipped from the glass. She seemed to be judging the accuracy of Clare's announcement.

"I'm Reed's wife, Mom," Clare whispered, unsure her mother believed her.

Ellie nodded as though accepting the inevitable, then she curiously studied the room. "This home is very nice," she murmured. "Of course it needs a woman's touch here and there, but really I'm quite—"

"Ellie."

Her husband's voice cut off the small talk.

"It seems you four have lots to discuss, so I think Gary and I'll be leaving," Erin said, stepping just inside the doorway. She hugged Clare and whispered, "Everything's going to work out just fine."

Clare wished she felt half as confident as her friend.

A silence fell over the room after Gary and Erin were gone. Clare's mother sat on the sofa, her father stood at his wife's side. Reed was at the other end of the room, before the fireplace, and Clare was positioned close to the kitchen.

"Coffee, anyone?" she asked brightly.

"That would be nice, dear."

Clare looked to her father and Reed, but both men ignored her, concentrating instead on each other, as if sizing up one another. Clare sighed and disappeared into the kitchen long enough to pour her mother a cup of coffee.

"Is it true?" Her father's question was directed at Reed.

Rarely a man of words, Reed nodded.

"There's never been an artist in the family," Ellie said conversationally, as though nothing were amiss. "It might be a nice change, don't you think, Leonard?"

"As a matter of fact, I don't," Clare's father returned abruptly.

"Dad, if you'd only listen."

"How long have you known him?" her father demanded next, slicing her with his eyes.

Clare bristled at his tone. She wasn't a child to be chastised for wrongdoing. "Long enough, Dad."

Her father, who'd always been the picture of serenity, rammed his fingers though his hair. His gaze skirted away from hers. "Did…he take advantage of you?"

It would have been a terrible mistake to have laughed, Clare realized, but she nearly did. "No." She couldn't help wondering what her father would say if she confessed how often she'd asked Reed to make love to her.

"Do you love him?" His fingers went through his hair once again.

"Oh, yes."

"What about you, young man? Do you love my daughter?"

"Very much." Clare was grateful Reed chose a verbal response. Although he didn't elaborate on his feelings, the message was concise and came straight from his heart.

"Do you make enough money to support her?"

Clearly her father had no idea how successful Reed was, nor was he taking into account that she made a living wage at the library. It was a question that could have offended her husband, but it didn't.

"He's famous, Leonard," her mother answered before Reed could. "Don't you remember there was that article about him in the *Washingtonian?* We both read it. You even asked me about Reed then, wanted to know if we'd ever met him. You seemed to be quite impressed?"

"I remember," her father muttered, but if he recalled reading the article, he took pains not to show it.

Clare moved so she was standing next to Reed. He slipped his arm around her waist and brought her close to his side. Clare was convinced the protective action was instinctive.

"Are you pregnant, Clare?" her father asked, his voice low and a bit uncertain. Pregnancy and childbirth were subjects that were uncomfortable to a man of his generation. His gaze studied the top of his shoes.

"I...don't know, but I'm hoping I am. Reed and I both want a family."

"You plan to live here?" was his next question.

"For now," Reed answered. "If Clare agrees I'd like to have another home built on this site within the next couple of years."

His arm tightened around her waist, and Clare pressed her head to his chest, drinking in his solid strength.

"I love Reed," she said softly, straightening. Reed's arms lent her courage to speak her mind. "I know our marriage came as a shock and I'm sorry for telling you the way I did, but you had to know sooner or later."

Her father said nothing.

"I really hope you'll accept Reed as my husband," she said, trying hard not to plead with her parents. "Because he's a wonderful man. I...realize you may not approve of my choice, but I can't live my life to please you and Mom."

"Of course we'll accept your marriage," her mother rushed to say, willing to do anything to keep the peace. "Won't we, Leonard?"

Her father seemed to be carefully weighing the decision.

"Reed Tonasket is a man of honor and pride. The happiest day of my life was when Reed agreed to marry me. That's right, Dad, I asked him. If you think Reed said or did anything to coerce me into this marriage, you're wrong."

"I see," her father said with a heavy sigh, and sat on the cushion next to his wife. The way he fell onto the sofa suggested his legs had gone out from under him.

"I don't think you do understand, Dad, and that makes

me sad—because you should be sharing in my joy instead of questioning my judgment. You raised me to be the woman I am, and all I'm asking is that you rest on your laurels and allow me to practice everything you taught me." Clare felt close to tears and rushed her words, wanting to finish before her voice betrayed her emotion. "I've made my choice of a husband and I'm very proud of the man he is. If you can't accept that then I'm sorry for you both. Not only will you have lost your daughter, but you'll have wasted the opportunity to know what a fine man Reed is."

Reed's hand was at her neck, and he squeezed gently as if he, too, shared her emotion.

The silence that followed was so loud it hurt Clare's ears. She watched as her father slowly stood. It looked as if he were in a stupor, not knowing what to do.

Clare's mother remained seated and stared up at her husband. She opened her mouth as if she wanted to say something, but if that was the case, she changed her mind.

After a moment, Leonard Gilroy crossed the living room until he stood directly in front of Reed. The two proud men met eye to eye.

Her father stretched out his hand. "Welcome to the family, Reed, and congratulations."

Clare sniffled once and then hugged her father with all her strength. "I love you, Daddy."

"You make a mighty convincing argument, sweetheart," her father whispered. "If I was angry, it was because I've always looked forward to walking my little girl down the aisle."

"I think you should," Reed said, surprising them both. "We were married by a justice of the peace. I wouldn't object to a religious ceremony and I don't think Clare would, either."

"You mean we could still have a wedding?" her mother asked excitedly.

"A small one," Clare agreed. "The sooner the better."

"I imagine we could pull one together in a few weeks." Ellie's eyes lit up with excitement at the prospect.

Clare nestled snug against her husband's side in the early-morning light. "You awake?" she whispered, rubbing her hand against his bare back.

She could feel Reed's grin since it was impossible for her to see it. "I am now."

"It went well with my parents, don't you think?"

"Very well," he agreed. Rolling onto his back, he reached for Clare, collecting her in his arms. "I was wrong about you, Clare Tonasket."

Clare agreed. "You made the mistake of underestimating me."

He chuckled. "Forget I ever said anything about you having a fragile spirit. You've got more tenacity than any ten women I know."

"You aren't angry I told them we're married, are you?" She lifted her head just enough to read his expression. From his small smile she realized he was teasing her. Her hair fell forward and he lovingly brushed it back.

"They had to find out sooner or later," he agreed. "I just wish you'd announced it with a bit more finesse."

"I'm through hiding the fact I'm your wife."

Reed slipped his arm around her waist and Clare leaned down and kissed him. "Talking about surprise announcements," she said, elevating her voice, "when did you decide you wanted to go through with a wedding ceremony?"

"It was a peace offering to appease your mother. Besides, your father had a good point. You're their only daughter and they didn't want to be cheated out of giving you a wedding."

"I don't feel cheated," she whispered. "I feel loved."

Reed slipped his hand to the small of her back. "We may have a daughter someday, and I'm going to want the privilege of escorting her to her husband."

"We may be proud parents sooner than either of us realizes if we have many more sessions like the ones recently."

Reed's eyes grew dark and serious. "Am I too demanding on you, Clare, because if I am…"

"You're not, trust me, you're not. Just don't let anyone know." She kissed his throat, working her way to his mouth. Reed groaned deep in his chest.

"Know what?" he asked breathlessly.

"What a shameless hussy your wife turned out to be."

"Sweet heaven, Clare, I love you. I never realized loving someone could be like this."

"I didn't, either," she admitted.

"My life was so empty without you. I couldn't go back to the way it was, not now." He buried his face in her neck. "The day will come when our children will marry. If it makes your parents happy to have us renew our vows so they can give us a wedding, then it's a small price to pay, don't you think?"

"I knew you were talented," Clare said, her lips scant inches above his, "I just didn't expect you to be brilliant."

"You've only scratched the surface of my many skills." He wove his fingers into her hair and directed her mouth back to his. Their kiss was slow and thorough. When she raised her head from the lengthy exchange, Clare drew in a deep, stabilizing breath.

Dawn was breaking over the horizon, a new day, fresh and untainted, a celebration that Clare felt certain would last all the days of their lives.

* * * * *

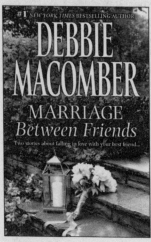

#1 *New York Times* Bestselling Author

DEBBIE MACOMBER

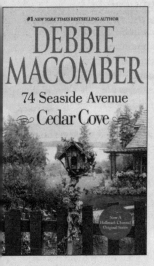

Do you remember Teri Miller? She works at Get Nailed, the beauty salon here in Cedar Cove. Well, Teri got married to Bobby Polgar, the famous chess champion, and they've moved into a beautiful house on Seaside Avenue.

Teri's my hairdresser, and she confided that something seems to be worrying Bobby. Rachel Pendergast also works at Get Nailed, and I've heard that she has *two* men seriously interested in her. And Linnette McAfee, who's Roy and Corrie's daughter, recently left town because her love life fell apart. We all know about *that* kind of trouble.

Sounds like there's a lot to catch up on! Teri says we should come by soon for a manicure and a chat....

Available wherever books are sold.

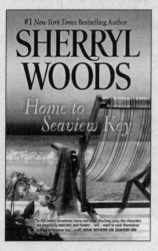

#1 *New York Times* bestselling author

ROBYN CARR

welcomes you back to Virgin River
with a moving story about survival, forgiveness—and
the power of love to heal a wounded spirit.

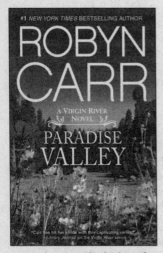

Marine corporal Rick Sudder is home early from Iraq—his tour ended abruptly on the battlefield. But can the passion and commitment of a young woman who has never given up on him mend his broken body and shattered heart?

Dan Brady has a questionable past, and he's looking for a place to start over. He'd like it to be Virgin River…if he can find a way in. But he never expects to find it in the arms of a woman who was as much an outcast as himself.

For a favorite son returned from war and an outsider looking for a home, Virgin River offers them a chance to make peace with the men they once were…and to find the dreams they thought they'd lost.

Available wherever books are sold.

Be sure to connect with us at:
Harlequin.com/Newsletters
Facebook.com/HarlequinBooks
Twitter.com/HarlequinBooks

HARLEQUIN® MIRA®
www.Harlequin.com

MRC1590

REQUEST YOUR FREE BOOKS!

2 FREE NOVELS
FROM THE ROMANCE COLLECTION
PLUS 2 FREE GIFTS!

YES! Please send me 2 FREE novels from the Romance Collection and my 2 FREE gifts (gifts are worth about $10). After receiving them, if I don't wish to receive any more books, I can return the shipping statement marked "cancel." If I don't cancel, I will receive 4 brand-new novels every month and be billed just $6.24 per book in the U.S. or $6.74 per book in Canada. That's a savings of at least 22% off the cover price. It's quite a bargain! Shipping and handling is just 50¢ per book in the U.S. and 75¢ per book in Canada.* I understand that accepting the 2 free books and gifts places me under no obligation to buy anything. I can always return a shipment and cancel at any time. Even if I never buy another book, the two free books and gifts are mine to keep forever.

194/394 MDN F4XY

Name	(PLEASE PRINT)	
Address		Apt. #
City	State/Prov.	Zip/Postal Code

Signature (if under 18, a parent or guardian must sign)

Mail to the **Harlequin® Reader Service:**
IN U.S.A.: P.O. Box 1867, Buffalo, NY 14240-1867
IN CANADA: P.O. Box 609, Fort Erie, Ontario L2A 5X3

Want to try two free books from another line?
Call 1-800-873-8635 or visit www.ReaderService.com.

* Terms and prices subject to change without notice. Prices do not include applicable taxes. Sales tax applicable in N.Y. Canadian residents will be charged applicable taxes. Offer not valid in Quebec. This offer is limited to one order per household. Not valid for current subscribers to the Romance Collection or the Romance/Suspense Collection. All orders subject to credit approval. Credit or debit balances in a customer's account(s) may be offset by any other outstanding balance owed by or to the customer. Please allow 4 to 6 weeks for delivery. Offer available while quantities last.

Your Privacy—The Harlequin® Reader Service is committed to protecting your privacy. Our Privacy Policy is available online at www.ReaderService.com or upon request from the Harlequin Reader Service.

We make a portion of our mailing list available to reputable third parties that offer products we believe may interest you. If you prefer that we not exchange your name with third parties, or if you wish to clarify or modify your communication preferences, please visit us at www.ReaderService.com/consumerchoice or write to us at Harlequin Reader Service Preference Service, P.O. Box 9062, Buffalo, NY 14269. Include your complete name and address.

ROM13R

DEBBIE MACOMBER

32988	OUT OF THE RAIN	___ $7.99 U.S.	___ $9.99 CAN.
32929	HANNAH'S LIST	___ $7.99 U.S.	___ $9.99 CAN.
32918	AN ENGAGEMENT IN SEATTLE	___ $7.99 U.S.	___ $9.99 CAN.
32911	THE MANNING SISTERS	___ $7.99 U.S.	___ $9.99 CAN.
32883	TWENTY WISHES	___ $7.99 U.S.	___ $9.99 CAN.
32882	THE SHOP ON BLOSSOM STREET	___ $7.99 U.S.	___ $9.99 CAN.
32858	HOME FOR THE HOLIDAYS	___ $7.99 U.S.	___ $9.99 CAN.
32828	ORCHARD VALLEY BRIDES	___ $7.99 U.S.	___ $9.99 CAN.
32798	ORCHARD VALLEY GROOMS	___ $7.99 U.S.	___ $9.99 CAN.
32783	THE MAN YOU'LL MARRY	___ $7.99 U.S.	___ $9.99 CAN.
32767	SUMMER ON BLOSSOM STREET	___ $7.99 U.S.	___ $9.99 CAN.
32743	THE SOONER THE BETTER	___ $7.99 U.S.	___ $9.99 CAN.
32702	FAIRY TALE WEDDINGS	___ $7.99 U.S.	___ $9.99 CAN.
32602	THE MANNING GROOMS	___ $7.99 U.S.	___ $7.99 CAN.
32569	ALWAYS DAKOTA	___ $7.99 U.S.	___ $7.99 CAN.
32474	THE MANNING BRIDES	___ $7.99 U.S.	___ $7.99 CAN.
32362	COUNTRY BRIDES	___ $7.99 U.S.	___ $9.50 CAN.
31458	CALL ME MRS. MIRACLE	___ $7.99 U.S.	___ $8.99 CAN.
31457	HEART OF TEXAS VOLUME 3	___ $7.99 U.S.	___ $8.99 CAN.
31441	HEART OF TEXAS VOLUME 2	___ $7.99 U.S.	___ $8.99 CAN.
31426	HEART OF TEXAS VOLUME 1	___ $7.99 U.S.	___ $9.99 CAN.
31424	MONTANA	___ $7.99 U.S.	___ $9.99 CAN.
31413	LOVE IN PLAIN SIGHT	___ $7.99 U.S.	___ $9.99 CAN.
31395	GLAD TIDINGS	___ $7.99 U.S.	___ $9.99 CAN.
31341	THE UNEXPECTED HUSBAND	___ $7.99 U.S.	___ $9.99 CAN.
31325	A TURN IN THE ROAD	___ $7.99 U.S.	___ $9.99 CAN.

(limited quantities available)

TOTAL AMOUNT	$ _____
POSTAGE & HANDLING	$ _____
($1.00 for 1 book, 50¢ for each additional)	
APPLICABLE TAXES*	$ _____
TOTAL PAYABLE	$ _____

(check or money order—please do not send cash)

To order, complete this form and send it, along with a check or money order for the total above, payable to Harlequin MIRA, to: **In the U.S.:** 3010 Walden Avenue, P.O. Box 9077, Buffalo, NY 14269-9077; **In Canada:** P.O. Box 636, Fort Erie, Ontario, L2A 5X3.

Name: _____
Address: _____ City: _____
State/Prov.: _____ Zip/Postal Code: _____
Account Number (if applicable): _____
075 CSAS

*New York residents remit applicable sales taxes.
*Canadian residents remit applicable GST and provincial taxes.

HARLEQUIN® MIRA®
www.Harlequin.com

MDM0214B